POISON

JOHN LESCROART

THORNDIKE PRESS
A part of Gale, a Cengage Company

Farmington Hills, Mich • San Francisco • New York • Waterville, Maine
Meriden, Conn • Mason, Ohio • Chicago

LIBRARY OF CONGRESS CIP DATA ON FILE.
CATALOGUING IN PUBLICATION FOR THIS BOOK
IS AVAILABLE FROM THE LIBRARY OF CONGRESS.

ISBN-13: 978-1-4328-4739-5 (hardcover)

Published in 2018 by arrangement with Atria Books, an imprint of Simon & Schuster, Inc.

Printed in the United States of America
1 2 3 4 5 6 7 22 21 20 19 18

To Lisa Marie Sawyer,
Again, and yet again

When skating over thin ice,
our safety is in our speed.

— Ralph Waldo Emerson

1

If opening day wasn't the happiest landmark in Dismas Hardy's year, he didn't know what was.

From the time he was eleven — when the Giants had arrived in San Francisco — until he was eighteen — the year before his father died — he had never missed attending the yearly ritual with his dad, first at Seals Stadium and then at Candlestick Park.

Adding to the mystique, in an era that pretty much ignored the concept of father-son bonding, Hardy's father had considered this time he spent with his only son a major priority, far more important than the vicissitudes of everyday life, including his own job or his son's time in the classroom. The renegade in Joe Hardy had believed that a man must keep his priorities straight, and some rules were made to be broken. He had no problem declaring Opening Day a de facto holiday, regardless of the opinion of the administrators at his son's schools.

He would pass this flexibility along to his son.

For Dismas, those days in the company of his father, watching big-league baseball in person, were among the most cherished experiences of his young life. It didn't matter that they had occurred in the cramped bandbox of Seals Stadium or the freezing wind tunnel that was Candlestick Park.

Great as those days had been, he thought that this one was better.

Part of it, of course, was AT&T Park, which to his mind was essentially the platonic ideal of the ballpark. (Although, of course, how could Plato have known?) His seats, courtesy of a client who'd moved to Oregon and sold his season tickets to Hardy to keep or sell off as he saw fit, were as good as it got — in the last row on the Club Level, fifty feet from the broadcast booths, shaded from the sun and occasional drizzle, mere steps from the closest bar.

He looked down at the sun-drenched field, warm and windless at the moment, a half hour to go until game time. Five minutes ago, the band Train had sung "Save Me, San Francisco" and now attendants were clearing the bandstand from the infield. Some of the players were still doing wind sprints or long toss out in left field.

Soon his son Vincent (impossibly, twenty-six years old and playing hooky from his job at Facebook) would return carrying two beers, a couple of bratwurst, and an order of garlic fries.

Hardy dabbed at his eye and took a breath against a wash of emotion. By all rights, he knew he shouldn't be here. He shouldn't be alive at all. About a year before, he'd taken two bullets — one to his chest that had bounced off a rib that deflected it away from his heart, and one superficially to the side of his head — bloody but not serious.

These last couple of bullet wounds made it four in his lifetime, surely more than the average allotted number for a mostly sedentary sixty-something lawyer, albeit a former Marine whose first experience of getting shot, in the shoulder, had come while he was pulling a guy who would become his brother-in-law out from under enemy fire in Vietnam.

But still . . .

Four?

Troglodyte that he was, Hardy had completely turned off his cell phone nearly an hour earlier, as soon as the Opening Day festivities and announcements had begun.

11

Vincent, who could probably survive without air for longer than he could live if he were not connected to the cloud or the World Wide Web or whatever, for the first four innings kept up a steady and knowledgeable patter with his father about the game, his job, his girlfriend Jennifer, and the general state of his physical and mental health — all good.

At the same time, his thumbs never seemed to stop tapping the face of his iPhone.

Finally, with the Giants coming up in the bottom of the fourth, Hardy could stand it no more. "Who are you talking to all this time?"

"Everybody."

"About?"

"Whatever."

"Work?"

"Sure. A little."

"I thought you were taking the day off."

"I am."

"But you're also working?"

"Dad. Really? Come on. That's the great thing about my job. I don't have to be there. I mean physically."

"So what about here, where you are physically?"

"What about it? I'm having a great day

with my old man, having some brewskis, watching the ball game. I'm totally here right now. Bottom of the fourth coming up, three to two, Padres. You're thinking about cutting back to half-time for the summer. The Beck's had two offers to change firms and turned them both down. Mom's joined a women's hiking club and you think they're pushing it too hard. But if you want, I can go dark."

"Not necessary."

"But you'd prefer it?"

"No," Hardy lied. In fact, he *would* have preferred it, but far more important to him was that he didn't alienate his son, to whom this was the norm, and who was, after all, living in the world in which he'd been raised. "I just need to get used to it. Multitasking in the modern age."

"But you already are. Here we are, watching the game, you and me catching up on the home stuff, enjoying our beer. I'd call that multitasking, too. Wouldn't you?" He looked down at his phone and chuckled.

"What?" Hardy asked.

"Just a text from Ron." His roommate.

"Saying?"

"You really want to know?"

"Sure."

"Okay. Why'd the cowboy buy a dachshund?"

"I give up. Why?"

"He wanted to get a long little doggie."

Hardy's lips twitched up slightly. "Good one," he said, though not, he thought, necessarily worth the interruption.

Like so much of the rest of it.

But continuing to push the conversation in that vein, he knew, was not going to be a fruitful line of discussion. He was just an old fart, unfamiliar and — it seemed suddenly, only in the past couple of years — slightly uncomfortable with the way so many of the young people he knew were living.

He was the one who had to get over it, change with the times, go with the flow. "Hey," he said, getting to his feet, "I'm on a mission for another beer. You want one?"

Vincent's thumbs were back flying over his phone's screen; looking up for the briefest of instants, he nodded absently. "Sounds great."

2

Another man who, during the previous year, had suffered a gunshot wound — although only one — was an SFPD homicide inspector named Eric Waverly.

Just as the Giants were taking the field in the top of the sixth inning on this beautiful Thursday afternoon, Waverly was a few miles to the west, near the panhandle of Golden Gate Park, ducking under a ribbon of yellow crime scene tape that responding officers had strung across the entrance to the six-unit apartment building on Stanyan Street. A couple of these uniforms were standing around downstairs in the small lobby with their sergeant from Park Station, but there wasn't any other police presence yet.

Waverly had been out finishing lunch with his mother — struggling with her divorce after twenty-six years of marriage — at a small French restaurant on Clement when his partner, Ken Yamashiro, texted him from downtown about the homicide. Waverly, relatively close to the crime scene, had hustled right over, beating the rest of the pack.

He had barely flashed his badge when one of the uniforms said, "Number four, upstairs."

The other one told him that the rest of the building was empty.

And the sergeant, perhaps redundantly, added, "It's not pretty."

Waverly knew that homicides actually were typically fairly antiseptic — something about the absolute finality of death transformed the corpse into an object of interest, but rarely of horror. Watching a man die was very emotional; looking at a dead man simply wasn't.

He took the stairs slowly, at a methodical pace. Since he'd been shot, he'd stopped taking stairs two or sometimes even three at a time the way he used to. His regular daily jog had turned into a walk, sometimes barely a stroll. He had given up jumping rope, given up sparring with the heavy bag. Any impact of feet on ground caused pain.

His doctor told him that his shoulder was completely healed, but if that were the case, Waverly wondered, why did it still plague him so? He was thirty-three years old, a natural-born athlete, and felt that he was altogether too young to let a physical condition negatively affect his performance and his life. But every time he tried to push it, his body pushed back.

Hard.

It really pissed him off. In fact, truth be told, he was angry now almost all the time, and didn't seem to be able to do anything about it. Stopping at the top of the first flight, he turned back and called out in a harsher tone than he perhaps intended. "Hey! If nobody's here, who called it in?"

"An old lady in the next building over. She heard the shots. Two of 'em. We've got her name and numbers. She said she'd be around."

Swell, Waverly thought. She'd be around. Except if she wasn't. Fucking clowns, he thought. Did they even train patrol officers anymore? This was a goddamn crime scene — hell, a homicide scene, and —

He felt blood pulsing in his ear.

He continued on down to where the door stood ajar. He wondered if it had been open when the officers arrived. And the front door to the building, too, for that matter. He'd have to ask. If they had noticed. Which they probably hadn't.

But he was up here now. He could have pushed the door open, but he kicked at it instead, harder than he needed to, and it opened all the way. He saw nothing in the short hallway. In the apartment's living room, directly in front of him, a bank of three windows let in a lot of light, cascading over a seat in the corner, over a sofa and coffee table against the left wall. The light reflecting off the hardwood floor glared up at him.

He brought his hand up, shading his face, stopping to let his eyes adjust. When he looked again, he saw the body. A circle of blood under the head had spread out over the cupped and ancient hardwood, haphazardly following the little gullies in the individual slats. The right-hand wall, in front of him, featured white cabinets under shelves of books that extended to the ceiling. On those cabinet doors, even to the naked eye, he could identify little splotches of white and red — undoubtedly where brain matter and blood adhered.

The sergeant downstairs hadn't been kidding about it not being pretty.

The victim, an Asian male, had apparently been shot twice, which comported with the neighbor's statement. One entry wound was clearly visible in the short hair just above the collar of his dress shirt. The second shot, under the middle of the jaw, would have been the coup de grâce that removed the top of the man's head.

To better view the carnage, he went down to one knee, then blinked and swallowed against the onset of another mild nausea attack, another side effect of his pain pills. Balancing himself, his hand on the floor, he willed himself up to his feet.

Walking back down to the lobby, his temper in check for the moment, he asked the responding officers if they'd like to try to locate the old woman who'd placed the 911 call and get her back there. Then, after asking a few more questions about the building as they'd found it, he left the sergeant guarding the entrance to the scene and went back upstairs to stand by the apartment door and wait for his partner to arrive.

Yamashiro showed up on the heels of the stripped-down three-person (budget, budget, budget) Crime Scene Investigation team, under the direction of the always sartorially splendid head of that unit, Len Faro. Before they'd all tromped in, four of them waited out on the staircase landing while today's photographer, Victoria Lacy, shot a few stills and five minutes' or more worth of video to document the scene before it got disturbed.

Now all five of the cops were standing over the body in the apartment's living room. After a decent interval of respect for the dead — say, four seconds — Faro decided not to wait for the coroner; he leaned down and, reaching into the back right pocket of the victim's khaki slacks, carefully removed a wallet. Straightening up, flipping it open to the driver's license, he said, "David Chang, thirty-one years old. Lives right here in this apartment. Ring a bell for anybody? No?"

He cast a glance to the cabinet doors with their spatter of gore, to the open archway that led into the kitchen, over to the reading chair under the front window. Finally, down again to the body resting in its darkening pool of blood, almost pure black now at its surface and where it gunneled in the slats.

Annoyed at something, Faro pulled at the perfectly trimmed soul patch under his lower lip, flapped the wallet closed and handed it to Waverly, then asked, "Anybody touch anything before you got here?"

"They say not. I think I believe 'em. This door wasn't locked or even closed when I got to it, but the outside door downstairs was both. It locks automatically on closing. I walked in about to here, touched nothing, and then turned around and walked out to wait for you."

The partners had cleared out of the apartment again to let Crime Scene work its magic. They had already gone downstairs, where they learned that the old lady who was their only witness had answered neither her doorbell nor her cell phone. The patrolmen who had let her walk away were confident that she'd be back any minute from wherever she'd gone.

"I love that," Waverly said. "They're confident." They were waiting in line for their drinks to be called at the Starbucks on Irving. "And what, you might ask, makes them so confident? Is it their years of experience rounding up and interviewing witnesses? Do they have any idea about how hard it is to get somebody to talk to us once they've had a while to think about the repercussions it might have? I don't know about you, but I'm taking it as a bad sign that she's not answering where she said she'd be. You?"

Yamashiro shrugged. "She'll probably show up, Eric. She's the one who called nine-one-one, remember? So we know she's not afraid to get involved. Maybe she'll turn out to be a good citizen."

"Yeah, and maybe the pope will canonize her like Mother Teresa. But I still wish they'd kept her here for us to interview her."

"I think you made that point clearly enough."

"Okay, yeah, but can you believe those fuckers? It's not like there's a lot to remember. We ought to write 'em up, get it on their record."

"I think that might be a little harsh."

"Fuck harsh. And fuck them. And who gets blamed if this all goes to shit and we never find her? Tell me that."

Yamashiro looked balefully across at his partner. "You've got to chill out a little, dude. Seriously."

Waverly met Yamashiro's gaze. "What's taking this coffee so goddamn long? Are they growing the fucking beans out in the back?"

3

With a win for the home team under his belt, Dismas Hardy hugged his son good-bye outside of MoMo's restaurant and considered dropping into the bar there for a postgame cocktail. But he'd already had those two beers at the game, and any more alcohol during the daylight hours would render him sloppy if not downright coma-tose. Somebody should do a study, he thought, about why drinks in the afternoon hit so much harder than they did at night. It was one of life's profound mysteries.

But rather than conducting more research on that topic, he shrugged, buttoned his suit coat, and turned west on Townsend, walk-ing into a growing afternoon breeze that seemed more biting than usual.

He hadn't gone more than a block when he remembered to turn on his cell phone and, on doing so, was immediately rewarded — if that was the word — with two text messages, six emails, and an equal number of voicemails.

Half of the voicemails were from his office, which undoubtedly meant Phyllis, his secretary, had been trying to reach him throughout the game. The concept of the managing partner of a law firm taking time off for recreation of any kind had never worked itself into Phyllis's psyche. She clearly believed that all that was needed for something bad to happen was Hardy's absence. And in that eventuality, the legal work they missed out on might go to another firm. And if that occurred often enough, the firm would find itself in big trouble; it might even go under. She knew that it was a brutal and competitive world out there, and if Hardy let down on his vigilance even for a second, there would be no telling what would happen, but whatever it was, it would be bad.

And it would all be Hardy's fault for having left the office.

Suddenly wishing he had stopped off at MoMo's after all, Hardy stepped into a doorway out of the wind and punched up his work number.

Phyllis answered on the first ring — of course — and without preamble Hardy said, "Three calls in three hours? Tell me somebody died."

"Didn't you listen to your voicemails?"

"No. I had my phone turned off."

"Then how could you have gotten your messages?"

"I couldn't, Phyllis. That was kind of the point. I was watching the ball game and, lo, the world did not end. Did somebody in fact die?"

"No."

"Well, there's a relief. So what up?"

He heard her exhale in frustration. "What up?" was not lawyerspeak, he well knew. Hardy remained a disappointment to her in so many ways. Maybe, he thought for the ten thousandth time, he should put her out of her misery and fire her. If only she weren't a brilliant organizer and mind reader . . .

"You got a call just after you left the office this morning from a woman named Abby Jarvis, who said she had just been arrested and she needed you to come down to the jail right away and help get her out. She sounded truly panicked, sir. Which was why I felt I had to keep trying to reach you. She said it was an emergency."

"And she was already in jail?"

"That's what she said."

"And when was that again? The call."

"Eleven forty-two a.m."

Hardy glanced down at his phone and made a face. "Four plus hours."

"Yes, sir. Do you know her?"

"She's a former client." Hardy didn't add that, except for the Christmas cards she'd sent him every year, he hadn't heard a word from Abby Jarvis for almost a decade, since he went to her wedding about a year after she'd gotten out of prison (two years early) after serving seventeen months for vehicular manslaughter. Since these Christmas cards eventually came to include her child, Veronica, as well, and had made a point of highlighting the fact that Abby had made it another year living clean and sober, Hardy had let himself entertain the always uncertain hope that her legal troubles were behind her.

But, judging from today's news, apparently not.

If she'd gotten all the way to being arrested, and not merely cited for some infraction, she was in the middle of something at least relatively serious. "Did she say," he asked, "what they'd brought her in for?"

"I thought I'd mentioned that."

"Not yet, no."

"It must have been on one of my voice-mails."

"I'm sure it was, Phyllis, but I think I've mentioned that I haven't had a chance to listen to them yet. How about you just say it again?"

Her exasperated sigh sang through the connection.

"Murder," she said at last. "They arrested her for murder."

4

Although he'd only been on his phone and tucked into a doorway for a few minutes, when Hardy stepped back out onto the sidewalk, the wind was gusting, kicking grit and dust up from the street into his face, while the temperature had dropped precipitously, perhaps fifteen degrees. Leaning into the gale, pulling the coat of his suit up tight around him with an impatient tug, he grimaced at the stabbing pain he'd just brought on at the site where the latest bullet had creased his rib.

Hardy knew that calls out of the jail were recorded. Arresting officers or other interested parties weren't supposed to listen to attorney-client calls, but they did lots of things they weren't supposed to. So the only time that Hardy would ever talk to a client about a case was face-to-face. Meanwhile, at Seventh and Harrison, the jail was only six blocks away — long, cold, blustery blocks, to be sure, three of them west into the teeth of the wind — but still, walking there offered better odds of talking to his prospective client sooner than any other option.

And so he walked, teeth clenched, eyes blinking, hands jammed into his coat pockets, silently swallowing a litany of obscenities.

The jail abutted the back of San Francisco's Hall of Justice, the four-story slate-gray block of stucco and glass that seemed to draw its architectural inspiration from any number of Cold War–era public buildings from the Eastern Bloc. To those who might be tempted to view the practice of criminal law as a glamorous or romantic profession, the Hall of Justice offered a mute yet powerful rebuttal.

The building was home to the district attorney's office and its investigators, the San Francisco Superior Court, and a random sampling of other police units, such as Homicide, Domestic Violence, Fraud, and Sex Crimes.

Early in his career, laboring on the prosecution side of the fence as an assistant district attorney, Hardy had worked for a couple of years in the Hall, up on the third floor. Over his years as a defense attorney, he'd also been involved in an almost un-countable number of trials — from DUIs and other misdemeanors to murders — in one or another of the myriad courtrooms, which for whatever obscure reason were called departments. So to say that he was comfortable in the building would be something of an understatement.

But today, though the Hall itself wasn't his destination, he decided to take the shortcut through it on his way to the jail. He passed without being challenged through the metal detector by the Bryant Street front doors. Eyes down to avoid seeing the inadvertent acquaintance who would delay him, he hung a right, crossed the lobby — which as always was throbbing with mostly unwashed humanity — then went out the back door, ignoring the big sign that said, "No Exit — Alarm Will Sound." Hardy wondered idly if they had ever installed the alarm or whether it had never worked, for over the last several years he was sure hundreds of people had used this exit unimpeded. The corridor outside led to the coroner's office on the right and the seven-story semicircular jail on the left.

One might suppose that, after a thousand or more regular appearances here checking in at the reception counter as an attorney visiting his clients, Hardy would be at least a vaguely familiar figure to the deputies at the gate and be accorded a degree of recognition or even welcome. But one would be wrong.

Defense attorneys had no leverage. Anything Hardy got would be at the mercy and even whim of any sheriff's deputy he encountered.

Today's desk sergeant was Bob Grassilli and Hardy had met him, identifying himself and checking in at least fifty times in the past couple of years. Nevertheless, when Hardy got to the counter, the sergeant looked him up and down as if he were a block of wood.

"Name, please."

"Dismas Hardy."

"To see?"

"A client of mine, Abby Jarvis. J-A-R-V-I-S." Abby was not technically his client yet, but Hardy wasn't going to open that can of worms.

Grassilli left the counter and went to a computer on one of the desks in the reception area, tapped the keys for a moment, shook his head, and then returned to the counter. "She's not in the system."

"She was just arrested this morning, Sergeant."

"What time?"

"She called me from here at quarter to twelve. She should have a cell by now."

"Maybe not. It's Opening Day, you know, and odds are there was a long line of drunks waiting to get processed ahead of her. It could be a few more hours. To say nothing about half our deputies being out at the game itself, so we're short-staffed. In any event, if she's got a cell already, I don't have it."

Hardy, his temper already pretty well frayed, grabbed at a breath to buy a minute and not explode. "Could I trouble you to please call intake and see where they've put her, Sergeant?" he asked with an exaggerated calm. "She's been here for almost five hours."

Grassilli checked his watch. "Your math's good," he said.

Never more aware of the leverage he didn't have, Hardy broke a cold smile. If he even inadvertently pissed off Sergeant Grassilli with a show of impatience, he might not get an opportunity to see Abby anytime today. "I'd really appreciate it if you could double-check for me. She's a

32

good kid, Sergeant, and she's scared to death."

Grassilli clearly did not appreciate this imposition on his precious time, but Hardy had obviously hit just the right obsequious tone. The sergeant sighed deeply, went back to his desk, picked up the phone. After a short discussion, he hung up and returned to the counter. "They're processing her in right now. Maybe another ten minutes."

"Thank you, Sergeant. I'd be happy to wait in the attorney-client conference room if it's not being used right now."

Grassilli gave him the dead eye for several long beats before he nodded once, then pointed off to Hardy's right. He pushed the button that allowed Hardy's access to the back and, in a startling display of largesse, allowed Hardy to proceed unescorted. "Second door on your left."

"Thank you, Sergeant. I know where it is. I've been here before."

Ten minutes?

In his dreams.

Hardy spent thirty-eight minutes cooling his heels in the large, semicircular space that was the attorneys' visiting room. The room was perennially cold and antiseptic in its fluorescent glare, its curving wall made of green-tinged glass block. It had something of the feel of a locker room without showers.

A brisk double knock on the door broke Hardy from his anger-stoked reverie as he sat in suspension at the metal table. That table, like the chair he sat on and the other two in the room, was bolted to the floor: jailed prisoners in their frustration and fury had been known to pick up large objects and try to throw them at their attorneys, their deputies, the walls.

Hardy all but jumped out of his chair. The door opened and a deputy stood in the doorway. "Are you Hardy?" he asked. "For Jarvis?"

"That's me."

The deputy was holding Abby by the upper arm out in the hallway behind him. Now he turned and brought her into Hardy's field of vision, all but pushing her into the room.

She could have been the poster child for someone who'd spent many hours of a long day being "processed" into the criminal justice system, and it wasn't pretty. Already decked out in one of the jail's orange jumpsuits, which seemed to swim on her, she appeared tiny, beaten down, scared, and helpless. In fact, without prior knowledge of who she was, he probably could not have picked her out as the naïve twenty-three-year-old he'd represented all those years ago.

Hardy was no stranger to the visceral wallop of seeing someone he'd known in other circumstances enter this room or one like it looking almost unrecognizable. But that didn't make him immune to registering the moment as a punch in the gut.

Or to dealing with the other standard indignities. "The shackles and cuffs aren't necessary," Hardy said gently. "I'll take full responsibility for my safety."

The deputy looked his prisoner up and down, then shrugged and said, "Your funeral."

Hardy and Abby waited, maintaining silent eye contact while the job got done, after which the deputy excused himself, gathered up the chains and other hardware, and closed the door on his way out.

Hardy came up out of his chair and around the table. Abby took a few tentative steps toward him and he found himself holding out his hands. Hesitating only for a second, she stepped into his embrace. He brought his arms up around her.

As he held her, her shoulders began to shake and a sob escaped, then another. He patted her back. "It's all right, Abby," he whispered. "It'll be all right."

She shook her head against him. "Nothing's all right." Extricating herself, she backed away and looked up into his face. "But thank God you're here."

"About the delay with me getting down here. I was —"

"It doesn't matter." She looked up into his eyes. "I'm just so sorry, Mr. Hardy," she said. "I am so, so sorry."

Hardy didn't like the sound of all these early apologies, since they indicated that she'd done something she regretted.

Well, he thought, whether it was from guilt of wrongdoing or self-pity that she now found herself in these straits, he'd know soon enough.

"It's been a while," he said, "but I think we'd gotten around to where you were calling me Diz. Why don't we pick it back up there?"

"I never could have killed him. Or even hurt him. He was an amazing man who'd never been anything but wonderful to me." She had gotten her tears and apologies under control and eventually taken one of the chairs along the short side of the table, diagonally across from Hardy.

After he'd gotten used to the jumpsuit, the tousled hair, the washed-out makeup, and the years since he'd last seen her in person, he realized that, now in her midthirties, she had grown into quite an attractive woman — perhaps more so, in fact, than she'd been in her twenties. The lines around her deep-set brown eyes brought character to what had been a nice-looking but really unremarkable face that had also lost the last of its baby fat, accentuating her cheeks, bringing into relief a mouth that was still generous, full-lipped.

In the past five minutes, Hardy had already learned that the deceased was Grant Wagner, the sixty-two-year-old fourth-generation owner of Pipes & Valves, a specialized plumbing and fixtures company where Abby had worked continuously as its bookkeeper almost from the day she was released from prison.

"I loved him."

Hardy raised an eyebrow.

But she shook her head. "Not like that."

"Like how, then?"

"Just as a guy, as a boss, as a friend. I mean, how many people would have hired me just out of prison and given me a chance? Guess zero and you're on the nose. And then kept me on all those years? Even during the recession, when everybody was getting laid off? But, no, I was one of the family. We'd all cut corners and wait for things to turn around and start going again. And that's what they did."

"How did you find him to begin with?"

"Pure luck. Gloria — his youngest daughter? — we were roommates and best friends all through college. Two accounting majors. Yuck, right? But we totally bonded as the only two people with personalities in the whole program. Then after the . . . after the accident, she came and saw me down at Chino as often as she could — like, every month or so the whole time I was in. She was my rock, Diz. Truly my rock. Then when I got out, Mrs. White — P&V's bookkeeper before me — she was getting set to retire and the timing was right and I started in under her and then took over when she left."

Hardy sat back. All this was well and good as far as it went. But Abby had just gotten herself arrested for Grant Wagner's murder. Somebody must have thought she had a reason to kill him, so he asked her, "Do you have any idea why anyone would suspect you of Mr. Wagner's murder?"

"I have a good guess." Sighing, she threw a glance at the ceiling. "How it started anyway, their suspicions. The inspectors." She paused and took another breath, then delivered it straight. "He left me a million dollars."

Holy shit, Hardy thought. "That's a good-sized hunk of money," he said.

"It is. But in context it's really not so . . . well, no, I guess it is, no matter what. But Grant had a lot of money. The company's worth somewhere around twenty-five million dollars. If they decide to look for a corporate buyer on the open market — say, a Kohler or a Home Depot — it might go for seventy-five or even a hundred million dollars. So, even though it sounds like a million is a lot, Gary's new salary is half that every year, and —"

"Gary?"

"The new CEO. The oldest son."

"Is he trying to sell the business?"

"Nobody knows yet. But anyway, as to my million . . . I thought it was wonderful, of course, except if it's why I got arrested for this, for killing Grant, and I think that might really be the reason. That, and me having been arrested before."

"You're right. That never helps."

"If I didn't have a previous record, I don't think they ever would have even looked at me. But it's, like, as soon as that got into

39

the picture, they decided it had to be me. But listen, I wasn't even going to quit working, so the million would have just made it easier for me and Veronica. It wouldn't change our lives in any real way. Don't get me wrong, I wasn't turning it down, but it was no reason for me to kill him."

"Veronica's your daughter, right? Is she all right? Do you know where she is now?"

"She's okay. She's with my mom. When I couldn't reach you, they gave me a second phone call, and I got through to my mom. She's a saint."

Hardy, relieved that these domestic issues seemed to be under control, brought the conversation back to the case. "So do you think that's it? The million dollars? That can't be all they have on you. They must have tried to talk to you. Did you make any statements? What did they ask you?"

"Well, the first time, they just asked me a lot about Grant. But just now, when they arrested me and told me about the indictment —"

"Indictment? You've been indicted? There was a grand jury indictment?"

"That's what they told me. But I don't know what that means."

It meant, thought Hardy, that there was a hell of a lot more going on here than

40

inheriting some money. At least twelve grand jurors must have thought that there was direct evidence tying Abby to this killing. "It means there's an awful lot I need to know if I'm going to represent you."

She gave that a long moment of consideration, then finally shrugged. "I honestly don't know what else there could be."

"Okay. At least maybe you can catch me up a little. How did this guy die?"

"Well, that's interesting, too. Because it changed. At first they said it was a heart attack, and then they went back and looked again . . ."

"Why did they do that?"

"Because Gloria asked them to. Grant was in great shape. He worked out every day. He'd evidently — like, two months ago — just had a major full-body workup — EKGs and MRIs, the works — and he passed with flying colors, so Gloria couldn't believe his heart would just go out, and she came down here and begged the district attorney to ask the medical examiner to take another look; and the second time around he found something else, because they told the family it was either suicide, which for some reason they decided it probably wasn't, or somebody killed him."

"And how long ago was that? The new

finding."

She lifted her shoulders, let them drop. "Well, Grant just died a month ago. So it must have been sometime in there." Suddenly, she sat up straighter. "But in terms of the inheritance, you know, I'm nowhere near the only person who stood to make money from this whole thing. I mean, the whole family's on the payroll, and everybody — I mean the kids — got a huge raise, like at least fifty thousand each . . . and that's right now, in salary, before any buyout or whatever."

"And how many kids are there again?"

"Four. Gary, Grace, Gene, and Gloria. Let's hear it for the G-Team. Except Gary's raise — plus the move up to president — was two hundred and fifty."

Hardy digested these facts. "So," he said at last, "I'm afraid I'm still not clear on why they picked you to arrest, Abby. They must have had something beyond the million dollars."

"If they do," she said, "I don't have any idea what it could be."

Across the room, a knock resounded, the door opened, and a new deputy stepped inside toward them.

"Can I help you?" Hardy asked. "We're not quite done here."

"If she doesn't come now, she misses dinner," he said. "Take it or leave it."

Hardy huffed out a breath in frustration. He had roughly a thousand other questions to ask Abby, including the sometimes prickly topic of what it would cost for her to remain his client. He knew that he would have to meet with her again tomorrow, when she would probably be arraigned. They would have to decide on some of the details before the arraignment: whether she could afford to retain him, her plea, a bail strategy if it was available. He needed much more information on the G-Team, including the former top G, Grant Wagner. On the company they all worked for. The extended family.

But the immediate issue was dinner. He looked his question at his potential client.

"No lunch, either," she said. "And now that he mentions it, I've got to say I'm starving."

Hardy gave her a bleak smile. "That settles it, then. Are you going to be okay here?"

She nodded. "I guess I'll have to be. When will I see you again?"

"I'll make sure, but probably tomorrow in court for your arraignment."

The deputy came forward, this time carrying a pair of handcuffs.

"Hands behind you," he said.

She gave Hardy one last look before the deputy turned her, unceremoniously clicked on the cuffs, and led her out the door and into the hallway.

5

Eric Waverly and Ken Yamashiro never did hook up with their elderly female witness who had called 911 on the David Chang homicide. And so they made essentially no progress on the case. This failure did not improve Waverly's mood to the extent that at around four thirty his partner told him to take the rest of the day off along with a chill pill and maybe tomorrow they'd have better luck being methodical and following up leads as they developed.

And by the way, Yamashiro added, really, maybe Eric needed to talk to somebody about his anger issues.

At Eric's two-bedroom duplex on California Street, his five-year-old elder son Jon kicked his latest tantrum into high gear. At issue was a Mowgli plastic drinking cup that three-year-old Michael had had the effrontery to usurp for his chocolate milk when he knew good and well that it was Jon's favorite cup and had been ever since they'd seen *The Jungle Book.*

And so Jon had, reasonably enough, grabbed it back from his younger brother, in the process dropping it and spilling its contents all over the floor.

This finally got their mother, Maddie, involved.

She awarded the refilled cup back to Michael because it wasn't really Jon's cup. It was a family cup that — all right, she'd admit, was Jon's favorite; but that didn't mean that Michael couldn't use it from time to time, like today, when he'd just happened to be the one who picked it up first.

"But it's *mine!*" Jon insisted at the top of his lungs. He then made the tragic mistake of trying to grab it back from Maddie. But she held on and Jon had gotten ahold of it again with both hands and pulled all at once, losing his grip on it and flipping the cup behind him, where it knocked their framed family portrait off the sideboard and onto the floor, where it shattered.

"Look what you've done! Look what you've done! Watch out for the glass!"

But of course, lurching again for the Mowgli cup, diving for it where it lay on the floor, Jon didn't watch out for the glass at all. And suddenly pure bedlam ensued and there was blood seemingly everywhere.

And this was the peaceful and serene oasis to which Eric opened the door.

"Jesus Christ! What the fuck is going on around here?"

Into the shocked sudden silence, Michael whined, "Daddy said a bad word."

By eight thirty the boys were bandaged and asleep. They'd mopped up the milk; gotten, they hoped, all of the glass off the floor. The family portrait was a dead loss.

Dinner had been hot dogs and sauerkraut and Kraft macaroni and cheese, washed down with a couple of glasses of milk, basically leftovers from the kids' dinner. Eric spent most of the meal recounting the many disappointments of the day: his mother's depression, the idiot patrolmen who'd let their one witness get away, Yamashiro's almost sublime indifference to the lack of progress on their cases, the madness greeting him when he got home.

And all of it colored by the goddamn unending pain where he'd been shot. He was starting to think that his shoulder would never heal. But he didn't want to tell anybody at work about it because they might think he was unable to keep up with the physical demands of the job. But, really, just between him and Maddie, the damn thing wasn't getting any better.

Pain, pain, pain. All of the time.

Rubbing his shoulder, he shook his head; then, in the middle of bringing some hot dog up to his mouth, he suddenly put the fork down, pushed back from the table, and stood up.

"Are you okay? Where are you going?" Maddie turned at the table, watching him.

He didn't answer her. Instead he reached up and opened the cupboard right above the refrigerator where they kept their hard liquor. Pulling a bottle of Bulleit bourbon down from the shelf, he took a glass from the drying rack by the sink and filled it a little over halfway.

"Do you really think you need that, hon?" she asked. "Didn't you just take your pills?"

"Yes, I just took my damn pills. But guess what? They're not working worth a shit."

She sighed.

"What?"

"Nothing."

"No, really. What?"

"It's just all your swearing lately. Even with the kids around."

"The kids were out of control when I got home, Maddie. What, am I not allowed to have a reaction to that kind of madness? After all I put up with all day? To say nothing of —"

"I know. The pain."

"You don't think it's real?"

"No. I believe it's real. I feel terrible for you. It's got to be awful." She hesitated, drew in a breath, decided to go on. "But you've got to figure out a way to deal with it without getting so mad about everything. Without swearing at everything."

He squeezed his glass so that his knuckles shone white. "It's my house," he whispered. "If I want to swear in my own goddamn house, I think I'm allowed to do that."

"That's not how you used to be, Eric."

"Well, no shit. You know why that is?"

She started to gather the plates and stand up. "Yes, I do. But I don't have to listen to you swear at me and have the kids be afraid of you."

"They're not afraid of me. And I'm not swearing at you. Don't be ridiculous."

"I'm not being ridiculous." Holding the plates, she was facing him. "Can I get by?"

He didn't move.

"Eric. Please. I know you're angry and I know you're hurting." She indicated his drink. "But that's not going to help. You need to figure out what to do. Not drink it away."

"You don't know."

"No, I don't. But I'm here for you, whatever you need. It's not always a picnic being with these children all day, either, you know. I need a partner here."

"That's what I am."

"Maybe not so much." Again she pointed at the drink. "And to be honest with you, that's not helping. Can I please get by?"

Shaking with pent-up rage, Eric turned. "You don't want me to have this drink?"

"I'm just saying I don't think it's going to help."

"Here, then, take it," he said. "Throw the goddamn thing in the sink."

She paused, put the plates down, then turned back and took the glass from him, placing it on the counter.

Eric stood immobile for a moment, shaking in fury. "Goddamn it!" And then, with no further warning, he slammed his fist into the wall between the kitchen and their tiny dining room, blasting a hole into and all the way through the drywall on both sides.

Maddie jumped back with a muffled scream and, in the back bedroom, one of the kids started to howl.

6

Gloria Wagner was on her second lemon drop at the Battery's high-end bar in one of the city's most exclusive venues, beautiful people at every seat. She was getting more and more upset, telling her fiancé Chad Loring that she'd placed multiple calls all day to both of the inspectors — Yamashiro and Waverly — who had come into the office that morning and arrested Abby. Neither had called her back. The whole thing was a travesty and she felt it was all her fault.

"How could any of it be your fault?"

"Because I'm the one who pressed for the second autopsy. I didn't believe my dad had just up and died of a heart attack."

"And you were right, as it turns out."

"But if I'd have known they'd go after Abby . . ."

"How about if they went after her because she did it, Glor?"

"No. I can't really believe that. If I would

have thought that . . ."

"What? You wouldn't have wanted to know if your dad was murdered or not? Of course you would have, whatever the fall-out."

"Yeah, but not Abby."

"Not the same Abby who killed that woman and crippled her kid?"

"That was ten years ago, Chad. More than that. And a total accident."

"Not so total. If she hadn't been drunk, it probably wouldn't have happened. Right?"

Gloria pouted and sipped at her drink. "You sound just like the cops."

"The cops are not always wrong, as it turns out."

"But she loved my dad. I know she did. She couldn't have killed him. Plus, she's a wonderful person. She's not a killer of anybody. And not my father especially."

"That's the hardest part to me," Chad said. "I mean, I didn't know him all that well, but I still thought he was a terrific guy. It's hard to imagine anybody deciding to kill him."

Gloria's eyes started to glisten with unspent tears. "It's one tragedy on top of another. First Dad and now Abby. And it's just all so wrong."

Chad tipped up his martini. "If it's not

Abby, could he have killed himself?"

"No. Not that way. He wouldn't have poisoned himself ever, I don't think."

"Why not?"

She shook her head. "Because it's Dad. He would have wanted to be sure, as in positive. Poison would have been too risky. I mean, it might not work. But even if he did go that way, or however he would have done it, more than that, there's no doubt he would have left some kind of note for the four of us, the kids. He would have explained, or tried to. Plus, definitely he would have had some instructions for each one of us about how we should be living and what we should do with the business. There's no way he would have just checked out."

"I agree. You're right. Okay, so if he didn't kill himself and it wasn't Abby, then who?"

"I don't want to be blaming people, Chad."

"Yeah, you do. That must have been why you've been calling the cops all day. You want to give them somebody else to think about."

"Not really. They've obviously already decided."

"But . . . ?"

"But I don't know if they've even glanced at Stacy, who was hurt and furious and felt

53

super-betrayed, and I can't really even say that I blame her."

"Yeah, but she and your dad broke up when? Two months ago?"

"Something like that. But if you remember, it was bad. And anything but mutual. I mean, Dad just decided it wasn't working and dumped her."

"And so she came back six weeks later and killed him?"

"At least she had a real reason, Chad. She hated him. He betrayed her. Which was nowhere near the case with Abby. And do you remember who Stacy works for?"

"No."

"*Probity.* Big Pharma. All the drugs in the world."

"Hmm," Chad said.

Gloria nodded. "Just sayin'."

In semidarkness, having come back downtown after a family dinner at home, Gene Wagner sat stewing at his desk on the second floor of the enormous P&V warehouse on Eighteenth Street and Sanchez in the Castro District.

The building's renovation, ten years before, had moved all of the private offices upstairs, vastly increasing the storage capacity and accessibility to their products down below on the ground floor. Five of the six new offices were identical in size, and each of those five — all in a row along the elevated walkway that looked out over the aisles down below — featured three wooden sides and an eight-foot glass wall into which a glass door had been set.

Signifying openness.

Grant's idea was that this arrangement would also promote a feeling of equality among the siblings. The only objective difference between the offices, after all, was proximity — in sibling age order — to their father's corner office, which was twice the size of all the others and which had no open glass wall. His father, Grant, the president, probably never supposed that closeness to his own big office could be a source of jealousy and conflict among his children.

His father, Gene knew, had in many ways been blind.

The way it worked in real life was that Gary — eldest child, heir apparent, and CEO — had the office next to Grant's. Then came the office of Grace, mother of four, who worked at most part-time as the sales and marketing director, a position and title that had no real meaning, since the source of almost all of the company's work was Grant's charisma and connections. Only next, three doors away from his father, and more than halfway down the length of the building, came the office of the chief financial officer, Gene.

Equality?

He thought not.

In any event, beyond his office, to his left as Gene sat fuming, was Gloria's. She was Gene's favorite sister, smart and efficient and a great person, but the idea that she somehow carried a burden equivalent to the ones shouldered by the other siblings in the company's business was ludicrous. In spite of her official title of "inventory specialist," she actually functioned more as a glorified secretary, doing piecemeal chores for whoever needed whatever. In fact, most of the time Gloria simply hung out, gossiping and laughing, in the office of Abby Jarvis, the bookkeeper, whose office was the last one down the line, farthest from Grant's.

Gene had come in tonight fully intending to get on Abby's computer and review some of the nuts-and-bolts decisions she'd made over the past months in the day-to-day running of the office — decisions that he assumed had evidently played a major role in her arrest this morning. Whatever she had done, Gene was confident he could get to the bottom of it. After all, he was a licensed certified public accountant and — Abby's and Gloria's bookkeeping degrees notwithstanding — the only one in the family or the company with any real financial background.

But when he'd arrived, the door to Gary's new digs — the big corner office formerly inhabited by his father — was yawning open, a dim light shining out from within. It drew him like a moth to a flame.

He had wondered for a second if Gary was back at work, too — or if he had, with all the drama of the day, simply forgotten to lock up.

But before he got there, he passed Gary's former office, its bookshelves empty, the desk pristine. Deserted. He knew the basic fact, of course, that his brother had moved to his father's office, but suddenly, in the otherwise empty building, the enormity and reality of it kicked in with a vengeance. He put his hand up against the glass wall, sucked in a breath, and only after a long moment got his bearings again.

Now, instead of being pulled toward it, he found he had to force himself to step into the sanctum sanctorum. Turning on the overhead light, he saw that the room was still comprised of the bones of his father's office, all dark wood and leather, with built-in floor-to-ceiling bookshelves, a custom liquor trolley, picture windows on the two outer walls, diplomas and awards and pictures with clients and some local celebrities.

But in only a few weeks Gary had already put his stamp on it: the Madison Bumgarner autographed baseball on the credenza; the framed picture of Gary's family where Grant's photo of his own nuclear family with all the sibs had been on the desk; the terrarium with the turtles; Gary's shotgun leaning in the corner.

Finally, Gene got himself seated back at the desk in his own office.

How had he let things come to this? With his father's death, his understanding was that everything would go on the same for a time, as in fact it had. But the future direction among his brother and sisters had been clear, or at least he thought it had been clear: they were going to position the company to sell and divide the proceeds equally. There would be enough for all of them to retire, to get off the treadmill, to live better lives. But now, suddenly, that plan seemed ephemeral at best, impossible at worst. Gary would never sell, because the company was his life, as it had been for their father. Gene did not and had never felt that way. To him,

P&V was where he worked. It was a job and eventually, perhaps, an escape route from having to work until he was an old man.

Or maybe not.

And meanwhile, somehow, the salary structure had shifted in the aftermath of Grant's death. His father had written down his suggestions for the succession, and big brother Gary had come out light-years ahead of the rest of them; his new salary, now that he would be both president and CEO, would increase by a quarter of a million dollars, while Gene and the girls got piddling raises of only $50,000, not even three thousand a month after taxes.

Gene and the girls!

As though the sisters' jobs were comparable, as though their salaries should be the same as his. Always Gene and the girls, an afterthought.

Whereas Gary always shone with a light all his own.

It was wrong. So wrong.

Gene had truly believed that his father's death was going to set him free. And now it seemed that it had just tightened the shackles.

7

Dismas Hardy's house, a "railroad style" Victorian on Thirty-fourth Avenue near Clement, was the only stand-alone home on a street otherwise packed with duplexes and apartment buildings. About ten years earlier, a fire had pretty much ruined the place, but he and Frannie had rebuilt on the same footprint, adding a second story for their bedroom and a spacious front porch that looked out over the expanse of their postage-stamp lawn.

With the wind having picked up and then died down after sunset, the night was comfortable in a frigid sort of way, and Hardy sat bundled in a down jacket on one of the Adirondack chairs under the porch's overhang. He'd brought his book — Daniel James Brown's *The Boys in the Boat* — out with him and turned on the porch light, but he hadn't yet gotten around to picking up where he'd left off. The book lay with its spine cracked, facedown on his lap.

He heard the creak of the front door opening, then Frannie's voice. "Oh, here you are."

"Here I am."

"Aren't you a little cold?"

"Only where my skin shows. Mostly I'm toasty."

She crossed over a few steps and put a hand against his cheek.

"That would be a bare-skin area," Hardy said.

"Decidedly not toasty, though. Are you all right?"

"Relatively. Probably." He paused. "Just pondering."

"About anything specific?"

"Don't worry. It's not the Neanderthals."

Over the past few weeks, spurred on by his friend Abe Glitsky's contention that Neanderthals had sailed the Mediterranean and were probably light-skinned with reddish or blond hair, Hardy had done a few hours of research into the topic, regaling Frannie with every new factoid or theory that he'd uncovered — many of them, in his opinion, mind-blowing. Intermarriage with *Homo sapiens,* language, weapons — amazing stuff, if true. And yet, inexplicably, he thought, Frannie did not share his

61

fascination, which of course did not extinguish, and quite possibly fanned, the flames of his enthusiasm.

Now she broke a tolerant smile and said, "Well, that's good to hear. I think you've pretty much pondered the Neanderthals to death."

"Not just death," Hardy corrected her. "Extinction."

"That, too. And now that we know you're not pondering Neanderthals anymore, that leaves a tiny little gap."

Hardy sighed. "I've tried not to think about it all night."

"I knew there was something."

"No flies on you." A last hesitation. "You know how I've solemnly sworn not to get involved in another murder case, no matter what?"

Frannie pulled the other Adirondack chair up behind her and sat on the front edge of it. "It vaguely rings a bell," she said. "Something about not wanting to get shot at anymore."

"To say nothing about actually getting hit. I mean," Hardy said, "I've got a thriving law practice with a partner and six associates, all happily billing away. I don't need murder cases to squeak by and pay the rent."

"You certainly don't. Damn straight."

"There you go. That ought to settle it."

Frannie reached out and put her hand over his. "So who is it?"

Hardy let out a breath. "Abby Jarvis."

Frannie frowned. "I don't remember her. Him?"

"Her. DUI manslaughter. I got her a good deal — first offense, yada yada. She was a young kid when it happened back in aught three, and she's been employed and sober ever since she got out of prison. I get a Christmas card from her every year at the office. She's got a seven-year-old daughter now, too."

"And she's up for murder?"

"Already arrested. I went and saw her at the jail after the game."

"And who'd she kill?"

Hardy gave her an out-from-under look. "Nobody, my dear. She didn't kill anybody."

Frannie broke a wide smile. "I know," she said. "I was kind of teasing you there."

"Got me," Hardy said. "My bad. Anyway, she's charged with killing her boss because in his will he left her a million dollars."

"That's a great boss."

"I thought so, too."

"So she was his lover?"

"I don't know. Apparently not. I don't

know the whole story yet. But she swears she didn't kill him . . ." He held up a hand. "I know, I know. That's what they all say. But in this case I'm tempted to give her the benefit of the doubt. That is, if I'm going to be involved at all, which is — as you may have guessed — why I'm out here pondering."

"But you've already seen her in jail. Doesn't that mean you're already her attorney of record?"

"No. Not technically. No retainer. Not even a handshake. I could pass her off tomorrow to any number of my well-qualified colleagues."

"But?"

"But none of them are going to have my history with her."

"And none of them will care as much."

"Sure they will," Hardy said. "It just wouldn't be as personal."

"Does that matter?"

"I truly don't know, Frannie. Sometimes I think so, and then I think I'm just being sentimental and stupid. Maybe I should just give her up and see how it feels. See how *I* feel."

Frannie sat back into the chair. "How much time do you have before you have to decide?"

"The arraignment's tomorrow morning. I've got to make up my mind by the next time I talk to her."

"Well," Frannie said. "There's a relief. At least it's not a tight deadline." She got to her feet, leaned over, and kissed him on the cheek. "I'm going up. Can I expect you shortly?"

"Couple more minutes."

Sleep wouldn't come.

Hardy could be as glib as he wanted with his wife, but now in the lonely darkness of his bedroom he found no solace in irony. Folding the covers back off his body, he checked the time and saw with some dismay that it was two thirty-four. Best case, he'd only log three or four hours tonight, and that's if he ever fell all the way to sleep to begin with. But clearly nothing was happening here in bed, so he rolled up to a sitting position, made sure the movement hadn't awakened Frannie, then got all the way up.

Downstairs, their family room behind the kitchen was home to his tropical fish collection. Sitting on the ratty couch across the way, he watched them swimming around in their semidarkness and let the soft bubbling soothe him.

There had been a time — it seemed not too long ago — when he'd chosen to believe that for all of its adversarial character, the practice of his profession was not inherently dangerous. Lawyers on both sides basically played by the rules most of the time; there was an underlying collegiality. Defendants, though frequently handicapped by poverty, ignorance, prejudice, drug addiction, mental health issues, lack of intelligence, and a host of other similar burdens, still rarely if ever became fixated on either the prosecutor who'd sent them to prison or the defense attorney who'd been unsuccessful in preventing their conviction; they tended to blame the system, not any individual lawyer.

That was the apparent norm, anyway.

But in Hardy's case, the norm seemed not to apply. Early in his career, the wife of a federal judge had shot Hardy when he'd been about to make an argument that would get his innocent client acquitted at the expense of her guilty husband. Later, his partner David Freeman was assaulted in the street and killed by a gang of thugs whose boss was involved in a civil suit with one of the firm's clients. Then the mother of the victim in Hardy's own brother-in-law's murder case wreaked her own vengeance after the jury had failed to convict him of killing her son: she shot Moses McGuire to death behind his bar as he was getting ready to pour her a drink. And finally, just last year, his daughter Rebecca's client, about to be exposed as guilty of the murder with which he'd been charged but not convicted, shot twice and very nearly killed Hardy before taking his own life.

In the wake of all of this real and personal violence, Hardy found that his worldview had shifted irrevocably. People could tell him that his own experiences were a fluke; this was, he thought, easy for them to say. The truth as Hardy had come to believe it, and other lawyers ignored it at their own peril, was that murder trials carried an inherent element of danger. Someone had already killed once. This was a good thing not to forget. And that killer might not necessarily have been the defendant, which meant that he or she was probably not in custody and therefore had little or no movement restriction. The actual killer could lie in wait, plan an ambush, ring Hardy's doorbell at home and shoot him where he stood, hire a professional killer. The possibilities were nearly endless.

Hardy stared at the fish swimming in the tank. They swam until they got to a wall, then they turned and swam until they got to another wall, then they swam . . . Hardy could relate.

8

As was his wont, Hardy arrived early at the Hall of Justice. He knew that court wouldn't convene until nine thirty and that his client might not be called for her arraignment until early afternoon. And that was if and only if she actually became his client and could pay him a substantial retainer. Murder trials weren't cheap, and if he was going to risk his life in Abby's defense. . .

Well, all right, he thought, that was probably an exaggeration — but he wasn't doing any part of it for charity, not this time around.

On that he was firm.

Grant's bequest to Abby in his will had been for a million dollars. But now that she had been arrested for his murder, she had no chance of seeing any of that money. Not unless and until he could get her acquitted. And she'd been working as a bookkeeper. Even if she had been relatively well paid, she was raising a daughter. Hardy thought it unlikely that she would have been able to save much.

He would find that out today. And a lot more as well.

But meanwhile, it was eight fifteen. He hadn't overslept; in fact he'd barely dozed all night. He hadn't been caught in traffic, either, or had an accident, or encountered another emergency at work. Even though he couldn't exactly remember the last time any of the potentially tardy-making things he worried about had made him late for court or for anything else, he'd be darned if he was going to let down his guard against any of the possibilities for random delay that he imagined stalked him like a panther, waiting for him to make the tiniest slip.

There was no use trying to meet with Abby at the jail before court. Between doing the count, getting the inmates breakfast, and moving the people with court appearances over to the Hall of Justice, there was no chance the deputies would take the time to permit an attorney visit. Hardy's best bet was to try to catch his client for a few minutes in the back corridor of the courthouse before her case was called. He'd go by there and hopefully work out (or not) some of the details of their professional relationship at around nine o'clock, but that left forty-five open minutes.

Two minutes later he was walking past the empty desks of DA Investigations all the way to the back. Turning left, he passed a couple more desks and finally came to a lone cubicle, set apart from the open workstations in the rest of the office. The upper half of the partition revealed the closely cropped graying hair of Hardy's best friend, Abe Glitsky, the only other human in attendance so far. Knocking on the wall, Hardy came around to the opening, by which time Glitsky had pushed his chair back, turned to face the open entrance, and lifted his mug of tea halfway to his mouth, which, as usual, was not creased in a smile.

Glitsky's father was Jewish and his mother had been African American, and the combination had given him light mocha skin and blue eyes. His facial arsenal, threatening and somehow compelling at the same time, included an impressive hook of a nose and a scar that bisected his lips at an angle. This had in fact been the result of a playground accident when he was a kid, but he never denied the persistent rumor that the scar had been a result of a knife fight early in his police career — and that he'd killed the other guy.

"I think it's time we resurrected your old nickname," Hardy said without preamble.

"Which one is that?"

"The Indian one. People Not Laughing."

Glitsky sipped at his mug. "I'm not sure I remember that one."

"Yes you do. Because whenever you're around, you are usually surrounded by people not laughing. Surely you recall that."

"Not too clearly. And don't call me Shirley, either." Glitsky put his mug down. "Are you getting any sleep? You look a little ragged."

"Thanks. You can tell?" Hardy dropped his briefcase onto the floor, then pulled a chair around and straddled it. "I was hoping it didn't show."

"Maybe not to the average mortal, but I'm a trained investigator. Nothing escapes." Glitsky reached again for his tea. "So is it just the usual existential angst or something specific?"

"More or less specific, I'd say. I've got a former client who looks like she's up for murder and don't see how I can't take her on."

"Sure you can. You tell her you're crazy busy. You're retiring. Your life coach has forbidden you to take murder cases."

"I don't have a life coach."

"No? I could have sworn. Well, I could give you a dozen reasons not to take her on."

"Just like I gave myself last night. None of them stuck."

Glitsky's face went through a few changes. Then he asked who the client was and what she'd done last time. After hearing about it, he scratched at his cheek and said, "There's always 'Just say no,' too."

Hardy grimaced. "I can't do that."

"Why not?"

"You'll scoff, but I really don't believe she would have done it."

Glitsky's lips turned down. "You're right. I'm scoffing. This is a woman who's already been to the joint?"

"Seventeen months," Hardy admitted.

"Plenty of time to master some new tricks in a rich learning environment."

Hardy shook his head. "That's just not who she is."

"What part of her is not who she is? And if she didn't do it, how come she got herself arrested? You think the grand jury was just bored and picked her name out of a hat?" Glitsky sat back, pulled an ankle up to rest on his knee. "Look, Diz. It's your life. Take the case if you want. But I seem to vaguely remember you swearing on a stack of Bibles that you weren't doing any more murder trials because these people tend to be — how can I put it? — toxic and dangerous. It's not just your client. It's everybody else involved, and somebody's already gotten himself killed, so the stakes are already your basic life-and-death. And any one of the bit players might get motivated to kill again, take out a lawyer who might be getting too close. And, by the way, in case they ring a bell, these are your own words I'm tossing back at you."

"Ah, that would explain the sudden eloquence."

"You laugh."

"No, actually. Not really. Those are all good reasons not to take her on. You're right."

"But . . ."

"But I don't know, Abe. I really don't know."

"Well, I know one thing."

"What's that?"

"Last time I checked, you didn't want to get shot anymore."

"Yeah, but honestly, in real life, that's probably not going to happen. Not again."

"True. No argument there. Probably not. Not very likely."

Hardy made a face. "Sounds like we're in

74

accord," he said.

In her jumpsuit, Abby sat on the concrete bench in one of the back hallway cages where they held prisoners before they entered the adjoining courtrooms. Hardy stood leaning against the wall across from her. She was line seven on the calendar for the day, which meant that, barring unforeseen delays, they'd probably get to her arraignment in the first hour or so.

In spite of all of Hardy's agonizing about it, taking care of their business hadn't proven to be much of an obstacle to overcome. Apparently, sometime after leaving Glitsky's office, he found that his gut and conscience had colluded and made his decision for him: he would be defending her if she could come up with a "friends-and-family" retainer of $25,000 to be applied against his rate of $500 an hour, with $5,000 for each day of trial. Hardy knew that the $25,000 wouldn't cover even a large fraction of what he would charge up front to take on a murder case. He wasn't exactly taking on her case for free, but this was about as close as he could get.

Nevertheless, to his surprise, she immediately accepted. She would have her mother hand deliver that first check to his office this afternoon. This was astounding, Hardy thought, given that she had no chance of seeing any of the $1 million from Grant Wagner until he'd gotten her acquitted. But if she had money, whatever the source, he wasn't going to make a stink about it. Not yet. So as to her mother bringing him her first payment, "Not necessary," Hardy told her. "She can put it in the regular mail. If it doesn't arrive, I'll know where to find you."

She almost got all the way to a smile. "Not funny," she said. Then: "So what's next? What do we do now?"

"Well, the procedure's pretty much like last time."

"I can't say that's my most treasured memory, Diz."

"I can understand that. Well, first up, they'll read you the charges. Then they'll want to hear your plea, which I'm assuming to be not guilty. Correct?"

"Yes. Of course."

"So you'll be saying that yourself, out loud, to the judge. 'Not guilty.' Short and sweet. But we might want to put that off, entering your plea. Time doesn't start to run until you've entered your plea, so we have to decide whether you'll waive time before we start that clock running."

She nodded, looked down hesitantly, then glanced across at him. "What about bail?"

Hardy clucked in frustration. "I will make an argument," he said, "but I have to tell you I think it's not too likely. You're not going to get bail of any amount on charges like that."

Although she'd perhaps been expecting this news, Hardy's verification of it took a visible toll. She put a hand up to her heart and grabbed to get a breath. "I wouldn't run away, Diz. They must know that. Not with my daughter . . ."

Hardy held up his hand. "Yes, but even if I could get the judge to take that into consideration, you've got a prior conviction."

"That again?"

"I'm afraid so. But, more specifically, I picked up the file this morning and the formal charge they've got you down for is murder for financial gain, and there's no bail on that. The DA will argue it's statutory, which means the judge has no discretion."

"Could we get the charge reduced somehow?"

"I can ask. I *will* ask. And I can keep asking as discovery comes in. Something might change. But I'm saying it would probably

77

be better if you don't get your hopes up."

Abby ran both hands back through her hair.

"The last big question," Hardy said, "is whether you want to waive time, which I highly recommend."

"Remind me again what that means."

"It means that you have the right to a speedy trial, within sixty working days of your entry of plea, which, if not today, will happen pretty quick. We've got that time to prepare for trial. If we waive that time, we give up that right and don't go to trial very soon."

"What's not very soon?"

Hardy took a long beat, then came out with a little bit of a lie. "Six months at least," he said. Then spoon-fed her what was closer to the truth, although still wildly optimistic. "Maybe a year. Or more."

Her hand went back to her chest as her head dropped in despair. When she looked back across at him, her eyes were glistening. "And all the time I'm in jail without bail?"

"Yes. I know," Hardy said gently. "This is a tough one."

"But you recommend it, this waiving time?"

"I do."

"As opposed to sixty days? How is that better?"

"Well, the short answer is that it's better because we'll have a better chance to win. We'll have time to do our own thorough investigation. Develop our own evidence, maybe a new theory of the case. The investigating officers might wig out or quit. Then again, some of their witnesses might change their testimony or forget what they'd originally said, or even might die; it's been known to happen."

"But still . . . a year?"

"As opposed to life in prison without parole if we don't win? It's really not much of a trade, Abby. And the odds are far, far better if we waive the time. We've got a much better chance, and we've got to remember that we're playing the long game here. A year against the rest of your life. It's really a no-brainer if you look at it from that perspective. Technically it's my decision. I can't put myself in a position where I don't give you a competent defense, but I want to be on the same page as you with this."

Abby brought her hands, prayerlike, up to her mouth. "I don't know how this can be happening to me again, Dismas. I didn't do anything wrong this time. I feel like any decision I make is going to be wrong just because I made it. I don't have any idea what I should do. What if I don't waive time?"

"Then it will depend on what their case looks like. If we can do it, we go to trial in a couple of months and fight with what we've got. But I have to tell you, Abby, if this case is long and complicated, I have to take the time to prepare for it."

"But if we force them to go forward, they've got to go with what they've got, too. Whatever little it is. Right?"

"Sure." Hardy nodded. "But remember, whatever they have was enough to convince the grand jury to indict you for it. Not a high bar, admittedly, but still, we'll need to put some kind of alternative scenario in front of a jury — *your* jury — and that's going to take time to develop evidence to support whatever it may be."

"I don't know if I can decide to do that, Dismas. Ask my mother to take care of Ronni full-time for a year? And she's not the easiest child, you know."

"I didn't. I don't know anything about her."

"Not that she's . . . well, I shouldn't make excuses for her." Seeming to gather herself, Abby drew a deep breath and began.

"They're pretty sure that she's somewhere on the spectrum. The autism spectrum. Asperger's. Whatever you want to call it. High-functioning, maybe brilliant, but also very challenging. They're saying she might improve as she gets older, but there aren't any guarantees with this type of thing. It doesn't seem possible I could ask my mother to take her full-time."

"So who's been watching Veronica while you've been at work all this time?"

"Well, we had a caregiver the first few years, until she was three. But that just got to be too expensive. Since then it's been Mom filling in whenever she can. I take her to school, but Mom picks her up and handles things until I get home from work. But that's only a couple of hours a day, maybe a few more on some weekends. Which is a far cry from full-time."

"All right. And where does your mother live?"

"With us. She moved in just after Ronni was born."

Hardy paused for a moment. "So I'd be correct assuming that there wasn't a husband in the picture back then?"

"Or ever." Abby shrugged. "No. When I got out of prison, I hadn't been with a man in forever . . . Anyway, I made another bad decision. One of my last ones, but . . . it came with its own consequences, and I couldn't . . . well, it's what it is, Dismas. And I love her."

"No judgment implied or stated, Abby. So it's just been you and your mom and Veronica? Ronni?"

"Just us."

"So it wouldn't uproot your mother's life if she took on a bigger role with Veronica."

This brought a small, bitter laugh. "That's easy for you to say." Then, more seriously: "She could probably handle it for a couple of months, but a year? I don't know if I could even ask her."

"Again," Hardy said, "not to beat a dead horse, Abby, but a year is not a lifetime. We need to get you acquitted here, and I haven't even seen their discovery yet. I'm not even sure what game we'd be playing, much less how to win it. There's no way anyone could be prepared in sixty days."

"I understand that," Abby said. "It makes sense. I just really don't know. Can the judge give us a break on deciding whether or not we're going to waive this time?"

"A few days, maybe more, if we're lucky," Hardy said. "But the clock's ticking right now."

"Don't worry. I hear it."

Hardy decided that this was as good as it was going to get. "All right, then." He crossed the cell and knocked at the door to the courtroom. When the bailiff opened the door, he turned back to his client. "See you when they bring you in, Abby. Hang in there."

Looking up from where she sat on the concrete bench, she nodded. She remained silent, shook her head again, and let it hang there as though awaiting the fall of the guillotine blade.

9

Even with the morning's pain pills on board, Eric Waverly felt his right hand throbbing under the Ace bandage he'd wrapped around it. Still, he wasn't going to call any more attention to it than it had thus far received. He'd already told Ken Yamashiro the falsehood that his son Jon had accidentally slammed their car door on it, and Eric did hate lying to his partner. Plus, he knew that he'd truly gotten away with something, punching the drywall and somehow not hitting one of the studs, which would have resulted in some broken bones at a minimum. As it was, his whole hand was swollen and probably would hurt for several days. And this, like nearly everything else that had happened in his life since he'd been shot, continued to fuel his simmering rage.

But he and Maddie had had a long talk last night in the wake of the punch, while he soaked his hand in the ice-water bath she'd laid out for him on the kitchen table. This constant anger, the swearing around the kids, the glare, the pain drugs, the drinking, the dark mood, and now trying to punch through the wall — she wanted him to know that it was getting too serious to ignore anymore. All of it frightened her, but the real source of her fear was what she saw as the escalation of his reactions into the physical realm. How close, she wanted to know, had he come to hitting *her* in his frustration and anger instead of the drywall?

That she even considered the possibility that he'd be capable of physically mistreating her had rocked him. If it had gotten to that point, they both agreed that he had to get his anger under control and make it stop. Beneath his tough cop exterior, Eric had always been a sweet guy, and Maddie didn't want to live in fear of him or his reactions. Maybe he should make an appointment with a therapist. Or, at the very least, if he wouldn't do that (and he wouldn't), how about if he just worked on tamping down his reactions: the swearing, the flares of temper, the striking out at physical things? How about cutting back on the pills and the booze, too?

He agreed. It was time to do something.

He could get this under control without help from a professional therapist. And in that vein, he would not even acknowledge the pain in his hand this morning. He would find a way to act cheerful and upbeat in the hope that this would fool himself and become how he really felt. You smile enough, pretty soon you're actually happy. They'd done studies. At least he'd try it.

And, in fact, one of his main frustrations from yesterday — the disappearance of the elderly witness in the David Chang homicide — had already proven to be moot.

Now they were sitting around a kitchen table in Betty Lou Honaker's apartment, the building next door to the crime scene on Stanyan Street. Betty Lou was spry and voluble. She dressed like a fashionable teenager, in blue jeans and pink tennis shoes, a black pullover sweater under a pink down vest.

She'd already apologized for not being available yesterday, but she'd gone on her walk and hadn't taken her cell phone, and then she'd stopped at a friend's house to visit and then had come home for a short while to shower and dress for her dinner date and again hadn't taken her phone, and hadn't even checked for messages in the interim. "I just can't live plugged in all the time. I don't know how these young people get anything done, with the texting and talking and taking pictures of themselves. I had a young man nearly run me over on my walk yesterday. I don't think he ever even saw me, texting away, blasting through the crosswalk. He didn't miss me by more than a foot. I smacked his car as he went by. It's illegal to text and drive, isn't it?"

"That's the theory," Eric said.

"I should have called in about him, too." Her eyes sparkled with enthusiasm. "It's funny. You go seventy-four years without ever once calling nine-one-one, and then in one day you get a couple of opportunities. Although I doubt if anybody would have bothered chasing after that young man. But he could easily have killed me and maybe not even noticed as he went texting by. Ah, well, but I do go on. I'm sorry. You're here to talk about the shooting."

"Yes, ma'am," Yamashiro said. "Did you know the victim? David Chang?"

"I didn't. I don't really know my neighbors anymore like I used to. When I first moved in here, back just after the Civil War, I knew everybody on the block, at least to talk to. Not that we were all friends exactly, of course, but we all knew one another. Now, except for Odene Mitchell on four . . . oh, listen to me."

"It's all right," Waverly said. "There's no hurry."

Betty Lou Honaker picked the thread right back up. "I was just getting ready to go out, when I heard this . . . well, it could only have been a shot, not that I've heard too many of them. Or any, even. But it was a nice day and I had these windows open." She gestured toward her kitchen sink with the windows above it. "And you know how fast the weather changes out here, so I thought it would be smart to close up before I went out. In any event, I was standing right there, and it wasn't like people say it sounds like a backfire or something. Who even knows what a backfire is anymore, anyway? I don't know that I've heard one in ten years." Impatient, she waved away her digression. "But the shots . . . with the second one, there wasn't any doubt. Not that there was before. The first one was so loud. It almost knocked me over."

"So they were close together, the shots?" Waverly asked.

"I couldn't swear to the exact time because it was like they say, it seemed to stand still. But it couldn't have been more than ten seconds, maybe less. *Bam.* And then I was holding my heart, I think, unable to move at all, wondering what . . . except I knew. And then the next one. *Bam.* It must have been the adjacent apartment in the building next door."

"And what did you do next?" Yamashiro asked.

"Well, for another minute or so — I don't really know how long it was — but for a while I just stood by the sink, waiting for another shot, I suppose. Kind of afraid to move, more than anything. Then I leaned over and looked down at the street to see if that's where it might have happened, even though it hadn't sounded like that. In any event, nothing was happening there. Then I figured that whoever had done the shooting was probably still in the building next door, and he'd probably want to get away as fast as he could, so I leaned over and was looking at the front door when he came out and headed off up the street."

The inspectors shared a glance.

"You saw the shooter?" Waverly asked.

"Well, I don't know that, if that's who he was. I didn't see any gun. But I did see a man come out of the front door and look both ways and start jogging down the sidewalk."

Waverly was first with his question. "So you saw his face?"

"Only just for a second, and looking down from up here. I can't say I'd recognize him if I saw him again; it might not even have been him. Although I think it probably must have been."

Waverly kept on. "So it was a male?"

"Yes."

"Could you tell what race?"

"White."

"Height and weight?"

"I think kind of normal." She went on. "He wasn't young, I'd bet, though I'm not really great at telling how old people are anymore. But definitely he wasn't a teenager, and maybe even was older than his twenties. Thick brown hair and some facial hair like he hadn't shaved in a few days, the way all the movie stars look nowadays, kind of unkempt."

"Clothes?"

"Nice pants, khaki. Nice plain blue shirt, too, long sleeves and collar. No jacket. Regular shoes."

"What do you mean, 'regular'?" Waverly asked.

"Not sneakers. Not boots. Shoes you'd go to work in, like you inspectors are wearing."

"Regular," Waverly said.

"Right. In fact, all in all, I'd say he was dressed like a normal business guy who was going to work at a store or in an office. Or had just come from there."

Waverly nodded. "Except unkempt."

"Only the way most men are nowadays. Not really dirty or anything like that."

"And even though he wasn't wearing a jacket," Yamashiro asked, "you didn't see a gun? Tucked into his belt or anything like that?"

"No. And given what I thought I'd just heard, believe it or not I actually looked. So it might not have been him, the shooter, after all. He might just have been one of the other neighbors, though I don't think I've ever seen him before around the building. Meanwhile, the shooter could have gone out a back door, and this other guy, the guy I saw, maybe he heard the gunshot and wanted to get out of there as fast as he could. I wouldn't have blamed him."

"So," Waverly continued, "you saw this man leave the building and jog off. Any car?"

"No. Not that I saw. But I just watched for a few seconds, then I thought he might turn around and see me looking down at him, and then he might want to get rid of any witnesses, so I backed away from the window, which was silly, I know, but . . . it was really pretty scary, the whole thing. And that's when I called nine-one-one."

"You did fine, ma'am," Yamashiro said. "Better than fine."

Yamashiro was stopping and starting in heavy traffic cutting across Golden Gate Park on their way to the home of David Chang's parents. "If an upstanding citizen like Ms. Honaker doesn't cheer you right up," he said, "there's no hope for you."

"She was good," Waverly admitted. "Unexpectedly."

"Well, unexpectedly or not, I mean, can you believe she actually saw the guy? I bet if we find a suspect, she could identify him, even though she said she probably couldn't."

"It wouldn't matter."

"Yeah, it would, Eric. An eyewitness matters."

"No gun, though, you notice," Waverly said. "And without a gun, there's no proving he's the shooter, even if he was and she nails him in a lineup."

Yamashiro wagged his head sadly back and forth. "I swear to God, Eric, you're like a turtle with a head cold. You just won't be consoled by good news, will you?"

"I would if it was good enough. That talk with Betty Lou Honaker really wasn't much. And this next stop looks to be a laugh riot, too. The parents of a dead guy — always a good time. If we ever get there."

Yamashiro glanced across the front seat. "As long as nothing is going to make you happy anyway," he said, "I might as well give up."

Waverly nodded. "Probably a good idea."

Wei and Jing Chang lived in the lower unit of a two-story duplex in the Sunset District, on Twenty-Eighth Avenue just north of Geary. Wei opened the door wearing a black business suit and tie. Sorrow exuding from his every pore, he invited the inspectors into the large and open living room and introduced them formally, with no Asian accent, to his wife and twenty-something daughter, Sara. Neither of the women looked like they had slept at all, and neither got up from the couch they shared.

Someone had laid out a tea service on a sideboard, but both inspectors declined the offer.

The introductions — such as they were — completed, Wei Chang clasped his hands behind his back and half turned to face the inspectors, who also remained standing. "Now that you are here, how can we help you?" he asked.

"Well, first," Waverly replied, "let me say that we are very sorry for your loss." Nodding sympathetically to Wei and then to the women, he went on. "Next, I have to ask: Do you know of anyone who might have had a reason to kill your son?"

"No. As far as I knew, he had no enemies. Jing and Sara both agree. We talked about this all day yesterday. We think someone must have come in to rob him. Is that something you're considering?"

"It's possible, of course," Waverly said, "but there was no sign of a forced entry into David's apartment, which makes us think he knew the person who shot him. Also, along those same lines, the shooting took place in the living room, which seems to indicate that they came back there together. Finally, David apparently felt comfortable enough to turn and face the other way in the shooter's presence, as though he didn't perceive any threat. So we don't think it was a burglary and robbery. And, let me be frank, the shooting had some elements that we'd associate with a drug killing. Two men who knew each other and fell out somehow over drugs."

Chang's nostrils flared and his eyes narrowed. "That is not possible. David did not use drugs. He didn't hang out with anyone who did drugs."

"You're sure?"

"One hundred percent."

On the couch, Sara spoke up. "It's ridiculous to say that David had anything to do with drugs. He had no use for drugs. None of his friends took drugs."

"Did he have many friends?" Yamashiro asked.

Sara gave him a fleeting look, then turned slightly and directed her answer to Waverly. "I don't know exactly. I'd say five or six guys. Mostly business acquaintances in his entrepreneur group who worked constantly, none of whom had time or the inclination, really, for drugs. It just wasn't part of that culture."

"Did he have a girlfriend?" Waverly asked.

Wei Chang shrugged his ignorance and looked over at his daughter. "No one in particular," she said.

"No breakups recently?" Yamashiro asked.

Again she answered in Waverly's direction. "Nothing serious. He dated occasionally, but he made no bones about it: he didn't want to commit to any woman until he could support whatever family they'd have. And he wasn't there yet."

"This entrepreneur group?" Yamashiro asked. "Is it like a formal thing, or just a bunch of guys? I mean, will there be a list of members, records of meetings, all that?"

Sara gave it a moment before turning to Waverly. "More informal, I think, but some of them will be in his contacts on his phone, and they'll know the other ones, I'm sure."

Since Waverly seemed to be the default focus of her attention, he took over. "Any other non-business friends?"

"Some, I guess. His college roommate Bill. Bill Kenney. They still hang out some-times, I think. Hung out." She ran a hand under her eye, wiped away a tear. "I can't believe someone did this to him. So you don't have any idea? Of a suspect, I mean. Of what really happened or why."

Waverly said, "Well, as you suggest, we'll be checking his phone and his computer, see if anything turns up. Plus, we'll be get-ting the crime scene reports from his apart-ment. Sometimes that can help paint a pic-ture."

"Of what, though?"

Waverly made a face. "That's the ques-tion. DNA, fingerprints, ballistics evidence, traces of stuff that can help tell us who's been in the apartment, at least. Which reminds me . . ." He gave her Betty Lou Honaker's description without mentioning the source.

Admittedly, it wasn't much, and after Sara had heard it, she answered with a bitter smile. "You've just about described everybody he hangs with."

"I thought that might be the case."

"So you've really got, essentially, nothing."

"Not yet, no. But please understand that it's early in the process. And I wanted to assure you — all of you — that we'll be working the case as hard as we can. Meanwhile, if anything else occurs to you that you think might be connected to David's death, no matter how small or seemingly insignificant, please let us know immediately. We're going to do everything in our power to find his killer and bring him to justice."

Back out in their car, Yamashiro said, "Sara didn't like me. I think there was a racial element to it."

"I doubt it."

"No. She didn't say a word to me. Even when I asked her direct questions. She answered to you. You must have noticed."

"Maybe she didn't understand your accent."

"Maybe that's it. Except I don't have one."

"That's what you think. I often find you very hard to understand."

"Fuck you. How's that for understand-able?"

"Clear, I must admit. So, does her being a racist have anything to do with her brother?"

"I wonder, that's all. If he hates Japanese people, too, his entrepreneur group might have wanted to let in a Japanese guy, and David might have vetoed or insulted him."

"So the guy then came back and killed him?"

"Or something. Just another possibility to keep in mind. I haven't worked out any of the details yet."

"No kidding. In its unrefined state, it might be the dumbest idea I've ever heard."

"Well, if nothing else, at least it seems to have put you in a better mood."

"Not really so much." Waverly broke a small grin. "Not at all, in fact."

10

All other things being equal, as line seven in the daily calendar, Abby Jarvis would normally have been called for her arraignment within an hour or so of court going into session. As it turned out, though, line two was a twenty-four-year-old, three-hundred-pound Samoan man named Kalolo Safale, who happened to notice that line one was not confined by hand and foot shackles the way that he was. In contrast to Kalolo, line one was also unaccompanied by bailiffs on both sides of him. It was just line one and his lawyer, two civilized people standing in the courtroom, neither of them chained like an animal.

Kalolo felt this inequality in their constraints was unfair. The more he thought about it, the angrier he became, so that by the time his line was called and he'd gotten to his place behind the defense table, flanked by his own two personal bailiffs, he was mumbling nonstop, a smoldering volcano of rage at the unfairness and racism of the system.

When the judge told Kalolo's attorney to get his client under control or he would reschedule their court appearance into the following week, it was the last straw. Kalolo, who had not yet taken a seat, erupted in a spew of Samoan invective at the judge. At the same time, he got his hands under the lip of the defense table and flipped it upside down as though it were weightless into the middle of the courtroom, almost hitting the court reporter with it, then tried to push his way through both of his bailiffs and his lawyer. He was also screaming now at the judge, who was banging his gavel and calling for order.

At last his bailiffs beat Kalolo into submission, but not before he had made it more than halfway to the judge's bench, overturning a couple more chairs and laptop computers and portable files and strewing loose papers from his attorney's binder and the rolling cabinets all over the place. Kalolo was bleeding heavily from the blows he'd taken to his head, and blood was spreading over the floor beneath where he lay, still shackled and out cold. The courtroom, with its upended furniture and debris that had settled seemingly everywhere in the bullpen, was in complete disarray and reeked of the pepper spray that the bailiffs had liberally distributed over everything during the melee. The judge ordered the courtroom cleared until it could be restored to its original condition.

In spite of Glitsky's Indian name of People Not Laughing, five of the six adults seated around the Hardy dinner table that night were cracking up at the story. Dismas, the lone holdout, said, "It really wasn't all that funny."

Wes Farrell wiped a tear from his cheek. "I'm sorry, but really? You *never* got called?"

"Never. Not once."

"That's a long day in the courtroom." Treya Glitsky, not exactly dripping sympathy, tried to arrange her smiling face.

"Tell me about it," Hardy said. "And then, after three more hours of cleanup and an hour and a half worth of lunch, they finally got all the way to us — we were next up — and then the judge said it had already been a long day, the place still stunk of pepper spray, and we should adjourn early for the weekend. To which, of course, I politely demurred. And almost got myself charged with contempt for my trouble."

"You probably weren't as polite as you thought you were being," Frannie said. "With your demurrer and all."

"Well, what was I supposed to do? Here's my poor client stuck in the slammer for the weekend now . . ."

"Where she was going to be anyway," Glitsky said, "no matter what you did."

"We don't know that," Hardy said.

Glitsky came back at him. "Special circumstances murder?" he asked. "We've got a pretty good idea."

"She wasn't getting out on bail, in any event, I'll tell you that," Farrell added. "So unless you were planning on a daring escape, she'd be back in her cell for the weekend anyway. Where she belongs, I might add."

Farrell's wife, Sam Duncan, finally spoke up. "Not to be a party pooper, but I think we're coming close to breaking the House Rule here."

This was a protocol they'd adopted several years before, just after Farrell, who had been Hardy's law partner, got elected district attorney, the city's top prosecutor. All of these men had long histories of cooperation, friendship, and — mostly — respect. But now two of them worked convicting criminals and putting them in jail while Hardy remained entrenched on the defense side. After Farrell's election, when a few initially friendly dinners had devolved into some pretty serious acrimony, the women got together and proposed the House Rule, forbidding discussion of active cases in which they might all be involved. Most of the time it worked very well. Although once in a while . . .

"Diz started it," Farrell said.

Sam gave him the cold eye. "Well, there's a mature response."

"Thank you."

"I think Sam was being sarcastic," Hardy said.

"Maybe I'm just tired."

"No sleep at all last night and then eight courtroom hours getting nothing accomplished? Why would that make you tired?" Frannie came up behind where Dismas was perched on a kitchen stool sipping a nightcap of the Macallan that probably wasn't a brilliant idea. She gave his shoulder muscles a few good squeezes. "Only a wimp would do it, but you might consider going up and lying down."

"It's one of the options I'm considering," Hardy said. "Meanwhile, you've got a half hour to cut that out."

"Or what?"

"Trouble will ensue."

"I'll risk it." She kept up the massage. "Wes and Abe seemed a little more hostile about your new client than usual tonight. Did you notice that?"

"It's because Abby's a second-timer. You know how that goes. If you've got any kind of a prior record, that whole presumption-of-innocence thing goes out the window. Not that it plays too great a role in real life anyway once you've gotten yourself convicted of almost anything, much less a homicide. And if you get arrested after that, whatever you're charged with, you're probably guilty to the average juror, and definitely guilty in the mind of a cop like Abe. Wes, pretty much the same thing."

"How about a defense attorney like you?"

Hardy didn't answer right away. Twenty seconds went by, and Frannie — digging in with her thumbs now — repeated, "How about a defense —"

"I heard you." He brought his glass up and took a sip. "But first, of course, it doesn't matter how I feel. They prove she did it or they don't. The actual fact of it doesn't really come into play."

Frannie stopped rubbing, resting her hands on his shoulders. "But yesterday the

104

actual fact of it seemed to be that you believed she didn't do it. And that seemed to matter in your decision to take her on or not."

"Yeah. Well, I had some unexpected free time pop up today, as I believe I've mentioned, and I had a chance to chat with Kathy Guerin, who caught the case and put it in before the grand jury."

"Not pretty?"

He shrugged and she kissed the top of his head.

"Let's say Abby didn't come across as the soul of cooperation when they were questioning her. The first time the inspectors talked to her, this guy Grant — the victim, her boss — hadn't even been ruled a murder. He'd died of an apparent heart attack and the questions they were asking her were all pretty routine, but still she came across as uncooperative, arrogant, and pretty snotty. Like they were only questioning her because of her past record. She didn't know anything about Grant's heart attack. Why should she? Why were they hassling her?"

"I can't really say I blame her for that. If she hadn't done anything and he'd died a natural death, what would they even have to talk to her about?"

Hardy shrugged again. "I understand why

105

she reacted that way, but it just wasn't how I'd ever perceived her. She really came across as tough and cold, when it would have cost her nothing to be a nice person, like she was, or pretends to be, with me."

"Maybe she was just afraid and got defensive."

"Maybe. But the bigger thing was the money."

Frannie came around and sat on the stool next to his.

"That's why they're giving her the Specials," Hardy said. "They're calling it murder for financial gain. Which carries no bail, then life in prison if you're guilty. No parole. As you may know."

"I've heard of it," Frannie said. "So what about the money? The million dollars?"

Hardy held up his hand. "Wait. So I went in this morning and told her about my fees to represent her and she didn't even blink. 'Twenty-five grand down? Sure. My mom will bring it right around this afternoon.' This is a single woman bookkeeper and her unemployed mother and a young daughter who needs to be cared for, living in the not-so-low-rent Marina District where it's got to set her back five grand a month. Let's get crazy and say she was making a hundred grand a year, which I doubt: Where does she get an extra twenty-five thousand dollars to pay me, and maybe more to come?"

"What about the million dollars?"

"Well, she's not going to see any of that money unless and until she gets acquitted. But if the call on Grant's death had remained heart attack, she would have gotten it, which is a pretty strong motive, I think you'll agree. And even without that, she seems to have plenty of savings. Reading between the lines of the later interrogations, it's clear that the inspectors thought — think — that she was embezzling from the company. I haven't seen the discovery yet, or the grand jury transcripts, but whatever they found, it seems it was enough to get her indicted."

"So her boss gave her this million dollars. Why?"

"That's a good question."

"And she was embezzling from him?"

"Allegedly. From the company, not himself directly. But yeah."

"So he caught her at it and was going to let her go?"

"Either that, or turn her in and get her arrested."

Frannie let out a couple of deep breaths. "Did anybody else have as good a motive?"

"Not that I've come across, but it's early

innings. I'll put Wyatt" —Wyatt Hunt, Hardy's investigator — "on it and get the big picture."

A little silence built again until Frannie broke it. "So now you've got a client who looks a lot more guilty than she did yesterday."

"A little, maybe."

Frannie ignored him. "Who is paying you' money from an unnamed and possibly illegal source at about a quarter of your normal billing rate . . ."

"Well, we don't —"

"I think we do. Isn't this exactly what you were so worried about getting involved in last night, but it was going to be okay because she really didn't do it, except now maybe in fact she did? What are the chances you could refer her to another lawyer?"

"I could, I'm sure, but —"

"But they wouldn't care as much as you do? But you haven't done enough murder trials? But you think the danger level of this one will somehow be different? These are not *my* arguments, you know. These were your very own words just last night."

Hardy met her gaze. "I know." He tipped up his Scotch, shook his head. "By which I mean I don't know. I don't have a clue."

"Just so we're clear," she said. She reached

out and patted him on the hand. "And it'll be clearer in the morning, if you'd like to try to get some sleep."

He nodded. "I don't see how that could hurt."

11

Gene was reasonably comfortable that in the long run he could get his younger sister, Gloria, on board with his plan to put the company up for sale soon, so he didn't feel any urgency about talking to her. The problem was going to be convincing second-born Grace, the sales and marketing director, who, with her bone-deep connection to their big brother Gary, was unlikely to vote for anything that didn't have Gary's full and complete approval. Their father's death seemed to have hit her the hardest of the four siblings to the extent that she hadn't shown up for work more than half a dozen times since the funeral, and Gene awoke on Saturday morning and suddenly had the idea to use those absences and her ongoing sadness as a pretext to drop by her house, something he normally did about every two years or so.

Ironically, though they had never been

particularly close emotionally, they lived only a few blocks from each other in the upper Noe Valley. When Grace had gotten married, she took her husband Jim's last name of Franklin, and now they had four children — six, seven, nine, and eleven years old. They all lived on Jersey Street in a beautifully restored ten-room Victorian, in stark contrast to Gene and Teri's dark and cold two-bedroom lower duplex.

For Gene, it was a very pleasant morning for the six- or seven-minute walk from his place. When he got to the bottom of the Victorian's front stairs — twenty-two steps from the sidewalk up to the porch — he stopped for a minute just to take in the grandeur of his older sister's home.

No wonder, he thought, that she didn't want to upset the status quo. Her house was worth three and a half million dollars minimum, and he knew that she and Jim had bought it ten years ago for around seven hundred thousand. Plus, Jim was a construction engineer and ran a small but prosperous company of his own. They simply didn't need money the way he did.

Of course, they didn't have a Teri in their household, either; Teri, who considered any day without buying something — clothes, shoes, appliances, kitchen items, gifts — a day without meaning, a lost opportunity.

Suddenly intimidated by the house, he almost walked on by, thinking it was a losing cause. In fact, he did walk completely past the bottom of the steps once before stopping, turning back around, and making the climb.

Talk about your mansion on a hill, he thought.

Grace opened the door with an expression he didn't expect, a bemused smile. "Well, this is another surprise. Did somebody put out a memo that I missed?"

"What do you mean?"

"I mean on any given Saturday morning, ninety-nine times out of a hundred I'm the soccer mom of the decade till mid-afternoon at one of the AYSO fields, but this morning my saint of a husband volunteered for that duty, and next thing I know, two of my brothers are knocking at my door when by all rights I shouldn't even be home."

"Is Gary here?"

"No. Joey. I just poured us some coffee, if you want to join us. Are you guys and Jim in cahoots about something?"

"Not that I know of."

"Well." Grace stepped back. "Come on in."

Joey Engle was already standing in the

hallway as Gene came inside. The two guys, only a few years apart, greeted each other with fist bumps, "Yo, bro," and a quick and perfunctory hug.

The family treated Joey as the little brother and considered him as such, but he wasn't related by blood to any of the Wagners, and as a wannabe tech mogul he had nothing to do with P&V's business, either. He lived by himself in a loft in SoMa and, after a few false starts with "surefire" apps, was still looking to make it large with the Next Big Idea.

To the nuclear family, Joey's connection to them, albeit convoluted, was nevertheless clearly understood and fairly straightforward. Joey had been an orphan and his aunt Ginger had adopted him. Although Ginger — another *G*! — was eight years older than Grant, the two had fallen madly in love and had gotten married in 1994, the year that she had adopted Joey. So he had come along with that package. As Grant's second wife, Ginger became the stepmother to the "G-Team" of siblings. By 2010, Ginger, though only sixty-four, started showing signs of early-onset Alzheimer's disease. For the past three years she'd been living in a full-service home in the Richmond District, in her own universe, all but completely oblivious to the world around her.

"You haven't been at work in so long," Gene was saying, "I decided to come over and make sure you were all right."

Grace held her coffee cup in both hands as though for protection. "I know," she said. "I should be going in and keeping up on things, but I just don't see the point, you know?"

"I do know," Gene said. "In spite of Gary trying to keep the ship on course, it feels to me so much like I'm just going through the motions. Like the spark's gone out of the place."

"Well, it has," Joey said.

"But what do you mean, 'in spite of Gary'?" Grace asked. "He's the one holding it all together, don't you think?"

"For now, yes. No question. I'm just thinking about the future."

"In what way?"

"In the way that, with Pops running the show, we were this well-oiled machine. Lean and mean. And we all knew what the eventual plan was."

"And that was what?"

Gene threw an apologetic glance at Joey

and said, "She's kidding."

"Kidding about what?" she asked. "I didn't know about any eventual plan. What was the eventual plan?"

"Come on, Grace," Gene said. "We were getting it all set up so one of the big chains could buy us. You knew that."

"Well, I knew we had talked about it, but I didn't think . . . it wasn't decided yet by a long shot. Not definitely, I mean."

"Well, that's really neither here nor there anyway. The point is now. And luckily, up to now, there hasn't been too much fallout in the marketplace with Pops . . . being gone . . . I mean, in terms of our client list and book value. But I think we have to be realistic and recognize that it's only a matter of time before that changes. Which means that right now we're at, or pretty damn close to, the peak. And if that's true, it means there's only one way we're going to go. As a business in terms of valuation. And here's a clue: it's not up."

"So what are you saying?" Grace asked.

Joey had been listening carefully. "He's saying we ought to put the word out on the street that we're ready to entertain offers. Subtly, of course, so nobody smells panic. But still . . ."

"Nobody's panicking," Grace said.

"Not yet, at least. Which again is why we should really think about moving on this."

"Does Gary want that?" Grace asked.

Gene picked up his coffee, took a sip, made a face. "With all the other fires he's been putting out, to tell you the truth, I don't know if he's thought too much about it yet. Which is one of the reasons I wanted to talk to you first." A little flattery wouldn't hurt, so he ladled it on. "He listens to you, Grace. We all do. So I really wanted to see if maybe you could talk to him and make him see the light. It's pretty clear that we've got to strike while the iron is hot, which is now, and I know that's what Pops would have wanted, too. That's what he was working for, that big payoff for all of us."

"You know that?"

"Absolutely."

"I don't know. How about you, Joey? Did you ever talk to Dad about that?"

The young stepbrother held up both hands, smiling to break the tension. "That's you guys. I carefully keep my nose out of all that. That said, Gene's point is a good one. P&V probably isn't ever going to be worth more than it is today. Or at least not for a long while."

"But I'm not sure I see why that matters. Don't you like working there, Gene?"

"Sure. I love it. I really do. But we're still, all of us, we're still wage slaves, putting in the hours, and if we got bought out . . . well, I mean, it would be way different. We could all do whatever we wanted."

Grace frowned. "But I'm already doing what I want. I think Gary is, too. And we're all very well paid." She shook her head. "I just don't think I've thought very much about this. I'm sorry, Gene. But you really think it would be better?"

"I do, yes."

"Well, I'm going to have to give it some more thought, then."

"That's all I'm asking," Gene said.

"What about you, Joey?" Grace asked. "You don't have any opinion?"

"No," Joey said. "I have an opinion, but I don't get to vote on it, so it doesn't matter."

"Except that I'm curious."

"Okay, to satisfy your curiosity only, I have to say that I'd go with Gene on this one. You'd each stand to make close to ten or fifteen million dollars, maybe more. How do you not decide to make that kind of money if you can? All you've got after that are more options, including starting another business if you want. It's just a no-lose proposition."

"But why change when everything is

working so well?" Grace asked.

"Because it could be so much better," Gene repeated himself.

Grace came right back at him. "Okay, possibly," she said, "but it could also be so much worse."

"She's going to be a tough sell," Joey said when the two men reached the sidewalk at the bottom of the steps. "She's not going to do anything that might piss Gary off, and Gary isn't going anywhere. What does Gloria say?"

"Gloria's probably with me, but she's not going to rock the boat until we've got three votes. That would be me and her and Grace if we could convince her."

"Well, from what I just heard, good luck with that," Joey said. They started walking. "You shouldn't ever have had four directors."

"I know. Easy to say now. But you forget, Pops wasn't ever going to die. So we had five all along, which worked perfectly. Nobody ever seemed to consider that something, someday, might change. If it hadn't been for Abby . . ."

"You think she did it?"

"Well, the cops do. Me? I don't know. I guess so. I never saw it coming, though.

That she'd have a reason to kill him. I thought, if anything, she might have had a crush on him."

Joey snorted in derision. "Hah. The rumor — what I hear — is that she was embezzling. You're the CFO. Didn't you see that?"

"No. I didn't oversee her day-to-day work. It never ever occurred to me. Since then, of course, I've taken a closer look, and there didn't seem too careful of an effort to hide what she was doing."

"So nobody checked?"

Gene shrugged. "We've always been a cash cow, as you may know — lots of cash in, cash out — so as long as we're not audited, nobody asks and nobody knows. And it wasn't all that much she was lifting anyway: maybe a hundred grand a year. She could have almost taken it out of petty cash, and in fact, sometimes, I think that's exactly what she did."

"Yeah, but a hundred a year for how many years?"

"That's not clear. Eight or nine."

"Since her kid was born," Joey opined. "So almost a million extra dollars, total. Could Dad really not have known?"

"No. He would have known. Eventually. So I think we have to assume he did."

"You mean he found out she was stealing

and called her on it?"

"No," Gene said. "If she was outright stealing from the company, Pops would have fired her right away and also changed his will, but instead he left her a million dollars. My theory is that he was part of it. It was a game they were playing, maybe him paying her in cash under the table so she could avoid the taxes. Or something like that."

"Then why did she kill him?"

"Maybe because she thought he was going to cut her off. Maybe she wanted more and he balked at it. Maybe it was a . . . a personal matter between them."

Joey stopped walking. "You're talking romantically?"

Gene shrugged. "Not impossible."

"Really? You think so?"

Another shrug. "Pops got around, for an old guy. Actually, for any kind of guy. No offense to Ginger."

"None taken. They might have still been married, technically, but she really isn't here, and by 'here' I mean anywhere."

"Maybe I should go pay her a visit," Gene said. "Be a good stepson."

"You could do that but, not to sound cruel, I really wouldn't bother," Joey replied. "She doesn't recognize anybody, Gene, and hasn't for years now. It's sad, but it's what it is. I wouldn't beat myself up over not seeing her. She wouldn't even know you were there. Besides, you're going to want to be saving your energy for the big battle. Something tells me that's where you're going to need it."

The two men walked on a few more steps. "That damned Abby," Gene said.

Joey shook his head, commiserating. "I hear you."

12

For a couple of hours on this Saturday morning, Waverly and Yamashiro had been downtown at the homicide detail on the fourth floor of the Hall of Justice, facing each other at their adjoining desks, slogging their way through the contacts in David Chang's cell phone. The people the victim had known were universally shocked and dismayed — some of them learning of his murder for the first time — but no one had even a small idea or random theory about why someone would have shot him.

Waverly was on a break between calls when the line on his desk chirped and he picked up. "Homicide."

"Hello. Is this the homicide department?"

Impatient in any event, and riding the wave of his pain meds, Waverly dripped sarcasm. "Yes, it is, though we call it the homicide detail, not the homicide department. But either way, yes, it's Homicide.

That's why I answered the phone the way I did, saying 'Homicide' and all. How can I help you?"

"I'm sorry. I don't know the protocol here. My name is Bill Kenney and I'm a little blown away and kind of upset at the moment. I just heard about one of my best friends, David Chang, getting shot. Killed. And I thought maybe I could help with the investigation somehow. I knew him pretty well — like, forever. So as soon as I heard, I called the police department number and they transferred me here to you. I don't know what I can do, if anything. But if I could help, I'd like to."

Kenney lived in the downstairs back room of a Victorian house in the upper Mission District that he shared with three other people, two women and another guy, all of whom were home when the inspectors arrived. All of them had known David Chang because he'd been a regular visitor, Kenney explained, and they all wanted to at least get an update on the progress of the case.

Yamashiro told them in the nicest possible way that they weren't at liberty to discuss the details of an open homicide investigation. What he didn't add was that that was because they were all acquaintances of the victim and hence all potential suspects. They probably weren't going to be getting the answers they were looking for, although the inspectors would be happy to take their names and other information and they would be contacted later.

In three minutes, the roommates had all dispersed to the far-flung reaches of the house. Bill Kenney, who perfectly fit Betty Lou Honaker's description of the possible gunman, remained and took a seat at the large circular table in the round dining room; the inspectors sat across from him. Waverly took out his pocket tape recorder, gave his standard introduction — his and Yamashiro's names, the date, the case and their badge numbers, the location, and the person they were talking to — and put it out on the table between them.

Yamashiro started in. "Mr. Kenney, you initiated contact with the police and we appreciate it. Can you tell us the last time you saw the victim, David Chang?"

"He was over here last Saturday. We watched some basketball in the afternoon and had a few beers and then played some video games until, I don't know, ten or eleven or somewhere in there. He took an Uber home."

"Did he talk about anything that was

bothering him?"

"No. He seemed his regular old self. He was into the Warriors game and then the tournament."

"What tournament was that?"

"Well, it wasn't really a tournament. We just called it that. Video games, you know?"

"Who won?" Waverly asked.

"I did."

"So, was there money involved?" Yamashiro asked.

"What do you mean?"

"I mean, did you bet on the games? Was there a pool? Like that."

"No. It was just for fun. We play a lot. If we bet, we'd be broke."

"Well, one of you would," Waverly said.

"But we didn't. Bet, I mean." Kenney crossed his arms and sat back, waiting. "Is that it?"

The two inspectors looked at one another. Waverly pushed at his aching shoulder. "Why don't you tell us why you called us and what your first thoughts were when you heard that David had been shot," he said.

"I couldn't imagine why anybody would shoot him. That was the main thing. He was this low-key, chill kind of person. I mean, last year we got jumped by some guys wanting our wallets, and David was all, like, 'No

125

problem, take what you want. Nice and easy.' But that's who he was. Like, if somebody was robbing him at his house, he just would have let it all happen. No fight, no struggle. So the whole thing just doesn't make any sense."

Yamashiro cleared his throat. "Where do you work, Bill?"

"Deloitte," he said. "Downtown."

"And you were there Thursday? All day?"

"Yeah. You don't think . . . ?"

"We're just covering the bases," Waverly said. "You were at work Thursday all day?"

Kenney didn't have to think about it. "Seven thirty to six," he said. "We gave a big presentation to one of our clients. I was in the middle of it. You can check if you need to."

"Thanks," Yamashiro said. "We'll do that. But meanwhile — and, again, you called us — is there anything else about David that you think might be relevant? Anything he might have been involved in that might have been dangerous or unusual?"

Kenney's face went through a few iterations while he thought about it. "Well, this wasn't dangerous, I don't think, in any way, but his entrepreneur group is a pretty wonky bunch. I don't think any of them were making any real money. But then, neither was

David. So it wasn't like he had anything worth taking."

"How about girlfriends? Boyfriends?"

Kenney shook his head. "No. He's not . . . he wasn't gay. He's had two or three girlfriends over the past couple of years, but the last relationship broke up at least a year ago. No drama, none that I saw, at least. He was talking about going on Tinder, but I hadn't heard anything about that recently."

"How about drugs?" Yamashiro asked.

Kenney found this amusing. "No. No chance. Not unless you include his Asian market stuff."

"What was that?"

"Just some teas and herbal medicines. All legal, I promise."

"What's that about?" Yamashiro asked.

"Just staying in touch with his culture more than anything. He figured since he was Chinese he should cook and heal himself with traditional herbs and spices because they wind up lining up better with his genetics. Or whatever."

Waverly came forward. "You're saying he was sick?"

"No. If he'd get, like, a cold or something, he liked to have this stuff on hand. He never made a big deal of it. Basically, he just drank tea instead of coffee. Which, you know, being Chinese, kind of made sense."

"So where'd he get this stuff?" Waverly asked.

"I don't know. Someplace in Chinatown, I'd imagine." Kenney allowed himself a small chuckle. "So how did we get on this?"

"Asking about drugs," Waverly said.

"Well, it's not like these are recreational drugs, and not at all like he was an addict or anything like that, either. If you look in his apartment, it's, like, maybe half a shelf on the spice rack in his kitchen, maybe less. Eight or ten jars. Was there some sign of drug use at his place? I mean, real drugs? Because that would be whack, since David's like one of the straightest, soberest guys I know."

As he had mentioned to the roommates earlier, Yamashiro was not there to answer questions but to ask them. So he broke a small smile. "Anything else you can think of?"

Suddenly, Kenney's expressive face shut down. "This is just so incredibly devastating. I mean, this is my best friend and now he's just gone — *boom!* Forever. I really don't know what to do with it."

"We're very sorry for your loss," Yamashiro said.

Waverly reached for the tape recorder. "If

128

anything else occurs to you, no matter how small or insignificant, please give us a call right away."

"I will," Kenney said. "I promise."

Waverly intoned the date and time and added, "The same people are present who were present at the beginning of this tape. End of tape."

Wyatt Hunt, Dismas Hardy's private investigator, lived in an enormous converted flower warehouse on Brannan Street, just around the corner from the Hall of Justice. High windows and eight thousand square feet of living space. He'd renovated the place into two areas. The back third was the apartment he shared with his wife, Tamara — two bedrooms, two baths, library, TV room, dining room, and kitchen. The larger area, with its twenty-foot ceiling, accommodated his hobbies — wind- and water surfing (four boards), guitars (seven electrics and two acoustics), free weights, computer snooping (mostly for business), and baseball and basketball, represented, respectively, by a backstop with some bats stuck in it and — the pièce de résistance — half of a professional basketball court complete with basket and net and a Golden State Warriors logo in the key that he'd bought for a song right after he'd moved in when the home team decided to replace its old court with something that had a little more bounce.

He also had his Mini Cooper parked in its spot just inside the commercial-sized garage door.

Hardy was in his weekend clothes — jeans, ancient Top-Siders, a USF sweatshirt. When he'd first arrived, he'd taken a few shots at the hoop, but the latest bullet wound in his side complained right away, and now he convinced himself that he was content just to watch as Hunt walked around the three-point line, doing his best Steph Curry imitation by sinking almost every damn shot he took, the show-off.

"It's really boring when you never miss," Hardy said. "Takes away all sense of mystery." He was standing under the basket, where he could retrieve the shots and pass them back out without expending too much effort, which he did again and waited while Hunt got the ball, dribbled once, jumped, and swished another one.

Ridiculous.

This time Hardy held on to the ball. "Okay," he said, "I declare you warmed up. You need to take a break before you wear yourself out."

Hunt hadn't broken even a little bit of a sweat. "One more," he said.

Hardy threw him the ball, which he took and dribbled out to the half-court line. Turning, barely taking the time to look, Hunt let the thing fly in a high arc that hit off the front of the basket and bounced off and away. "There you go," Hardy said. "Human fallibility on full display. Did you miss on purpose to make me feel better?"

"I can't tell you."

"Why not?"

"Because no matter what I said, you wouldn't believe me."

Hunt had picked up the ball on his way in and now dribbled as they walked back to the apartment side of the warehouse. Without warning, when they reached the three-point line, he pivoted, spun, jumped, and shot, and hit pure air within the rim. "I hate to go in on a sour note," he said by way of apology.

"Yeah," Hardy said. "That would have been awful."

Now they were sitting in Hunt's kitchen with their respective coffees in front of them. Hunt's brow was furrowed, a quizzical look on his face. "I'm not getting this," he said. "She supposedly killed this guy with poison?"

"Right."

"That's really not the most foolproof way to kill somebody."

"I know."

"And what was the name again? The poison."

"According to Kathy Guerin, he was killed with aconite."

"I've never heard of aconite."

"Join the club. It's got about ten names. It's also known as the 'queen of all poisons.' Wolfsbane. Monkshood. Devil's Helmet. Take your pick."

"I like wolfsbane."

"That's my favorite, too."

"So what happened? Did they find a supply of it at her house?"

"No. But if she had it at any time, it wouldn't have been hard to get rid of."

Hunt's frown deepened. "Okay. I'm trying to understand this, Diz. They charged her with murder, right? I'm trying to figure out what they had on her to get to that. How did they decide that it wasn't a suicide? All things being equal, it sounds like suicide is as good a bet as murder."

"For what it's worth, the ME agrees with you. The formal ruling is 'homicide/suicide equivocal.' "

"But even with that, the grand jury indicted her?"

"Yes, they did."

"Based on what?"

Hardy brought Hunt up to speed: the million-dollar inheritance from Grant, sufficient access to slip him poison, and — according to Guerin, at least — a great motive. It seems Abby was embezzling money from the firm. The police theory was that Grant caught her at it.

"All right," Hunt said when he'd finished. "All of that, taken together, might mean she's not a saint, but it doesn't make her a murderer, either."

"I'm glad to hear you say that, how the evidence strikes a regular citizen like yourself."

"What evidence? I didn't hear any evidence. Like, for example, how'd he get this lethal dose inside him?"

"Evidently he drank it, like a tea."

Hunt sat back and crossed his arms. "So they chatted while she made him tea? Did anybody see her make this tea? I mean, is there any evidentiary case that puts her with him?"

"Her office was just down the hall from his. She'd go in from time to time, most days, usually in the later afternoon, and they'd take a break together, just the two of them. He was a big tea drinker — five or six cups a day — and evidently Abby and Grant made their own exotic blends. He had a cabinet in his office with all kinds of different teas."

"And that's where they found the wolfsbane?"

"No. They haven't found it."

"So in theory, then, couldn't it have been anybody in the office? Or anybody who knew about this tea collection?"

"Yeah. But there's another little wrinkle I think you'll like."

"Hit me."

"Wolfsbane leaves aren't poisonous. You dry them and drink them and nothing happens. Maybe you get a little buzz. The poison is in the root."

"And where do you get that? The root."

"Anywhere you want, really. Believe it or not, it's not a controlled substance. If you know where to find it, you can just go buy it. So herbal shops, some Asian markets. Lots of online sites. But again, there wasn't any of that — the root — in Grant's cabinet. But that didn't really matter, either, because he evidently took the poison at his home. That's where they found him dead."

"And had she been there, to his house?"

"Well, yes, evidently, but not necessarily on the night he died. At least, there's no proof that she was there that night, and she denies it in any event." Hardy hesitated. "I must tell you, Wyatt, I think they indicted her because they really didn't have anybody else to look at."

Hunt reached for his coffee cup. "Do you want to hear the good news?" he asked.

"Always."

"Well, this sounds to me like there's really very little case. It ought to be a walk in the park for a professional litigator like yourself."

"Except for the indictment, I'd agree with you. But you know once these things get in front of a jury, all bets about real evidence are off."

Just then the kitchen door from the outside back alley opened.

"Dismas Hardy," Tamara said as she put her grocery bag down. "As I live and breathe."

Hunt's wife was seven months pregnant and insanely beautiful. "You've got to stop taking those ugly pills," Hardy told her. "They're just not working."

With a tolerant smile, she leaned over and kissed him on the cheek. "You're looking rather hale and hearty yourself. Can it be

135

that, last time we saw you, you were in the hospital?"

"That sounds right," Hardy said. "I've been laying low."

Hunt popped in. "Yeah, but still, we went out back to shoot some hoops and he used that old 'I got shot' excuse out on the court."

"Twice," Hardy said. "I got shot twice."

13

Hardy's basic instructions to Hunt were to find plausible alternatives that he could present to the jury at the trial, including other potential suspects whom the police might have overlooked, and possible still-unknown or undiscovered motives for Grant to have killed himself. It did not hurt that Hunt had a long-standing and strong relationship with Lieutenant Devin Juhle, head of the homicide detail; at least he might get slightly more cooperative access to the inspectors who had drawn the case, two veterans named Waverly and Yamashiro.

Meanwhile, since Wyatt Hunt's place was less than two blocks from the Hall of Justice and the jail, Hardy went to the DA's office to pick up whatever discovery had now become available. Twenty minutes after that, Hardy was back in the circular and sterile attorney visiting room greeting his client, who had already taken on what he thought of as the jailhouse pallor. This time she came in without handcuffs and so was spared that slight indignity, but her general demeanor at first glance — a kind of furtive wariness — suggested that she hadn't yet completely adjusted to her time behind bars.

"How are they treating you?"

"Like they do."

He'd stood up by his chair when she entered, and now when the guard closed the door behind her, she crossed the space between them. "If you want me to be honest," she said, "I could use a real hug."

Nodding with acceptance, Hardy stepped forward and put his arms around her. She leaned into him and held him far more tightly than she had the last time they'd met here. Up close, holding her, he was struck by the strong smell of bleach, disinfectant, and laundry soap. After ten or fifteen seconds, he patted her back gently, but she leaned in against him and tightened her hold on him. "No," she whispered. "Please."

She pressed her face and body against him with enough pressure to cause him some pain where one of the bullets had creased his ribs. Again he nodded, this time all but to himself, and the embrace went on for another twenty seconds, perhaps half a minute. He was going to let it go on as long as she felt like she needed it.

Finally, with a sigh, she let up her hold on him and stepped back. She looked up at his face. "I'm sorry. I just needed some human contact."

"Not a problem," he told her. "Hugs come with the program. Free." He sat back down and she followed suit. "So, how are you holding up?" he asked her.

"Better, I think. Trying, anyway. In spite of needing that hug. Ronni and Mom came by to visit this morning and that helped. Maybe helped all of us."

"How are they doing?"

"All right, which, given Ronni's issues, is kind of a miracle. She doesn't really understand why I'm here, because she knows I didn't kill anybody, but she knows there'll be a trial and that I'll get off. Especially since it was Grant."

"So she knew Grant?"

"Of course. Grant was like her uncle."

"So he'd visit with her and you? Was this a regular thing?"

"Not formally. But he'd come by maybe once a month or so, take us all to dinner, frequently to places I could never afford. So she — Ronni — she knows I would never have done anything to hurt Grant."

"That's good."

"It is. But I'm afraid it might turn into a problem for you and me."

"How's that?"

"Well, this whole thing you talked about yesterday, with me waiving time."

"What about it?"

Abby scratched at the metal surface of the table. "Ronni can understand that I have to go on trial because the police have got it wrong, what happened to Grant. But since she thinks it's impossible that I killed him, and she's right, she sees the whole thing as kind of a formality that we just have to get out of the way, and then I'll be back home. The idea of having to wait for a year or more? I couldn't really even bring it up, and I can't see ever agreeing to let things drag on for that long with me in jail. I think Ronni might really freak out, to say nothing about my mom."

Hardy tried to keep the disappointment out of his expression. He forced a small grin, which disappeared as quickly as it had arrived. "Well, as I told you yesterday, Abby, it's really my decision, and if you really want me to represent you, you're going to have to give me enough time to get ready. We don't even have the grand jury transcript yet. Neither one of us has any idea of what we're up against. The idea of waiving time is something your family is going to have to handle. I can't represent you unless you do, and, frankly, I can't think of any other lawyer who'd agree to do it, either."

"I think I understand what you're saying," she said. "But look at it this way. They don't have anything on me now — not really — do they? I mean, in terms of real evidence. I didn't buy any poison, for example, so nobody's going to show up proving I did. And I certainly didn't go to Grant's house the night he died. So, really, there isn't very much."

Hardy chuckled. "My private investigator just told me the same thing."

"So that's a good thing, right? If they take a year and still that's all they've got, they can't convict me, can they? So we'll have the same chance in sixty days as we will a year from now or longer. Right?"

"In theory, perfectly right," Hardy said. "But juries are notoriously unpredictable. You can tell them they need physical evidence, a smoking gun — that every single stitch of evidence must be proved beyond a reasonable doubt — and still they tend to think that, since you've been arrested, you must have done something wrong, and probably what you've been charged with."

"Okay, but my point is that even with all

you're saying, we're still as well off not waiving time as holding everything off for a year."

Hardy chuffed out a breath in frustration. "Well," he said, "we've got until Monday to make that decision, and if that's what you want to do, after I've seen all the discovery, I'll consider it. Because as far as I know so far, you are right. The evidence is slim."

"Good. Thank you."

"You're welcome." Sitting back, he took a beat. "But I must tell you," he went on, "that even though the physical evidence is light, there's a thing called circumstantial evidence, and enough of that can be pretty damn persuasive."

"Enough to convict an innocent person?"

With a dead flat affect, Hardy nodded. "It's been known to happen." A pause. "And since we're on the subject, Abby, I need to ask you a few questions, just so I know what we'll be dealing with."

"That sounds ominous enough."

"It might, but it's necessary."

Abby filled her lungs, let the air out in a rush. "Okay."

"Okay, let's take the big one first: the embezzling accusation."

Hardy told her what Guerin had told him: that there was money missing from the company and evidence that Abby had taken it.

Her face clouded with anger. "That is just bullshit, Diz. There wasn't any embezzling ever. Grant knew all about it from the beginning, right after Ronni was born. In fact, it was his idea completely. It was a tax thing. And, okay, so maybe it wasn't completely legal. Who did it hurt? And what was I supposed to do, look this totally generous gift horse in the mouth?"

"But you did take money out of the corporation?"

Abby leaned back and gave him a look. "Are you going to tell me you're shocked to hear that small businesses sometimes play some accounting games to, for example, avoid taxes?"

"And that's what this was about?"

"It was one of the things, sure. We made less profit, so we paid less taxes. We'd give discounts to certain customers in return for payments in cash. And in my case there would sometimes be leftover money on a cash deal where I'd short the invoice and take the extra cash. I could draw you a diagram, but you're a business guy with a small company: I think you get the picture. My point is that the business, P&V, has a very large cash element and Grant knew every step of the process. I mean, technically, maybe it was shady, but as I said, who did it hurt?"

"But there was —"

She interrupted him. "Wait. Why in the world would I want to hurt the guy who is making my life so much better than it would be otherwise? Can anybody tell me that?"

"Well, how about, since there's no record of any of these cash transactions — and I'm right there, right?"

"Yes."

"Okay. What about — just making the argument — what about if Grant didn't know about you taking the cash —"

"But he did!"

"So you say."

"I do say, Dismas. Goddamn it. Don't you believe me?"

"Of course I believe you. But the prosecution is going to have a different interpretation. Which is this: What if he didn't know, and there was just so much cash flowing in and out that you could take as much as you wanted and it was never a problem for the business, and everything was just running along smoothly until recently, when — I don't know — the company got audited to attract potential buyers, for example? Or Grant suddenly became aware that you were skimming cash against discounted invoices or something like that?"

Abby shook her head against this onslaught. "But that wasn't it. That wasn't what happened at all. Grant knew all along. He was part of it. There *was* no crisis. Nothing changed. It was just that Grant died. Otherwise nobody would even have looked."

"And why, again, did Grant just want you to have all this extra money? At considerable risk to his reputation and to his company, I might add."

She leaned all the way back against her chair and crossed her arms over her chest, her face set in a childlike and stubborn pout.

Hardy let the silence lengthen, his eyes occasionally meeting hers, holding her gaze until she would look away. Finally, after a small eternity, he bent toward her, his voice barely audible, and said, "Tell me this, Abby: Why was it so important that no one knew he was Ronni's father? Why is it still so important?"

For an instant her whole body seemed to stiffen as though an electric jolt had run through her. She swallowed, then let out a heavy breath. "You don't know that," she said. "You can't know that."

"No, but I can make the assumption, and I won't be the only one. Were you still involved with him when he died?"

Suddenly she snapped at him. "Stop talking about this as though it was a fact. You don't know anything about us. Ronni's father was a guy I didn't even know and I still don't. I already told you this. It was a one-night stand and a mistake."

"So it wasn't your husband?"

"No. Bill was another mistake. I was already a couple of months pregnant when I met him. It turned out he didn't want a baby. I should have told him before we got married, but I thought I could . . . well, never mind. I couldn't. Another stupid mistake. The only thing good to come out of all that was Ronni. But her father isn't Grant."

Hardy had his hands clasped on the table in front of him. He looked down, tapped his thumbs together a few times, then raised his eyes toward his client. "This can cut both ways, Abby. First, even with Grant dead, they've got his DNA and either side can run a paternity test to prove he's Ronni's father.

"On the one hand, it explains why he would give you the money from the firm, and it gives you a reason not to kill your daughter's father, who is coincidentally the golden goose. On the other hand, a prosecutor could argue that someone in a fraught emotional relationship is much more likely to have killed Grant, since nobody else on the planet seemed to have the slightest reason to do so.

"But the most important thing is that you have to tell me the truth before I can do anything. It's bad luck to bullshit your lawyer and time for it to stop right now. And if you can't trust me with that information, I'm afraid I'm not going to be able to keep on representing you." He tried to dredge up a neutral expression. "I'll give you a couple of minutes."

Standing up, Hardy walked the short twenty feet over to the door she'd come in through, which led back into the jail proper. He looked at his watch, the second hand sweeping inexorably around. After two minutes and eight seconds, he turned with a sigh. "I'll stick with you through the arraignment on Monday, of course. I've got several excellent colleagues who I'm sure will do a fine job and we'll get you set up with one of them." He gave it another ten seconds. "I'm going to knock for the guard now," he said.

He saw her drop her head, then whirl around.

"Wait!"

■ ■ ■ ■

"It was all my fault," she said. "I knew he was married. I knew he was the father of my best friend. I knew what I felt about women, and what generally happened to the women, who slept with their potential bosses. So there we were, Grant and I, having my job interview. I was only a week out of prison. Gloria had set it all up, so it was basically up to me not to blow it. I got to the warehouse around four — this was before the whole new configuration, so Grant's office was downstairs in the back — and we sat down and just started talking.

"I told him a little about my background, and the accident and how I'd killed that poor woman and hurt her son so badly, and how I was going to be sober the rest of my life and still never be able to pay back the people I'd hurt. But I was sure going to try by never being anyone's burden again.

"Then we — Grant and I — we got on to surviving prison after all that. And I guess after what I'd told him, he felt comfortable telling me about some of the personal stuff in his life. How he and Peggy — that was his first wife — had the four kids in quick succession and then, when he was thirty-six, she died suddenly of a cranial aneurysm. Which left him building the company pretty much on his own, getting married again, moving on.

"Anyway, long story short, by the time we looked at a clock, it was seven thirty and I felt kind of madly in love with him, inappropriate and ridiculous as that was. He asked me if I had plans for dinner, and when I didn't, he suggested we order in and so we got Chinese. After all those prison meals, talk about heaven. In any event, after we finished eating, we somehow found ourselves on the couch together. And that was that."

Without having to ask, Hardy could see that Abby didn't share his vision, but he didn't think that this was such a pretty or romantic story. Here was a young, poor, unemployed woman, emotionally vulnerable after a spell in prison, looking for a job from a wealthy, much older married man who had traded that job — no matter how either of them spun it — for sexual favors. She had used the word *inappropriate* in referring to herself, but Hardy felt that she was pure as the driven snow in comparison to Grant Wagner's behavior toward her.

But he wasn't there to judge either of them. His job was to get to the bottom of the facts of the current relationship between Abby and Grant so that he wouldn't be blindsided during the trial in case these details came to light or he even decided to bring them up himself. "And by 'that was that,' " he said, "you mean that was when Ronni was conceived?"

"No, not that night, exactly. More like sometime in the next few weeks."

"But after that first night, I'm gathering he hired you."

She hung her head. "I know that sounds bad, but it wasn't like you're thinking."

"No? How was it, then?"

"I was qualified. My degree was in accounting and bookkeeping. He told me I was hired within an hour of meeting him at that first interview, so that really didn't play any kind of a role in our relationship."

Hardy wanted to box her ears or, failing that, scream at her: Of course it did, you idiot!

Instead, mild and controlled, he said, "And what about the second wife?"

Her face scrunched up in a show of disappointment. "I know. Ginger. I felt bad about Ginger. But the truth is that they had a solid working marriage. They got along very well with each other: they had Joey — Ginger's boy — that they were raising together with

Grant and Peggy's kids. And Grant made it clear early on that if we were going to go on seeing one another, it couldn't threaten his marriage to Ginger. She's much older than he is, you know? Eight years, and now she's got Alzheimer's. Actually, she's had it for a while, which is a tragedy, but the fact is that she's in a full-time facility and doesn't really know who she is, so she's not much in the picture anymore."

"But you and Grant, while she was still in the picture, you were still seeing one another romantically?"

She nodded with an embarrassed expression. "When we could. Sometimes. Not so often anymore as we used to."

"Was that a source of conflict between the two of you?"

"No. We had an understanding. We didn't have conflict."

"Never?"

She hesitated, took on a look of distaste. "Since this appears to be tell-all time, you'll find out anyway. But he got another girlfriend six or eight months ago. Stacy Holland. They've since broken up, but we had a few bad nights about it."

"Did you play a role in that breakup?"

"What do you mean?"

"I mean, did you ask Grant to break it off

151

with this woman?"

"I did. I didn't think it was right or fair that he was seeing her."

"Sharing him with Ginger was all right, but it wasn't all right sharing him with Stacy?"

"Ginger wasn't really there the last few years. I thought when she died something might change."

"With you and Grant?"

"Yes."

"That he might marry you? Something like that?"

"It had come up. If the time was ever right."

"And what happened with Stacy? Did you tell Grant he had to break up with her or else?"

"Or else what?"

"I'm asking you."

"No. You're asking did I threaten Grant in some way? No. I just told him that Stacy in the picture made me uncomfortable. He said Stacy was with me kind of the way I'd been with Ginger."

"The second wife?"

Clearly, Abby didn't like that terminology. "I said I didn't want to share him anymore. It was either going to be me or her. Not both. And he chose me."

Hardy thought to himself: So he said. Or so you said. But if not . . . another excellent motive to kill and a mark in the ledger against bringing any of this up at the trial. "And how did Stacy feel about this breakup?" he asked.

"Upset, I would guess. Grant said it was really hard to handle her: she was so furious. She felt like he'd betrayed her."

"Is it possible that she felt betrayed enough by Grant to decide to kill him?"

Abby's mouth formed a silent O. This was either the first time she'd considered that possibility, or she wanted Hardy to believe it was. "I don't know," she said. "I never met her. But that really might be worth looking into."

"I will, don't worry. But if you can handle another few minutes, I'm still curious about a few things."

"I'll check my datebook," she said, breaking out a weary smile. Grabbing a quick breath, she took a beat. "Sure, I'm good. Let's go."

Hardy flashed a tight, humorless grin, and charged right ahead. "I think it's not unlikely that the prosecution is going to try to paint the money you took out of the company as a blackmail payment. As long as Grant kept giving you money, you wouldn't disclose his paternity of Ronni, so he'd get to keep his marriage to Ginger intact, among other things. It wouldn't upset the rest of the family. It wouldn't undermine his authority as the CEO with his other kids, the so-called G-Team. What's your answer to that?"

"My answer? It wasn't anything like blackmail. I never threatened him in any way. He came up with the idea for the money."

"Why didn't he just pay you more? Or admit the paternity?"

"Well, in strictly business terms, he couldn't really justify a superlarge payment without raising suspicions. I was already at about the top of what a bookkeeper realistically could make. And admitting the paternity — I think I said this before — would have probably meant breaking up with Ginger, or screwing up Joey, or both. And he didn't want to do that."

"Yeah, but what about screwing up Abby?"

She nodded. "I know. I can see why you ask that."

"Well?"

"Well, I guess the main thing is we made a deal, right from the beginning when I found out I was pregnant. I told him right away."

"And how did he take the news?"

"Very well. He said he'd support me whatever I wanted to do. It was my decision."

"You mean an abortion?"

"Or put her up for adoption. Or even keep her and raise her as I did. Whatever I decided, he still wanted to see me."

Somewhere in the telling, tears had overflowed onto Abby's cheeks, and now she wiped them away, one side, then the other. "But he really hoped that, if I kept the baby, I wouldn't ask him to change his life. He'd made a deathbed promise to Peggy that he'd never do anything to threaten the G-Team. They'd always be his only acknowledged children. The same reason is why he never had Joey become involved with the business. He loved me, and he'd help support Ronni, but that was how it was going to have to be if we were going to be together."

"And you were okay with that?"

"Obviously. I didn't want to have to put him through that pain. And I didn't want to be a home wrecker. I just wanted my baby and to know that Grant loved me."

"And you agreed to all these conditions, disadvantageous as they were?"

"I didn't feel that they were. It was what I wanted, too."

"You didn't feel that, as Ronni's father,

Grant had an absolute obligation to support her? California law would have been on your side on that one, almost without any discussion."

"Maybe. But that's just not how he and I decided we were going to do it. And it worked, Dismas. It's worked for all these years."

Be that as it may, Hardy thought it was beyond a terrible deal for Abby and her daughter (who might in fact be one of Grant's legitimate heirs), and the idea that she would agree to this arrangement spoke volumes about her lack of self-esteem.

But also, since the strategic decision of whether or not a suspect would testify in a trial was always a major one, he was marginally satisfied with the turn this discussion had taken. Whether or not he would get Abby on the witness stand to tell this story, her situation with Grant Wagner was so egregiously unfair that, all by itself, it gave Abby a motive for killing him. Now he was aware of this minefield and would perhaps be able to avoid it.

And that was even if nothing had changed in the past month — since Grant had broken up with Stacy Holland, say — and he and Abby were going along as usual with Abby essentially a concubine, raising her

156

autistic child without any acknowledgment from her father, working at a day job for Grant and taking a large portion of her pay in illegal embezzled cash.

Living life under those conditions, Hardy thought, might drive a saint to commit murder.

But imagine how much stronger the motive to kill her lover would be if the status quo was changing — if Grant decided to cut off the flow of illicit money, maybe to hook up with Stacy Holland, perhaps even to lay off the clerk who'd been cooking the books all these years.

Facing that kind of betrayal, with no power, no influence, no leverage, and no hope, Abby's grab for the million dollars Grant had left her in his will might have felt completely justified, and she had to act quickly while that bequest was still in effect.

That was how any jury Hardy could imagine would see it.

It was how he was even tempted to start seeing it himself.

14

His brow creased in anger, Gary Wagner put his cell phone down on the desk in his home office, sat still for a moment fuming, then pushed back his black leather rolling chair. He stood up, drew in a breath and let it out, then walked across the room to the window that looked out over his backyard.

On this warm and sunny Saturday afternoon, it was a beautiful view and one that, most of the time, soothed him. Unlike his siblings, Gary had made the decision years ago to leave the hustle and hassle and chill of the city and move down the peninsula to Hillsborough. He and Eileen pushed the envelope on what they could afford back then and bought themselves a three-bedroom foreclosure on three-fourths of an acre for a million six, which at the time had seemed like all the money in the world. Now, as he stared across the green grass, over the pool, and into the shaded expanse out to the back hedge, he knew that he was living in and currently looking out at a total of at least $4 million of real estate, possibly quite a bit more.

But, as usual, more money didn't seem to make him any happier.

"That didn't sound like a very pleasant discussion," his wife said from the doorway.

He turned away from the window. "My love, are you spying on me?"

"You get to a certain volume, the sound kind of carries. I could have left the house and not heard you, but that seemed a bit extreme." She walked across the Persian rug covering the hardwood and laid a gentle palm against his cheek. "Is everything all right? Because it doesn't sound like it."

Something went out of Gary's shoulders. "That was Grace. It seems like Gene and Joey stopped by her place this morning and tried to talk her into going along on the question of putting P&V up for sale."

"Joey? What was he doing there?"

"Yeah, I know. Or rather, I don't know. But Gene . . ."

"Gene's just a crab."

"Well, maybe not *just*. If he's going to Grace and trying to get her into backing him up while he orchestrates some kind of coup, he moves into the realm of true menace."

"And that's what he went there to talk about?"

"That's what Grace said. Evidently, he's already got Gloria on board."

" 'On board.' Say it like that and it does sound like a conspiracy."

"That's because that's what it is. You can't call it anything else."

"Couldn't you just buy him out? Or them? All of them if you need to."

"Wouldn't that be nice?"

"Well?"

"Well, good idea, but I couldn't offer them anything like what we'd eventually get on a bid from any of the big guys. Not for a few years at least. As of right now, we're nowhere near that, especially after Pops . . ." At the mention of his father, more of his pent-up energy seemed to seep out of his posture.

"But I thought . . . Didn't you say that things were going pretty well? I mean, I know there have been some hiccups, but . . ."

"Day to day, yeah, sure, things are okay. We're in the black. It's all good as far as it goes. But we've got a huge issue that isn't going away anytime soon."

Suddenly and obviously concerned, Eileen

lowered herself onto the ottoman in front of Gary's dark leather reading chair. Her hand went to her chest. "What kind of issue?"

Gary hesitated. "Legal," he said. "Accounting."

"Serious?"

He shrugged. "As a legal matter, potentially, maybe. But in terms of the company's salability, it's a monster. As part of any sale, the buyer would insist on seeing the books. We get audited — and we'd have to if we put ourselves up on the block — we could take a pretty good hit in terms of valuation. We'd be nowhere near where we are today, not even close."

"Okay, now you are scaring me. What does Gene say about it?"

"He's more or less oblivious."

"But how can he be? He's the CFO."

"Yes, he is, but he's a long way from being the bookkeeper."

"What do you mean? Do you mean it was Abby after all? Are you saying she was doing something illegal?"

"Irregular at best. Probably illegal, too. They charged her with embezzling tens of thousands of dollars. God knows what else we'll find when we take a hard look at everything she's done over the years."

"So" — Eileen paused, her hand now at

her throat — "are you saying she killed your father? I never thought —"

"I don't know if I'm all the way to believing that yet, but she was definitely taking money out of the company. A lot of it. For a long time."

"Oh my God."

"Yeah. It's not pretty."

"Did your father know?"

"Not that I know of. Nobody did. She claims it was a long-standing agreement between her and Pops to save her on taxes, but there's no proof of that."

"When did you find this out?"

"After the grand jury charged her with grand theft. But the bottom line is our financials are going to be way off if anybody wants to look at them closely. So I can't let that happen."

"Can you explain that to Gene? And your sisters, too?"

"I could do that, but I'm not sure they'd believe me. I'm still not a hundred percent sure that *I* believe it. But Grant must have noticed. He knew every tiny detail of what happened every day. A box of Kleenex couldn't have gone missing without him spotting it."

"How could Abby have taken all this money without him catching?"

162

Gary cocked his head, gave her a piercing look. "I think we can figure that one out, Eileen. Don't you? He *did* know what was going on. He was letting her have the money. And we both know why."

It didn't take her long to do the math. "That would make Abby's autistic daughter —"

"Veronica," Gary said.

"Okay, Veronica. You're saying she might actually inherit?"

"That's not impossible. If Abby starts talking about paternity and gets picky about it, the law is clearly on her side."

"So you're saying that Veronica is your half sister?"

"She might be. She probably is. Abby could find out easily enough, if she hasn't already."

"She must know."

Gary shrugged. "You'd think so. You'd also think she'd have been motivated to find out for sure, wouldn't you? And this is regardless of whether Abby gets convicted of killing Pops. Which, God help me, I still just can't get my head around. I've always thought she was the soul of loyalty, especially to Pops."

"So what happened? Did he find out what

she'd been up to? Was he going to cut her off?"

"Well, she never talked about it, but what was she going to say? For the record, she seemed as devastated as any of us. Maybe more than some."

After a relatively long pause, Eileen looked up at her husband. "Let me ask you something," she said.

"Anything."

"You're not going to like it."

"All right, I'm prepared."

"What if we just called it quits?"

"And what good would that do?"

"It would take away all this stress and give us a few million dollars, Gary. Maybe nowhere near what we could get if there weren't all of these problems, but we could at least talk about it."

"Now you're sounding like Gene."

"Is he so wrong?"

"Well, from a strictly business perspective, this is not a good time to sell, so, yes, he's wrong there. By comparison, if we let all this stuff shake out in two, maybe three years, we might get ten times what we could bring home today. So that strikes me as worth the wait. But beyond that, what would I do?"

"You could cut a deal to stay on as president during the transition and maybe a couple of years after that."

"And then sign a noncompetition agreement that would keep me out of the only business I know?"

Eileen shook her head. "You could run any business, Gary. Don't kid yourself."

"But this is who I am. Like Pops before me and his dad before him. P&V is ours, hon. Our baby. I don't want to give it up, not unless the money becomes truly stupid, and maybe not even then. And there's simply no reason to."

His wife exhaled in frustration. "You don't exactly sound open-minded about it."

"That's probably because I'm not. You don't think I've thought about this? A lot?"

"No. I'm sure you have. But maybe you haven't thought enough about your siblings and what they want."

"I have, Eileen. Of course I have. I feel a tremendous responsibility to them. But what they want doesn't make sense. Not at this moment, anyway. Gene's just creating a false crisis, as though we don't have enough of one already with Pops' passing. I just need more time. They should see that."

"I'm sure they're trying to understand, Gary."

"Well, they should be trying harder."

■ ■ ■ ■

As lieutenant of Homicide, Devin Juhle had a private office with a door that closed should the need arise. In his office now, catching up on paperwork, Juhle frowned at the knock on that door: he was in here on the weekend, after all, because the odds were decent, all things being equal, that he would be left alone and allowed to actually finish something.

"It better be good," he said in a testy tone.

The door opened and his friend Wyatt Hunt poked his head in, grinning like a Labrador retriever. "Hey!"

With a pained expression, Juhle closed the binder in front of him. "I've got my cell phone with me, so you could have called and made an appointment like other people."

"I know. But we're friends. Besides, I called your home first and Connie said you were down here, so I thought I'd make your day with a surprise visit. It's one of the perks of living so close. I can just drop by with no warning. You busy?"

Juhle motioned to the stack of in-box paper, the wall of binders at the edge of his desk. "No. As you can see, I'm just whiling

166

away the afternoon. What do you want?"

"Nothing much. I just thought we'd catch up on stuff, maybe go grab a cup of coffee."

"No. Really. I do have some work I was hoping to finish. What's up?"

Smiling broadly, Hunt came all the way into the room and closed the door behind him, then took one of the chairs. "I pulled an assignment with Diz Hardy on Abby Jarvis and I thought I'd ask politely if I could have a small chat with the inspectors who worked that case. Yamashiro and Waverly, in case you lost track."

Juhle pointed to the whiteboard on the wall opposite him over Hunt's shoulder. "Yep. That's who I've got working it. But thanks for the reminder."

"So?"

"So what?"

"So you know how inspectors are. In the normal course of events, they're not going to want to cooperate with a private investigator working for the defense unless and until somebody greases the wheels a little bit. Tells them I'm okay. Like that."

"What makes you think you're okay? You just told me you're working for the defense, which means you're working to help get their suspect off, are you not?"

"No. Absolutely not." Feigning pain at this

gross misinterpretation of his motives, Hunt put his right hand over his heart. "I'm surprised — hurt, even — that you could even say that."

"Didn't you just tell me you're working for the defense?"

"Technically, perhaps, sure. But mainly I'm working to see that justice is done. Same thing as they are."

This finally brought a smile to Juhle's face. "It would be fun to watch their reaction when I tell them that."

"So you'll talk to them for me? Maybe make an introduction?"

"Will that take you out of my office and leave me free to do the hard work for which the citizens of this great city pay me?"

"It will."

In a flash, Juhle was up out of his chair and coming around his desk. "In that case, let's see if they're available."

Eric Waverly evidently had some kind of conflict and hadn't come back to work after lunch, but Ken Yamashiro stood up and shook hands with Hunt in a friendly enough manner when Juhle introduced him. As soon as the lieutenant had gone, however, the apparent camaraderie between professionals all but vanished.

"The Jarvis matter is old news to us," Yamashiro replied in his "I'm a cop" voice before Hunt could get much of a word in — before he'd even sat down in the chair next to the desk. "We've got a couple of new cases that are taking up pretty much all our time."

Making himself comfortable sitting down, Hunt went for conciliation. "Always. That's just the way it is. But I understand that Jarvis just got herself arrested only a couple of days ago. Thursday, I think it was. I gather you guys brought her in. Am I right on that?"

A shrug. "She got herself indicted. That's what happens. Nothing out of the ordinary."

"Really? I heard the coroner originally ruled the victim died of a heart attack."

"Yeah. He got that wrong. But he eventually found the poison."

"Right. But how about you guys? From the discovery I've seen so far, there wasn't any poison where Jarvis lived, or anyplace else that I saw."

"Poison." Yamashiro shrugged again. "You flush it down the toilet, it's gone. Or put it in the garbage. We're talking almost four weeks ago. A lot of time to clean up and get rid of stuff."

"But, as you say, it was gone."

Yamashiro leaned back in his chair, folded his hands over his stomach. "What's your point?"

"My point is that Jarvis got indicted, so there must have been something to convince the grand jury that she was guilty. I'm just wondering what that might have been."

"You'll have to wait for the grand jury transcript."

"But they must have had something."

"When you get the file," Yamashiro said, "take a look at her checking account. That ought to get your attention."

"Okay. But I was wondering about other stuff, before you even saw the checking account yourselves."

"What do you mean?"

"I mean other suspects."

Yamashiro appeared to cogitate for a few seconds. "Not really, no. You know she's done time, don't you? Jarvis."

"Yeah, but vehicular manslaughter seems a long way from murder by poison."

"Yeah, but it's a long way from sainthood, too."

Hunt scratched at his cheek. "All right, how about this: I noticed the name Stacy Holland in your field notes, but not much in the way of follow-up, which of course made sense, since you already had a suspect.

170

But who was she?"

"Nobody. An old girlfriend. Out of the picture long ago."

"I only saw a short interview. Did you ever follow up with her?"

"No. But we didn't follow up with Snow White or any of the dwarfs, either. Why? Because they weren't part of it. As far as we could tell, Stacy hadn't seen or talked to our victim in a month. They broke up. What were we supposed to talk to her about? Especially since we had Jarvis, who — trust me on this — did it."

"Do you know? Did she go to his house the night he died?"

"Look . . . Hunt, is it?"

"Wyatt Hunt."

"Okay. So listen, Hunt. This murder went down a month ago, but everybody more or less remembers where they were that night. Except Jarvis, who said she was pretty sure she hadn't been there — at Grant's place — either that day or the day before. But her own mother's calendar has Jarvis out that night, getting home from work, as she calls it, at around nine. And her cell phone mysteriously went dead between seven and nine p.m. So that doesn't prove she was there, but it sure as hell doesn't mean she wasn't. Beyond that, our victim didn't have any security system to speak of, much less a video cam on the property."

Hunt sat still for a few seconds. "Do you have any reason to believe he didn't kill himself?"

"I do."

"What's that?"

"First and foremost, because Jarvis killed him. Second, though, he was actively involved in getting his company up for sale. Into it. None of his kids report anything like depression or anxiety or anything. He was a happy guy getting ready to cash out of a lifetime of work. He left no note, no hint, no nothing. Oh, and one last thing: the poison. If he's killing himself, he's not using poison, because it wouldn't have been certain enough. He owned four guns, and he would have used one of them and made sure. He just didn't do it."

"Well, thanks." Hunt stood and extended a hand. "You've been a help. I appreciate it."

"No problem," Yamashiro said. "Maybe see you at the trial."

"I wouldn't be surprised."

15

She opened the inner door of her Valencia Street duplex. On the stoop through the still-locked outer glass door was a ruggedly good-looking, casually dressed hunk of a guy roughly her age. He wore a neutral expression that somehow came across as friendly. Still, she had lived alone in the Mission District long enough to know that you just never could tell for sure. So, keeping her hand on the inner door, she opened it slightly more and took a better look. Nothing set off any of her private alarms. "Yes?" she asked.

"Stacy Holland?"

"That's me. Who are you?"

The man already had a business card out, and he held it up for her to see through the upper pane of glass. "My name is Wyatt Hunt and I'm a private investigator. I'd like to ask you a couple of questions if I might."

"What about?"

"Grant Wagner."

"Are you with the police?"

"No, ma'am. As I said, I'm a private investigator."

For a moment she said nothing. Then: "Do you mind stepping back and handing me your card?"

"Not at all."

She reached down and unlocked the outer door, then pushed it open an inch or two with her right hand. Hunt slipped his card to her, noting that she locked the door again while she looked, her left hand remaining firmly on the inner door. This was, he thought, a woman who had had some problems with men perhaps getting too close to her too quickly.

He waited longer than he would have predicted — perhaps nearly a minute.

Though apparently satisfied with her perusal, the woman hesitated before she reached down and threw the lock, pushing the door open toward him, her hand still on the inner door, holding it open, but to Hunt's eye ready in an instant to slam it closed in his face.

He took hold of the outer door, waiting until her body language became more welcoming. "If you'd be more comfortable with me standing out here, I'd be fine with that."

That softened her resolve. She gave him an apologetic smile and backed up a step. "I'm sorry," she said. "Just being paranoid. You can come on in."

Still, he noticed that she didn't yet turn her back to him. Rather, backing up another step, she swung the door open. "Go ahead," she said when he came abreast of her, "in there." Gesturing with her left hand, she pointed him toward a large, well-appointed living room brightly lit up by the afternoon sun. "Sit anywhere you'd like."

He took the couch on the far side and watched her as she chose where she would sit, which turned out to be sideways to him on an ottoman just across the coffee table. She was a shoulder-length brunette wearing a mid-thigh multicolored sleeveless dress and low-heeled black pumps. Her arms and legs revealed enough to let Hunt know that she worked out regularly, perhaps even religiously. Her face was lightly made up, probably because it didn't need more: coral lipstick, a hint of eye shadow. She had a half-carat stud diamond earring in each ear.

"Is this a good time?" Hunt asked her. "It looks like you were getting ready to go out."

She glanced at her elegant watch, made a

small apologetic moue. "I've got about a half hour. I'm just ready so soon because I hate being late. Dinner's not supposed to be until seven thirty anyway, and here it is not even six. You're probably keeping me from being unfashionably early and then having to wait around for everybody else, so I should thank you."

Hunt, playing along, said, "You're welcome."

She was not a mincer of words. She nodded, acknowledging his pleasantry, then said, "You wanted to talk about Grant Wagner. You know we broke up a month before he died?"

"Yes, I did know that. And, forgive me, but I understand it was not so much the two of you mutually breaking up as it was his idea."

"All right."

"Well?"

"I didn't hear a question."

"The question is: Who broke up with who?"

"You're correct. He broke up with me. It was unexpected and unpleasant. Heartbreaking, really. We'd been together almost six months, we'd talked about getting married, and I thought we were in love. But let me ask you something."

"Of course."

"Your card says you are a private investigator. Who are you working for?"

"Dismas Hardy. He's the lawyer for Abby Jarvis."

She sat back as though satisfied. "Ahh. The trusted bookkeeper. And now, evidently, his killer, too."

"That's a long way yet from being established."

"Which means you're looking for other suspects. Which is why you're here."

Hunt flashed her a low-watt grin. "Busted," he said. "But if you'd like to tell me something that eliminates you from consideration as Grant's killer, I'd be happy to hear it."

"Like what?"

"Like, for example, if you were out of town the day or even the week he got killed."

"This is ridiculous, and wouldn't that be convenient? But I'm afraid not. Although I hadn't seen him for several weeks before the day they found him. I don't think you'll be able to find anybody who said I did. Even Abby."

"Did you know her?"

"No."

"Ever meet her?"

"No. Although — full disclosure — a day

177

or so after we broke up, I stalked her when she left work, just to see what she looked like."

"How'd that go?"

"She's a little on the heavy side, if you ask me."

"When did you find out about Grant's involvement with her?"

"Pretty much from the beginning. He didn't want to lie to me. Wanted everything to be aboveboard and on the table."

"And how did he characterize their relationship when he told you about it?"

This caused her to pause. "Long-standing, amicable, more or less permanent, but the passion was gone." A first sign of emotion: her eyes flashed, there a moment, then gone. "Ha! Passionate enough, I'd say, when push came to shove."

Hunt held off for a beat. "So he basically reneged on his promises to you?"

She seemed to find some humor in that interpretation. "And because of that I decided I had to kill him? Really? I don't think so. I gave up deciding I wanted to kill men who betrayed me with my first and still only husband. And I didn't kill him, either."

"And how about suicide?"

Throwing her head back, she let out a genuine laugh. "Are you kidding? I wasn't

178

going to be killing myself over any man, even one as charming as Grant Wagner."

"No," Hunt said. "Not you. Grant."

"Grant?" Clearly, the idea had never occurred to her. The amusement in her face morphed to pure disbelief. "*Grant?* What in the world for?"

"I don't know. The coroner's report doesn't rule it out, so it's worth pursuing. I gather you don't think that was very likely."

"No. More than that. Impossible is more like it." She leaned in toward Hunt. "You don't understand. He had everything. He was rich and healthy, adored by his children, and his business was thriving."

"Still . . ."

"No," she said. "Just plain no. Not Grant, not ever."

"Okay. So let me ask you this: What do you know about aconite?"

"Aconite? Is that what killed him? I know a little about it, of course. I work in pharmaceutical sales. You might as well know that. I don't sell aconite, specifically — I'm not aware of anyone who does — but I'm familiar with it, since I need to know about drugs for my work. If I were going to poison somebody, including myself, aconite wouldn't even be in the top ten of my choices. But even if he'd known about something relatively foolproof — say, cyanide or a combination of Elavil and alcohol — he still wouldn't ever have killed himself. I don't care what the coroner says, you can rule out suicide."

Hunt sat back on the couch. Stacy had just supplied him with two or three reasons why in a reasonable world she should remain high on his list of possible suspects, and yet ironically he found himself becoming more convinced that she had nothing to do with Grant Wagner's death.

But that did not mean she might not have some relevant insights that could still prove useful. "So what about the kids?" Hunt asked. "You just said they all adored him."

"They do. They did."

"All of them, equally?"

After considering for a moment, she said, "None of them could possibly have killed him. Let's say that. They all had great jobs and good pay. Maybe Gary, the oldest, maybe he had the best deal, since he was in line to take over; but the other three, they really had nothing to complain about, and I never heard that they did. Complain, I mean. They loved him."

"So you knew them personally?"

"I'd met them all, yes."

"How'd they treat you?"

"Actually, very nicely. Everybody was incredibly welcoming. Surprisingly."

"You didn't expect that?"

"No. I would have understood if they didn't."

"And why wouldn't they accept you? Because you were taking Abby's place?"

Shaking her head, she said, "Abby wasn't on that side of things. She wasn't really part of the family that anyone acknowledged."

"So who else was there?"

"Well, Ginger, of course." In a few words, she filled Hunt in on the situation with Grant's senile wife, ensconced now and for the past four years in a nursing home. "So I thought Joey, at least, wouldn't be very cool with me suddenly coming into the picture, but he was fine with it."

Hunt broke a bemused smile. "I think I'm going to need a scorecard to keep up with the players here. Who's Joey?"

"Ginger's adopted son. Part of the family but not part of the business. Which was fine with him. He does his own thing."

"Which is?"

"Tech stuff. Start-ups. Smart kid. Anyway, I thought he might object to Grant and me being together, but he knows his mom isn't coming back. It turned out not to be an issue, which I was so glad of."

Hunt looked around the room for a moment, then finally across to the sophisticated, intelligent, trim, attractive woman sitting across the coffee table from him.

Why in the world, he wondered, did she consent to become involved with a man who was already married and who was simultaneously involved with the mother of another of his children?

She caught his glance. "I know what you're thinking," she said. "You're wondering why I would get involved in all that potential drama? Right?"

"Something like that."

"I'm thirty-eight years old and divorced. I've still got my looks, such as they are, but they'll be gone soon enough. If Grant would have brought me on, I believed that before too long I would have been at the top of the pecking order. I would have inherited a good chunk of change — a small fortune, really — when he died. Meanwhile, Abby would have stayed second, where she's always been. And Ginger's going to die in the next year or two as well. Meanwhile, Grant was already using the 'M' word around me. That's where I would have been. You might not understand. It was complicated, but I couldn't let him get away." She sighed. "I should have given Abby more

182

credit. If I had known how she was going to play it, I might have killed her."

"You . . . ?"

She held up a hand. "That was a joke, mostly. But, honestly, I just never really saw her as a threat."

"And you never wanted to punish Grant for choosing Abby over you? And get Abby accused of his murder in the bargain?"

She barked a shallow laugh with no humor behind it. "Mr. Hunt. The lawyer you work for can probably make a jury believe that that's what might have happened," she said. "But that's not what it was. He'd chosen her. I wasn't getting him back. I never even saw him for the last month of his life." Much to Hunt's surprise, she dabbed at one eye, then the other. "I'm sorry," she said. "I still miss him a lot."

16

Hardy and Frannie considered themselves fortunate to have one of their favorite restaurants — the Pacific Cafe — at the corner of Geary and Thirty-Fourth Avenue, so close to their home. No parking hassles, no need to designate a sober driver. Tables miraculously appearing for them even when the place was packed, which it usually was.

Now, hand in hand, sated and relaxed, they were walking home in the darkened twilight. Except for their two-story stand-alone rebuilt Victorian, every other building on the street was either an apartment house or a duplex, all of them shoulder to shoulder right out to the sidewalks. By contrast, the Hardys maintained a small lawn, bisected by a footpath to their front porch and set behind a white picket fence, so that even from a distance as they approached, it was easy to pick out their house from the apartment clones.

And now they were across the street, coming close.

Hardy stopped in mid-stride and put his free hand on Frannie's arm. "Did we leave the kitchen light on?" Their kitchen was at the back of the house.

"I don't think so. In fact, I'm sure we didn't. It was still light out when we left."

"Hmm."

Hardy took a quick look at the cars parked at every free spot up and down the street. There was no obvious sign such as glinting, glimmering glass on the ground that any of them had been broken into. Over the past three or four years — ever since the San Francisco Police Department had stopped investigating car burglaries as a matter of policy — there had been an epidemic of broken car windows and missing property throughout the Richmond, and almost every other district, to say nothing of an apparently brisk trade in residential breaking and entering. In spite of the Neighborhood Watch signs posted on the corners at each end of the block, Hardy was aware of no fewer than four burglaries here within the past year. One of his neighbors had even been shot, though fortunately not killed, when he'd walked in on the crime in progress.

"Maybe we installed a timer and forgot about it," Hardy said.

"I think I'd remember. What do you want to do?"

"I'll just casually mosey on over and knock on the front door and let him escape out the back."

"If there's somebody."

"Right. Do you want to come with me?"

"As opposed to waiting out here alone? I think I'll stick with you."

"Let's do it."

They crossed the street, opened the fence gate, walked up the path onto the porch. Opening the screen door, Hardy banged and waited.

Footsteps. Not retreating. Not escaping out the back.

The porch light flicked on above them.

From inside: "Just a minute. Who is it?"

Hardy rolled his eyes at his wife. "Jesus, Vinnie," he said. "Open the goddamn door!"

"You guys are getting paranoid."

"Not so much," Hardy said. "Paranoid is when there is nothing to worry about. This was a light on in our house when we'd left it off. You could have called us and let us know you were coming over."

"I could have, and in fact I did. Text and

voicemail, and you didn't answer."

"That's because your mother and I sometimes like to have a dinner that isn't interrupted by our phones."

"Well," Vin said, "I hate to tell you that you're not in the majority of humanity anymore on this one. You know, don't you, that you could have left your phone on buzz and no sound and then you would have at least gotten my text and avoided all this pain and suffering?"

"How about if we didn't want to get texted, either?" Hardy asked. "Bizarre though that might be."

"All right," Frannie said. "I think that you two gentlemen are going to have to agree to disagree on this one. Meanwhile" — she touched her son's arm — "were we expecting you to come by tonight? Not that you're not always welcome. But usually you give us some warning."

"I know, I just . . ." His lips went tight holding back some emotion. "I had a shitty day. Really, really shitty. I thought seeing you guys might help."

"What happened?" Hardy asked. "Everything okay at work?"

"Work's fine." He sighed. "I just found out today that a friend of mine, David Chang — you've heard me talk about him

— he got himself killed a couple of days ago."

"Oh my God," Frannie said. "I'm so sorry, Vinnie. What happened?"

Her son opened his mouth to speak, but no sound came out. He tried it again. "Somebody shot him. It's so weird to even say it."

Frannie's hand went to her mouth. "That is so horrible. How did it happen? Was it an accident?"

Vincent shook his head. "No. Not an accident. It was pretty definitely a murder."

"They're sure about that?" Hardy asked.

"No doubt. Evidently it was like an execution, really. Two shots in the head."

"And this was one of your regular pals?" Hardy asked.

"Yeah."

"Do you know? Do they have any idea who did it?"

"Not yet. They're saying it might have been somebody he knew, which is, like, impossible to believe."

"Why do they think that?"

"I don't know, Dad. That's just what I read. Evidently there wasn't any sign of a struggle or anything. He let whoever it was into his apartment and the next thing you know they're in the living room and then he's dead. With a second shot to make sure."

"Was he into drugs?"

"Why does everybody ask that?"

"Probably because people in the drug business often wind up killing one another. But you're saying he wasn't?"

"Not that I ever saw or heard of. The whole thing is just so surreal. I mean, people I know don't get killed for no reason. It doesn't make any sense. David couldn't have been any threat to anybody. He was the most regular, normal guy." He turned to his father. "Do you think this just could have been a mistake?"

"It could, of course. Possibly. Although, from what you describe, that doesn't really seem very likely. Two guys in the same room. Two shots in the head. You've got to assume somebody meant it to happen."

Vincent rubbed a hand across his forehead. "I'm just flipped out about this. Things like this aren't supposed to happen. Not to David. Not to guys I know. It doesn't seem possible."

"I hear you," Hardy said. As they'd been talking, they'd migrated into the living room, and now Hardy was sitting in his reading chair, Frannie and Vin on their own chairs across from him. "But if somebody shot him," Hardy said, "there must have

189

been some reason. How'd you hear about it?"

"Bill Kenney, one of our friends. He heard about it and called the police, who came down and talked to him this morning."

"Is he a suspect?"

"If he is, he doesn't know it. He was trying to help the cops."

"Doesn't mean he's not a suspect," Hardy said.

Frannie spoke up. "Your father is a little bit cynical about the police sometimes."

"I've noticed that," Vin said. "But I still don't think Bill's a suspect."

"Well," Hardy said. "We shall see."

The three of them stayed up talking over a few nightcaps each until nearly midnight, and then Frannie went into the family room and opened the futon they kept ready for the occasional unexpected visit, like tonight's, from one of their children.

Upstairs in their own bedroom, Hardy was in bed first. Wide awake, his hands crossed behind his head, he had his eyes closed, but he wasn't fooling his wife. She got in bed and snuggled up against him. "What are you thinking?" she asked.

"I'm not," he said. "I was sleeping. You just woke me up."

"You still had your reading light on."

"Darn. I knew I'd forgotten something." He let out a heavy breath. "I hate this."

"I know. Me, too. Do you think the killer is somebody Vinnie knows?"

"To the second degree of separation, anyway. Which is way too close for my taste."

"So what do you think he should do?"

"Do? He should not do a damn thing, except keep going in to work and not develop an interest in finding out who done it after all. Fortunately, this guy Chang and he weren't really all that close. I don't see Vin letting it get too personal. At least, I hope it doesn't. Maybe I'll call Abe, find out what I can."

Frannie pushed away from him and came up on her elbow. "I've got a better one. How about maybe you don't start, either? You have nothing to do with this Chang case. You've already got Abby and her case. I think that's plenty at any given moment. How about let the cops do their job and hope they find somebody to arrest before too long? How about that?"

"You're right. That is what ought to happen."

"That's what *will* happen, Dismas, if you just let it. You can lead by example here, and just let it alone. *Completely* alone, just like Vin should."

"You are one hundred percent right," Hardy said.

"I know I am."

"I'm going to turn off my light now and go to sleep."

"That," Frannie said, "is an excellent idea."

17

Vincent had gotten up and absconded to parts unknown by the time Hardy came downstairs. Frannie entered the kitchen in her hiking clothes about fifteen minutes later, and Hardy made them both an enormous omelette in his black cast-iron pan: mushrooms, arugula, some diced Italian dry salami and cheese. They discussed the irony that he'd spiked the eggs with a cheese from Cowgirl Creamery named Mt. Tam, and that Frannie was going out to climb the very same Mount Tamalpais with her women's hiking group in the next half hour or so.

What a wacky world.

So he was alone and had killed two pleasant hours at home reading a C. J. Box novel, stopping on a high note when he laughed aloud after coming across the line "Nothing spells trouble like two drunk cowboys with a rocket launcher." Figuring it wasn't going to get better than that anytime soon, he put the book down and finally decided on his ill-fated meeting with his best and testiest friend Abe.

Hardy had told Frannie — and when he said it, he had meant it — that he wasn't going to talk to Glitsky about the David Chang murder. Nosiree. The fact that Chang happened to be a distant acquaintance of his son Vincent was nowhere near reason enough for Hardy to even pretend to be involved, even as a matter of idle curiosity. And so he would be beyond neutral — uninterested, even. That case had nothing whatsoever to do with his client or his business. He would not mention it to Abe.

On the other hand, barring a run on short-tempered Samoan warriors in the courtroom, his client Abby Jarvis was up for arraignment first thing tomorrow morning, and Hardy, for all of his reservations about the true nature of her relationship with Grant Wagner, still could not understand why the grand jury had in its wisdom decided to indict Abby.

Hardy had simply not seen one shred of physical evidence that Abby had poisoned Grant. In spite of the fact that all witnesses seemed to believe that Grant was the kind of guy who would never choose poison as a means to kill himself because he would have chosen something that was automatic and quick, such as a gun, to Hardy it was moderately reasonable to assume that Grant had in fact taken his own life. He was unwilling to abandon that conclusion out of hand.

He could imagine himself making an argument to the jury.

Absent any hard evidence to the contrary — and there wasn't any he was aware of — Hardy found it plausible to believe that, for whatever reason, Grant had just had enough with living. It happened. Women troubles, kid problems, business and legal issues — the weight of them all had finally done him in.

He had been sixty-two years old, probably not as virile as he'd once been or liked to think he was; haunted by guilt at the abandonment of his second wife to an Alzheimer's facility; under pressure from Abby to legitimize their relationship and all the conflicts that would bring with his "real" family; maybe even brokenhearted over the breakup with Stacy Holland, who, according to Wyatt Hunt, was formidably sensuous.

At every turn, Hardy found another pressure point in Grant Wagner's life. He had no trouble believing, and the facts fully supported him, that Grant had come home from work one day and mixed himself up a pot of wolfsbane root, then sat down and fallen asleep, never to awaken.

Easy, painless, final — an end to his earthly suffering. And an ending that Grant knew — or at least believed — would be ruled a heart attack. Which meant that the G-Team would inherit the company. Which meant that Abby and her child would get their million dollars. Which meant he'd have taken care of his business and gone out like the man he was: responsible, fair, in control.

And, given those elements, the aconite would have been every bit as good as a firearm, maybe better.

The suicide argument didn't sing loudly to Hardy, but, he reminded himself, it only took one juror out of twelve to keep his client from being convicted.

And yet, the grand jury had indicted Abby.

Hardy, who'd put on dozens of serious trials in his career, could not recall a less impressive set of facts behind an indictment. Either his own mental acuity was slipping, which he didn't believe, or . . .

Walking up the steps to Glitsky's duplex at a little after noon, he broke into a grin:

either he was closing his eyes to a situation he did not wish to acknowledge, or he was unaware of the caliber of disaster indicated by the presence of a pool table in his community.

The Music Man's pool table, in this case, being Abby's earlier conviction for DUI and vehicular manslaughter. Her previous criminal record, he believed, was coloring and prejudicing every aspect of this case. It hadn't come in to the grand jury and probably wouldn't come up at trial, but it seemed to be a presence hovering over every move the prosecution made. He thought that, maybe, his friend Glitsky could help him put it all into an off-the-record perspective so he'd have a better idea of what he was fighting against when he got to the courtroom the next morning.

If only he'd known . . .

Voices were raised before he'd been there ten minutes. Glitsky, who normally shunned all forms of profanity, brought his hand down flat and hard on the kitchen table and said, "That is such utter *horseshit.* I can't believe you've got the chutzpah to even try to float that by me."

"What? I'm simply asking you —"

Glitsky cut him off. "You're simply asking me to consider the possibility that she is in-

197

nocent. Yes, I heard you. Lack of evidence. Blah blah blah. But I'm not going there. And you know what? You insult my intelligence by even asking me. Seriously. Lord above." Glitsky pushed his chair back and stood up in the cramped kitchen. He took two steps into the edge of the living room, then spun back around and looked down on Hardy where he sat. "I mean, go ahead and defend her if you're in the mood. Or, even better, if she's paying you, psyche yourself up on whatever story you decide to tell and go along for the ride. But don't give me that 'factually innocent' crap, Diz, and ask me to buy it. I can't do it. And you know why? Because I subscribe to the 'Don't be stupid' view of life. Maybe you ought to try it."

"You show me some physical evidence and maybe I would."

"Yeah, here we go, as though physical evidence is the whole ball game."

"Yeah? Well, this just in: the Supreme Court's made a few rulings on that issue, and guess what? It pretty much *is* the whole ball game. You might want to check it out."

"You might want to bite me." Glitsky pointed a finger. "You're drinking your own Kool-Aid, dude, and I don't want any part of it." He pulled his chair around, brought it back up to the table, and straddled it backward.

Hardy took the cue to push his own chair back and start to rise. "Yeah, well, thanks. You've been a big help."

"I could be," Glitsky said, "and save you a lot of heartache. Do you want to know how I know she's guilty? You want to hear about some real evidence, if you've got the nerve?"

Hardy settled back down, his eyes fierce and guarded.

"Just to get a take on what this really looks like if you don't happen to be blinded by what you want to see. Let me tell you what's already there, in plain sight. Are you ready for that?"

"Sure. Enlighten me."

"All right. One, and you can laugh all day about it if you want, but it's a fact. The woman's already a criminal."

"Oh, Jesus Christ, Abe, what's that got to —"

Glitsky held up his palm and raised his voice. "She's killed somebody before, Diz. She knows what it feels like. Killing somebody else is not going to intimidate her."

"That's got nothing to do with these charges."

"Right. How about that she's a drunk?"

"Again, nothing remotely connected. And,

by the way, she's been sober for ten years."

"Says she. But the fact remains, even if it's true, she's still an alcoholic."

"No. She's a reformed alcoholic," Hardy said. "And I'm still waiting for something that sounds like evidence."

"Okay, then maybe you forgot about the victim, the guy she embezzled from, the same sweetheart of a guy who gave her a job despite her criminal record when nobody else would. Whom she undeniably repaid by ripping him off."

"He knew all about —"

"Oh, spare me. He found out she was stealing from him and that's why she had to kill him, because an unrepentant criminal probably didn't want to go back to the joint when he found out she was fiddling with the books."

"Yeah, except have I mentioned that he knew about the money? Which was going to help her raise the kid?"

"Oh. Good plan. Except that, by embezzling the money, she was exposing her kid to being raised in the foster system when she inevitably got caught. But, like all criminals — did I mention that she was a criminal? — she went for what was easy rather than for what was right. And, by the way, while we're on motive: not only was hers excellent, but nobody else on the planet seems to have one."

Hardy leaned back in his chair. He shook his head. "All this is nothing, Abe. Nothing."

"No? Well, then, how about this? Isn't it a hell of a coincidence that whoever chose to kill this guy did it with tea, which your client made for him every day? What? Are we out of guns and knives in San Francisco? So let's even say that somebody else did have a motive and did just happen to decide to kill our victim with poison: How in the world did this person get close enough to the victim to see that he drank the tea without getting suspicious? I mean, really. Your supposed killer knocked on the door and said, 'Here, try this tea. I promise it's not poison.' She did it, Diz. She had a great reason — *several* great reasons — to do it. And, meanwhile, have you seen the videos of her statements to police?"

"Not yet, no."

"Well, when you do, I think you'll agree that your sweet and innocent client comes across as snotty and indignant and self-righteous and a world-class liar who is obviously lying about having no special relationship with the victim and had never taken a dime from his company or anybody else. I

201

think even your Supreme Court counts lying as a strong, even compelling form of evidence, does it not? And she's been lying about every little thing to hide the fact, the plain, true fact, that she is a career criminal with substance abuse problems, an embezzler, and a murderer at least twice. Take it all together, there's no other rational way to look at this, Diz. So you go ahead and defend her — although how you live with your job is something I'll never understand. I'm just trying to tell you what any jury is going to see and believe. But don't try to sell your snake oil to me. It really, really, really pisses me off."

Thinking, that really went well, Hardy descended Glitsky's steps and stepped out onto the sidewalk, now bathed in bright, warm, shade-free sunlight. He took off his jacket and slung it over his shoulder, only at that moment realizing that a parking space directly in front of Abe's duplex remained open. It had been there when he arrived on foot forty-five minutes ago, and this was only amusing because he had considered himself relatively lucky to find a parking place near Park Presidio, a bit less than a mile from Glitsky's, and he'd taken it. He wondered, as he often did at these kinds of occurrences, whether that place would have still been there if he had not taken the earlier spot, if he had just trusted in fate and bet that the closer spot would be empty when he arrived. He was pretty sure it wouldn't have been.

In any event, by the time he got to his car after a brisk and health-inducing ten-minute walk, he didn't need his jacket over his shoulder anymore. Or anywhere else. He threw it across onto the passenger seat and slid into the driver's seat, noting that the internal temperature of the car was a hundred and forty degrees or so. He put the key in the ignition, opened the windows, and turned the AC on to max.

At around one o'clock, Hardy crossed the lobby by Phyllis's reception desk just outside his office. Off to his right, he heard subliminal sounds of activity, although nothing like when the office hummed on a workday. Down the hall, somebody was copying something. He fancied he even heard the *tap tap tap* of several keyboards. A male voice — Graham Russo? — struck a bass note as he patiently explained something on a telephone call.

Sunday afternoon, and all the busy little beavers hard at work.

Sighing, he went to his door and used his key to open it, then, living large, decided in Phyllis's absence to leave it open so he could continue to enjoy the background symphony. Almost without thought, he walked over to the cherry cabinet mounted on the wall to his right and opened its doors, sliding them back to reveal a dartboard. Grabbing one set of tungsten beauties with turquoise blue flights, he walked back eight feet to the foot-long cherry line in his otherwise light hardwood floor.

After a couple of rounds, he was painting the 20 with regularity and felt prepared both spiritually and physically to begin a round of "301." A couple of years before, he'd thrown a perfect game — 20 down to bull's-eye without missing a shot — and the memory still served as both a challenge and a rebuke. After five starts today, however, he'd missed, respectively, on 14, 16, 17 (twice), and even the first 20, which was flatly unacceptable. He was, to put it bluntly, not "in the zone."

But he pulled the darts from the board again and went back to the line and turned. However he scored, darts tended to clear his mind, and now he stood in a kind of trance, something obscure about the next day's arraignment of Abby Jarvis flitting at the edges of his consciousness. He closed his eyes, fingered his dart. Whatever it was, it would come.

"Daddy?"

Opening his eyes, he broke a welcoming smile.

"My darlin' girl."

"What are you doing in here on a Sunday?"

"I might ask you the same thing."

"Well, I'm a third-year associate and I work almost every Sunday, and you are the managing partner, who doesn't have to work at all."

"Perish the thought. And I *am* working."

"On the dart game. Yes, I can see that."

"On a case, too. The arraignment's tomorrow. Abby Jarvis. Murder."

"I'd heard the rumor. How bad is it?"

"Your uncle Abe thinks it's a slam dunk, even with no physical evidence."

"Well, you know, once you get arrested, you did it."

Hardy's smile widened. "Of course. How could I forget? Anyway, I figured your mom went hiking and Vin's probably working, so I'd be a slacker if I didn't put in a few hours."

But at the mention of her brother's name, Rebecca's face darkened. "Did you hear about his friend? Vinnie's?"

"I did. So you've talked to him?"

"He called me this morning. Just wanting to talk."

"Yeah, he stayed with us last night. He was pretty shook up."

"He still was this morning."

"I wouldn't doubt it. Your friend gets killed, it messes with your world. But let me ask you: Did you get the impression he was inclined to find out a little more about what happened?"

"Maybe a little. I told him that was a bad idea."

"As did your mother and I last night. Several times. But the fact that he called you to talk about it some more makes me think he didn't hear us too well. I really don't want to see him start trying to figure out who killed this guy."

"David Chang."

"Yeah, him."

She shook her head. "I think I talked him out of that. Besides, he's seen what's happened to you, and to Uncle Abe, for that matter."

"Well, let's hope all that's made an impression."

"I'm sure it has," she said. "I know it has for me."

The object of his father's and his sister's concern — Vincent Hardy — had spent the latter part of the morning and early afternoon in his condo and on his laptop, as usual. He'd put in those four-plus hours schmoozing on Skype with three of the Facebook recruit candidates he'd been courting for the past month or so, extolling the benefits awaiting them if they chose to come on board with the company. All three were also fielding similar offers from Google and Oracle. He knew that the final decision in some measure was going to come down to the relationship these young geniuses formed with their respective recruiters — for example, him.

Surprisingly, money did not seem to be an overriding factor; Vincent knew that all of the jobs started at a comfortable six figures.

About midway through the third interview, he felt his energy and enthusiasm for the task at hand starting to wane. He'd had some of his parents' good Peet's French roast coffee before he left their house, then had another large Starbucks next door after he parked in his Douglass Street condo's underground garage, and finally a third full cup from his Keurig machine after he'd finished up on the first call.

He didn't need any more coffee.

What was claiming his attention and softening his focus was not caffeine withdrawal, fatigue, or boredom with this phone call but a fresh wave of reaction to the murder of David Chang. In five minutes he'd managed to extricate himself from the call with Bonnie Becker without leading her to suspect that she was not his complete and absolute priority on this Sunday afternoon.

After he'd ended the call, he immediately went looking on the Net for all the details he could find related to the murder of his friend David Chang. They were few and far between, providing little more information than he'd already learned from Bill Kenney. There were no suspects and no theories, just the bare fact of the killing in his apartment.

This didn't seem right.

It wouldn't surprise Vincent, who was, after all, the son of a defense attorney, to learn that the cops in actual practice no longer truly investigated many murders in San Francisco, much as they didn't investigate car thefts and break-ins at all. If it wasn't a sexy or high-profile case, inspectors would be assigned, of course, but they didn't spend as much time looking for motives and suspects as they did making sure that the paperwork was in order so that the city's budgetary and political ass was covered in case somebody, somewhere, suddenly decided to care.

David had been killed last Thursday and here it was Sunday and they'd discovered essentially nothing? He asked himself: How hard could they be trying? Had the cops gone through David's cell phone and computer with forensic techs, picking them apart for the smallest inconsistency or clue? There could definitely be a lead there. Vincent knew for a fact that the police hadn't made a complete canvass of David's friends, because he was one of them — maybe not in the first rank, but how would they know that? — and no one had called to question him about how he'd spent last Thursday, for example.

Oh, yeah, he recalled: Opening Day.

The more he considered it, though, the more it galled him, until finally he looked up from the screen he'd been staring at for hours, saw that it was a beautiful day outside, and jumped up from the stool in his kitchen, deciding to go take in some of that sunshine.

Maybe stumble upon something the police had missed.

He was just getting up to the entryway of David's apartment when a young woman came out the front door, pulled it closed behind her, and turned around, almost walking into him.

"Oh, I'm sorry, excuse . . . Vincent?"

It only took a half second for recognition to kick in. David's sister. "Sara," he said. It shouldn't have been too much of a surprise, but somehow it was. After giving her a quick hug, Vincent grabbed and gently held on to her shoulders for a beat. "This is pretty awful, isn't it? I'm so sorry."

Exuding weariness, she bobbed her head in a muted nod.

"How are you holding up?"

She shrugged. "It comes and goes."

"I hear you."

"What are you doing here?"

"I don't have any real reason, to tell you the truth. I guess it doesn't seem like the cops are doing too much to find out what was going on."

"Tell me about it."

"I don't really know what I was thinking. Maybe I'd pick up some vibes or something.

Were you just up at his place?"

She nodded. "But I couldn't get in."

"There's cops up there?"

"No. I knocked and nobody answered."

"But you have a key?"

"Yes, in case he locked himself out, which he sometimes did, but . . ." She stopped, a hint of mischievousness in her eyes. "Can we just do that?"

But when they were standing in front of the upstairs apartment's door, Vincent balked. He knew that neither he nor Sara had any right to enter the apartment. Even if the cops were not still inside, it might still be some sort of crime scene. He'd heard enough of his father's rants about the sanctity of crime scenes to know that what he and Sara had been contemplating was among the very worst of bad ideas. And what if the cops came back or the landlord caught him inside? If nothing else, his father would kill him, and that would be so awkward.

She had the key out and offered it to him, but after another moment of hesitation he shook his head no. "Call me a wimp, but I don't think I can do it after all."

His decision seemed to relieve her. She let out some of the breath she'd been holding.

"Probably that's best. I didn't know what I came down here to look for anyway. If anything. Maybe I just wanted to feel his presence somehow, you know? Does that make any sense?"

"It does. To me, anyhow. Going inside isn't going to help anything, and it might even hurt. No, it would hurt. It never helps anything."

"So, now what?" she asked.

"Now," he said, "I guess we just try to suck it up and let the cops do what they do in their own sweet time."

18

Eric Waverly had Sara Chang on his mind as well.

When he'd been interviewing the family, he had of course noticed that she had directed all of her answers to him and not to Ken, who had asked the questions. But he did not think, as his partner had surmised, that this was because of her prejudice against the Japanese. Maybe his reasoning was clouded by his pain or the pills he was taking to combat it, but Eric had come away with the distinct impression that, albeit with great subtlety, she'd been coming on to him. Then, as he was formally shaking hands all around, saying good-bye, she had taken his hand in both of hers and without question held on to it, looking into his eyes — perhaps pleadingly — for far longer than it should have taken.

In his seven years of marriage, Eric had never been unfaithful to Maddie and had never really thought about it or been seriously tempted. And although for some reason he didn't understand, their intimacy had taken a hit after he'd been shot — again, the pain pills, the pain itself, his post-traumatic stress about the situation itself — he had been figuring that he would just give them both time to let things shake out and then they'd get back to normal.

But it didn't seem to be happening. For the past few months it was like he was a sick child and Maddie was his nurse, and that was about as non-sexy a relationship as he could imagine. She was taking care of the kids and taking care of him, and he knew that he was mostly a burden to her.

Sara, on the other hand, was young and she was in mourning. Over his years as a cop, Eric had watched grief exerting its own erotic undertow among the survivors. Life is unpredictable, and my sweet brother is suddenly dead, and I'm a fool to let life and experience pass me by. So let us make love and make merry while we still can.

He'd seen it more than once.

He'd told Maddie he was going downtown to work on some backlogged cases, which was vague enough to be true, although in fact he didn't go into the office at all. Instead, he'd cruised through the Tenderloin and finally hooked up with his confidential informant whose second source of income came through the sale of Oxycontin. Eric had popped a couple of the pills out of the dozen he'd bought and washed them down with a Diet Coke, then headed out and parked in the lot that faced the beach.

There, as the pills took effect, his thoughts turned to Sara Chang.

She picked up on the second ring. "Hello, Inspector."

"Ms. Chang."

"Sara, please. I'm glad to hear from you. Have you found out something about David?"

"I'm not sure. I was hoping I could run a few ideas by you and, between us, maybe we could make a bit of progress on the investigation."

"What about your partner? Is he with you?"

"No. It's Sunday. He's taking some time off. Weekend hours."

"But not for you?"

"Some cases get under your skin and you can't let them go."

"And David's is one of those?"

"It appears so. Is now a convenient time?"

"Now would be fine." She paused, then her voice came out smaller. "I should tell

215

you, I went by David's apartment earlier."

"Earlier when?"

"Today. A couple of hours ago."

"Why did you do that?"

"I don't know. I know that sounds weird, but it's the real answer. I thought I'd be able to, I don't know . . . I don't know," she repeated. "It probably makes no sense. It's just something I thought I wanted to see."

"You didn't try to go in, did you?"

"No. But I'd be curious to see what might be there. He's been on my mind all day. David. I still can't believe that someone he knew killed him."

"Where are you now?" Eric asked.

"Back home. My apartment."

"Where's that?"

She gave him the address. Fourteenth Avenue near Irving. An easy swing back on the way to David's apartment on Stanyan.

"How about if I pick you up in ten or fifteen and we go by there. You can wait down on the curb. I'm pretty sure I'll recognize you."

"I'll be there."

"Good."

"And, oh, Inspector?"

"Eric."

"Really. I can call you that?"

"You're Sara, I'm Eric. Works for me."

216

"Good."

"It is. What were you going to say?"

"Just thank you."

"For what?"

"For caring."

"Where's the rug?" she asked.

Waverly explained that the crime scene team had rolled up the throw rug that had covered the floor in the center of the apartment's living room and taken it away to the lab. He did not go on to tell her that someone, probably the landlord, had also cleaned up the blood and the spatter, both from the floor and from the white cabinets under the bookshelves. They'd also left the three street-facing windows open a couple of inches each for ventilation, and, with the curtains open, the late afternoon sun lit up the room as it had on the day Waverly had first seen the body. The result was that the place really had very little of the feel or the smell of the scene of a brutal murder.

Even though the Oxy had kicked in nicely, Waverly rubbed his sore shoulder as he lowered himself onto one corner of the couch. Sara had come in behind him and put a hand up to her mouth, stopping in the doorway where the hall opened into the living room.

"This is where it happened?" she asked.

Waverly nodded. "You can see why we think it must have been someone he knew."

After a few seconds she inclined her head in acknowledgment. "I never realized the room was so small. It never felt crowded or anything."

"Have you been here a lot?"

"Some. He was my brother, after all. We helped each other move into our places."

"Went to the same parties?"

"Not so much. He was older, you know. Six years." She wiped a rogue tear as it fell onto her cheek. "I'm sorry. I'm not being much help."

"You're doing fine. Nobody says this stuff is easy." He looked around the room. "Anything here seem out of place to you? Wrong somehow? Even the slightest little thing?"

Letting out a breath, she moved forward and eased herself down on the other end of the couch. She was wearing low black heels and a light-tan skirt that came halfway up her thighs, and then a couple of inches higher when she sat. Turning to her right, she showcased a bosom that strained at her tangerine silk blouse. Taking her time, she scanned the room right to left — the shelves, the cabinets — before finally coming around to Waverly. "It's just his living room," she said. "It looks the same."

"Okay. Let's you and me poke around a little more." Straightening, he pushed up against the couch's arm and grimaced.

"Are you all right?"

"I'm fine. Just some problems with my shoulder." He pointed to the other doorway to their right. "How about the kitchen?"

"Let's see." She led the way. It was a narrow room with counters on both sides, another door out to the entrance hallway, which they'd passed coming in, and a window in the far wall that looked out onto an open skylight that ran inside the center of the building.

She got to the door and turned around by the window. "What are we looking for here?"

Waverly opened the refrigerator. "Probably nothing," he said, peering inside. "Anything obvious, and even not so obvious, Crime Scene would have logged it in and taken it downtown." Closing the refrigerator door, he leaned up against one of the counters. "I got the impression you just felt like you needed some closure, walking through this place one last time. Wasn't that why you came by earlier: just to let yourself in and look around?"

Her eyes were glistening, another tear or two about to spill over. "That's really what

I felt. Does that make any sense?"

"It doesn't have to make sense, Sara. It's what you're feeling. Crime Scene's clearly done here. We're not compromising any evidence or violating the sanctity of the place. So if being here somehow makes things easier for you, who's it hurt? Take your time. Look around."

She nodded. "You are so not my idea of what a cop is like. In a good way."

"Well, thank you, I think. But please don't tell anybody. Word gets out and my reputation goes in the tank."

"You're not supposed to be sympathetic?"

He smiled over at her. "It never hurts, but it's not exactly the first prerequisite to becoming an inspector."

"Well, thank you anyway. Can I ask you something?"

"Sure."

"What happened to your shoulder?"

He looked down, surprised that he'd been rubbing the site of his wound. "I got shot last year. Being stupid."

"I doubt that."

He went to shrug again, and again, unbidden, he grimaced. "You had to be there. I stopped paying enough attention for two seconds and that was all he needed."

"And it's still painful?"

"I must admit, it has its moments."

"Are you taking anything for it?"

"Sure. Some prescribed meds, for all the good they're doing."

She took a step toward him and laid a palm flat, light as a feather, against the place where he'd been rubbing. He was wearing a lightweight Tommy Bahama Hawaiian shirt, tucked in. She pushed gently against the fabric.

"Is this it?" she asked. "You can still feel it."

He nodded. "It made a pretty good hole. All in all, though, I'd have to say I was lucky."

"But it still hurts?"

"It's all right. Really."

"But maybe not as good as you hoped it would be?"

"Maybe not, but I don't seem to see any other options."

After a moment of hesitation, looking up at him, she said, "Here." With her right hand still up against the wound site, she put her left hand onto his right shoulder and pushed him back, brushing up against him in the narrow space. "Let me by."

He watched her turn around and open one of the kitchen cabinet doors. Reaching inside, she took down an apothecary jar nearly filled with what looked like loose tea. After reading the Chinese script on the label, she put it up where it had been and took down another jar that was almost identical to the first. Then she put that back and reached for the next one.

"What are you looking for?" he asked.

She was looking at the next jar, and the next. "Just checking. David doesn't need any of this anymore. But none of this is what you need, either."

"For what?"

"Pain. Inflammation."

"But I don't —"

"How do you know if you don't try? And you've already said your prescription medication isn't working."

"Well, it's —"

"It's denial, is what it is." She checked the last jar and put it back in its place on the shelf. "When we're done here, we can stop by my place and pick up some of what you need, and if it works, we can get you more where that came from."

Her apartment was smaller than her brother's, a studio with a kitchen, a space for a table and four chairs, and the bedroom and adjoining bathroom. She had him sit in one of the chairs while she put water on to boil, then disappeared for a moment only to return with a couple of bottles that she placed on the table in front of him.

"I hope you don't want me to drink that," he said.

"This isn't to drink. This is for healing the scar. Vitamin E and aloe vera. It's not all magic Chinese herbs. So now I need you to come over here and take off your shirt."

"I don't —"

"Yes you do." Gently she patted his back. "Up. Shirt off."

He got to his feet, unbuttoned his shirt, and hung it over his chair, then crossed to the ottoman, where he sat again.

Pouring lotion into her hand, she went around behind him and viewed the damage. "Ouch," she said. "It's worse in the back."

"Exit wound."

She rubbed some of the lotion onto his back. "You need to apply this every day," she said. "Is anybody taking care of this at your home?"

"It's not a big part of the program, not that there is much of a program to speak of."

"That is wrong," she said. "Don't let me rub this too hard."

He leaned back into the pressure. "You'll be the first to know."

She kneaded the wound site, both thumbs working at the scar tissue. "Oh, the water! Don't move," she said, then walked back into the kitchen, rinsed her hands, and poured the near-boiling water over the herbs she'd picked out from her own collection and already placed in the strainer above the heavy mug. When she'd filled it, she brought it back over to him. "Drink while it's hot," she said.

"What is this?"

"It is my uncle's special pain mixture. My uncle is a famous herbalist. He has a store here in Chinatown. I take it for migraines. It is magical. Try it and you'll see."

"In one glass I'll see?"

"Maybe a few. Over a few days. I will give you some to take home. If it helps, we can go see my uncle and get you a regular supply."

"Sounds good."

"Yes. Quiet now. Drink. I'll finish with your back."

When he'd finished the tea, he reached out and put the mug on the windowsill. "Done."

"Good." She came around, went over to the table, and poured some more lotion into her hands. Returning, she came and stood in front of him, rubbing her hands together, reaching out, her breasts a foot or less in front of his face. She put her hands on the wound site. Some of the lotion dripped down his arm and she scooped it back up. "It would be better if you were leaning back. Maybe over on the bed."

She backed up a step and he got to his feet.

Looking down, she asked him, "What have we got here?"

"I'm afraid you've got me a little turned on."

Without changing her expression, she said, "If you must know, I am, too, a little bit. We can ignore that for now. Go over to the bed."

It was a double bed, and Waverly took a few steps over and sat on the edge of it. Sara went into the bathroom for a couple of seconds and came back with a towel. "Here," she said after she'd spread it out on the bed, "lay down crossways here."

He did as instructed. She had room to sit on the bed alongside him and began rubbing in the oil. "Close your eyes. Just relax."

As she'd done with his back, she kneaded the scar tissue around the wound.

He had his eyes closed and kept them that way as he felt her hands stop. A second later she lay one of her hands, palm down and flat, on his stomach. The other hand went to his belt, unbuckling it. "Is this all right? Just say stop if you want to stop me."

He couldn't get an answer out.

The belt undone, she slid her hand under it and took hold of him, squeezing and holding on for a few seconds. Then she let go.

He felt her stand up. She went around to where his legs draped off the other side of the bed, then put her hands on both sides of his belt and pulled.

He opened his eyes to see her stepping out of her skirt.

She smiled up at him, then put her hands on him and stroked a few times with her oiled hands. "That's a boy," she said.

Climbing up onto the bed, pulling up to straddle him, she hesitated, barely touching him for a few more seconds.

"I'm so ready," she said, then with a shiver lowered herself onto him.

19

On Monday morning, after he'd cleared the metal detector at the Hall of Justice, Dismas Hardy considered going upstairs and dropping in on the district attorney, his former partner Wes Farrell. After all, he still had half an hour to kill before court went into session, and Wes was usually good company.

But Hardy's reception at Abe Glitsky's home yesterday afternoon, after he'd broached the subject of Abby Jarvis, gave him pause. Something about the case had gotten under Glitsky's skin, and Abe was just a bystander. Farrell, by contrast, at the very least would have been aware of the decision to put Abby's case before the grand jury even if he had not personally made the call. He wasn't going to be inclined to listen to Hardy's arguments about the evidence being light. In fact, if anything, he'd be more on the defensive about the indictment than Glitsky had been.

So Hardy bought a cup of coffee in the lobby and walked up the stairs to the second floor, yawning vast and nearly empty in front of him. Over to his left, though, he heard the elevator doors open, and there, coming around the corner surrounded by a posse of five people, was none other than the district attorney himself, who, upon seeing Hardy, stopped short and broke into a smile.

"So much for the element of surprise," he said, "How you doing, Diz? I believe you know most of my colleagues here: Paul, Kathy, Inspectors Yamashiro and Waverly, and of course our lovely and indispensable Treya."

Treya being Farrell's secretary as well as Glitsky's wife.

What, Hardy wondered, were all these people doing here? And furthermore, what was Wes himself doing here? "So, who were you hoping to surprise?" he asked.

"I'm afraid that would be you," Farrell replied.

"Well, I'm flattered at all the attention, of course, but I'm not sure what it's about. This Jarvis arraignment."

"Right. To sort of let you know, since you seem to have more than your normal doubts, that this wasn't some paint-by-numbers deal and that this district attorney's office stands one hundred percent behind the indictment."

Hardy all but rolled his eyes.

Farrell pushed on. "I just happened to be talking to Abe yesterday after you left him, and after we got off the phone, I thought it might be a good idea to put on a show of prosecutorial zeal to drive home the point that we think this is a righteous arrest and indictment."

"Maybe not so much, Wes."

"How can you say that when you haven't even seen the transcripts from the grand jury?"

"I've talked to my client. She didn't do it, plain and simple. The medical examiner himself ruled it a possible suicide after first not seeing any sign of a crime at all. It's just an egregious jump to go from all that ambiguity to a charge of first-degree murder with special circumstances. I mean, look at it: it's completely absurd, especially with the lack of any physical evidence — any that I've seen or heard of, anyway."

"So the grand jury just got it wrong?"

"It wouldn't be the first time, as you know, and it won't be the last."

"We don't think so."

"Clearly," Hardy said, "since you're bringing down all the troops like this. Do you really think you're going to intimidate me?"

Kathy Guerin spoke up for her boss. "Nothing like that, Mr. Hardy. That's not our intention at all. We're here to put on a show of solidarity and support for the grand jury and the prosecution team."

"Well, you're putting on a show all right." Hardy found himself truly angry at this grandstanding. "But if you ask me," he went on, "it's a shit show. And now, if you'll all excuse me, I'm going inside and getting ready to talk to the judge."

Fifteen minutes later Hardy stood up at his desk in the courtroom, next to his client in her prison garb in Department 22 of the Superior Court. Behind him in the gallery, Farrell, Treya, another assistant district attorney named Paul Stier, and the two inspectors sat projecting their negative karma his way. At the other desk inside the rail next to him, Kathy Guerin fiddled with some paper and looked as though she'd be prosecuting Abby when the case got to trial.

"Dismas Hardy appearing specially for the defense," he said.

Judge Magnus Brekkubruns removed his tortoiseshell eyeglasses and looked over them with a hint of impatience. "Waiting for Mr. Green, Mr. Hardy?" he asked.

"Not exactly, Your Honor." The judge's question was a code known to all of the legal professionals in the room. Mr. Green was money — Hardy's payment, without which he would presumably not be Abby's attorney. If Hardy had not informed the judge at the outset that his was a "special" appearance, then it would be considered a "general" one, and Hardy would be the attorney of record and mandated to remain in that role unless and until a judge ruled that he could quit. "Ms. Jarvis and I are just working out some of the final details of my representation."

"All right, Mr. Hardy. So noted. But I'd like the point settled before we go too much further. Is that clear?"

"It is, Your Honor. Thank you."

Hardy touched Abby on the shoulder and she got to her feet.

"Ms. Jarvis," the judge intoned, "you are charged with first-degree murder and murder for financial gain, which makes this a special-circumstances case." He went on to read the rest of the indictment, then finished up. "Do you understand these charges that I've read to you? Mr. Hardy, is your client ready to enter a plea?"

"No, Your Honor. May we have a week for plea and counsel?"

"All right, but if you haven't come to terms with your client by then, I'll have to appoint somebody else and move on."

Hardy knew that that appearance would be crunch time for the time waiver. He had already, on his own, made the decision while shooting darts the day before that he didn't care what Abby thought about it: he was going to waive time and she could decide to fire him or not. She hadn't liked it when he told her about it the night before, but that was her problem, not his. And in the end she'd gone along with it, because she didn't really have a choice. For his part, Hardy wasn't walking headfirst into the firestorm of a murder trial without taking all the time he needed to prepare his defense.

If it took him a year, so be it.

Although he did have a potential alternative strategy up his sleeve, brought on by his fury at Farrell and his really unprofessional decision to attend the arraignment in a show of force.

So they finished up what would normally be the last of the administrative details of scheduling. Since all of this stuff was completely expected, it caused not a ripple of response in the courtroom. But Hardy, still at a low simmer over the presence of Farrell and his minions, wasn't ready yet to call it a day. He half turned to make sure that the gang was still all there, then cleared his throat.

Judge Brekkubruns had his gavel in his hand, about to slam it down and call the next line, when Hardy spoke up. "Excuse me, Your Honor," he said. "If it please the court."

The gavel went down with exaggerated slowness. "Yes, Mr. Hardy."

"There is the matter of bail."

The judge's eyebrows came together in a frown.

Kathy Guerin piped up. "This is a special-circumstances case, Counsel. No bail is allowed."

Hardy said, "I believe Counsel is mistaken, Your Honor. No bail is permitted in a death penalty case, but I'm sure the district attorney is aware that there hasn't been a death penalty case in San Francisco in twenty-some years."

Guerin dropped the veneer of collegiality. "And I'm sure Counsel is aware," she said, "that the courts have interpreted the section to apply to any case where the People could ask for the death penalty whether we do or not. This is a special-circumstances

233

case, which could be a death penalty, though we are not asking for that. There is no bail."

"True as far as it goes, Your Honor," Hardy said, "and almost correct. But the actual code section — Penal Code 1270.5 — says that there is no bail in such a case quote 'when proof of guilt is evident or the presumption great.' The prosecution's case, from everything that I've been able to learn, has not remotely met that standard. I'd be happy to loan Ms. Guerin my copy of the Penal Code, if she'd like to look it up."

This brought Guerin to her feet. Her face had already colored slightly, and Hardy thought this might get worse in the next moments. "I actually have a copy of the code, Your Honor, and perhaps Mr. Hardy would like to read the portion of the grand jury transcript that sets forth in great detail the evidence which squarely pins this murder on his client. The defendant has been indicted by the grand jury, and that alone meets the standard."

Hardy, the soul of calm, shook his head. "Well, now, Your Honor, we've gone from mere shoddy analysis to a downright misrepresentation designed to mislead the court. That same code section says, and I quote here, that 'the finding of an indictment does not add to the strength of the proof or the presumptions to be drawn therefrom.' My client is entitled to bail, or at least a bail hearing, and I respectfully insist that it be provided to her."

Guerin could barely stutter in response. "The grand jury made that decision," she said.

Hardy shot back, "The statute is clear, Your Honor. Bail can only be denied when the evidence is clear and the presumption of guilt is great. The prosecution has met neither of those criteria. And meanwhile we're talking here about keeping my client — a single mother with a young child — in custody for perhaps a year or more when in fact there is no clear evidence that a murder has even been committed. How could there be a clearer demonstration of when bail must be allowed?" Then Hardy dropped his big bomb, the word every judge hates to hear: "The undue hardship that no possibility of bail places upon the defense may very well prove to be an appealable issue at a later date."

This was not true, or at the very least probably not true, and Hardy knew it. But he also knew that having a high-profile trial reversed on appeal is the nightmare of every judge. Brekkubruns hadn't been on the bench too long — he probably wasn't yet forty — and from his tightened-down facial expression, obviously the thought that he could irrevocably screw up a decision at the arraignment stage over a minor issue such as a bail hearing struck him as seriously disturbing.

And Hardy figured, while he was at it, pumped up on adrenaline and ostensibly ahead on points, he might as well push his luck and try to land another blow or two and put Wes and his team on notice that if they were going to screw around with him, they could expect payment in kind.

"Also, Your Honor," he went on, "I'd like the record to reflect the presence in this courtroom not only of the district attorney himself but two of his assistants as well as both of the inspectors who handled the investigation and arrest of my client. For a simple arraignment, Your Honor, this smacks of an attempt to intimidate the court."

"Your Honor, objection! It's nothing of the kind." Guerin had turned briefly to check back with Farrell for something he might signal to her in the way of a response, but her boss merely spread his hands and made a "What can I do?" face. This was absurd, Farrell thought, but Hardy was running with it and, it seemed, he had the judge's attention. If the judge believed for a minute that Farrell had come down there with his troops in an effort to somehow intimidate the court — that is, the judge himself — things could get ugly in a hurry.

As district attorney, Farrell was not without power in regard to the judiciary. Each party in a case has the onetime option to issue a challenge against the judge and have the case moved to another judge. The district attorney was a party to every criminal case, so the DA could effectively challenge judges on every criminal case, end their career in the Hall of Justice, and send them off to hear only civil cases. In modern history, very few trial judges without significant criminal law experience had ever been promoted to the Court of Appeals.

And Hardy had just reminded Brekkubruns of all of this. Which meant that if the judge felt like he was being threatened, Hardy and the judge were for the moment at least some kind of allies.

For a fleeting instant, Hardy thrilled to the possibility that Brekkubruns might speak directly to Farrell out in the gallery and perhaps ask him what he and his team were doing there, where in fact they had every right to be. Hardy had given Farrell's presence there a spin and it had knocked the district attorney and his people down a few pegs, but that was likely all he was going to get.

Buying himself some time, the judge took off his glasses again and wiped a handkerchief across his brow. "At issue before the court is the question of bail. Mr. Hardy, do you have a motion?"

"Yes, Your Honor. I'd like to request a hearing on the question of bail for my client."

"Your Honor!" Guerin's voice was shrill. "This is unconscionable. Bail is not permitted in a special-circumstances case. The defendant has been indicted, which by itself meets the evidence standard."

"Your Honor," Hardy replied, "that is quite simply not true. The standard for denying bail in a special-circumstances case has not been met. Further, as a single mother living with her special-needs daughter, Ms. Jarvis is clearly not a flight risk."

Brekkubruns straightened up at the bench. "This is the first I've heard of special needs."

"Veronica has Asperger's syndrome, Your Honor. Her mother is not about to leave her daughter to flee the country or even the jurisdiction. Bail is totally appropriate in this case, Your Honor, and I'd like to request a hearing at the court's earliest convenience if you're not ready to make a ruling today."

"How about a week from today? Same time, same station. Would that be convenient for all parties?"

"Fine by me, Your Honor."

"Ms. Guerin?"

"A full-blown hearing? Your Honor, Mr. Hardy can't be serious."

Brekkubruns's eyes closed down slightly into a squint, his mouth going tight. "Mr. Hardy makes a colorable argument that in this case, in spite of the special circumstances alleged by the prosecution, bail may be appropriate for this defendant. It seems to me that with all the firepower the district attorney has brought into this courtroom today, plus the weight of the grand jury indictment to buttress the People's position, a hearing would not be overly burdensome. That is my ruling. I'll expect to see all parties here a week from today."

Hardy risked a quick glance over his shoulder. Catching Farrell's eye, he inclined his head an eighth of an inch, driving home a victory nail. He'd drawn first blood and everybody knew it.

Farrell, his hands in his lap, out of sight from the bench, gave him half a grin in ironic acknowledgment, then turned a hand over and flipped him off.

Sweet, Hardy thought.

Waverly and Yamashiro stopped by Lieutenant Juhle's office to fill him in on how they'd spent their day so far, in the courtroom. Both men sat in chairs they'd unfolded in front of the lieutenant's desk. Yamashiro was doing most of the talking. When he'd finished, Juhle was frowning.

"I'm not sure I get it," he said. "Farrell didn't want you to testify? You weren't called as witnesses?"

"Nothing like that," Yamashiro said. "He just wanted us both to be there with him and a couple of other DAs."

"Out in the gallery?"

"Yep."

Behind his desk, slumped down in his leather chair, Juhle scratched at his cheek. "Wasn't this the case where they thought it was a heart attack first?"

"That's the one."

"And, refresh me, why did they go back and look again?"

"One of his daughters went to Farrell directly and convinced him to go back to the ME."

"Okay. And why was that?"

"What do you mean?"

240

"I mean she must have suspected some-body killed him or he killed himself. Right? The guy's in his sixties and he dies of a heart attack. Big deal. Happens every day. Shouldn't raise any kind of flag. But she thought it was something else, and she was apparently right. And then . . . what was it? She fingered the bookkeeper because of all of these financial irregularities?"

"Uh" — Yamashiro cleared his throat — "not exactly. She and Jarvis — the book-keeper — they're friends, or they were."

"So" — Juhle looked confused — "who else was she looking at?"

Finally, Waverly — bleary-eyed, guilt-ridden, and short-tempered — spoke up. "She just wanted to know why her father died, Devin. He'd just had a medical workup and everything was peachy. He shouldn't have died when he did. She just couldn't believe it and, what the hell, it was only a couple more scans for the ME. So he found it."

"And once you guys started looking, she stuck out? This Jarvis woman?"

"Like a sore thumb," Waverly snapped.

"The grand jury thought so, too, Dev," Yamashiro reminded Juhle with a touch of defensiveness.

Waverly doubled down on the vibe, clipping out his words, his face blotching with anger. "Am I hearing you've got a problem with this thing, too?"

Juhle rolled his chair forward up to his desk and held up a palm. "Easy, Eric. Are you feeling all right? You need a minute?"

"I'm fine."

"Well, then get your shit under control. Nobody's accusing anybody of anything. I'm just trying to understand why Farrell decided he needed to have you guys and a couple of DAs sitting with him in the gallery, and one of the reasons that occurs to me is that he doesn't have a whole lot of faith in the case itself. Do you think that could be a possibility, Eric?"

"The case is rock solid," Waverly said.

"But it seems the indictment might not have struck Farrell as enough, right? If it was, he doesn't need you guys down there with him, does he?"

"That's his problem," Yamashiro said.

"I agree," Juhle said. "But I would just like to know which way the wind is blowing. He's taking two of my experienced inspectors out of the field — call it four man-hours — I'd like to think he's got a good reason."

"You want my opinion," Yamashiro said, "it's something to do with her attorney."

"And who's that?"

"Dismas Hardy. He and Farrell used to be partners. I think he was just spitting in Hardy's eye. You remember that PI you brought by on Saturday? Wyatt Hunt?"

"Sure. What about him?"

"He was fishing for other suspects in this same case. Working for Hardy."

Waverly turned to his partner. "When did this happen?"

"You weren't here. It wasn't important."

"Yeah? Except here we are, talking about it."

"Never mind that, you two," Juhle said. He came back to Yamashiro. "Was Hunt down at the arraignment?"

Yamashiro shook his head no. "But he's on it. I promise you."

Juhle nodded with a bemused look. "The old SODDIT defense," he sighed, referring to the acronym for *some other dude did it.* "So who else is Hunt looking at?"

"An ex-girlfriend. Probably most of the dead guy's kids, if they'll talk to him. Nobody even remotely as good for it as Jarvis, though."

"Sure. Hence the indictment." But Juhle leaned back, fingers templed over his mouth, obviously troubled by something. "Did you guys get a chance to interview the

243

daughter who wanted the redo on the autopsy?"

The two inspectors threw an embarrassed look at one another.

"I'm taking that as a no," Juhle said.

Waverly started to explain. "She wasn't —"

But Juhle cut him off. "I'm just saying that it sounds like she didn't have any suspicion of Jarvis, since they were friends. But she must have thought something was squirrelly someplace or she never would have gone to Farrell. She might be worth talking to. That's all I'm saying."

"It sounds to me," Waverly said, "like you're saying we missed something."

Juhle exhaled heavily in exasperation. "What I am doing is running out of patience, but — for the record — I'm just playing out the string here, Eric. You guys get invited to a standard arraignment for no apparent reason except to throw some defense attorney off his feed and all I can figure is that the DA isn't all that confident about the merits of the case. Which reflects back on this department. And then I hear about this woman who started this whole ball rolling and you haven't interviewed her yet. And I'm wondering if that's where the problem might be."

His arms crossed over his chest, Waverly said, "There *is* no problem."

"That's what you keep saying, Eric. And I'm saying it couldn't hurt to talk to her."

Yamashiro, the voice of reason, came back at Juhle. "We've already got a suspect in custody, Devin. What's our excuse to take up this woman's, the daughter's, time?"

"I don't know, Ken. Be creative. Tell her you're working to make the case against Jarvis even stronger. This isn't rocket science, guys. But what we really don't want is Dismas Hardy pulling something out of his ass at the trial that we never saw coming just because we refused to look."

Yamashiro nodded in agreement. "Or even at the bail hearing," he said.

This stopped Juhle dead. "What bail hearing?" he asked. "I thought this was specials."

"It is."

"So what's with the bail hearing?"

Yamashiro gave him the short version, at the end of which Juhle's frown had turned to a deep scowl. "You're telling me the judge may grant bail?"

"Not impossible," Yamashiro said.

Juhle shook his head in apparent disbelief. "You guys," he said, "really need to go talk to this woman. I mean, like, yesterday."

20

Wyatt Hunt was already there, in the cramped seating area in the office in front of her desk, talking to Gloria. "But after you heard that Abby had been arrested —"

"Heard? Are you kidding? I was here. Her office is just there, through that wall. And they just came in and put her in handcuffs and took her away. None of us could believe it."

"Did you try to stop them?"

"Not at the time, no. It never occurred to me or any of us that they were actually here to arrest her. They went in, just talking to her at first, and next thing you know — Gene and I were in Gary's office trying to decide what to do — they're downstairs and stuffing her in the back of a police car."

"So then what did you do?"

"What could I do? I mean, I was in shock. I couldn't even think of anything to ask them while they were still here or tell them to stop. And since, I've called those inspectors so many times," she said, "wanting to know what they had done to her and what we could do to help her out. And how many callbacks did I get from them? You want to guess?"

"I'm thinking it's a low number."

Gloria let out a little chortle. "Try zero. Still, to this day. No callbacks."

"Have you tried to go see her in jail?"

"No. I feel . . . well, to some extent I know it's my fault she's there, and she must think that, too. That I have abandoned her. But I'm her friend still. Besides, can you just do that, go see somebody at the jail?"

Hunt nodded. "There's regular visiting hours every day."

"There are? You mean you can just go in?"

A snap of his fingers. "Just like that."

"I have to do that." Gloria pushed back and forth on her ergonomic chair. "I need to explain to her . . ."

"What, exactly?"

"Well, that I don't think she's guilty. I wish the inspectors would have just spent a little more time talking to us. Any of us could have told them this was wrong. At least so soon. There were a lot of other possibilities. How could they have been sure enough to arrest her?"

"Do you suspect someone else?"

Gloria's eyes opened wide in surprise. "Why do you ask me that?"

"Well, first, because you seem pretty sure it wasn't Abby, and next, because you're the one who got the DA to ask the medical examiner to rerun his diagnostics about your father's death, which meant you thought something about the first test was funky."

She hung her head for a moment. "I shouldn't have done that. If I'd known what was going to happen to Abby . . ."

"Even if she did kill your father?"

She paused, reflecting. "I don't know," she said at last, then released a heavy breath. "I don't know."

"Gloria," Hunt said in a gentle tone. "You just said that there were a lot of other possibilities. A lot? Really?"

"I don't know about 'a lot.' Maybe that's an exaggeration. Some, though."

"Like who?"

She seemed to shrink back into her chair, glancing over at the door to make sure it was closed. Barely beyond a whisper, she said, "Well, I mean, this is terrible . . ."

Hunt waited.

Finally, she looked up and over at him. "I really didn't want to find out he'd been murdered or had killed himself. Those were the last things I wanted. My idea was to find out for sure. That was all. That it was really a heart attack. I never expected them to find anything like they did."

"And why was that so important?"

She lowered her voice even further. "Because I didn't want to live thinking it might have been one of my brothers or sister." She checked the door, came back to Hunt, let out a deep breath.

"And now?"

Another sigh. "And now everybody thinks it's Abby, and I really don't know. Plus," she said, then stopped.

"Plus what?"

"God. I feel like, with every word, I'm getting somebody else in trouble."

Hunt kept silent, put on his understanding face.

"He had a girlfriend, too," she said at last.

"Stacy?"

"You know about her?"

"I talked to her over the weekend."

"Pops treated her pretty badly," Gloria said. "How did she seem about that to you?"

"Sad. Bitter."

"Betrayed?"

"Maybe a little of that. Your father had been important to her, but she made no bones about that. Do you have any reason to think she might have . . . done something?"

"Not really. It's just that when suddenly the door got opened and we realized that somebody had killed Pops, I think all of us thought it could have been her. And for me it was easier thinking it might have been her than . . . than the other alternatives."

"She told me she hadn't seen him in the month before. Do you have any reason to believe that's not true?"

"I don't know. I don't have any proof that she did. And I don't think he ever mentioned her to me again after . . . after they broke up. And he would have, I think. If she'd come by, even just to visit."

"So that leaves . . . ?"

"God. I hate to even think about that possibility. I mean, it's really unthinkable. We're the G-Team. We're all in this together. None of us could have . . . except Abby couldn't . . . it's all such a mess. I never should have . . ." She shook her head in disappointment.

Although at what, precisely, Hunt couldn't say.

Gary didn't know who the guy in Gloria's office had been, but the presence alone

250

made him uncomfortable. He felt that Gloria was clearly in Gene's camp on the "sell soon" scenario, but she was also surprisingly reluctant to accept as fact Abby's involvement in their father's murder, which meant that his youngest sister very possibly harbored some doubts about their other siblings, maybe even about himself.

The whole thing was a mess.

Getting up from his desk, he went out to the catwalk that looked down into the warehouse, walked past his old empty office, then past Gene's — and wondered where his brother was this fine morning. He finally tapped on Gloria's enormous glass window and came to her door, which was open. "Got a second?"

Warned by his knock, she was already looking up expectantly. "Sure. What's up?"

"Just checking out how you're doing. It seems to be just the two of us in here this morning."

"I'm fine," she said, "given everything. But we're way behind on ordering and we'll be out of basics pretty quick if I don't get some kind of jump on this stuff soon. How about you?"

"Everything still feels pretty surreal."

"It does to me, too. I just figure I'll keep coming in and doing my work and things will get normal again eventually."

"Have you heard anything from Gene?"

"When?"

"This morning."

"No. Why?"

"Just that he's not in yet and no call, which is a little strange. I thought it was him in there with you earlier."

"No. That was a private investigator with Abby's lawyer's office."

"Really? What did he know?"

"He's trying to find another suspect who killed Pops."

"And he came to you? Why was that?"

"I think basically because I don't think Abby did it, so I was essentially on the same side as her lawyer. Plus, I'm the one who wanted the second autopsy. He wanted to know why that was."

"It's a good question, Glor. I've wondered about it myself."

She shrugged. "I don't think I've realized it myself until this morning, until he asked."

"And? What did you come up with?"

"That I didn't want to prove that Pops had been murdered, but that he hadn't been."

"But that didn't work out."

"No."

"And so you don't think it was Abby. Who

else does that leave?"

"I don't know, Gary. I can't believe it was any one of us . . ."

"Us?" Gary's voice suddenly resonated like thunder. "What do you mean, 'us'? We all loved Pops, Gloria."

"That's why I say I can't believe it. When I really think about it. But then I know someone did —"

"Okay, then how about Abby, even if she was your friend?"

Gloria was shaking her head. "It wasn't her. I know it wasn't her."

"How can you know that, Gloria?"

"I just do. I know her. She wouldn't kill a fly. And she loved Pops."

"She was also blackmailing him, somehow, about her kid."

"That's just not true, Gary, although the police seem to believe it. That wasn't the way it was. It wasn't the way they were."

"All right, so who does that leave, if it's not any of us and it's not Abby?"

She looked up at her brother, a plea in her eyes. "Stacy."

"Did you tell that to this private eye?"

"Yes. He'd already talked to her. He didn't think she was a very likely suspect, either."

Gary nodded, got his voice back under calm control. "You know, everybody's been saying that Pops would never have killed himself because if he wanted to be sure, he would have done it another way, right?"

"Right."

"Well, what if he just made a mistake? What if he just took down the wrong jar of tea and mixed up a strong cup and drank it all off, maybe even had another, and then went to sleep? That way it's not Abby, it's none of us, and it isn't Stacy, either. Don't you think that's at least a possibility? It's still a tragedy, yeah — maybe worse that way than if somebody did kill him — but there's no killer in the picture. It's just Pops making a mistake. And I know, he didn't make many of them, but maybe just this once . . . you might try thinking about it in those terms, Glor. Where nobody did anything wrong. For your own peace of mind, at least."

She let out a soft sigh, met her eldest brother's eyes, and nodded. "Okay." After a pause she added, "But then it's more important than ever to help Abby get off."

"You're right," Gary said. "She's part of the family, too, all these years. I'm sure we could all work together — I mean the G-Team as the kind of solid unit we are — and find a way to help her. Maybe with her legal bills. Something, anyway."

"Would you be behind that? Really?"

"We'd have to work out the details, but absolutely." Thinking that this was a small price to pay to make her his ally and effectively cut Gene out of the pack.

She got up, came around the desk, and put her arms around him. "You are such a great brother," she said.

He leaned down and kissed the top of her head. "We're a great team," he said in his most confident tone. "We'll make it work."

21

Quietly savoring his victory in the courtroom, Dismas Hardy hung back, taking a seat in the gallery of Department 22, making sure that he gave Farrell and friends ample opportunity to leave the hallway and disappear into their various offices. He knew he had a half hour or more before Abby would be delivered back to the jail, where he looked forward to doing a little postmortem with his client. And possibly crowing just a little bit.

Each time he thought about Farrell flipping him off — he couldn't help it — a tiny twitch tickled at the corners of his lips.

Finally, he took hold of his heavy briefcase and got to his feet. A minute later he was out in the hallway, crowded wall to wall as it often was during business hours with attorneys, clients, cops, families, reporters, and courthouse groupies of all stripes. Today's menagerie featured more than a few members of the Gypsy Joker Motorcycle Club, clogging up the pinch that led to the elevators.

Hardy, no stranger to navigating similar waters, inched his way along the wall, avoiding all eye contact, and made it unmolested to the stairway, where he decided to take advantage of the opportunity for exercise and use the steps.

Out on the sidewalk between the morgue and the jail, he checked his watch, saw that he still had plenty of time before he could expect Abby to be available at the jail, and so instead turned right and let himself inside the offices of the medical examiner.

For about half a century, San Francisco's medical examiner had been a Georgia-born, heavily accented gentleman named John Strout. Hardy, having worked as both a cop and an assistant DA in his twenties, had gotten to know Strout fairly well, and a visit to him was usually entertaining and quite often surprising.

For example, it was probably illegal to own many of them, but Strout nevertheless collected guns and knives, pokers and blunt objects and assorted other murder weapons, and kept them in a museum-worthy glass case in his office. The bookshelves identified him, also, as a student of many other gadgets of the torture-and-execution game dating back to the Middle Ages, the centerpiece being a skeleton that had been seated and fitted at the neck with a red silk garrote from the Spanish Inquisition. It was rumored that he kept a live hand grenade on his desk and would often reach for it and give it a rub as though it were a favorite pet.

But finally, the previous year, fighting convention to the end, Strout had retired at the age of seventy-nine. The new guy was Amit Patel, from the looks of him still somewhere south of forty. He had, of course, taken over Strout's old office, but the place might have been the dark side of the moon for all of its resemblance to the way it had been. The bookshelves, for example, at a glance contained actual books on forensics and poisons, various texts on general medicine and psychiatry, the *Compendium of Drug Therapy,* Stephen Jay Gould's *Structure of Evolutionary Theory,* Stephen Hawking's *Brief History of Time,* and perhaps a couple of hundred more. Beyond that, Patel seemed to understand that the job entailed frequent meetings with human beings, and he'd furnished the office with three comfortable chairs around a mahogany coffee table.

As soon as he entered the room, Hardy must have somehow telegraphed his reaction to the change, because Patel broke into a warm smile and said, "I knew I couldn't compete with the way Dr. Strout had it, so I went with the tried-and-true. I hope it's not too discouraging."

"Not at all. It's almost a relief. That hand grenade, did you ever see that? As many times as I was in here, it made me nervous every time."

"You didn't hear, then?"

"What's that?"

"He handed it over to the bomb squad when he left the office. Evidently didn't want it around his house where somebody might pick it up and pull the pin by mistake."

"Smart."

"It was. Especially considering that when the bomb squad took it out to be safe about it, they went ahead and pulled the pin and detonated the darn thing. The rumors about it being live turned out to be true. Which just goes to show you, you can't be too careful."

"Wow," Hardy said. "When I think of how many times I've been right here in this room with that thing. I thought about pulling the pin as a joke maybe a dozen times. It gives one pause."

"Indeed it does. If it's reassuring to you, I make it a point not to have live ammunition of any kind in this room. I confess that I even get nervous when inspectors and officers come in with their hardware, but there's not much I can do about that."

"No. I suppose not."

Touching the side of his head just over his right ear, Patel asked, "So, speaking of firearms and not meaning to pry, how long's it been since you got yourself shot?"

"A little over . . ." Hardy paused, broke a bit of a grin. "I like to pretend that it's not so obvious," he said.

Patel shrugged. "It would depend on who's looking, I suppose. But for me, especially with my job" — another shrug — "there might as well be a sign pointing to the scar. It really couldn't be anything else. Is the pain in your side from the same incident?"

This really put Hardy back on his heels. "I'm also pretending that I'm not favoring that side, either."

"Well, again, perhaps. I understand if even talking about it is painful."

"No. I'm impressed. And to answer your question: yes, it's from the same incident. One of my daughter's ex-clients shot me through a hollow-core door — twice, as it turns out. I've convinced myself that I was lucky he couldn't see me when he pulled the trigger."

"It sounds like, and it looks like you were." With an expansive sweeping gesture, Patel offered Hardy one of the chairs. "But enough of these pleasantries, pleasant though they may be. You didn't come here for my Sherlock Holmes impersonation. How can I help you?"

Hardy settled into his chair. "I'm handling the defense of Abby Jarvis in the Grant Wagner case, and since there were so many forensic issues that have already come up, I thought maybe you could kind of walk me through how you got to where we are now. I should also say at the outset — full disclosure — that I'll almost undoubtedly be calling you as a witness and I wanted to give you a heads-up on that."

"That's very considerate of you. Because of the incorrect initial autopsy result of heart attack, I would imagine?"

"That first, yes. But actually the second result might be just as persuasive. 'Homicide/suicide equivocal' isn't exactly a ringing victory for the prosecution out of the gate. I'm going to try pretty hard to get you to say that Mr. Wagner killed himself."

"He very well may have. That's something we can't really ever know from the forensic evidence alone, in any event."

Hardy came forward in his chair. "Dr. Patel . . ."

"Amit, please."

"All right, Amit. Nothing you found in either of the scans indicated that it might not be suicide? Made it lean more toward homicide?"

"No, not that I can think of."

"Well, as you can imagine, that's the answer I'd like to hear from you at the trial."

"Of course. Though I'm sure that the prosecution will have me admit — because it, too, is true — that there is nothing that rules out homicide in any of the scans, either. Mr. Wagner died after ingesting aconite."

"As a tea?"

Patel paused. "There is no clear indication of that. It might have been some kind of herbal decoction made from aconite root. It may have been a tea; it may even have been in the form of an overdose with pills."

"Really? Is there such a pill?"

"I don't know. It's a rare enough drug to begin with because the danger from overdose is so great. I'd wager it doesn't see much use here in the US, certainly among

Western practitioners. Maybe they manufacture it as a pill somewhere in the East — China or Indonesia, maybe even India — but although it's in the literature, I've never run across it here."

"Okay, so stay with me here. If it was a pill, or if we could locate a local source for a pill, then we're talking about a very probable overdose situation, aren't we? Which is to say, a suicide."

"I see what you mean." Patel considered for a moment. "If he had access to such a pill or pills, I'd have to say it would sway me in that direction, too. I mean, his alleged murderer wouldn't very likely have stuffed some pills down his throat, would he? Or she? I don't see how that would have played out without signs of struggle or duress, and there was no indication of that. But as far as I know, as I said, there is no pill."

Hardy sat back, pensive. "Can I ask you one more?"

"Sure."

"When it's not being used as a poison, what is this stuff's therapeutic value? What does it treat?"

"Fever and inflammation. Like aspirin but homeopathic — and, of course, way more dangerous. It's not called the 'queen of all poisons' for nothing. Did you know that the Japanese used it to poison their arrows when they hunted bear? The Eskimos after seals, same thing with their harpoons. I mean, this stuff brings down big game and works in a hurry."

"But I haven't heard anybody saying that Wagner had any medical issues. So why would he have taken it, period?"

"Good question," Patel said. "It's not impossible he just liked the taste of the tea."

"He was a complete tea junkie," Abby told him after they'd gotten settled next to one another at the round table in the attorneys' visiting room at the jail. "I'd make him a cup at the office two or three days a week near close of business. It wasn't like this was a secret we were trying to keep from anybody. He probably had twenty or thirty different types of tea at work at all times. In fact, unusual or rare teas were like the default gift if you wanted to get on Grant's good side. He was a real aficionado."

"And you're telling me the G-Team knew this?"

"Everybody knew it. Do you think that's what happened? Somebody made him tea out of the poison?"

"It's starting to look like it, which doesn't

mean somebody gave it to him. He might have just brewed up a cup by himself and that was it."

"But they didn't find any of that stuff, the poison, in his house, did they?"

"Not that I've come across yet. The crime scene report says they didn't. Leaves, yes, at his office, but it's the root that's poisonous, not the leaves. But I'm assuming he had lots of different teas at his home as well, right?"

"Lots."

"That's what I was afraid of." Hardy clucked in frustration.

"What?" Abby asked. "What's the problem?"

"The problem is that we can make a very good argument that this was either a suicide or an accidental overdose. The forensic evidence from the medical examiner supports both of those theories, so we'd be in relatively good shape."

"But?"

"But if it were either of those, the poison would still have been there."

"What do you mean?"

"I mean, give it some thought, Abby. Grant most probably didn't make himself some tea at his home with the very last portion of root of aconite. And if that's true, the remainder of it would have still been there at his house, in his tea cabinet, right? There would have been a trace of it some-where — in a baggie or one of his tea jars. But in fact there was none of it there anywhere, which means someone — his murderer — wanting to remove all the evidence and make it look like a heart at-tack, took it away and possibly even cleaned out Grant's cup or mug or whatever it was before he left. No sign of the aconite at his house therefore means it was in all likeli-hood a murder after all, and not an accident or a suicide."

"That's not the answer we want," Abby said.

"No, it's not." Hardy let out a breath, then shot his client a look. "But it does lead to something else we have to talk about."

She sighed wearily. "And what's that?"

"What you were doing on the night that Grant died."

"I already told the police I don't remem-ber."

"I know that." Hardy pushed back a little from the table. Crossing his arms, he settled a deep stare on her.

"What? Why are you looking at me like that? Do you think I'm lying?"

"Let's go for the short answer: yes."

"Diz. It was six or seven weeks ago. How am I going to remember one random day back that far?"

"It wasn't random. It was Wednesday, February twenty-fourth."

"Okay, and why would I remember that, out of all the other days?"

"Because you learned about his death the very next day. If you'd been with him the night before, of course you'd remember. Of course it would have made an impression. How could it not have?"

"Nobody can prove that."

Hardy shook his head. "I don't want to tell you how guilty that makes you sound. It's not a question of whether they can prove it, Abby. It's what were you in actual fact doing that night. Because, according to your own mother's calendar — religiously kept up, by the way — you didn't get home until nine o'clock that night. The prosecution, trust me, is going to mention this fact at the trial. And people are going to wonder what you were doing all that time after you got off work at five o'clock."

"How do you know I was off at five? I was probably just working late, catching up on things. I don't remember exactly."

"Catching up on things," Hardy repeated, disdain all but dripping off him. He took a

267

deep breath to calm himself. "As I said, Abby," he began, "I've just come from a visit to Dr. Patel, the medical examiner. It turns out that one of the things he discovered doing the original autopsy that kind of got lost in all the drama around the second version was that Grant had had sex a few hours, maybe only one or two hours, before he died."

Hardy kept up the thousand-yard stare, watching her slowly collapse as she caved into herself, her head dropping, her shoulders heaving once, twice.

When she finally looked back over at him, tears had overflowed onto her cheeks. "I swear to you, Dismas, he was totally fine when I left," she whispered. "That was, like, around eight o'clock and he was exactly like he always was."

"And how was that, Abby?" he asked.

"Wonderful."

22

After the two cops left their lieutenant's office with very clear orders to go and interview Gloria Wagner right away, without any discussion — without one word — they both returned to the wide-open room around the corner from Juhle's office that was the home of the homicide detail. Their desks faced one another hard up against one of the windows that looked down on Bryant Street, four floors below them.

Yamashiro picked up the phone at his desk and put in a call for a city-issued vehicle that they needed because he'd dropped his morning car off for an oil change. Waverly stood, impatient and smoldering, shifting his weight from foot to foot, until finally he shook his head and said, "Pit stop," and walked away.

Fifteen minutes and still very few words later, Yamashiro pulled their new ride into an open bit of curb space in an alley a few blocks south of the Hall of Justice and turned off the engine.

"What's here?" Waverly asked. "Why are we stopping?"

"Because we need to talk."

"What about?"

"About how long we're going to go on like this. Because I'm about done putting up with it."

"With what?"

"See if you can guess, Eric. The attitude, the bullshit, the anger, all of the above. You pick one."

Waverly sat facing forward in the passenger seat, arms folded across his chest. His eyes were on the alley in front of them. "So you think it's me, huh?"

"I think you need to figure out what's happening with you, yeah. I think you've got some post-traumatic stuff going on. It probably wouldn't kill you to talk to a professional."

"Yeah, 'cause it's all me. It's not you, having this PI come by over the weekend and dicking around with our cases, and you don't even mention it to me. Were you ever going to bring that up on your own, or was that some special secret between you and Juhle?"

"Perfect example," Yamashiro said. "Everything's about you and your paranoia."

"You're saying that wasn't anything? Talking to a PI and not telling your partner?"

"That's exactly what I'm saying, Eric. The guy was nothing. The discussion was nothing. I gave him nothing."

"It didn't sound like it. And funny how Juhle knew about it."

"He didn't just know about it, Eric. The guy is Juhle's pal. He brought him around and introduced him. There was no threat."

"Yeah, except it cut me out pretty well, didn't it?"

"Dude. You weren't at work. Remember? If you had been, you would have met the guy, too. But as I say, that's a perfect example. You gotta talk to somebody. And while we're at it, let me ask you one thing: Are you on something?"

"Fuck you."

"Yeah, there's a good answer."

"I got pain pills that I'm taking. Prescribed."

"Is that all?"

"What all do you want?"

"I want the truth."

"The truth is, I'm on what the doctor ordered."

"And nothing else?"

"I don't have to answer that."

"I think you just did. And while we're at it, how'd you really hurt your hand? You slammed it in your car door? Really? How'd that happen, exactly? You want to give me the play-by-play?"

Waverly sat up straight, his hands now resting on the dashboard.

"Dude, listen to me," Yamashiro said in his most reasonable tone. "We've been partners for five years. I knew you before you got shot and I see you now and you can like it or not, but you're not the same person. So I'm giving you fair warning before you get called in and busted by somebody else who sees what's going on. Juhle, for example. He's not blind. You don't think he's got a clue? You heard how he talked to you in there this morning — he's feeling you out. Why? Because you're bleeding your shit out everywhere. You don't think people see that, you're wrong.

"And if Juhle wants a blood sample — and, believe me, that's in your future — then when you fail it, it's not your needing counseling voluntarily, it's suspension at a minimum. You want to deal with that? You want that on your record? To say nothing about how you're scoring, which might mean jail. A cop in jail isn't a pretty picture. And I'm telling you, all that is close right

272

now. And it's not me who's the threat, Eric. The threat is inside you, whatever's eating you up. And time's running out. I'm not shitting you. You need to get straight, get some help. I'm telling you. I'm your friend and I'm telling you."

Waverly wiped a hand over his forehead, then killed some time by opening the window on his side. Crossing his arms again, he stared off out in front of them at the alley. He pursed his lips, then tightened his mouth down. High on his cheek, a muscle worked in his jaw. "I'm a fucking mess, Ken," he said at last. "I don't have any idea what I'm going to do."

So, with one thing and another, Waverly talking about most if not all of his issues and how they were going to address them, they didn't get to Gloria's office until around eleven fifteen. She wasn't exactly overjoyed to see them.

"I don't believe this," she said, standing up behind her desk when they knocked at her office door. "Do you know how many times I've called you guys? And now suddenly you just drop in and show up with no notice when I'm getting ready to head out to lunch, which is going to be at the jail to visit Abby Jarvis, who by the way didn't kill

273

my father. I don't know what you expect me to do for you, but my general rule is if I call somebody more than once and they don't even give me the courtesy of calling back, then I'm not too inclined to feel cooperative."

"We apologize for not getting back to you," Yamashiro said. "We've had our hands full following up other leads, and since we generally aren't permitted to talk about the course of an investigation, we don't typically get back to witnesses or other concerned parties unless there's something specific to report."

"Yes, well, meanwhile you went ahead and arrested the wrong person in this case."

"Is that what you were calling about?" Waverly asked. "You've got some information that implicates somebody else?"

"No. I just know it wasn't Abby. And in fact, I was talking about this with my brother this morning, and we agreed: Isn't it possible that nobody killed my father? That he wasn't killed at all? That it was an accident? Or even, maybe, that he killed himself? Why do you have to have a killer?"

"You'll pardon me for saying so, ma'am," Yamashiro said, "but that sounds just a bit funny coming from the person who pressed the medical examiner after his first verdict.

At that time you must have suspected something. Isn't that right?"

"That got misunderstood. I just wanted to be sure."

"So you must have thought somebody killed him at that time," Waverly said. "And you were right."

"I shouldn't have done that. It just got you guys thinking that Abby . . . because she had that accident . . ."

Waverly spoke in a calm and measured tone. "It's not just that — not even mostly that. You have probably heard that she was embezzling from your company for the past several years. We're talking about maybe hundreds of thousands of dollars."

Gloria was scornful. "I read in the paper that they were saying that, but it's just not true."

Yamashiro piled on. "I'm afraid it was exactly like that, Ms. Wagner. And while we're at it, did you know that your father's will left her a million dollars more? And of course he had to die before she could collect on that."

Gloria looked at them as if they were speaking a foreign language. "I'm sure there's some explanation for all of that. That's just not who Abby is."

"No?" Waverly asked. "Then maybe we

could go back to the question we asked earlier. Is there someone else you think might be implicated here? Is there some new information we're not aware of?"

"No, but . . . I mean, not specifically. The main thing I've come to believe is that it was some form of accident, an overdose or something like that."

"So what's changed?" Yamashiro asked.

"What do you mean?"

"I mean, since you pressed to have the second scan on the autopsy. Since we arrested Ms. Jarvis. At one point, when you were pushing for that other scan, you must have thought — strongly thought — that your father didn't just die of a heart attack. Now you're saying that's exactly what you think. So what's changed?"

"More than that," Waverly added, "you just said you didn't have any specific new information. We'll take nonspecific, whatever you think it is."

Gloria put her hands palms down on her desk and, hanging her head, put her weight on them. Her shoulders rose and fell. Drawing in another breath, she looked up, and her face suddenly brightened as her eldest brother appeared behind the inspectors in her doorway.

"Gentlemen," Gary said, shaking hands.

"I don't mean to be interrupting, but is everything all right down here?" He looked across the room at his sister. "Gloria?"

"Fine," she said.

Yamashiro said, "We're just following up on some phone messages your sister left us. We were hoping to talk to her to clarify our case against Ms. Jarvis, but she tells us that now she may have some other information implicating someone else."

"Actually, no," Gloria objected. "I never said that. I just said it was nothing specific. It just wasn't Abby."

"Didn't we make it clear to you gentlemen?" Gary asked. "Grant knew everything that was happening in this business. It would have been impossible for her to be taking that money without him knowing about it. It was a little squirrelly, okay, maybe even illegal, but she and Pops — Grant, that is — knew all about it. It wasn't any reason for her to have killed him."

"On the other hand," Yamashiro said, "it may very well have been a reason to have killed him at that. I think the grand jury kind of saw it our way."

"In any event," Waverly put in, "we said we'd be glad to take whatever she has, even if it isn't specific."

"That's the point, though," Gloria said.

"It's nothing specific, except I feel very strongly that it wasn't Abby. I think if you guys had talked to me a little more before deciding it was her, you might not have made her your suspect."

"Which," Waverly answered her, "is part of why we're here now. If you have other suspicions . . ."

"Curiosity, more like," she said. "Like . . . okay, I might as well say it . . . like Stacy Holland."

Gary was shaking his head in disapproval. "Gloria . . ."

But she came right back at him — at all of them. "Listen. I talked to somebody from Abby's defense team this morning and he told me that you guys barely even talked to her."

"Wyatt Hunt?" Yamashiro asked.

"Right," Gloria said. "So I've got to wonder why you guys haven't even looked at Stacy when she had every opportunity and plenty of reasons still —"

Yamashiro held up a hand. "First, we talked enough to Ms. Holland to eliminate her as a viable suspect. Second, we follow every lead in a case, no matter where it comes from or where it goes. Now, if you have something that categorically clears Ms. Jarvis, we'd love to hear about that . . . if she was out of town or had some other solid alibi, something like that. Even if you have a lead that might take us in another direction, we would certainly follow that up. But I haven't heard anything like that. Do you have anything like that?"

But Gloria remained adamant. "It's not her. I just don't believe it."

Yamashiro huffed out a frustrated breath. "All right, then. Thanks to both of you for your time."

"If you get anything more specific," Waverly added, "please give us a call. I promise, we just want the truth."

Back in their car, Yamashiro said, "She's got something else."

"Maybe, but not enough to get Jarvis off or she would have told us."

"True." He hit the ignition. "But then, if that's the case, what was she calling us about? To tell us we'd made a mistake?"

"Maybe."

"You think we ought to go make another call on this Stacy Holland person?"

"What for? We've already got a suspect. If we go talk to her, it's pretty damn close to harassment before we even start." Waverly paused for a beat. "Okay," he said, "I've got another theory. About Gloria."

"Hit me."

"She thought it was in the family. Originally, I mean. Now, she doesn't want it to be Abby, but if she tells us why and we buy it, it very well might fall back onto somebody in the family. And she doesn't want that, either. So she's stuck. If she frees Abby, it opens the door to one of her sibs. And while that might have been great in theory when she first heard about her dad dying, seeing Jarvis get arrested makes it all a lot more real. She just wishes she could back out, but she can't. But she definitely knows or suspects something she's not telling us, and, blood being thicker than water, I don't think it's about Stacy Holland. That's just wishful thinking that it's not somebody closer to home."

Yamashiro drove for a moment, then looked across at his partner. "Good theory, Eric, but we're not going there. You know why? Because it fucking well *is* Jarvis. I don't care what Gloria Wagner's got up her sleeve or why Farrell felt like he needed us in the courtroom with him today. We got a righteous suspect with a righteous indictment. If somebody — even, say, Juhle, for example — wants us to go work some theories on the defense side of the case, finding all the ways you and me might have

280

screwed this up, they can all just bite us. As far as I'm concerned, our live case is David Chang. And we've got a list of at least six people we need to interview and I say we get on them. How does that sound?"

Waverly, unconsciously, was rubbing his shoulder. But he nodded and said, "Good enough."

His partner cast him another glance. "How are you feeling?"

"Holding up."

"If you weren't holding up, would you tell me?"

Waverly broke his first smile, a weary one, of the day. "Probably not."

"You need a pill?"

"Always."

"Feel free. I won't bust you."

"Least of my worries," Waverly said.

23

Still a little before noon.

Gary and Gloria remained in her office, debriefing one another on the inspectors' visit now only recently ended, when Gene showed up at her door. He came in, friendly enough, and sat down, and they'd just about gotten him caught up on all the recent developments, when Grace appeared in the doorway as well.

Wasting no time, Gary took the opportunity to invite the rarely assembled G-Team all down to his large office, where there was more room and maybe — since they were all present and accounted for — he could take advantage of this chance to clear the air about the company's immediate future once and for all.

When his door had closed behind them, Gary took his chair and waited while the others took theirs. He started off on a conciliatory note. "I can't tell you all how glad I am that we're all here in the same room together at last. I know we've all been doing our jobs day to day and keeping busy, but I think it's important that we all try to keep up the communication amongst ourselves so we don't let resentments build up and ruin what makes it great to work here with our own company. I don't want us to forget how lucky we all are."

An obviously disgruntled Gene shifted uncomfortably in his chair between the two women, who seemed relaxed and attentive.

Gary didn't want to pause too long to give Gene, for example, the chance to interrupt. "I don't mean to criticize Pops or any of the decisions he made while he was alive," he said, "but I've been in this office now for a little over a month, and I've got to tell you all that I'm beginning to think he made a mistake on our salaries."

"No shit," Gene said.

"I know." Gary nodded at his younger brother. "I don't blame you for feeling that way, Gene. I'd feel the same if I were in your shoes, and that's exactly what I wanted to address first while we're all together. In fact, I probably should have called a formal meeting like this one earlier as a high priority, but, frankly, I've been swamped trying to keep the ship afloat, as I know all of us have been."

"Well, not so much me, to be fair," Grace said. "But I'm ready to start coming back in a little more regularly, keep up my side of things."

"You're doing fine, Grace," Gary said. "We're all dealing with the change and the pain of this in different ways, I know." He turned to Gene. "Little brother," he said, "I don't blame you for being a little pissed off. This hasn't started off too fairly, and I don't blame any of you if you're unhappy with the new order. It just hasn't been my focus, and now I think I realize that it should have been. So what I'm proposing today is that I live off my salary as president and take my CEO salary, which you all know is $250,000, and divide that equally among all of us, which comes to $62,500 each, on top of the $50,000 raise we all got last month. That puts us all on the same playing field and I think is a much more fair distribution."

"But you're doing both of those jobs," Grace said.

"Well, I am, but they're pretty much one and the same, Grace. Otherwise, I feel like I'm just taking money out of your pockets, and that's just wrong."

Grace came back at him. "But we don't

need —"

"Like hell we don't!" Gene exploded. "Maybe you and James don't need more. Teri and I could use more every day. Or else, what am I working for? But, hey, if you want, Grace, tell you what: you can have the three of us split your share and you can stay where you are."

Gloria stepped in to protect her sister. "She doesn't want that, Gene. She's just trying to be fair."

"Fair, fair, fair," Gene said. "This whole thing hasn't been fair since Pops died."

"Well," Grace shot back, "you're just coming across as selfish, Gene. What are we doing — extra, I mean — to suddenly earn that much more money? Whereas Gary is actually in here every day trying to keep it all together."

"I don't know if you've noticed, Grace, but I'm in here every day, too. And Gary's making half a million a year, while we — all of us — even with the bump last month, we're barely making two hundred K. You want to tell me how that's fair? Because I don't see it."

"He earns more because he does more."

"No," Gary finally broke in. "That's not really true. I think Gene is right here. The only way we can be really equal, as the

G-Team has always been, is that we all make pretty close to the same salaries. I know that I don't have any desire to break us up and I hope we all pretty much feel the same way."

"Well, I do," Gloria said.

Grace chirped in. "Me too."

"Gene?" Gary asked.

"It's a decent start," he conceded. "I'll need to run the numbers, but at first glance they sound doable. I think it's a good move, Gar. Effective when?"

"I'd go with the next pay period if it's all the same to you guys. It's not an issue for me." He met the eyes of each of his siblings. "But I'll tell you what is a bit of an issue for me, and that is the long-term plan for the company." When nobody spoke, he went on: "We all know that Pops was thinking about putting us on the block in the next year, year and a half, where he was looking at somewhere in the range of seventy million and up. By contrast — with the legal problems involving some of Abby's, shall we say, bookkeeping practices, to say nothing of Pops's death muddying the waters — I think, Gene, that even you'll agree that our valuation is in the toilet — twenty-five to thirty million tops — and is likely to remain there for a while, at least until we're audited and clear up whatever tax issues we've got left. I expect that we're talking about an eighteen-month, maybe two-year interval.

"So the bottom line is that if we're willing to give ourselves those two years to get back to where we were just a couple of months ago, we stand to make forty to fifty million dollars more than we could hope to see if we went on the market in the next few months. That's a probable minimum of ten million extra dollars for each of us, free and clear, and to me that's worth a bit of patience on our part. I would hope that these new salary distributions that I've suggested here today would mitigate any individual financial hardship over that short term.

"Anyway, that's my position, and if anybody has any comments, I'm open to hearing them."

"I've got some," Gene said.

Gary nodded at him, a tolerant smile playing around his mouth. "I thought you might."

"First, I think your valuation as of today is low. I think we could get forty now, which is the ten million you're talking about. Each. Why do you want to wait?"

"Because in two years, Gene, we're talking a probable valuation more in line with what it was before Pops died, of eighty mil-

287

lion, which is twenty million each; that is, ten million *more* for each of us. I think that's worth waiting for."

"If you could guarantee it. But you keep using the word 'probable.' What if the valuation doesn't go up? Or even goes down? What if we're as high as we're ever going to be right now, or even lower?"

"That's a possibility, of course. None of this is definite, because shit happens. We all just got a lesson in that. So, yeah, it's a risk but, given the possible reward, I believe that it's one worth taking. We get back to where we were as a company and all other things being equal, we become a hot acquisition target again. And that's when we pull the trigger, not before."

"But you admit that we could probably get ten million each today?"

"That's a high guesstimate, but you know the numbers as well or better than I do, Gene, and I'm sure we could get close to there. Seven or eight, anyway."

"Well, I say we should position ourselves for that and go for it while we still have any value at all. And as soon as we can."

"You really want to do that?"

"I do. Seven million is a hell of a lot to walk away from on the off chance that it will turn into seventeen in two years. And I think our sisters here probably agree with me."

Gary held open his hands, palms up. "If that's the case, then that's what we'll do. Far be it from me to try to dictate to all of you. Nobody's trying to railroad anybody into this. It's a big decision. Grace, what do you think? Put us up for sale now or wait a couple of years?"

Grace looked from one brother to the other. Finally, with a look that seemed to beg Gene's forgiveness, she shook her head no. "I think it's a better idea to wait."

Gary nodded soberly. "Gloria."

She didn't hesitate for an instant. "I'm sorry, Gene," she said, "but I'm afraid I'm with the others on this. I think we ought to wait until we're back in shape and then see where we are in the market."

Gene slumped in his chair, defeated.

Gary eased himself back to sit on his desk. "If things are that tight for cash, Gene," he said, "there are any number of things we could do to help, including buying you out now if that's what you'd prefer. That would be a couple of million at least, which ought to help."

"A couple of million? Weren't we just saying each share would be closer to ten?"

"I think we got to seven," Gary said, "but

that's only if we all went in and sold out lock, stock, and barrel. There's no way we could divest any one of us for close to that in the here and now, not with all the flux we're facing. We need to hold on to most of our working capital, so any one share would have to be steeply discounted. But I'm sure that if you really want out now, we could come to some accommodation."

Gene, his face cast in bitterness, looked up at his older brother. "Thanks for the offer, Gary, but I think I'll just hang on for now with the rest of you and see if I can help right the ship."

"It was the saddest thing," Gloria said to Abby through the window in the jail's visiting room. "I had no idea that things were that bad with Gene, that he feels like he needs to cash out now just to live, but to put the company up for sale when it's having all these financial problems just seemed ridiculous."

After absorbing that for a moment, Abby asked, "Does everybody blame me?"

"Nobody thinks you killed Pops, if that's what you mean."

"That's so good to hear, but I mean about the financial stuff."

"Look, Abby. We all know you couldn't

have done anything without Pops knowing. Clearly, whatever you did, he wanted you to do." She paused for a moment, framing her answer. "I think everybody just wishes that you and Pops . . . well, that the whole payout thing with you would have been a little more transparent. Now the auditors are telling us that it's calling into question all of our accounting over most of the past decade, not just in terms of payroll, but where else Pops might have been avoiding taxes, dealing in cash, all of that. It's not very pretty, and the rumor is that it's going to get worse before it gets better. It just would have been so much better if we'd had some idea it was going on."

"He didn't want the G-Team to be involved. He didn't think you guys would go along with it, or at the very least you'd resent it."

"I wouldn't have, Abby. If I'd known all the details . . ."

"What details?"

"We've all kind of figured it out about Veronica. It's the only thing that made sense. We kind of suspected something might be going on, but you never referred to it, Pops never talked about it, and we all sort of left it alone." Gloria looked down to where her hands rested on the sill of the glass window separating them. She let out a frustrated breath and raised her gaze, looking into Abby's face. "It is a little painful to know you couldn't feel like you could share that with me. I mean, when I heard that . . . I mean, if nothing else, it makes Veronica our half sister. That's a huge deal. How could you think that wouldn't matter to us?"

"Your dad wanted to keep her separate from the G-Team. He promised your mother on her deathbed that you, the G-Team, would always come first. We — your dad and I — decided that nobody really needed to know about Veronica. Would it serve any real purpose? We decided that it didn't have to. He'd take care of both of us, forever and then some. Anyway, the person it's really hurt is me. I wouldn't be in here now if they didn't think I was blackmailing your dad and embezzling from the company. Which, I promise you, I wasn't."

"No. I never thought that. Nobody thinks that."

"Well, somebody does."

"Okay. But none of the G-Team does, anyway."

"But everybody else."

"That's so wrong," Gloria said. "Just so wrong."

"Maybe you can tell that to my lawyer."

"Your own lawyer doesn't believe you?"

Her lips barely curved into a bitter little smile. "Let's say that lately he's been on the fence."

"Then you should get another one."

She shook her head. "It doesn't matter. He even says it doesn't matter whether he believes I'm guilty or not. It's whether they can prove it, and he says with what they've got in terms of real evidence, they shouldn't be able to."

"That's not very heartening, is it?"

A shrug. "He's trying to get me out of here on bail, which is more than a lot of other lawyers would even try for. Plus, we have a relationship, a professional relationship, from the . . . the last time."

"But he thinks you did it?"

"Not really. Or at least I hope not. If he's leaning that way, he'll get over it. He just didn't want to hear that I was at your dad's earlier on the night he died."

Gloria sat back in her chair. "I didn't know that, either. Is that true?"

Another shrug. "It was a date," Abby said. "After Stacy, we were working things out."

Gloria couldn't say anything for a second or two. "How was he?"

"Fine. Healthy. In a good mood. Why?"

After another bubble of silence, Gloria said, "Well, mostly because people have been talking about the possibility that he killed himself."

"No chance, Gloria. He didn't kill himself — not on purpose. Somebody came there after I left and got him to drink the tea they'd brought along."

"You don't think it might have just been a mistake? An accidental overdose?"

"No. And for what it's worth, my lawyer, Mr. Hardy, doesn't think that, either."

"Why not? Does he know something we don't?"

Abby nodded. "The police never found any of the poison at his house. Mr. Hardy thinks that whoever gave it to him must have cleaned up afterward and taken it away. Otherwise, if he'd just mixed up his own tea, there would have been some trace of it, or maybe more than just a trace."

"Did he mention . . . Was he expecting somebody else?"

"I know. Wouldn't that have been nice? I've tried to remember if he said anything about that a hundred times. But, really, not a word."

Gloria looked one way, then the other, down along the row of seats, each of them holding a visitor talking to an inmate through a window just like the one she was talking through. A shiver ran through her bones, although whether from the temperature in the building or her emotional reaction to this place, she couldn't have said. Leaning forward in her chair again, she lowered her voice. "So, does your Mr. Hardy really think he can get you out of here on bail?"

"I guess he thinks there's some chance or I don't think he'd be going through the motions."

"And in the meanwhile, Ab, how are you dealing with all of this?"

"I'm all right," she said. "Remember, I've had practice."

"And Ronni? How's she?"

"Pretty good, given the circumstances. She came by with Mom for a couple of visits here over the weekend, and I think that helped them both almost more than it helped me. They're both being brave. They're my strength right now. And it's so nice to see you. Thank you so much for coming."

Gloria shrugged that away. "I'm sorry it's taken me so long to get down here. Like I said, things at the office have been a little . . . well . . . you know."

"Don't worry about that. I do know

you've got a million of your own things you're dealing with. But you're down here now. I can't tell you how much that means to me."

"Well, I feel sometimes like this whole thing is somehow my fault, and, given that, it's the least I can do."

On this mild and sunny afternoon, the walk from the Hall of Justice at Seventh and Bryant down to the P&V warehouse at Eighteenth and Sanchez would have normally taken about fifteen minutes, but Gloria — famished — stopped at her favorite burrito joint on Mission and stood drinking her Diet Coke and eating her fantastic double-spicy *machaca* at the counter while she tried to let things calm down a bit in her head. It might have been an unlikely way to settle her stomach, but, after the first few bites, it seemed to be working.

The day wasn't even half-done and it had already been an emotional roller coaster, first with the unexpected visit of Wyatt Hunt, then the police inspectors, then the impromptu G-Team meeting that had given her the stomachache in the first place, which had only been exacerbated by her long-overdue visit to Abby at the jail. At her first sight of Abby in her orange jumpsuit, Gloria had been struck with such a visceral response that she thought she might either faint or vomit. Or both.

This was all so unbelievable, so terrible, and Gloria was beating herself up over it. Why hadn't she kept her mouth shut about her father's death in the first place? All of the apologizing in the world couldn't change the simple fact that she had been the prime mover behind this murder investigation. Without her interference, Abby wouldn't be in jail, and without Abby's history and financial arrangement with Grant going public in the wake of her arrest, the company wouldn't be under audit. The G-Team wouldn't have all this division, drama, and rancor.

Then suddenly, in mid-bite, another wave of dizziness washed over her, so strong that she needed to take hold of the counter to keep herself from doubling completely over. An unconscious moan escaped her, and the guy a ways down the counter looked over and asked if she was all right.

Tight-lipped, she swallowed and nodded yes.

He pointed at her burrito. "Watch out for that double heat," he said. "It's serious shit."

Nodding again, she put her mouth to her straw and sipped.

It wasn't so much that she remembered — it had never truly been out of her mind since Abby had first mentioned it — as the import of it finally worked its way to the surface. *Abby had been at her dad's on the night of his death.*

Gloria was almost certain that the inspectors did not have this information and that it might prove to be crucially important. And while it was true that Abby had admitted it casually enough and her apparent lack of concern about it might therefore speak to her innocence, nevertheless the gravity of the admission itself seemed to tip the scales — for Gloria, at least, and for the first time in favor of her guilt.

How could Abby have let so much time pass without mentioning that supremely relevant point to anyone? Had she, in fact, lied to the inspectors about her alibi for the night of Grant's death? She must have. And wasn't a lie of that magnitude a sign of her true character?

Gloria had always been disposed to believe Abby because she thought that she knew her, who she was, her essential honesty and the goodness of her character. But now, all at once, the lie seemed to undermine all of that. If she was capable of lying about where she had been that night — and clearly she was and had — she could lie about anything, including her true relationship with Grant and the unreported money. Suddenly this new lens with which to view Abby's story revealed an entirely different picture that comported perfectly with that of the inspectors.

Abby had killed Gloria's beloved father, and she had done it for the money he had left her. That was why it had to look like a heart attack.

Back in her office, she kept the lights off and closed the door, then went to sit at her desk and think. Finally, she flicked on the green banker's lamp that sat on her desk and pulled the business card out from where she'd tucked it under one of her paper-weights.

When the number she'd punched up went to voicemail, she listened to the message and then said, "Inspector Waverly, this is Gloria Wagner. I've just come back from visiting Abby Jarvis in jail and she told me that she had been to my father's house on the night he was killed. I don't know if you already had this information, but I thought it might be important, and wanted to let you know right away."

24

Devin Juhle had his office door closed in the late afternoon. He'd read some portions of the city's human resources handbook earlier in the day — it was still lying face-down on his desk — and now was considering the situation with Eric Waverly.

He had nothing but sympathy for the man, who was obviously going through a very hard time.

And who could blame him? He'd been shot in the line of duty and nearly died from blood loss. After having been pronounced physically fit to return to work, he came back on duty six months ago, but almost from day one started displaying some unpleasant personality traits that made him, to say the least, hard to be around.

In the relatively close-knit group that made up the homicide detail — there were only fourteen inspectors in the unit — it didn't take long before his negativity and anger boiled over and scalded nearly every one of his colleagues. These weren't the type of people who cried about slings and arrows and other things and came running to their lieutenant, but underneath his hard-ass persona, Juhle prided himself on cultivating a smidge of sensitivity to nuance, and over the months he had picked up from casual remarks and more pointed witticisms that Eric had pretty much alienated himself from everybody else in the unit.

Finally, this morning, during their meeting when Juhle wound up sending Eric and his partner out to talk to Gloria Wagner, Juhle had gotten a fairly decent taste of the bitterness himself, and also a tickling, unarticulated, growing unease that Eric might be under the influence of some controlled substance. The thought of that, and its possible ramifications, made Juhle's stomach churn. But he was starting to think he was going to have to address that issue as well if something didn't change, and change quickly.

Hence, the tentative dip into the fetid pond of human resources. If Juhle were going to do anything formal regarding Waverly — and he hadn't quite decided that yet — he would have to document every single step he took. That would be tedious and probably get ugly, but otherwise, the San Francisco Police Officers Association would flay him and somehow turn him into the villain who was prosecuting a wounded hero.

No, Juhle thought. If he was going to start any kind of proceedings against Eric, he was going to need a specific incident, something he could point at as conduct unbecoming. It wasn't time yet, he told himself, aware that this was very possibly wishful thinking. But maybe Eric would start feeling better and his mood would improve. Soon.

It could happen, Juhle was thinking as a knock at the door derailed his train of thought. "It's open."

Speak of the devil, he thought, as first Yamashiro and then Waverly came through the door and over to the folding chairs in front of his desk, where they stopped. "Gentlemen," he said. "What goes?"

In the secret code that so many partners develop, Eric had apparently been appointed spokesman for this meeting. "Couple of things," he began. "As you suggested, we went out to P&V this morning and talked to Gloria Wagner, Grant's daughter and the woman who asked for the second scan on her dad."

"Sure. I remember. And how'd that go?"

"Not so great, to tell you the truth."

Yamashiro took over. "She mostly just wanted us to know that we'd made a mistake arresting Abby Jarvis. She said she knew that it definitely wasn't her, but she couldn't seem to dredge up some reason she thought that."

"Basically," Waverly said, "she said she wanted the second scan to eliminate her siblings so she wouldn't have to live with uncertainty about whether or not one of them had killed their father. But then she'd somehow been convinced that what we had on Abby wasn't enough, either, and we had nothing on her brothers and sister, so probably her father had just had an accident and drank the wrong tea, or too much of it, or something. Oh, and by the way, we should be looking for other suspects, since it couldn't have been anybody who worked at P&V."

"It was all a little disjointed by the end," Yamashiro said. "I think she was just feeling guilty that she'd opened a can of worms after the poison ruling and wished she could've taken it back."

"So," Juhle said with some disappointment. "Long story short, no new information?"

"That's what we thought, too," said Wa-

303

verly, who seemed suddenly and unexpectedly upbeat to Juhle, his perennial discontent nowhere to be seen. They had come upon something that had pumped them up.

"Do you want me to guess?" Juhle asked.

"You won't believe it," Eric said.

"I'll try. Let's hear it."

"After we left, Gloria went on down to the jail and visited Jarvis, where she — Jarvis — made a big mistake and admitted she'd been at Grant Wagner's place on the night he died."

"Farrell didn't already have that?" Juhle asked, incredulous.

"Nope."

"Not exactly a smoking gun," Yamashiro said, "but a nice, big missing piece of the puzzle. As soon as Gloria heard about it, right after she left the jail, she put in a call to Eric and told us. If Farrell needed any more, this ought to do it. You want my opinion, it's huge."

"And even better," Waverly enthused, "because when we first interviewed Jarvis, she told us she'd been working at P&V that night. So we've got her absolutely dead to rights lying to us, which I promise the jury is going to hear. And last time I checked, juries don't like people who lie to cops. And also — get this — Gloria with no hesitation told us that she'd testify. It might have just been a moment of weakness, but Jarvis told Gloria point-blank that she'd been there, and now Gloria's ready to tell the world. We got her, Dev. She's nailed."

"That's a good day," Juhle said. "Nice going."

The two inspectors both nodded in acknowledgment, and then Waverly said, "There's one other thing I wanted to run by you."

"Shoot."

Throwing a quick look at his partner for encouragement, Waverly came back to his lieutenant. "Well, I don't know if you've noticed anything these past few months, but since I got back, I've been trying to deal with some residual pain from when I got shot. It's just not going away the way it's supposed to. Plus . . ." He hesitated. "Well, there's been some other issues, maybe some post-traumatic stuff, like that. Anger. The whole thing really pisses me off, and I can't seem to get a handle on it.

"Anyway, bottom line is I decided I'm going to want to be talking to somebody, missing some work probably. I don't know, whoever it is might recommend that I take a little more time off, maybe a month, maybe more. But whatever it is, I'm thinking I probably want to go ahead and do it. Get so I'm a little more myself again."

Juhle sat back in his chair, nodding. "That's a gutsy call, Eric."

Waverly shrugged that away.

"And I think it's a good one."

"Well." Eric suddenly seemed at a loss for words.

Yamashiro took up the slack. "I wanted you to know that I'm fine going solo if it's not for too long. Meanwhile, we don't even know if they'll be recommending some admin time off after all. We're just letting you know we're on the same page with this, Eric and me. Whatever it takes."

"That's good to hear," Juhle said. "And, Eric, of course, you do what you need to do. I'm sorry to hear about the pain. That's a bitch. You got a time frame?"

Waverly shook his head. "I only just today realized I had to make a move, Dev. I figured I'd talk to some people, then make an appointment, put whatever program it's going to be in gear. Then we'll see where it goes."

Juhle nodded again. "That sounds like a plan. You've got my blessing. Just make sure you both keep me in the loop." He straightened up behind his desk, moved the human resources booklet over to the side, and turned it facedown. Coming back to his inspectors, he said, "I'm glad you guys came by and you, Eric, made this decision. Ken, we'll see what shakes out on the partner front, but short term I don't think I see any problem. And, again, good work on the Wagner case today. That's good stuff. I'd be happy to let you guys run down and give Farrell the news in person. You'll make his day that started out so bad. Or, Eric, maybe you'd just rather go on home and get a little rest."

Pushing at his throbbing shoulder, Waverly managed a tolerant smile. "I think I can handle another hour or two. Though I might let Kenny run down to Farrell's by himself."

"All right. Whatever works. But keep me informed, would you?"

It was a dismissal, and the two inspectors stood up. In an abundance of enthusiasm, Yamashiro leaned over the desk to shake Juhle's hand, and the lieutenant got to his feet, hand extended. Meanwhile, next to him, Waverly half turned and glanced up at the whiteboard on the wall directly across from Juhle's desk. The whiteboard contained all the active cases that the homicide team was working, and the inspectors assigned to each of them.

After the handshake, Ken Yamashiro

started to walk past his partner toward the office door on his way out, but Waverly stood blocking him, rooted to his spot, his face a study in confusion.

"You all right, Eric?" Ken asked. He turned back, his own eyes following Eric's gaze.

"What?" Juhle asked. "What, guys? Really."

Finally Eric found his voice. He motioned to the whiteboard. "Is this some kind of joke? Or what?" he asked.

"What are you talking about?" Juhle asked. "There's nothing funny up there."

"You're telling me somebody killed Stacy Holland?"

"Yeah. A few hours ago."

"Holy shit," Yamashiro said.

"How'd she get it?" Waverly asked.

"She was shot in her apartment. Why? What's going on? Do you guys know her?"

The two inspectors whom Juhle had assigned to the Holland homicide were Darrel Bracco and Debra Schiff, and — along with a few uniformed officers — they were standing in the doorway to Stacy's Valencia Street duplex when Waverly and Yamashiro showed up there, sirens screaming, at a little before five o'clock. A couple of black-and-white police cars and a coroner's van were already double-parked on the asphalt, and Yamashiro pulled up behind them. Perhaps a dozen onlookers stood around on the sidewalk, behind the yellow crime scene tape.

Schiff and Bracco didn't evince a whole lot of obvious enthusiasm for the latest arrivals: they waited at the top of the fourteen steps and let the new guys climb up and come to them.

After perfunctory nods of greeting all around, Schiff said, "Sorry you wasted all your time hurrying on out here, but Crime Scene isn't going to be done with the place for a few hours more at least. We barely got a glimpse ourselves. What's your connection here? Juhle says you knew her. Stacy Holland."

"She's the ex-girlfriend of one of our vics, Grant Wagner."

The name drew a whistle from Bracco. "High-voltage visibility," he said. "The heart attack guy, right?"

Yamashiro nodded. "That's him."

"And she — Holland — is somehow with him?" Schiff asked.

"Was," Waverly said. "They broke up a month or so before he got killed. If we didn't already have a righteous suspect in the slammer, she was on the short list for the next round of suspects."

"You mean as Wagner's killer?" Schiff asked.

"Well" — Waverly backpedaled a bit — "as I said, we've got his killer locked up, so we never got that far down the list. But her suddenly getting herself shot . . . it's a little coincidental, to say the least." He chinned toward the duplex door. "So, how'd it go down in there? Did you guys get any kind of a good look?"

Schiff brushed her short strawberry-blond hair out of her eyes and shot her partner a glance. If they were going to be sharing information with this second team of inspectors, she and her partner both ought to be involved.

Bracco took the cue. "If I had to guess on first impressions, it was somebody she knew. No sign of forced entry, and both the front doors are pretty seriously double bolted, as you'll see. Whoever it was, she let him in."

"A guy, then, you're thinking?" Yamashiro asked.

Bracco shook his head. "Figure of speech. I have no idea. Could have just as easily been a woman. In any event, from the looks of it, they were both sitting on the couch, maybe three feet apart. The killer used one of the throw pillows to muffle the sound; the stuffing's all over the place. Shot her once in the side, then a head shot behind her ear."

"Any idea when it happened?"

Schiff and Bracco exchanged another look. Schiff said, "Best guess is sometime last night, but it could have been as long ago as Saturday. Anytime this weekend, tell you the truth. Crime Scene will close up that window, but for now we don't know."

"Well, we might," Yamashiro said.

Bracco squinted at him. "How's that?"

"A private eye named Wyatt Hunt."

"Sure. I know him. What about him?"

"He might have come here to talk to Ms. Holland on Saturday afternoon."

"Might have?" Mystified, Bracco asked, "About what?"

"This connection she had with Grant Wagner."

"I don't get it," Schiff said. "So she was still a suspect?"

"No. Our suspect is Abby Jarvis and Hunt was working for her. Her attorney, anyway."

"And he came here to talk to Ms. Holland?"

"Maybe," Yamashiro said. "He didn't call me back afterwards and report in, so I don't know if he ever really made it. But he left

311

me the impression he was going to talk to her."

"Hmm," Bracco said. "Talk about co-incidence. We need to find out about that."

"It's already on my list," Yamashiro said.

"Well, not to get all pissy around turf," Schiff said, "but maybe talking to Hunt ought to be on our list, since last I heard this is still our case."

Yamashiro reached over and subtly put a restraining hand on Waverly's arm, keeping his volatile partner in check.

"Absolutely," Yamashiro said, "except where it intersects with Wagner, if it does. You want to talk to Hunt, you've got our blessing. And meanwhile everybody shares information. We appreciate your help. Good?"

"Good enough," Bracco said.

"So back on this, if you don't mind: When did you get the call?"

"Nine-one-one? A little after noon today."

"How'd somebody think to look?"

Schiff shook her head. "That wasn't it," she said. "Her cleaning lady had her own key and today was her day. She's pretty flipped out, as you can imagine. But, to her credit, she hung around until we got here, sitting on these steps. She said she didn't touch anything and I believe her. Since then we let her go, but my guess is she'd be available."

Yamashiro left Waverly off downtown at a few minutes before six o'clock. Now, ten minutes later, and filled with guilt and self-loathing, Eric sat in his own car in the lot behind the Hall of Justice.

Having sex with Sara Chang was, in his opinion, the worst thing he'd ever done in his life, and if he were going to turn things around and get back to feeling like the good person he really was, he was going to have to put a stop to any repetition of that kind of behavior.

That much was clear. Period.

Another question for which he didn't really have an answer was what to do now about Maddie. He wasn't sure if he would ever confess what he'd done to her, or even if he should. What would be the point? Plus, it would unnecessarily hurt her, and she didn't deserve that. To say nothing of the fact that in his heart, in spite of all the hard times lately, he loved her. They were committed to each other, to their family. He knew that it was he who'd been so difficult to live with for at least the past year, and just today, thanks to Ken, he'd finally made the decision that he would seek counseling and try to get out from under the cloud of misery, pain, and anger that had just about ruined his life.

And finally, definitively, he was going to break the hold that the Oxy had taken over him. The unbelievably stupid risks he'd already taken, doing business with street vermin — how long could that go on without one of them blowing the whistle on him? So that was ending, too. Right now — today.

The last remaining problem, though, was the pain — the pain that had started the whole downward spiral and now continued to plague him.

His hand still throbbed; his shoulder incessantly burned.

But, fortunately, there was a possible solution. Fraught, perhaps, with a bit of risk, but he'd been living with so much risk for so long now that, in comparison, it was nothing.

The fact was that the medicinal herbal tea that Sara had made for him to combat the pain had been surprisingly, even miraculously, effective. And it carried the extra benefit that it was apparently plentiful and legal. With the help of that tea, he felt that he could wean himself off the Oxy and gradually cut his dosage to where he could get back to a drug-free and pain-free life.

Of course, the risk was that, to guarantee access to the tea, he was going to have to go back and get in contact again with Sara. And that would entail some explaining, at least. He would have to tell her that it had been a mistake, that they couldn't see one another that way again, but he would be most grateful if she could put him together with her source for the tea to help him beat his addiction to the truly life-threatening Oxy.

The more he considered it, the more he didn't really think it would bother her very much. After all, she was young and very attractive, undoubtedly with her pick of younger, more vibrant guys. Whereas he was old, comparatively soft, perennially pain-wracked. He had neither the time nor the inclination for a real relationship with her.

She would understand that.

He pulled out his cell phone and made the call. "Sara. It's Eric Waverly."

"Eric. I am so glad to hear your voice. I have been thinking about us all day, thinking you won't call. How can you miss someone so bad when you hardly even know them?"

"I know. I should say I *don't* know. I'm

glad to hear you, too. I was hoping to see you."

"Yes. Yes."

"If you were home . . . if I could stop by for a few minutes. I'm done for the day. There is something I hoped we could talk about."

"Of course. Whatever you want. As long as you want. Now is a good time. I am here. I will see you soon?"

"Ten, maybe fifteen minutes."

"I am waiting."

"Okay," he said. "I'll see you then."

"I will be waiting," she said again. "Come soon. Please."

25

Dismas Hardy decided to swing by the Little Shamrock on his way home. It was one of the oldest bars in the city, founded in 1893 and so technically into its third century of operation, and after a series of barter-like deals with his now-deceased brother-in-law Moses McGuire, Hardy had finally attained a majority ownership.

But he didn't typically stop in to be a boss and check on the help. After all these years, the place essentially ran all by itself, a fact that was brought home to him as he pushed through the door at a few minutes after six o'clock. Even on the traditionally slow Monday night, every stool at the bar was taken, as were the chairs at the few tables scattered around the room. Standing patrons were scattered here and there in the small spaces left up front, and seated on the dilapidated couches under Tiffany lamps in the back. Hardy guessed that the dart room, around the corner and into its low-ceilinged shed, was probably packed as well.

Weaving his way through the crowd, Hardy patted a few shoulders as he passed some of the regulars he'd come to know. When he got to the end of the bar, he shrugged out of his suit coat, hung it on the coatrack, lifted the lid of the ordering station, and suddenly found himself working with Annette as her backup bartender.

He stayed behind the bar for the better part of an hour, until the pre-dinner crush had passed, then reemerged on the customer side of the bar with his suit coat back on. In his lawyer persona, he took one of the barstools that had become free and ordered a club soda.

"Going large," Annette said.

"Can't be too careful," Hardy said. "I've got too many friends with DUIs and I'd just as soon not join the club."

"You're the boss," she said, and grabbed a pint glass, filling it with ice. She was squeezing the lime over it when Hardy's phone rang, Wyatt Hunt's name on the screen. "I better get this," he said. "Hold my spot, if you would."

He hated cell phones in bars — in fact, in most public spaces — and when he picked up, he said, "Wyatt, hold on a second" into the phone, got up off his stool, and headed for the front door.

Outside, the sun nearly down on his left, the dusk still surprisingly clement, he brought the phone up to his ear. "No overtime pay for working late," he said, "though, for the record, I'm impressed by your work ethic. What's going on?"

"Are you sitting down?"

"No, but I was about twenty seconds ago. I could go back inside."

"You might need to," Hunt said. "All kidding aside, I just finished a rather lengthy interview with Darrel Bracco."

"He's a good guy. What did he know?"

"It isn't good news, Diz. Somebody shot Stacy Holland over the weekend."

"Stacy Holland?"

"Grant Wagner's former girlfriend."

"No. I know who she is." Hardy paused. "Somebody shot her? Just randomly? Was she in a fight?"

"No sign of that. No struggle, evidently. And apparently not random. In her living room. Two shots. And somebody who must have known her. Did I already tell you, when I saw her on Saturday, she was pretty damn proactive about not letting strangers into her duplex? I thought she was going to keep me out on the porch all day in spite of my innate natural charm."

"Hard to believe."

"It is."

"Does Bracco have any ideas?"

"Other than wanting to make sure it wasn't me who killed her? I don't think so."

"Stacy Holland," Hardy said again. "I'm trying to fit this into something we already know. Do we think — does Bracco think — it had anything to do with the Wagner case?"

"I don't know. It would be pretty strange if it didn't, wouldn't you think?"

"Not quite impossible, but pretty close. Thank God my client is already in jail."

"That's a good point. If she wasn't, she'd immediately jump to the head of the suspect line as Stacy's killer, wouldn't she?"

"That's how I'd play it if I worked in Homicide."

"That's assuming, though, that there is a connection to Grant Wagner."

"Right. But Grant was poisoned and she was shot. Different MO."

"Still not impossible."

"No."

Hardy was silent so long that Hunt said, "Diz? You still there?"

"I'm here."

"I thought I'd lost you."

"No such luck."

"So?" Hunt asked. "What are we going to do?"

"For the moment, I'm going to assume that the same person killed Grant and Stacy. Same or different MO, I don't care."

"But we don't know that."

"I know."

"Do we have any real reason to believe it?"

"Not really. Except, first, the coincidence factor, which is huge to the point where it's simply not believable. Second, but maybe more important for us, is that it's the only scenario that helps Abby. We know for a fact that she didn't kill Stacy, since she was in jail, right?"

"Right."

"Therefore, we're going to choose to believe that Abby didn't kill Grant, either. And the Stacy killing is much fresher, where Bracco and Schiff might actually have a chance to get themselves some righteous evidence. They might even welcome some cooperation from us."

"That's a good one," Hunt said.

"Okay, not likely, I admit. But we can make the offer. And you might want to have a casual little talk with your friend Devin."

"To what end?"

"I don't know for sure. Just make him

aware of the situation. Maybe he'll come to the conclusion that he's assigned the wrong teams to the wrong cases. Or at the very least that one team of inspectors — I don't care which one — should be handling both the Wagner case and Stacy. Because they're probably related."

"He's not going to do that, Diz. No chance. Not unless he buys into our home-grown little theory, which he won't because there's no evidence for it. And even then, probably not. I mean, as recently as an hour ago, Bracco probably had me down for a suspect myself."

"Yeah, but in his heart he didn't really believe that."

"I wouldn't be so sure."

"Well, if they pursue that, it won't pan out. I wouldn't worry about it."

"That's heartening. Thanks."

"You're welcome," Hardy said. "Think nothing of it."

"I don't know," Frannie said. "It might be a little over-the-top."

"But look." Hardy took a sip of his Pinot Noir. "A couple of years ago, who would have thought that we would be sitting at home at our table on a weeknight eating quail? Back then, everybody would have

said that quail were over-the-top, especially at home. And yet . . . here we are. And they are delicious, by the way."

"Okay, point taken. But nowadays you can just go out and buy as many quail as you want. Plus, they're so easy to cook. Not the same thing, I believe, as ortolan, which is not exactly commonplace. I don't even know if they exist here."

"I'm sure they do; or, if not, I'm sure they could be imported. We could get in on the cutting edge of ortolan importing. We could make a fortune."

Frannie sighed in amused exasperation. "Another fortune idea, and we've had so many. Do you even know what an ortolan looks like?"

"Vaguely. It's a small songbird, I know that."

"What got you thinking about them?"

"I was reading where Tony Bourdain had some and said it was the most incredible thing he'd ever eaten in his life, and believe me, Tony's eaten some good shit."

"So he's 'Tony' now? I tend to think of him as Anthony."

"He goes by 'Tony' to his friends, and I've bought enough of his books and downloads and everything else that I'm definitely his friend."

"So, how does he get his ortolan?"

"In France. Where they're illegal, too. Which just adds to the mystique. You really don't know about them?"

"Strangely enough. Assuming you're willing to run the risk of poaching illegal songbirds, how do you get ahold of one of them? If they're so small, wouldn't they get all blown apart if you shot them?"

"Sure. Which is why you don't shoot them. You capture them alive."

"Of course you do. How could I not have known? And then what?"

"Then you feed them wheat and figs for about a month."

"Wheat and figs. Normal household staples."

"Easily available if you're motivated. Anyway, after the month or so of this diet, they double in size, which is when you're ready to prepare them."

"I can't wait to hear how."

"Okay. The first step is, you have to kill them humanely, of course. So you drown them."

"Drown them?"

"Right. In Armagnac. Which, for the record, is how I wouldn't mind going myself."

"I'll keep it in mind when the time comes.

But really? Armagnac?"

"If you're not a purist, you could probably get away with Cognac, or even Scotch, but if we do it, I'd go with Armagnac." Hardy cut another bite of quail and brought it up to his mouth. "Okay, now your dead ortolan is ready to be plucked, so you do that, then throw it in a superhot oven for five minutes. Note that you don't clean it out. You don't remove the organs."

"I do note that."

"Good. Now you're ready. The bird's in the oven. So you go get out your dining hood."

"Where did we put those darn things anyway?"

"We'll get some new ones. So you sit down with the ortolan on the plate in front of you, and you cover your head with your dining hood. Then you lift the bird in your hand by its head and deliver it whole to your mouth, where first you savor the aroma released under the hood, and then bite down on the neck, severing the head."

"By now," Frannie said, "I'm getting a little bit queasy."

Hardy waved that off. "But here's the best part. When you start chewing, the little bones in the bird kind of tear up the inside of your mouth, which starts to bleed."

Frannie put down her fork. "Please."

"No, listen. So your own blood in your mouth mixes with the blood and the organs of the ortolan that you're thoroughly chewing, and you are thereby transported into heavenly bliss."

Frannie cocked her head, looking at her husband. She lifted her wineglass and took a sip. "How much of that is even remotely true?"

"Every word, except I'm not a hundred percent sure you can substitute Scotch for the Armagnac. Otherwise," he said, "it's good to go."

"If we could just get our hands on some ortolan."

"That is the bottleneck," Hardy said. "Finding a reliable ortolan supplier."

"Maybe," Frannie said, "we could get the crack dealers to carry it. If crack dealers carried ortolan, you could get them on any street corner in the city."

"No good," Hardy said. "Nobody cares about crack because it only kills people. If it harmed little birds on street corners, the public uproar would force a dramatic police crackdown on drug dealers. After all, ortolan is probably a gateway food: first ortolan, then foie gras."

■ ■ ■ ■

He was sitting again at the end of the couch in very dim light in the family room behind the kitchen, holding his Armagnac in a brandy snifter, vaguely aware of his tropical fish swimming around in their tank across the way.

He heard the water stop running in the kitchen sink, and a moment later Frannie appeared, backlit in the doorway. "I've been thinking about your theory," she said.

"Importing ortolan?"

"No. We'll save that one for another day. I'm talking about the same person killing this poor Stacy woman and Grant Wagner."

"That makes two of us. Am I completely out of whack?"

"Actually, the more I think about it, the more I find it fairly compelling. And maybe not just as a theory but as to really what happened. I mean, unless you believe that it's a coincidence, which is some kind of a stretch. You mind if I turn on the lights?"

"Go for it."

She hit the wall switch. "Better," she said. "Did you ever notice that when you're trying to figure things out in the dark, things tend to look bleakest? Daytime comes around or you turn on the lights and suddenly not so much."

"You might be onto something there. I was just sitting here, stewing, and slowly getting worked up over my original worry about taking on another murder case, where the actual killer walks around free as a breeze until he decides he needs to take me out because I might get my client off and that would open the door for another investigation that might be a threat to him. Another two minutes sitting here in the dark and I'm pretty sure I would have gotten into real anguish. For which, basically, I blame Paul Simon."

"Paul Simon?"

" 'Hello darkness, my old friend'?"

"Ah."

"When in fact, as you point out, darkness isn't really anybody's old friend. But because of that song, everybody in my generation subconsciously thinks it is. So I come in here and sit in the dark and worry that somebody's going to shoot me someday. Paul's fault entirely. Now, with the lights on, that whole scenario seems pretty farfetched." As though suddenly aware of the presence of his snifter at his side, Hardy lifted it and took a small sip.

Frannie came into the room and sat at the

other end of the couch. "But really," she said.

Hardy swallowed and nodded. "I know. I've been trying to think it through, starting with what we know for sure, what if anything it tells us, then what we might be able to do with it."

"And?"

"And here's really pretty much all I've got, and I'm afraid it's a little slimmer pickin's than I was hoping for when I first heard about Stacy. So what do we know? Abby didn't kill Stacy. That's it. And the question remains: Did she kill Grant? For which we don't have an answer."

"But you think not."

Hardy grimaced. "More like hope not. But let's say she didn't. Can we then assume that the same person killed Grant and then Stacy?"

"I don't see how. You'd have to have some reason, and I don't see one."

"I don't, either. Stacy hadn't seen Grant for a month before he got killed. Everybody seems to agree about that. And now, another month after he's dead, somebody kills her. Any kind of connection has got to be tenuous at best."

"So, what's the next step?"

"For me? I have to tell you, the idea of

leaving this completely alone doesn't really appeal. The good news is that Wyatt talked to Stacy on Saturday."

"Why is that good? Doesn't that make him a possible suspect?"

"In theory, yes. In practice, no. They'll find out she was killed sometime late Saturday or Sunday or this morning — because that's when it probably went down — and then he's completely off the hook. But the good news about that is that he went to see her as part of our investigation into Grant's murder. Therefore — are you following me here? — tenuous as it may be, there is a connection in the record between Grant Wagner's death and Stacy. The homicide guys can't pretend it doesn't exist. And it's possible that if they start looking in that direction, they'll actually find something. In any event, worst case, I can try to get it admitted in court as an alternative theory of the entire case."

"And a judge will let that in?"

Hardy broke a grin. "Realistically, not a chance in hell. Not remotely admissible with what we have now, but poke around a little and who knows? Stranger things have happened."

"And in the meanwhile, what?"

"Good question. Maybe I want to call Wes

and tell him his case has taken another major credibility hit and he should drop the specials and let Abby out on bail."

"Okay, that's a bad idea."

"Really?"

"Really. In so many ways and I think you know all of them. Next?"

"Next I get Wyatt investigating Stacy's murder on his own. Find out everything about her. See where she intersects with Grant and people who knew Grant. Pretend our theory that the same person killed Stacy and Grant is true and try to prove it."

Frannie took this in for a moment, then asked: "Do we know that she didn't kill herself out of remorse for having killed Grant?"

Hardy shook his head. "Two shots," he said. "No gun left in the room. No chance."

Vincent and Rebecca Hardy, fifteen months apart in age, considered themselves "Irish twins," and in reality they were half siblings. In any case, they were close, and saw each other frequently on their own, without reference to their parents.

Tonight was one of those nights. At ten thirty they were finishing up a late fish dinner at Lord Stanley restaurant on Polk and Broadway. The third member of their party was Bill Kenney, who'd called Vincent in frustration earlier in the evening. After his initial interview with homicide inspectors, Bill had been waiting to get some word on the progress, if any, of the David Chang case, and he hadn't heard a thing and wondered if Vincent had.

Although he and his sister had already made plans for dinner together, fitting Bill in wasn't any big deal.

But when they got there and were seated, it wasn't all — or even any — David Chang. After the introductions — Rebecca hadn't met Bill before — they talked first about their respective jobs and were starting to get into the crazy political season when they were saved by the restaurant's owners, Carrie and Rupert Blease, who through their wonderful and talented manager, Elizabeth, were offering them a few amuse-bouches that took their collective breaths away.

When they'd finally exhausted the four extra free courses, Bill thanked Vincent for inviting him along at the last minute and said it was really nice to meet Rebecca. As a defense attorney, was she aware of the David Chang case?

"Just what I read in the paper, which wasn't much," she said. "I found out more from Vinnie here when he called me and told me about it yesterday. I gather you still haven't heard much back from the inspectors."

" 'Much' would be an overstatement," Bill said. "I don't think they've done very much at all in the line of looking. Like, nothing."

"I know they didn't do much as of yesterday," Vin said. "I went by David's apartment and ran into Sara, his sister, there. There wasn't any sign of them checking out the place."

"You went by . . . ?" Rebecca asked.

Vincent waved off her objection. "I know. I know. Dad would freak if he knew. But it turns out we didn't even try to get in. Messing with the crime scene and all that. But you'd think the inspectors might have come by, though there wasn't any sign of it."

"So how do you get their attention?" Bill asked.

"Well," Vinnie said, "you already tried, didn't you? You called them, right?"

"As soon as I heard. But then they just came by and acted like they thought it might have been me. The guy who shot him, I mean. Which was totally ridiculous."

"Well," Rebecca said, "I hate to say it, but this sounds relatively normal to me. They're going to have to wait for lab results and the crime scene reports before they'll probably have anything they can even start with."

"Well, what about his phone?" Bill asked. "They could go through his contacts and call everybody, which I know they didn't do, since I never got that call."

"Me neither," Vincent said.

"Okay, but they might be going through his actual phone records first, see who he called and when, maybe in his last couple of days. They're also looking for unusual calls, like from an escort service or somebody who's not in the contact list." Rebecca held up her hand. "I don't mean to sound like I'm apologizing for these guys, but they've undoubtedly got other cases going on at the same time, so until they get something to work with, they're kind of stuck. Unless the killer made some egregious mistake: left his fingerprints all around, like that. But from what you guys tell me, this was like a professional hit."

"It makes no sense, though," Bill said. "He had nothing worth killing him over. The inspectors told me that nothing appeared to be stolen."

Vincent suddenly came forward. "Maybe he knew something."

Rebecca nodded. "There you go. That's an idea."

"But what?" Bill asked.

"I think that's exactly the kind of thing Daddy doesn't really want us to get too involved in," she said to Vincent. Then turned to Bill. "Although if you've already called the inspectors, you could probably call them again without taking too much flak."

"And then what?"

"I don't know. You might suggest what we've said here, about maybe David Chang knew something. That might lead to some questions they could ask his contacts."

"The entrepreneur guys. Maybe Dave got the Big Idea and told it to the wrong guy."

Rebecca and Vincent shared a look. Bill was tilting at windmills here, but it might make him feel better.

"Maybe something like that," Vin said.

"So what was up with his sister?" Rebecca asked him. "You said you met her at her brother's apartment. What was she doing?"

"I think just trying to get used to the idea that he was gone. To deal with it."

"Did she have ideas about why?"

"Nothing. She was in the same boat as we all are."

"So, Rebecca," Bill asked, "you're in this business. Let me ask you this: Will they really listen to me if I call them up and make some suggestions?"

"Honestly," she said, "that would be a hell of a long shot. I'd give them a little more time to find something on their own. Some evidence, DNA, ballistics, maybe stuff they've brought to the lab. I'm sure they'll be going through their normal routines."

"But if they don't find anything?"

She shrugged. "That happens, too, I'm afraid."

"Maybe we could call some mutual friends," Bill said. "See what they know. Then, if we get something, we pass it on to the inspectors."

"I think I'd let the inspectors do that if I were you guys."

"But they're not getting anything done," Bill said.

"Actually," Rebecca said, "we don't know that. And beyond that, cops don't share information even with good friends or relatives of the victim. Telling people what you know or what you plan to do is a great way to screw up an investigation. Since you're not in the immediate family, even if you're his best friend, they're not going to keep you updated. Which is a shame, but as I say, they're probably pretty busy. Do you know his sister, Sara? If they're talking to anyone, they might keep her in the loop."

"Also," Vincent said, "she might know

something she doesn't know she knows."

Rebecca shook her head. "Not really your job to find out what that is, Vin. Or Dave's other friends, either. You know what I'm saying?"

"I do," Vincent said. "Channeling our dear father."

"Who, in this case, isn't all wrong."

"Although, on this stuff," he persisted, "you must admit he's a little bit paranoid. But don't worry, I get it. I know what I'm doing. I'll be careful. Nobody's going to do anything stupid."

26

First thing next morning, Devin Juhle almost didn't take a call from his friend Wyatt Hunt but then did at the last second. While they were talking, he got up and closed and locked the door to his office. After arguing with Wyatt for fifteen minutes, he hung up and stared at his whiteboard with the names Wagner and Holland still prominently displayed.

If he were perfectly consistent, he knew he should have erased Wagner as soon as they'd placed Abby Jarvis under arrest, since that technically ended the homicide detail's role in the case; but with one thing and another, he just hadn't gotten around to it, which now he was taking as some kind of sign.

Not that he was seriously tempted to believe Hunt's theory.

Juhle knew that people in law enforcement, himself included, generally didn't want to believe that coincidences existed, but in reality they did happen every so often, and this was undoubtedly one of those times. Stacy Holland had been one of Grant Wagner's girlfriends, true, but that relationship had apparently been no part of her life over the last month or so of *his* life, and so the fact that someone had killed her in no way could be automatically construed as having to do with his death as well.

Still, he had to admit that Waverly and Yamashiro — both of them stone professionals — had gotten themselves exercised in a hurry when they saw Holland's name on the whiteboard.

Finally he got to his feet, came around his desk, unlocked his door, and went out into the hall that opened into the wide-open space that was the detail. The four inspectors sat working at their front-to-front desks on opposite sides of the room — Waverly and Yamashiro by the Bryant Street windows, Bracco and Schiff over by the interrogation rooms. The former team was closer and Juhle headed in their direction, then cocked his head at the latter, indicating they should come on over and join the party.

Everybody arrived at the same time and Juhle started right in. "I just got a call from my PI acquaintance, Wyatt Hunt, who some of you know. And he gave me an earful of malarkey about the Stacy Holland homicide being related to Grant Wagner and, that being the case, how I ought to reassign Holland to you guys." He nodded at Waverly and Yamashiro. "He didn't have any evidence that such a connection existed, but I think he did make a good point that I should talk to all of you to make sure the lines of communication are open." He spread his hands. "So here we are."

Debra Schiff crossed her arms defensively. "Nobody's hiding anything from anybody else here, Dev. We all hung at Stacy's apartment after Crime Scene finished last night. If there's any connection to Wagner, it's not jumping out at us." She looked around. "Am I right, here?"

Nods all around.

"And if something does come up," Bracco said, "we share and share alike."

Juhle said, "I'm not accusing anybody of anything. It's just that Hunt told me that he's going to be called as a witness in the Abby Jarvis trial for Wagner's murder — whenever that happens — and maybe we'd want to know that he's going to testify that he interviewed Holland and they're going to try to get in what she said as part of that case."

"Yeah," Schiff said, "but it's hearsay and the witness is dead. Nobody's ever going to let that in, so if they try to get it in, Guerin keeps it out. So what?"

"So what," Juhle said, "is now that Holland got herself killed, Hunt's boss is going to try to get the jury to believe that the same person — not his client — killed both her and Wagner. And we're going to want to be able to say, and in fact prove, that we investigated that coincidental connection and found nothing tying them together. Not that we expected to, since we've already got an indicted suspect for Wagner. But among ourselves we want to cover all the bases."

Juhle looked around at his inspectors. "The fact that we've already got Jarvis in jail for Wagner is also the reason, if anybody's wondering, why I'm not reassigning this thing to Kenny and Eric. That would send a message that we weren't confident about our indicted suspect. So officially I'm not going to acknowledge any connection or even suspected connection. But I think we'd be smart to keep our asses covered in case this does come up in the Wagner trial." Juhle allowed himself a tight little smile. "I know that's all of your favorites. CYA. But that's the world we're living in. Anybody have any questions?"

■ ■ ■ ■

Yamashiro looked up across his desk at his partner, who had just returned with a steaming cup of something. "That stuff smells just awful," he said. "Does it taste as bad as it smells?"

"I don't care how it tastes."

"I would if it smelled like that."

Eric lowered his voice. "You wouldn't if you were trying to get off the prescription stuff, believe me. It works."

"What is it?"

"Some kind of Chinese herb." Eric pulled the half-filled baggie of it out of his desk drawer. "You brew it up like tea."

"Let me see."

He tossed it over the desks. Ken opened the baggie and gave it a smell. "Subtle overtones of cannabis," he said. "Not that I'd know from personal experience."

"I don't think so."

Yamashiro took another sniff. "Where'd you get it?" he asked.

"This pal of mine who's into this stuff."

"Like David Chang and Grant Wagner? Both dead, by the way."

"Not like them. No."

"Since when do you have a Chinese pal? I

didn't think you had any friends, Asian or otherwise, besides me, and I don't really like you much."

"I have many friends," Eric said. "More than you could imagine."

"Yeah?" Ken raised an eyebrow, then tossed the baggie back across to Eric. "If I were you, I'd watch out for aconite."

"Funny."

"Not so much. Not if it *is* aconite."

"It isn't."

"It still smells awful."

"Get used to it."

An hour later Waverly put his phone down into its receiver and knocked on the desk to get his partner's attention. They'd been spending their time following up on David Chang's entrepreneur group, making appointments to talk in the afternoon to six out of the ten of them they'd identified.

Ken held up his index finger; he'd be done in a minute.

In the middle of his last call, Eric had received by interoffice delivery a padded envelope from the lab. Upon opening it, among some computer printouts and some crime scene photographs, he pulled out a sealed baggie containing the two bullets that had killed David Chang. Through the plastic, one of them was badly damaged, flattened almost beyond recognition, but the other seemed more or less intact.

Seeing them both right there in front of him, Waverly took another sip of his now-cold tea, made a sour face, and pushed himself all the way back in his chair, staring into the middle distance with an unfocused gaze.

Yamashiro hung up and knocked on his own desk to get Eric's attention back. "Yo."

"I'm here."

"What's up now?"

Waverly held up the bullets. "Let's get out of here," he said. "We need to go down to the lab."

27

Hunt's company, the Hunt Club, worked out of the upstairs offices of the Audiffred Building right above Boulevard Restaurant on Mission Street. He'd been in business now for about ten years and the number of employees had ranged from three to eight, although for the past four or five months it had hovered at six, including himself and Tamara, who'd be leaving the day-to-day operation for maternity leave in a month or so.

He got the call from Gloria Wagner on his voicemail while he was talking to Juhle in his office about the Holland-Wagner connection, one that seemed relatively sound to Hunt — albeit with all the usual caveats about coincidence. In spite of Juhle's professional intransigence, Hunt had the feeling that the lieutenant was more open to the idea than he was letting on. Maybe Hunt could meet him for lunch in the next day or two and get his real take on the topic.

Gloria's message was short and to the point: "Mr. Hunt, I feel really bad but I wanted you to know that I'm not so sure about Abby anymore and I wanted to tell you about it. Could you please give me a call when you get a second?"

He almost punched up Gloria's number to get right back to her, but since his game plan for the day had been to go down to P&V to have a few conversations with the G-Team anyway, he thought he'd just drop in on her: it was always preferable to show up rather than phone in. People could hide behind the phone, or simply hang up, and neither of those options were available on a personal visit.

There was also, of course, the surprise factor of showing up, which, depending on the circumstances, could be unnerving and therefore revealing. There was nothing like eyeballing a subject's reaction to help you uncover things they might not want to tell you straight out.

He got up from his desk and happened to glance at his gun safe hulking in the corner. Without too much thought, knees cracking, he squatted and worked the combination, reaching in for his favorite firearm — a .380 ACP Sig Sauer P232 — and its holster. This wasn't by any means a big gun, but Hunt found it comfortable and easy to shoot with accuracy — though, fortunately, to date he'd only had one occasion to use it.

He pulled out the gun and a full magazine and placed them on top of the safe, then stood up to slip on the holster. He'd just gotten it on when he turned around to see the lovely and pregnant Tamara standing by the door to his office, hands on her hips, her mouth pursed with concern.

"Is there something you've forgotten to tell me about? You're going out carrying?"

"I guess I am."

"I thought you were just going to interview the P&V people."

"I am."

"And they're a particularly dangerous bunch?"

"I don't like to think so, but after this Stacy Holland thing we learned about yesterday, somebody somewhere has got a gun and seems ready to use it. The Boy Scout in me would just rather be prepared."

"If the Holland thing is in fact even part of the Jarvis case."

"Right. I was just trying to sell that idea to Devin for the past twenty minutes, and I think I might have convinced myself a little more in the bargain."

Tamara stepped into the room and crossed over to him. "I can't say that this doesn't make me nervous."

"Well . . . I'm sorry about that, but I'm just being cautious. I haven't really analyzed the danger quotient, if any. There probably isn't any. But I've got to go with my gut. It would be silly to own a gun and find yourself in a place where you might need it and, whoops, left it in the safe. Right?"

"Okay. I know. Okay."

He leaned in and kissed her. "I'll call in when I'm done over there."

"That'd be good." She kissed him again, a quick and light one. "Be careful."

"Always." He reached for the gun, slapped in the magazine, and jacked a round into the chamber. Then, clicking off the safety, he tucked it into the holster at the back of his belt.

Intent on the computer at the side of her desk, Gloria seemed to be engrossed in some of the intricacies involved in her day job. Hunt watched her for a few seconds before he realized that she wasn't going to look up on her own, so he knocked on her open door. She nearly jumped out of her chair, then turned and said in ill-disguised exasperation, "Mr. Hunt. I didn't mean you had to come all the way down here again."

"I was in the neighborhood anyway," he lied, "and I just got around to hearing your voicemail, so I thought I'd just stop by."

"No, it's fine. I just . . ." She let out a deep sigh. "It's fine, although I don't want to take too much of your time."

"No problem. How can I help you?"

"Well, as I said in my message, it's about Abby. Please." She gestured at the chairs in front of her desk. "Have a seat."

Hunt did as he was told, then put on a neutral expression. "What about Abby?"

"Well, you remember yesterday when you told me I could visit her at the jail? So in the afternoon that's what I did. And she seemed, I don't know, somewhat different to me."

"Different how?"

"Again, I can't say exactly. Harder some-how, tougher. Not the person I thought I knew."

"A couple of nights in jail can toughen a person right up," Hunt said. "Especially Abby, since she'd already spent time in prison. You get back to your defensive self pretty fast."

"Yes, well, that wasn't exactly it, either."

Suddenly aware of his gun pressing into the small of his back, Hunt inched up, then

349

leaned forward in his chair and brought his hands together in front of him. "I'm sorry," he said. "Wasn't exactly what?"

"God," Gloria exclaimed, "this is just so horrible." She brought her eyes up and her gaze met Hunt's. "She told me she'd been at Pops' house on the night he died, which none of us had ever known before and . . . I don't know. She'd never mentioned that, and it's the kind of thing . . . I mean, how could she not have told us that right after he died? How could she not have seen how important it was? And then suddenly I was . . . it was like a tipping point, where I looked at her as if I were seeing the real Abby for the first time. I mean, if she'd been there . . ."

Hunt waited to see if she was going to add anything to her narrative. When it appeared that she wasn't, he said, "If she'd been there, and she had just told you she had, then you started to believe she might have actually killed him."

Closing her eyes, she sighed again. "Yes. Yes, that's it. But at some point you have to admit to yourself, if somebody's hiding something, there must be something to hide. Does that make sense?"

"As far as it goes, I suppose. But what's being hidden doesn't necessarily have to be the worst-case scenario."

"I guess that's true. But in this case . . ." She brought her shoulders up in an elaborate shrug. "In any event, I wanted you to know that I called the inspectors and told them about it, too. Her admission that she was there that night."

This wasn't the best news Hunt had ever heard, but he smiled with apparent understanding. "Well, then I do especially appreciate your getting back to me. They must have been happy to have heard from you."

"They thought it might be important at the trial, I think."

"They're probably right," Hunt said. "But while I'm here, I do have some news on another front, which I'm afraid you're going to find troubling: about Stacy Holland."

"What about her?"

Hunt hesitated for an instant, then came out with it. "Somebody shot her over the weekend. She's dead."

For an instant Gloria went completely still, after which her mouth dropped open, almost in caricature. Her eyes went out of focus, tried to come back, failed.

"Needless to say," Hunt went on in the face of her reaction, "Abby couldn't have been the one to shoot her, since she was locked up in jail."

351

"Well, then who . . . ?"

"Nobody knows."

"What do the police think?"

"What do you mean?"

"I mean, do you think that might have had anything to do with my father?"

"I don't know," Hunt said. "What do *you* think?"

"Just hearing about it, I'd say it must have." Still in shock, Gloria sat looking through where Hunt sat. "But I can't really believe it. It doesn't necessarily mean it has to involve Pops."

"No. You're right. Although it's the first thing that comes to mind, isn't it?" Hunt met her gaze, held it for a minute, then got up, went over to the door, and closed it. "Gloria," he said, turning around, "the last time I was here, you told me you'd asked for the second round of scans because you wanted to eliminate your siblings as suspects."

"Not so much that as I wanted to eliminate everybody. I didn't want anybody to have killed him, period. It's just so horrible to imagine. And now you say Stacy . . ."

Hunt held up a hand. "Gloria, you're just not making any sense. The coroner said it was a heart attack. He just died. No one suspected any foul play until you asked for

352

the second round of tests. You couldn't have asked to eliminate people because there wasn't anyone to eliminate. So why did you ask for the second round? Who did you think had done something to do with Grant?"

Her eyes grew wide.

Hunt went on. "Mr. Hardy — Abby's lawyer? — Mr. Hardy and I believe that there has to be some connection between Stacy's death and your father's. Of course, as you say, that's not automatically true, but you just seemed to jump to that conclusion yourself."

"Yes? Okay. What do you want me to do about that?"

"Please answer the question: Who did you suspect had done something to Grant?"

"I don't know. Nobody. I just wasn't thinking."

Hunt knew better than to try to push her further. He'd have to come back later. "Well," he said, "we'll let that go for the time being, but I really need you to think about that. In the meantime, and I don't mean to frighten you, but I'd like you to be more than normally cautious. Don't talk to anybody about this stuff — anybody — except maybe the police if they come talk to you again. Don't get into speculations with your family or friends over who might have done what. Remember that if there is a connection between Stacy's death and your father's, then there's a motivated killer out there who might not hesitate to kill again."

"Now you're really scaring me."

"Scared isn't bad. Scared can be a positive thing," Hunt said, but thought to himself: Scared is better than dead.

Dismas Hardy hadn't planned on visiting Abby this morning — he was at his office in the middle of writing his bail motion for the following Monday and wanted to give it his full attention — but when Hunt called to tell him about Abby's less-than-brilliant decision to tell Gloria Wagner about her visit to Grant on his last night on earth, he felt that some client massaging was in order.

The warden had barely taken off her handcuffs and left the circular attorneys' visiting room, when Hardy stood up and with some theatrics held up both hands. "What in the world do you think you are doing?" he asked.

As he thought it might, this got a rise. Abby's eyes flashed with anger. "What have I been doing? I've been wasting away in this hellhole. What's it look like I've been doing? I've been waiting for somebody like you maybe to get me out of here."

"You want to tell me how I'm supposed to do that when you keep digging yourself a deeper hole? What the hell, Abby. Are you thinking at all?"

"Am I thinking? Am I thinking? I'm thinking all the time, Diz. I've got nothing to do but think, think, think. I'm thinking about me and my momma and my baby and how the hell I got here and if I'm ever getting out. How 'bout that?

"And I'm thinking about Grant being gone and I'm just lost and I don't give a shit what you're down here honking at me about, because this is just so not right. I didn't do what they're saying and I don't belong here and if you're here to bust my chops about some legal stupidity I didn't know anything about, then why don't you call the warden and just get yourself out of here and leave me alone. Just please leave me alone."

Hardy watched her turn around and walk back over to the door, where she stood facing away from him.

He took a few steps around the table toward her. "All right," he said. "I believe that round goes to you."

Her shoulders settled and she hung her head. "I am so, so tired." She turned around. "What did I do wrong this time?"

Hardy gave her the short version: that her admission to Gloria did not help her situation. "The point is," he concluded, "that you can tell that stuff to me. I'm your attorney, so our conversations are privileged. You remember that, I'm sure. But if you do tell me something that could negatively impact your case — like, you were at Grant's on the night of his murder — that doesn't mean it's out there in the big world. You can't go telling it to somebody else, like Gloria Wagner."

"But Gloria's my one real friend. She can't believe I killed Grant."

"Well, according to my private investigator, it turns out that what she couldn't believe more than the fact of your innocence is the fact that you were there and had nothing to do with Grant's murder. She couldn't believe that you didn't say anything about that — to her, at least — a little earlier. She doesn't understand that."

"What was I supposed to say?"

"Maybe you would have said something like you couldn't believe he had a heart attack: he seemed fine and healthy while you were with him. And if you must know," he added, "I find that a little bit odd myself. That the issue never came up."

Abby's fatigue seemed to overwhelm her for a moment. Sighing heavily, she closed her eyes, took another breath, finally reached out, and put a hand on Hardy's arm. "It's not like when we got the news we all sat around Indian style in a circle and shared our feelings. This was their beloved Pops and he'd just out of the blue up and died. All the sibs were wrecked. Nobody was asking me how I felt about it or whether or when I'd seen him last. It just never came up. And that's the plain truth, like it or not."

"I don't mind the truth," Hardy said. "I just wish the inspectors didn't know it."

"Well, I'm sorry about that. I shouldn't have told Gloria. I see that now. But I thought she was on my side."

"Okay, but while we're on this stuff, you also shouldn't have lied to the inspectors when they asked you what you'd been doing that night. If you wanted to give me a reason you felt that was necessary, that might be helpful when we talk about it at the trial. Should we sit down?"

Another weary sigh. "Good idea."

All but collapsing onto the nearest chair, Abby waited for her lawyer to get settled, then said, "That was a mistake. I shouldn't have done that. But I didn't think there was any way that could get out. And at the time,

I knew the inspectors were starting to focus on me as their suspect because of the . . . because of my record. I didn't want to give them anything else. And then, of course," she added bitterly, "I did."

Hardy reached out and put his hand over hers on the table. "Well, it's water under the bridge, Abby. There's nothing we can do about that now except try not to make the same type of mistake again." Hardy gave her a moment to digest that, then went on. "But the good news is that it might not turn out to be as important as it looks."

She flashed him a quizzical look. "How can that be?"

"There's been a new development that I'm hoping might make some people rethink their positions. Somebody killed Stacy Holland over the weekend."

"What?" She put her other hand over his. "Are you kidding me?"

"Not even a little. Shot her twice."

"Do they have a suspect?"

"Not that I've heard."

"Oh my God. I mean, poor Stacy, but . . ."

"Yeah," Hardy said. "I know how you feel."

They shared a look.

"It's got to be whoever killed Grant, don't you think?"

"That's a possibility. At the very least, it muddies the water around your case."

Abby put her hand over her heart. "Thank God," she said. "That's the first ray of hope I've had in here. Finally, maybe the police are going to be looking at someone else. They'll have to, won't they?"

"Don't lose that hope," Hardy said, "but I don't know if they're there yet. You're still their suspect for Grant's death, and they're not going to give that up without a fight. But the connection between Grant's death and Stacy's is going to be pretty hard for them to ignore, if not impossible."

"No," she said. "They'll get him. You wait. He'll make a mistake or something." She leaned forward, looking into his eyes. "This has got to be some kind of sign. At least between you and me, Diz. I'm telling you, I swear to God, that I didn't do anything to hurt Grant, much less kill him. I loved him. And this person who killed Stacy, this is the universe giving you notice that I'm telling the truth. You know it wasn't me, and it wasn't me because it was this other person who killed Stacy. I know you see that now. I know you do."

28

As he walked through the back door of the Hall of Justice on his way to meet Glitsky for lunch, Hardy basked in the knowledge that Abby was right. He couldn't prove it yet and it wasn't based on logic, but he now absolutely believed that she hadn't murdered Grant.

In the past twenty minutes, he'd gone from moderate skepticism about Abby's guilt to downright certainty that she was innocent. Her unfeigned reaction to the news about Stacy had been utterly convincing to him: she believed that Grant's killer was also Stacy's killer and was out there in the world, doing more damage. And whether or not she was correct, that belief, more than any denial, convinced him that she was telling the truth.

While defense attorneys were fond of saying that it really didn't matter and they really didn't care about whether their clients were factually guilty or not, basic human nature kicked in when you sincerely believed that you were defending an innocent person.

The stakes went way up.

Hardy wound his way up some stairs and through a maze of familiar corridors and got to Abe Glitsky's cubicle in the district attorney's investigative division, where his best friend was sitting on the edge of his desk. "You're late," Glitsky said.

Hardy checked his watch. "Five minutes or less doesn't count. I had to see my client and she's more important than you. Innocent and falsely accused as she is."

"Don't start. You've incurred some serious wrath around here lately on her behalf."

"I predict that it's going to get worse before it gets better. But I thought that you and I might have a cordial lunch and bury the hatchet, at least between us."

"There is no hatchet. We agree to disagree about certain topics and maintain our tenuous friendship. But I have to tell you that Wes is pretty seriously angry with you. You should be prepared should you run into him at Lou's. If he's eating there, which he may be."

"I'll be ready," Hardy said. "But be forewarned, I'm slightly perturbed at him, too. If we run into each other, I can't promise I won't pop him."

In a rare display, Glitsky broke a smile. "That'll be fun to watch. That and your subsequent arrest for assault and battery. But, all in all, I'd try to resist the temptation."

They fell into step together, heading out through the desk-cluttered room.

"He started it, you know," Hardy said.

Glitsky cast him a sidelong glance. "Well, as long as you're being mature about it."

Directly across the street from the Hall, Lou the Greek's was packed, but Hardy and Glitsky fell into the camp of super-regulars and they hadn't waited by the front door for more than a few minutes before they found themselves seated in one of the booths under the high windows along the far right-hand wall. Because Lou's was half-underground, these windows looked onto the alley outside at street level with its dumpsters and debris and occasional homeless campsite, with all of the hygienic moments attending thereto that one would expect.

Adding to Lou's considerable downmarket charm was its menu featuring one and only one item, the Special, changeable by the day. Every day Lou's wife, Chui, the "executive chef," in ongoing homage to her husband's Greek heritage and her own Chinese, would introduce a culinary creation borrowing from these cuisines, so you'd often see a special of hot-and-sour dolmas or taramosalata-filled pot stickers with hoisin sauce; General Tso's lamb shish kabob or the ever popular yeanling clay bowl, a noodle dish whose exact but vaguely Hellenic protein ingredients were better left unspecified.

But what Lou's lacked in selection, it made up for in convenience. No decisions were called for, so there was no unseemly dawdling over the menu choices. Patrons coming in knew they were going to get the Special, whatever it was, and most days it was filling, surprisingly tasty, sometimes actually delicious, and usually delivered to the table within minutes.

It didn't hurt that cocktails, beer, and wine were sometimes cheaper than wholesale and they, too, got delivered quickly.

Hardy nursed his Black and Tan, turning his pint glass on the table in front of him and waiting while Glitsky drank off an inch of his twenty-ounce Arnold Palmer — equal parts lemonade and iced tea.

When he put the glass down, Glitsky nodded and said, "Yep. That's a coincidence all right. But this just in: Coincidences happen."

"You never accepted that idea when you were a cop."

Glitsky straightened up in mock affront. "I'm still a cop."

"Only by the wildest stretch of the definition. But let's not quibble. We've got a woman in a serious relationship with a guy who gets murdered, and two months later somebody kills her. I know that back in your real cop days in Homicide, if you had a suspect in jail for the first murder, the second one would make you nervous."

"It might, okay. But maybe not so much if one murder's a poisoning and the second is a gunshot." Lifting his glass, Glitsky took another long, slow drink. "How did Juhle put these two cases together?"

"He didn't. Wyatt Hunt tells me that that was another coincidence. Like it or not. Juhle had Stacy Holland on his whiteboard and one of his teams — Waverly and Yamashiro — happened to be in his office and recognized the name."

"So wait a minute. There was nothing at the scene — Holland's, I mean — tying her up with your guy, Wagner?"

"No. That was Schiff and Bracco at Holland's, and they had no clue about any connection until the other guys showed up."

Glitsky turned his glass around in its little circle of condensation. "You'll note that at least I'm taking this seriously."

"Noted. Thank you."

"Okay. Let's say that if I'm Schiff or Bracco —"

"Debra Schiff's a woman, Abe. You couldn't be her."

"Sure I could. This is San Francisco. I could have a sex change and be a woman next month if I wanted to. But all right, say I'm Bracco and something else comes up while I'm looking into my case — the gunshot — that has even the slightest tangential connection to your case — the poisoning. Then I'd be jumping on it with both feet. But until I came upon that something independently, I'm going to chalk it up to one of those rare coincidences and not put in any time on it." He lowered his voice, speaking now friend to friend. "Don't get me wrong, Diz. I can understand why you're all pumped up around this. There's a connection going one way — Wagner to Holland — but not necessarily the other. Logically, it falls in on itself. You know this, maybe better than me. Now possibly Wyatt Hunt will make some connection, and then you're in business. Meanwhile, I've got to believe that this Holland person had a life of her own. You said she was attractive. Things happen, as you know, sometimes especially with attractive women. She might have had any number of enemies for a boatload of reasons. We just don't know. I don't know. You don't know. Juhle doesn't know."

"All God's children don't know."

"Essentially," Glitsky said. "True." He shrugged. "But on a happier note . . ."

Their waitress arrived with their plates. "Today's Special," she said. "Kung pao *garides*. Enjoy."

Glitsky looked down at the steaming bowl in front of him, smelled appreciatively, then leaned in toward Hardy and spoke in a conspiratorial tone. "This looks suspiciously just like actual kung pao shrimp."

"Not too surprising," Hardy replied, "since *garides* are shrimp. Maybe twenty years along and Chui's running out of new ideas. You can't just throw peanuts and hot peppers into Greek shrimp and call it kung pao, can you?"

"I never would." Glitsky picked up his chopsticks, separated them, and was about to dig in when he stopped. "And in the small-world department," he said, raising a hand to flag down Devin Juhle and Wyatt

Hunt, who had just come through the door, "here comes company."

A minute later the new guys had joined them in their booth. After a short but intense discussion of the authenticity of the day's Special, Hunt started in on Stacy Holland and the reason he'd invited his friend Devin to lunch: so that he could pitch him again on the idea of somehow merging the investigations into her death and that of Grant Wagner, since, according to Hunt, there was such a great chance that they were in fact related.

But he hadn't gotten too far before Juhle cut him off. "No, no, no. Not to interrupt you, but this is just a nonstarter, Wyatt, as I've been saying all along. Even your boss here, to say nothing of Lieutenant Glitsky, will agree that, since we already have an indicted suspect on Wagner, I can't very well assign Waverly and Yamashiro to Holland to see if they can connect those dots."

"You could," Hardy said in the mildest of tones, "talk to Wes Farrell and have him drop the charges against my client due to lack of evidence. Then you wouldn't have that conflict."

Juhle shot Hardy the cold eye. "Probably not," he said.

"No. I didn't really think so."

Hunt jumped in with another try. "It wouldn't have to be overt."

Juhle shook his head. "It's not happening, guys. My position, and the district attorney's, is that Abby Jarvis killed Grant Wagner. And that somebody else — completely unrelated — killed Stacy Holland. Shot twice, once in the head. No poison involved. I have talked to both teams of inspectors — Waverly and Yamashiro, and Schiff and Bracco — and they are aware of the situation and will share any information that might become relevant if something changes, but right now we're going ahead with the way I've got it assigned. These murders are unrelated events. Nobody's trying to stonewall anybody here, but as of this moment there is no reason to believe that Stacy Holland's death is in any way connected to Grant Wagner's. End of story."

"Hear! Hear!" Glitsky said. "At last, the voice of reason."

29

A couple of miles south, Waverly and Yamashiro were having soft drinks and microwaved hamburgers in the lobby of Building 606 at the former naval shipyard at Hunters Point, the home of San Francisco's forensic laboratory.

The inspectors had arrived without an appointment about ninety minutes earlier, and although they had characterized their interest and request as urgent, the staff at the lab had heard that song before and didn't seem inclined to dance to it.

30

Gene Wagner thought the loft apartments where his stepbrother Joey lived south of Market were not all they were cracked up to be. All of that urban living glamour that seemed to appeal to so many of his contemporaries just did not speak to him. Joey's place, for example, was mostly glass except for the occasional metal wall, which — apparently in random fashion — had been painted in teal, maroon, and red.

And parking!

Gene remembered why he didn't often visit Joey at his home. Parking on the street was just flatly impossible, and the nearest garage was four blocks away with a special all-day onetime rate of only $22. Insane. Even his prayer to the parking goddess had failed: "Gladys, Gladys full of grace. Help me find a parking space."

Didn't do shit.

But Joey had called him and asked if he'd

mind coming around to discuss a few things, some of them family related, and he wanted some advice if Gene could spare the time. This was a little bit out of the ordinary: Joey had always been extremely independent in his life choices. But the two of them had had a good talk together at Grace's just a few days before; it had felt like a real connection. And now was definitely a time when Gene felt that these family connections had taken on a new importance.

He rang the doorbell, said hello, waited for the buzz, and let himself into the lobby, whose glass walls completely exposed it to the street. The elevator door was stainless steel and opened with an unnatural silence as soon as he pushed the button. Whisked to the fourth floor in about three seconds with no sense of movement, he stepped out into the wide, cold, stone-tiled hallway.

Joey stood in his doorway, waiting. The two men exchanged their customary fist bump, followed by a quick hug. Then Gene followed inside where the floor-to-ceiling windows added to the open-air and, in his opinion, chilly motif. Stopping in the all-white-and-stainless-steel kitchen-dining area, Joey said, "Thanks for coming out. Can I get you anything? Coffee, tea, Coke, water, beer?"

"Is it too early for a beer?"

"It's not just for breakfast anymore," Joey said. "I'm already a couple ahead of you." Reaching into the refrigerator, he pulled out a couple of bottles. "Pliny the Elder," he said. "Best beer on the planet."

Gene whistled, aware of the beer's near-mythic status among the millennials and its limited availability. "How'd you get any of it?"

"Connections," he said, then broke a smile, "and the very occasional bribe."

He opened both bottles, gave one to Gene, and led the way into the living room: low white leather couches, a couple of matching ottomans, a wall-mounted television, and, of course, enormous windows on two sides, meeting at the corner of the building and providing a limited but still dramatic cityscape view to the south — the new residential skyscrapers by the Bay Bridge, the lights of AT&T Park just beyond.

"Can I ask you something?" Gene said.

"Sure."

"Do you ever feel a little bit . . . exposed living here?"

"Not really," Joey said. "There aren't that many Peeping Toms here four stories up. Besides, there are shades if I want privacy. I like the light."

"That's good, 'cause you've got lots of it."

"Lucky me." Joey held up his beer bottle and they both clinked and drank.

"Okay," Gene said. "Now I see why people are killing each other over this stuff. Wow."

"Yeah," Joey said. "It's good." He took in a breath and blew out a sigh. "Hey, thanks for coming."

"No sweat." He settled himself down onto one of the couches and waited for Joey to follow suit. "So, what's up?"

Joey flashed him a smile, took another sip of beer. "This is probably not a good time, but then, I don't know if there ever is a good time. I'm having a bit of a crisis around money."

Gene chuckled without any mirth. "Join the club, bro. What kind of crisis?"

"I'm running out of cash to live on month to month. If something doesn't break soon on Gamma . . ." This was the app — something about a connection to a universal high-speed gaming portal — that Joey had been developing for the better part of the last two years.

"I thought you were getting close on that."

"I am. I'm nearly ready to go. A couple of glitches cleaned up and I'm done."

"But . . . ?"

"But now suddenly . . . well, maybe you know that Silicon Valley isn't just fickle. It's completely unpredictable. And the people I've been talking to . . . after all the early interest, now some of them seem to be thinking I'm not the Next New Thing. Maybe I've been too slow. I don't know what's happened. But I've had a couple of investors, you know . . ."

"I didn't know that. Who were they?"

"Just some guys I knew in school who believed I was onto something and went out on the VC side. It wasn't a lot, but —"

"How much was it exactly, Joey? 'A lot' is a relatively subjective term."

Joey blew out again in frustration. "A million four hundred K."

Gene's eyebrows went up. This was significantly more than he thought Joey had been involved with. Far from being some kind of nerd hobby, the business was potentially substantial and Joey was out there playing with the big boys. He'd even garnered some serious venture capital money along the way. Which now appeared to have dried up.

"You've spent a million four in the past two years?"

"I know it seems high, but the expenses . . ."

Gene held up a hand. He knew that Joey

374

had paid in the neighborhood of two million for this apartment alone, so that should have given him a clue, but he had just not given the matter much thought. Joey had his projects: he was a smart guy; nobody knew exactly what he did.

So, yes, the expenses.

But Gene just said, "Okay, never mind that. We can talk about all those details later. The point is, you're in over your head."

"I am. I'm embarrassed as hell and ashamed of myself, to tell you the truth. And I still think — hell, I *know* — that Gamma can make it. When they first signed on, my friends were talking thirty, thirty-five million for the IPO alone, and I still think that's ballpark, but I can't get the goddamn thing picked up. I don't understand what's happened. I know I'm up on the technology. I know it's *right there,* Gene. But something's happening behind the scenes. I'm pretty sure that's it. But meanwhile my VC guys are bailing on me."

Gene took a long pull at his beer, leaned back on the couch, and closed his eyes.

"It's . . ." Joey began.

Gene opened his eyes and held up his hand. "Give me a minute."

"I never thought it was going to come to

this," Joey said. "Especially when we got the news about Pops. The original news, I mean. The heart attack." He hesitated. "This sounds terrible, but his death wouldn't have been that bad a thing for me, moneywise. I hate to admit it, but there you are. It's what it was."

"Which was what, exactly?"

"You don't already know?"

"No offense, but none of us was paying much attention to you, Joey, not with all the turmoil and the succession issues at P&V."

"Well, I understand that. But just so you know, so you don't think I'm the most irresponsible idiot in the world, I knew that Pops had taken out a separate life insurance policy with me and Mom as beneficiaries, with her staying under care in her nursing home until she dies. We're talking three and a half mill, with me as executor. Some of that cash, at least, was going to get me out of this hole. Except then Gloria goes and asks for the redo, and now — between the coroner calling it a possible suicide and Abby charged with murder — the insurance company, who of course never wants to pay anything to anyone ever, is dragging its feet. And we've got a whole new world and I don't plan on seeing any part of that money for a year at least, or however long this thing with Abby drags out." He tipped up his bottle of beer, finishing it off. " 'Nother one?"

"Sure."

When Joey came back, he handed Gene his beer and continued. "So, in a fair world," he said, "Pops's insurance payment money would have arrived just in time and everything would have been okay. But then Abby . . . or Gloria . . . I don't know who to blame more."

"I'm going with Abby."

"You think she killed him?" Joey asked.

"I do. This embezzlement thing caught up to her."

"And Pops really didn't know about that?"

"No way. He wasn't going to get bogged down in these details. Hell, Joey, I'm the CFO and I didn't know any better. That's the beauty of working with a lot of cash. It comes and goes, and as long as the bills get paid, nobody has to know. Unless something like this happens."

"Well," Joey said, "that's what I thought, too." He was sitting across from Gene on one of the ottomans and took a slug of beer. "Which brings me to my idea."

"I'm listening."

"From what I hear and gather from you G-Teamers, Abby was lifting about ten

377

grand a month, and her salary was around eight. Does that sound about right?"

"It varied, as far as we can tell, but I think that's in the general neighborhood, yeah."

"So P&V has been able to absorb that every month for years without anybody even noticing. Without it affecting the day-to-day running of the business at all."

Gene sat back and pulled on his beer. "I think I see where you're going here."

A brittle smile. "I thought you might. I'm not the most subtle guy on the block, but I really do think this might be something P&V could do."

"Give you that money every month instead of Abby?"

Joey nodded. "That's what I'm saying. Except it would all be aboveboard and on the books this time around. And call it whatever you want — an outright gift or a loan against the insurance when it comes in. Or, my personal favorite, an investment in exchange for equity in Gamma."

"And for how long would this go on? Your eighteen grand a month."

"Till Abby's convicted or Gamma attracts another buyer. Say a year, maybe two, tops." Joey's voice took on an edge. "This is do-able, Gene. I'm not asking for charity. There are any number of ways that this could work."

"And a few where it might not."

This time the smile took and held. "I wasn't trying to pretend there weren't."

"No. I know that." Gene tipped up his beer. "You know, this wouldn't be my decision alone."

"Right. Of course. It's G-Team all the way."

"But you've already softened up Grace with that visit to her on Saturday when I came by. And Gloria feels guilty because her interference is what held up your insurance, so she'll want to help any way she can."

Joey nodded in acknowledgment. "Lining up my ducks," he said.

"And a pretty good job of it."

"Thanks. So, what do you say?"

"I say that, on first glance, it's a reasonable suggestion and certainly worth doing if we can make the numbers work, and it sounds like we can."

"Okay, then." Joey reached out and, holding out his beer bottle, clinked it against Gene's again. "Here's to us and to the bright new future."

They both drank.

■ ■ ■ ■

Gene was at the front door on the way out when he suddenly stopped and turned around. "Hey, I don't know if you've already heard, but somebody killed Stacy Holland over the weekend. Shot her in her apartment." ·

Joey straightened up, a study in surprise. "Really?"

"Really."

"What is that about?"

"Nobody seems to know."

"Any sign that it had anything to do with Pops?"

"Why would it?"

"No idea. I'm sure it didn't. Except she was his girlfriend once upon a time. They might make something up. Who knows? Have the inspectors been around?"

"No. And I wouldn't have known myself if Gloria hadn't heard about it this morning."

"How'd she do that?"

"Evidently Abby's lawyer has a private investigator and they're trying to dig up another suspect for who killed Pops. Thinking it might be the same person who killed Stacy."

"I doubt it," Joey said.

"Me too. That would be a hell of a long shot, wouldn't it?"

"Too remote to think about," Joey said. "If I were you, unless I heard from the cops again, I'd just leave it all alone."

"That's my plan," Gene said.

"Sounds like a good one. I'd stick with it."

"I will. And I'll be back to you before too long, maybe the next couple of days."

"You're the man, Gene. I can't thank you enough."

"Well," Gene said, "let's see if we can make this thing work for all of us." He lifted a hand as the elevator opened. "Adios."

31

In his office, sitting behind his desk, Devin Juhle glanced up at the clock on his wall: 3:23. It had already been a long day and suddenly it looked as though it was going to get to be a lot longer.

He looked at Waverly sitting across from him, drinking some noxious liquid that was supposedly just the thing for pain, and asked him: "So, Eric, to fill me in on the background, how did this idea occur to you?"

Eric sipped at his tea. "Actually, it shouldn't have taken as long as it did. I was at the desk this morning catching up on business, when they brought in the slugs from the Chang murder and I realized that we had two killings in a few days with essentially the same profile — two shots, close range, once in the head, in their own apartments, with no sign of struggle. Both guns .40-caliber Glocks. Okay, not an uncom-

"You don't need fancy lab equipment. You can see the striations clearly with a plain old magnifying glass. They match up. Let's not waste time arguing about whether it's the same bullets from the same gun. It's the same gun, I promise you. Therefore, for our purposes, it's the same shooter.

"And what I'm saying here is that, since Ken and Eric pulled Chang first, then made this rock-solid connection between Chang and Holland, it makes sense to put them on Holland and let them run with it — unless you and Darrel have got something going on Holland that we need to know about. But I haven't heard about much progress on that front, unless I'm missing something. The point is that I don't want everybody running around stepping on each other's toes."

"With all due respect, Dev," Bracco said, "that's just bullshit and you know it."

"Watch it, Darrel!"

"You know what I think?" Schiff said. "I think this is really about Grant Wagner."

"Really?" Juhle asked. "And how's that?"

"How's that is that the last time we talked about Holland, you said that you didn't want to send a message that we weren't confident about our indicted suspect on Wagner, Abby Jarvis, already in the slam-

386

mon weapon, but still, it's not like this scenario grows on trees. I figured, what could it hurt to take a look at the other slugs in Holland and run ballistics to see if we had a match with Chang? And we did."

Yamashiro, antsy and pumped up with this new information, shifted in his chair. "And we would have been here four hours ago if we could have goosed somebody in the lab to move a little faster, but good luck with that."

"Well, you got this now," Juhle said. "I wouldn't worry too much about the timing. This is pretty damn good police work. I don't know the last time I've actually seen ballistics turn out much of anything important, but this is the real deal."

"Thank you," Waverly said.

"You're welcome. But while we're on this, Eric, and while it's just the three of us here before Schiff and Bracco arrive, I thought you were in the process of taking some time off, or at least talking to somebody."

"That's still my intention, Dev, but for the moment we're in the middle of this thing and it's just starting to heat up."

"Right. But that's pretty much always going to be the way it is, isn't it? Some case is always going to be heating up. How's the pain today?"

383

"I'm dealing with it." Waverly held up his cup.

"That's not exactly what I asked, is it?"

"No, sir."

"No, it isn't. And maybe you remember that just the other day you were in here and told me you thought you needed help dealing with pain and anger and post-traumatic stress and, no offense, I don't see that changing your brand of tea is going to do you much long-term good in that regard. What do you think?"

"I think you're right, but I also think I'd like to follow this one where it leads, at least for a few more days."

Juhle turned his head. "Ken? Are you up for that, too?"

Yamashiro nodded. "Eric's a big boy. It took the patience of a saint down there at the lab earlier, and nobody killed anybody else. A couple more days shouldn't hurt anything. But Eric knows what he's got to do."

"Let's hope so." Juhle came back to Waverly. "And sooner rather than later. I don't want to find myself in the position of being the heavy here and having to do something official. That would really piss me off. At both of you. I hope I'm making myself clear."

The inspectors simultaneously answered, "Yes, sir."

"Good to know," Juhle said. "Now, where are those other guys? Meanwhile, Eric, why don't you take this opportunity to go rinse that cup out and take it back to your desk so it's not here stinking up the joint when the fun starts. Jesus."

Now the four inspectors — Waverly, Yamashiro, Schiff, and Bracco — were clustered in front of Juhle's desk, the party in full swing.

Debra Schiff was going on in a heated tone, standing, her arms crossed over her chest. She was on the defensive after hearing about Waverly's deduction that resulted in the ballistics match. Of course, she could have made the same deduction about the similar crime scenarios if she'd known anything about the Chang case, but she hadn't known anything about that, another factor influencing her bad mood. She was saying, "Even if it turns out to be the same killer —"

"Of course it's the same killer," Bracco shot back.

"Is it? Are we sure? How sure are we it's even the same gun?"

"That's established, Debra,"

384
385

mer. So you didn't want to acknowledge any connection between Holland and Wagner. But now, suddenly, you've got a way to put Eric and Ken on Holland because of the perfectly legitimate connection to Chang. Do you really think, Devin, that Abby Jarvis is innocent — that we got the wrong person in jail here?"

Juhle's head was throbbing and he rubbed his hands over his temples. "No," he said with great weariness. "I don't think that. What I think is that the grand jury indicted Jarvis and the DA is taking her to trial for murdering Wagner. That's all we need to know about that."

Vincent Hardy believed that one of the great perks about working for Facebook was the shuttle that picked him up near his apartment in the city and dropped him at the campus down in Mountain View, then took him back home when he was ready to go. The drive each way usually took somewhere near an hour, depending on traffic, and provided a perfect opportunity to chill, or sleep, or listen to music, or catch up on work, or your friends, or the news in the greater world.

Probably the biggest oddity about the shuttle was its soft policy regarding verbal communication: talking wouldn't get you fired, but because so much actual Facebook work was done on the shuttle, it was frowned upon.

Being a sociable guy, Vincent wasn't always the biggest fan of this policy, but today it suited him well. He was sitting in the back row, stuck in rush-hour traffic on 101, his laptop open, methodically going through the chains of emails that he'd received over the past couple of years where David Chang's name appeared, either as the recipient or sender or within somebody's else's message.

It was turning into not too much of a fruitful inquiry.

Vincent had met David about three years before through Bill Kenney, and had really only come to know him as a source of potential candidates for tech employment when he'd been working as a headhunter in the city right after graduating from college. After he'd come to Facebook, Vincent placed two of David's pals — Joan Singh and Michal Novo — and kept the lines of communication open, since David's entrepreneur group attracted the same kinds of people that Vincent tended to be looking for professionally.

But most of the emails that Vincent had

received weren't about future employment or anything as serious as that. David Chang himself made his money in website design, augmented by substantial day-trading, but his passion was video games and tournaments that he put together, almost always with Bill. Vincent had gone to a few of these and had had a good time, enjoying both the games and the people, but he tended to be more of an active outdoor guy and never became one of the regulars, even though David had continued to include him among the couple of dozen other names on the invitation list.

After he'd finished with the seventh and last individual email chain, which he'd received in the middle of March, Vincent considered sending out a blast to all of the recipients of the email.

And asking them what?

On reflection, he realized that this was precisely the kind of behavior that his father had cautioned him to avoid. Besides, out of the seven email chains featuring David Chang's name that he'd perused, there were perhaps a total of a hundred names: gamers and/or entrepreneurs.

And those were just the emails to Vincent. David probably had a couple of hundred other contacts like Vincent, each of whom would have a similar chain of emails, possibly a total of a thousand names, or even more. What was anybody supposed to do with that amount of information? If the task was doable and the knowledge useful at all — and it very well might not be — it was definitely police work, and he was reasonably sure they were or would soon be on it. And without his help.

As the shuttle started moving again, albeit slowly, Vincent closed up his laptop.

Waste of time.

At six thirty or so, Devin Juhle finally got out from behind his desk and made it a point to walk out into the homicide detail, which was blessedly deserted.

To reduce the risk of running into someone he knew inside the building, he took the outside stairs down to the street level, then crossed Bryant and walked another block down the alley that ran along the side of Lou the Greek's. Turning left onto Brannan, pushed along by the wind that was just coming up with a vengeance, he got to the next corner and continued on another hundred feet or so until he got to a heavy steel door. Taking one last glance in both directions, he pushed the doorbell and heard the deep tones of church bells resound inside the building.

"C'mon," he said. "C'mon."

He was about to ring again when the door opened and Tamara Hunt greeted him with a smile and said, "We've got to stop meeting like this."

"Hello, my dear." He gave her a quick buss on the cheek. "How's the bump?"

"Kicking up a storm." Closing the door behind them, Tamara led the way through the recreation side of the warehouse, through another door, and into their living quarters. Wyatt looked up from where he sat on the couch, stringing an acoustic guitar. "Hey," he said.

"Hey, yourself."

"I'll be done here in a minute."

"Take your time."

Tamara asked Juhle if she could get him anything and he declined. Sitting down on one of Hunt's reclining chairs, he pushed himself back so that he was almost lying down. "If I fall asleep here, wake me up when you're done."

Hunt said, "I can listen just fine while I'm doing this."

"I'm sure you can, but I'd like your full attention."

"Coming up in five."

Juhle checked his watch, then closed his

eyes, wondering if his being here was a good idea after all. It certainly was unorthodox, but with his new information about the ballistics match between the David Chang and Stacy Holland homicides, somehow his conscience had gotten engaged. He'd already spent a good portion of the early afternoon having lunch with Wyatt, holding fast to the position that there was no evidentiary link between Stacy Holland's death and Grant Wagner's, and therefore that nothing had changed regarding Abby Jarvis.

She was still their righteous suspect.

And yet . . .

Eric Waverly had admitted that with all of his stress and ongoing pain, he hadn't been operating on all cylinders over the past months, which included the time he'd gotten involved with the Wagner homicide. He and Yamashiro had followed the most obvious trail — true — and it had led to Abby, but there was little to no doubt that they had been influenced by her past criminal record and the evidence of embezzlement to put her onto the fast-track front burner as their main suspect. Had they truly investigated according to Hoyle? Had they actually considered any other suspects at all? Certainly Wes Farrell's display of prosecutorial strength at the arraignment argued strongly — from Juhle's perspective — that the district attorney, his protestations to the contrary notwithstanding, was at least a little bit defensive about the grand jury indictment.

Bwang! Bwang!

Opening his eyes, Juhle saw that Hunt was tightening up the strings, getting the instrument in tune. Not that Juhle, being functionally tone-deaf, thought he'd be able to tell when the job was done.

Bwaanng!

He told himself that the real reason he'd come over here to Wyatt's was as a hedge against error regarding Abby Jarvis. Stacy Holland's murder might not have any logical connection to Grant Wagner's. And certainly there was even less reason to believe that David Chang's death intersected Grant's. But what Chang's murder did provide was another angle for triangulation. Chang and Holland had the same shooter, so they were inexorably connected. And this meant they must in all likelihood have had some relationship, although what that was exactly remained hidden.

Juhle thought it would be bad luck to forget that — coincidence or no — Holland had been Wagner's girlfriend, intimately involved with his life and, to some extent, his family. Waverly and Yamashiro, Abby's arresting officers, might not find themselves sufficiently motivated to look for a way that their initial conclusion about Abby had been wrong — even if confronted by plausible evidence that this was true.

This was, Juhle told himself, the reason he'd felt compelled to come over here to Wyatt's: to avoid error. To that end, he had decided to tell Wyatt about the ballistics match — a fact to which he would have no access in the normal course of events.

It galled him that, because his inspectors had moved so quickly on Abby, he found himself in this position. To avoid the appearance that he had developed a shaken faith in Abby's actual guilt, he couldn't assign any of his inspectors to that case again, since it was technically closed.

Suddenly, Hunt strummed a few chords in quick succession. Tamara called in from the kitchen. "Sounds good, babe."

Hunt ran through a scale or two, made a few adjustments, then strummed some full chords. Breaking into a satisfied smile, he said, "I love this puppy." He placed it carefully faceup on the couch next to him, gathered up the old strings, and got up to drop them into a wastebasket in the corner. Sitting back down on the front of the couch, elbows on his knees, he nodded at Juhle. "Okay," he said, "talk to me."

The whole story didn't take two minutes to tell. When Juhle finished, Wyatt said, "So earlier today you're all over Abby being guilty as hell and there's not a chance that Holland is part of that case, and now you've got this other guy Chang, who is one more step removed from Wagner but is definitely part of Holland, shot by the same guy."

"Right. And I'm not pretending I can tell you what to do with any of this. But I'm hamstrung with Abby Jarvis because she's our suspect, and that's the end of that story."

"Does Chang get you any closer to Abby?"

"I don't see how. Not yet, anyway."

Hunt sat back, pensive. "But in your heart you think there's something more going on with these three cases."

Juhle broke a small grin. "I'll deny it till the day I die. And I've never been here telling you about it, either."

Hunt waved that off. "Goes without saying. But if that's the case, how did I find out about the ballistics match?"

"I don't know. You're the private eye. You've got contacts. Somebody leaked it. But if you want to know the truth, you don't have to tell anybody that you know. Your boss, maybe."

"My boss, undoubtedly. Just to be up-front with you. With appropriate disclaimers, of course."

"It's my ass if this gets out, Wyatt."

"I get it. I'll be discreet. Promise. So will Diz."

Hunt met Juhle's gaze. "You really don't think Abby did it, do you?"

Juhle hesitated, perhaps searching for the right words. "I'm willing to consider that possibility. Off the record and unofficially. Let's put it that way. If it's not Abby, I don't want to let the real killer get away with it. Simple as that."

"And they don't bother you, the different MOs?"

"A little, yeah. I could see somebody doing Grant with poison. But after you decide that you're really serious about killing somebody else, how are you supposed to get them to drink the tea? There are better ways to go about it. Like you shoot them."

32

"Hey, Vin. It's your dad. If the mood strikes, give me a call back. I ought to be around on my cell. Thanks."

No point, Dismas Hardy thought, in telegraphing your sense of urgency, which at the moment is acute, to your son who already thinks you are paranoid.

So he stood on his front porch, cell phone in his hand, waiting for it, hoping for it, to buzz.

They'd repaired the streetlight on his end of the block sometime in the past day or so, and he felt oddly exposed with his front lawn now all lit up and the porch light on overhead. On top of that, it had suddenly gotten cold enough so that he was exhaling a cloud of vapor with every breath, although he had on his jeans and a Giants World Champions sweatshirt and was moderately comfortable. So he thought he'd stay out longer on the chance that Vin would check his voicemail and get right back to him while he was outside where Frannie couldn't hear the phone ring or the ensuing conversation.

When Wyatt Hunt had called twenty minutes earlier, at first the news had sounded like it was nothing if not positive — Devin Juhle going outside of protocol to surreptitiously clue them in on the details of an ongoing investigation to which they would normally have no access. This was not by any stretch of the imagination a common occurrence, and to Hardy it spoke volumes about the weakness of the prosecution's case against his client.

With all of these doubts about Abby's guilt, even within the homicide department itself, Hardy now was well-nigh certain that, one way or the other, whether or not he chose to waive time, the case would crumble before it ever got to trial. And with any luck at all, in spite of the restrictions Wyatt had laid out for him respecting Juhle's sharing of this information, he might even be able to find a way to cobble some of these coincidental facts together into an argument in time for her bail hearing to get her out of jail.

Then Wyatt had said, "So all we need is some back-ass connection from this guy

Chang to Grant Wagner and by extension Stacy Holland which, if nothing else, would establish —"

And Hardy had cut him off. "Whoa up, Wyatt. What'd you say the guy's name was?"

"Chang. David Chang. He's —"

"I know who he is. He's a friend of Vincent's, Wyatt, is who he is. My son Vincent." Hardy, testy and curt, toned himself down a notch. "Was, anyway. You're telling me his killer also shot Stacy Holland? Shit."

And now his son, who lived on his computer and was never *not* plugged in, wouldn't pick up his goddamn cell phone.

Hardy huffed a swirl of vapor out around him and then looked down at his own hand, clutching his cell phone so tightly that his knuckles burned white.

The front door to his house opened behind him. "Are you all right? You're standing out here like a statue."

He felt something go out of his shoulders. Turning around, he reached out to put his arms around his wife and brought her into his embrace. "I'm not all right at all. I'm overreacting, panic-stricken, and paranoid. But otherwise fine."

"Do you want to talk about it?" she asked.

"It makes no sense."

"Lots of what scares us doesn't, right?"

"Maybe not, but I don't want to worry you with it."

"Too late for that now. Do you want to come in?"

Vincent finally called back after Hardy and Frannie had talked it all out. He'd been out at a movie and was actually in the neighborhood if they wanted him to stop by. The parents said that they thought that might be nice. But no pressure.

Now the three of them were gathered in the kitchen as they often were, Hardy and Vincent on barstools and Frannie having boosted herself up onto the counter by the stove.

"So," Vincent was saying, "this means what exactly?"

"I can't say for sure. Other than that your friend David and this woman might have known the same guy, or even might have known one another. It seems reasonable to assume that these two shootings weren't completely random, but where they intersect is anybody's guess."

"Okay."

"Well, maybe not so okay."

"What do you mean?"

Hardy laid out the details. "So we've got Stacy Holland," he concluded, "involved with the victim in the case I'm working on, and also connected to your friend David. I guess what I'm saying is that this co-incidence factor makes me a little nervous."

"So David knew Stacy's boyfriend?"

"No. Not that we know of."

Vincent made a face. "I'm still not sure I get it. Why are you worried?"

"I told you. I don't know. Maybe it's just that you know the victim of one murder, and I'm working on a case about the victim of another one."

"But they're not related to each other, are they? That you know about. Or am I missing something?"

"That's the point, Vin. They clearly are related to each other. We just don't know how. And that makes it incredibly danger-ous to just go poking around. You can easily find yourself in the middle of something and never see it coming. This is a situation where ignorance is not, in fact, bliss. This is the real deal, Vin, I'm not just being para-noid."

"Says the man who's been shot in the middle of two separate cases," Frannie added. "For the record, I'm with your father on this."

"Okay," Vincent said. "So I'm gather-ing . . . Is there something you want me to do about any of this?"

Hardy sighed. "I guess what I'm asking is that I'd like you to humor your mom and me. And just let me reiterate that you should stay as far away from any of David's friends and acquaintances as you can."

"Because . . . ? One of his friends or acquaintances shot him?"

"Somebody who knew him, anyway."

"And therefore might shoot me? Is that what you're saying?"

Defensive, Hardy said, "I'm not saying it's likely. But suddenly here you are, involved to some degree in two separate homicides . . ."

"How am I involved in your case?"

"Because *I'm* involved in my case."

"Dad." Vincent hung his head and looked out from under his brows. "Mom. Come on. You both admit that there's no connection between your case and David. And the only guy I'd ever see about David is Bill Kenney. In fact, I saw him last night and he didn't even come close to shooting me."

"It's not funny," Frannie snapped.

"Why'd you see Bill, anyway?" Hardy asked.

"To find out what he'd heard about David, which was essentially nothing. And the supposedly ongoing investigation. But really, guys, I promise, Bill did not kill anybody." He held up his hands. "But okay, I get it. You guys are nervous. You've got two murders that are related, but two — David and your guy, Dad — who just aren't. At least that I can see. But I can let it go. You've got more information than Bill anyway, and now you've got Wyatt working on David, too, so if I'm curious about any of this I'll come to you. How about that?"

"It would be deeply appreciated," Hardy said. "And, for the record, even if you don't follow the logic here, I find it pretty compelling. And so does your mother."

Vincent took a moment before nodding his head. "Okay," he said. "It's not like I'm hanging every day with David's pals. But hey!" Dismounting from his stool, he went around the bar top to the dining room table, where he picked up his computer and came back into the kitchen.

"What's that?" Hardy asked.

"This," Vincent said, "is what we call a laptop."

Hardy gave him a blistering smile. "Everybody's a wise guy. What do you have on the laptop?"

Vincent's fingers flew over the keypad. "I was just checking this out on the ride home. David Chang's email chains to me, inviting me to stuff, over the last couple of years. Since I met him, actually."

Hardy all but rolled his eyes. "And what did you plan to do with this information?"

Vincent shrugged. "I didn't know. But you know knowledge is power and all. I thought I might see something that meant something."

"And then what?" Frannie asked. "This is exactly what your father was talking about."

Vincent held up a hand again. "All I did was look at some files, Mom, which is all we're doing now."

"Okay," Hardy said. "Looking for what, though?"

"Here," Vincent said, stepping back. "Check it out. What's the woman's name again? Stephanie?"

"Stacy," Hardy said. "No 'e.' Holland."

"I loaded the email chains up all together so I can search them all at once." Vincent typed in the name and pressed Enter. "Nope," he said. "So he might have known her, but he never invited her to any of his parties."

"What kind of parties?" Hardy asked.

"Techs and game tournaments. Pretty fun stuff. But this Stacy never got invited. At least in the same chains I did, and I know I never met her. So that's not the connection.

Give me one of the names from your case, Dad."

"How about Wagner?"

"Wagner it is. Nope."

"Jarvis."

"Nope. But remember, this isn't David's whole contact list, either. This is just from emails he sent to me." Vincent straightened up, eyes alight. "And you know, actually, now that I'm thinking of this, the cops ought to check his full contact list against this Stacy Holland. They find a name on both of them, they might have something."

"That's a good call, Vin, but they're probably already on it. But I'll mention it to Wyatt and he can put a bug in Juhle's ear about it and make sure it happens. Meanwhile" — he gestured at the computer screen — "what, again, Vin, were you going to do with any of this?"

"I didn't have a plan, Dad, honest. I just thought I'd see if something struck me. Now, because you're worried about it — and you, too, Mom — I'm going to delete this folder immediately and never think of it again."

"Well, wait," Hardy said. "Why don't you email it to me before you let it go, since I'll never get any of those names in discovery. Every little bit helps. Or might."

"Sure. Got it. Son aims to please." Vincent's hands went back to the keypad. He hit a few keys, then picked up his computer and held it so that both parents could see. "Here you go," he said. "All gone."

Frannie went upstairs while Hardy fed his tropical fish. Then, walking down the long hallway in his house, he double-checked the dead bolt on the front door and came back through the house, turning off lights all the way up through the kitchen again. Finally, he double-checked the dead bolt on the back door.

All secure.

Upstairs, Frannie was still dressed, sitting propped up against the headboard, her arms crossed over her chest. Her red and glistening eyes stopped Hardy at the foot of the bed, where he sat and then turned to her. Meeting her look, he sucked in a deep breath and let it all out, shaking his head in apparent commiseration.

"I'm sorry," he said.

She nodded in acknowledgment of what he'd left unsaid. "I've been sitting here . . ." She stopped, made to start again, but instead closed her eyes and let a sob escape.

Hardy got to his feet and came around the bed. "Fran . . ." He sat down on the mattress at her hip.

She shook her head, her shoulders heaving again and again.

It took her a while to regain her control. At last she opened her eyes. "I've been pretending that this is how we need to live. I've been pretty good at it." She reached down and put a hand over his. "But I don't think I can do it anymore."

"We don't have to . . ."

She raised her hand and put it gently against his mouth. "Shh. Let me say." She grabbed another breath. "All these times you have agonized over whether or not you should take this case or that case, when somebody needs you and you feel you're the only one who can save them. And oftentimes you are, Diz. The only one. You're so good at what you do. And I know you love it, even if it's exhausting and all-consuming. It's what you were born to do.

"And even those times where the case, where what you were doing, put you in real danger — we always accepted it as the cost of doing the job. I mean, just look at yourself now. A bullet scar in your head, a bullet scar in your chest.

"Well, okay, that's your choice. That's the price you decide you can pay to do what you do. And I see that every time it tears you up inside, making that decision to go back into it again, take another case, save another poor soul, even if you know there might be danger involved. You might get hurt. You might even get killed.

"But it's who you are. This is what you do. You're a grown-up and though it cuts out a piece of my heart every time you make the choice — the noble, the right, the good choice — I live in fear. Real fear, because I can see what has happened before, and it can and maybe will happen again. But because I love and support you, I keep letting it happen. It's a risk I take, while you take your own different kind of risk. And we're adults, and it's our choice for the two of us."

She wiped at the wet spots high on her cheeks. "But last year Rebecca . . . because she got involved in one of your cases, it almost happened to Rebecca, too, and now this year here is Vincent . . ."

A fresh wave of tears broke from her eyes.

Hardy sat helpless and mute. Her hand still held tightly on to one of his.

Finally she started again. "I can go along and let you live your life and take your risks, but now, somehow, in some obscure way, I feel that our son is in danger, too. And that it's got something to do with your case."

"Fran, I —"

"No. What I'm saying is I can't let that happen. We — you and I — can't let it happen. We can't leave our boy in danger, even when — especially when — we can't even define exactly what that danger is. Except we know that it's real. It may not be logical, we might not understand it perfectly, but you know and I know there's no denying it. Whatever is happening with all these cases, they're connected somehow and that means Vincent is too close to whatever is orbiting around out there. It's dangerous and it's real, and we can't let it go on."

Hardy hung his head, put his other hand over Frannie's. "I don't know what I can say."

"It doesn't matter what you say. It's what you have to do."

"Which is what?"

She took a breath, met his gaze, nodded. "I think you need to quit."

"What do you mean, 'quit'?"

"I mean just stop. Drop this case."

"Retire?"

She shook her head. "I'm not saying that. Not yet, although that's not out of the question, either. It's not like we need the money. You could stop tomorrow and we've got enough to last until we're ninety. Without even being too careful about it."

"It's not the money, it's —"

"It's not worth it anymore, Dismas. Not with what's at stake."

"But I can't just —"

Her eyes flashed with anger. "*Of course you can!* This is our son's *life* we're talking about, and you're telling me you can't do anything as simple as quitting one stupid case? What are we supposed to do with that? I can't accept that answer. How about that? You have to drop it, that's all there is to it. Don't you see? Get out of it while we still can. With our lives."

"Come on, Fran, I think that's a little —"

"*Goddamn it!*" She slapped both of her hands down at her sides, her face now a mask of pure fury. "Goddamn it!" Shouting at him. "Listen to yourself. I'm being a little extreme, right? Well, wrong. I'm the one thinking clearly here. How can you not see that? This is what has to happen. And it has to happen *soon. Right away.*"

Hardy, shocked by her vehemence, brought his hands up on both sides of his face. "That thought has never occurred to me."

"Well, it's high time it did. This can't go on. I can't live with this anymore. I can't have *my children* living like this."

"And what about my client? What about Abby? I just abandon her?"

Frannie's voice softened. "Yes. You just abandon her. You help her pick a new lawyer. You get out of it. She hasn't even paid you yet, has she? You don't owe her anything. You even told the judge at her arraignment that you were temporary. Abby Jarvis is nowhere near as important as our son's life."

"No one's saying she is, but —"

"No! There's always a 'but.' Don't you see that? There's always an argument why you have to stay. And you're always the one making it, finding some way to justify why you've got to take on another case, another challenge. But this time I'm not listening. I'm through with it, with all of it, and you've got to be, too. It's over, Diz. It's got to be over."

"I don't know if I can say that, Fran. This is who I am."

"No it's not. It's the job you do. It's nothing to do with the person you are."

"It's more than that; it's —"

"I don't want to hear about it. I don't want to argue because you are a professional arguer and you always win. I'm simply telling you what has to happen, and you can say yes and stay or say no and go. It's your choice."

Hardy's hand gripped at his roiling stomach. "You're not talking you and me . . ."

She folded her arms again across her chest. "I love you," she said. "I will always love you, but this can't go on. I can't live like this any longer."

Hardy sat still as a stone while his pulse pounded in his ears. Unsteadily, he got to his feet and walked over to the bedroom door, where he stopped and turned around.

"Where are you going?" Frannie asked.

"Downstairs," he said. "I need to think."

33

The way Eric Waverly saw it, he had to prioritize between Sara Chang and the magic Chinese drugs of which she was the sole source, and because of which he hadn't needed to take any of the extra Oxy that he'd been scoring illegally since the last time he'd bought it.

He couldn't believe how well the tea worked. The pain persisted but on a much lower level. Because of that, his anger seemed somehow easier to control as well. He didn't know whether the stuff was more or less a placebo, but whatever it was and however it worked, he didn't want to risk running out of it. Ever.

Or at least until he was finally and completely healed.

That, he decided, was the main thing.

She was not the main thing.

He didn't for a moment kid himself that he loved Sara or that their physical dalliances were anything more than recreational. And because of that, in the normal course of events, they would undoubtedly stop seeing each other before too long. (The guilt and lies to Maddie were already becoming emotionally burdensome as well: he didn't like to think of himself as a cheating husband and couldn't imagine himself carrying on the affair for very much longer.)

So while he and Sara were still an item of sorts and comfortable hanging out together, he needed to get her to show him where these magic herbs originated so that he could purchase them without her help or intercession after they ended their relationship.

He told Yamashiro that he was going to visit Sara for another interview about her brother this morning, so the two inspectors made plans to meet up in Homicide around lunchtime. In the meanwhile the two of them dallied at her apartment for an hour or so, and when they were done, she brewed him another cup of tea — his second of the morning on top of the one he'd had at home — and Waverly brought up the topic.

"I'm just afraid I'm going to run out of this stuff someday," he told her. "Then what am I going to do?"

"That's no problem," Sara said. "I go

resupply for myself every month or so. At least."

"Why do you need it?"

"Migraine. My time of the month. Both. Believe me, I make sure I never run out, so you don't have to worry."

"I'm not worried, but I am curious. This stuff is truly magic, as far as I can tell. I can't believe you don't need a prescription for it."

She giggled at the notion. "My *yeye* would love that idea. After all the years — still now — when Western medicine hardly recognizes Chinese healing. Or the herbs. Imagine, to need a prescription for any of it. Ha."

"Yeye? What is *yeye?"*

"Not what — who. My grandfather. My father's father. His shop is in the middle of Chinatown, right on Grant."

"Does it have a name? The shop?"

She laughed again. "Chang. Same as him. But you'd never find it unless you know the Chinese symbol."

"I'd love to see it. See what else he's got."

"Oh, he's got everything."

"We should go there someday, pay him a visit. In fact, are you hungry?"

She gave him an amused, flirtatious look. "I think after our . . . exercise this morn-

415

ing . . . I have in fact worked up an appetite for food, too."

"So. How do you feel about dim sum?"

They ate superb dim sum at the Imperial Palace and by the time they finished at around ten thirty, all the tourist and local shops on Grant Avenue were open and the street itself was clogged with pedestrians making their way through the morning fog.

Sara was right. Waverly never would have picked out her grandfather's shop without her help: it was down an almost invisible alley off Grant Avenue, a block or two up from the Chinatown Gate on Bush. There were no English letters on either the one window or the glass in the door — and in fact it looked to Waverly like nothing so much as the back door or perhaps service entrance to another one of Chinatown's buildings.

But Sara walked right up to the door and pushed it open to the sound of a tinkling bell. The windows on the alley and in the door provided dim light inside, and the air seemed infused with an almost overwhelming and not altogether pleasant herbal scent. As soon as they stepped inside, an elderly Chinese man in black slacks and a white shirt stood up from behind a table that featured an old-fashioned scale and a similarly out-of-date cash register.

Sara's *yeye*'s eyes lit up when he saw his granddaughter, and the two of them hugged and said their hellos in what Waverly supposed was Mandarin. Then another embrace and a short and more serious discussion in a minor key, no doubt sharing condolences about David, the deceased brother and grandson.

At last — tears still in her eyes — Sara turned and gave Eric a weak and apologetic smile. Switching to English, she turned back to her *yeye* and said, "This is a friend of mine, Eric. He wanted to come by to thank you in person for your SPT blend. He has had bad pain in his shoulder for a long time, and after only a few days with SPT it is much better."

"I'm so glad it's working for you," the herbalist said in nearly unaccented English. "People have mixed results — although my good granddaughter swears by my SPT, so I keep a good stock on hand."

"What is it?"

"It's my own mix of herbs, actually a secret recipe from my father before me, and his father before him: ginkgo, *ma huang,* which is called ephedra in English, then lotus seed, and *fu zi.* Very powerful."

"And the mix, the tea, it's called SPT?" If Waverly was going to be buying this on his own now or in the future, he wanted to make sure he had the right name.

Grandfather and granddaughter shared an amused glance. "That is a little joke on the Caucasian name," Mr. Chang said. "Easy to remember. 'SPT' is for 'special pain tea.' "

Waverly chuckled. "Good name," he said. "As you say, easy to remember. And so I don't wind up taking all of Sara's, I was hoping I could buy my own supply and have it on hand."

"Of course. But I must warn you, please be careful with how often you use the tea. It works because, as I say, it is very strong. Toxic in too big a dose. Although the *fu zi* I use, the main active ingredient as you would say, I prepare it specially first. Boil the leaves for at least an hour. Then dry. And never ever use the root untreated." He wagged a finger in front of his face. "Very dangerous."

"I'll keep it in mind," Eric said, "but mostly I just think I'll let you mix it up."

"Good idea." He hesitated a moment. "Sometimes people — Western people — don't believe that these herbs, they have real power. They want to try their own blend. If they want to use *fu zi* in the tea, I tell them use extra care, but if the FDA doesn't issue a formal warning, some people just won't believe. Stupid." He shook his head at the idiocy and turned to Sara. "I still worry some about David's friend. With the bad arthritis? Do you remember him?"

"No."

"Well, he was like that. Make tea stronger, stronger, use root of *fu zi*. Bad idea. I won't blend it up that strong here so he took some extra home to make there as strong as he wants."

"And you just sell this *fu zi* root over the counter?"

The old man smiled. "That's what I do, sell herbal medicines. Different blends work for different people. I know that, so I don't judge. And David said the strong dose was working for his friend, so that's good. But still, I don't recommend making your own."

"I believe you," Eric said. "I'll go with your own SPT mix. In fact, if you don't mind, could I buy some today? Take it out with me now? So I can stop borrowing from Sara."

"I don't mind," she said.

"Still. It never hurts to have backup."

The old man looked to Sara as if for permission and she gave him a small nod.

"Okay," he said. "Let me go in the back. Give me a minute."

Waverly, his eyes by now accustomed to the dimness, scanned the shelves all around the tiny shop. "This place is amazing," he said. "Who knew it was even here? It's like a whole different world."

"It is, I know."

"You don't mind that I'm ordering my own stash of the SPT, do you?"

"Why would I? It only makes sense. And you don't want to run out."

"No. Or overdose, it seems."

Suddenly, Waverly went still.

"Eric? What is it?" Sara asked.

"Nothing," he said. "Or maybe something. I don't know."

"What?" she repeated.

"Another one of my cases. A guy who was poisoned. Nothing to do with why we're here today, and no connection to David that I know of. But suddenly . . . talking about overdoses . . ."

Sara's *yeye* came out of the back room with a small plain brown paper lunch bag, which he handed to Eric. "Here we are. This will be good for about a month. No more than four cups a day. I hope it continues to work for you."

"Thank you. Can I ask you a question?"

"Of course."

"The ingredients in the SPT? Lotus seed

and what else?"

"Ginkgo and *ma huang,* which is ephedra in English, and *fu zi.*"

"Do you know what *fu zi* is in English?"

"Yes, of course. It's called aconite."

At his desk in the homicide detail, Yamashiro leaned all the way back in his chair, looking up at his partner. "You've got to be kidding me. You think that's the source for the stuff that killed Wagner?"

"I've got no way to prove it, but I'd bet my badge on it."

"And so this grandfather — in theory this means he could identify our guy."

"Well, in theory, maybe. He described him for me pretty much in exactly the same words as Betty Lou Honaker. Mid-thirties, medium-dark hair, medium-sized, stubbly beard, nothing particularly remarkable about his clothes — in short, your typical millennial male. Almost without question, I'm thinking he's the one who shot David."

But Yamashiro didn't like this. "So he scores this aconite and then shoots David Chang? Am I missing something here?"

"No. Here's what I think. Follow me. And the great thing is, this gives us a motive, too. For the different MOs."

"Who are we talking about now?"

421

"Our shooter. And the aconite guy, who is one and the same. I think he found out about the aconite somehow from David Chang and decided that it was exactly what he had in mind for killing Grant Wagner and making it look like a heart attack — which, you remember, almost worked. In fact, it did work for a while."

"Okay."

"Okay, so everything's peachy — Grant Wagner has died of natural causes — which is good for Abby Jarvis and anybody else who happens to be in the line of succession, since the insurance money or special bequests — like the Jarvis million dollars — start to flow soon after the natural death. But then Gloria goes and screws it all up, exacerbated — and I hate to say this — exacerbated by our Jarvis arrest . . ."

Yamashiro jerked forward in his chair, his palms up. "Whoa, now. Whoa. I don't think we're anywhere near there yet."

But Waverly stood his ground. "I don't like it any more than you do, Ken, but if I'm right on this aconite guy, it means it couldn't have been Jarvis. And it also explains the gunshots for his second round of victims."

"How's that?"

"Chang was with him when he bought the

aconite in Chinatown. As long as Grant Wagner was being considered a natural death, no sweat. So what? So our guy bought some super-toxic aconite root for his homemade tea. Big fucking deal. But then —"

Yamashiro, following the narrative, picked it right up. "Then the aconite shows up as the cause of death and . . . yeah, I get it. I see where you're going. Anybody who puts aconite together with our guy becomes a threat who needs to be eliminated."

"That's how I read it."

"Which explains the MO. This guy was a friend, or at least an acquaintance, of David Chang's. So he drops by, sweet as you please — buds — and Chang lets him in and then turns his back for a second — and why wouldn't he? — as he's going to make some tea or get some other drinks for the two of them, being the good host — and then *blam.*"

"Blam," Waverly repeated. "Shit."

"That, too." Yamashiro glanced at his computer screen, then back up to his partner. "I've been sitting here, going through a thumb drive of Chang's hard drive, which came in this morning, hoping some name is going to pop up for me. You know how many people he has on his contacts list?"

423

"I'm guessing a lot."

"One thousand two hundred and seventeen. And you don't even want to know about who he sent emails to. Call it another two grand on top of that, although some of those will be dupes from the contacts. And of course a good portion of them aren't even real names but email addresses and usernames. One of them is probably his killer, wouldn't you say?"

"Likely."

"But what are we supposed to do? Interview three thousand people, even assuming that we could identify them?"

Waverly shook his head, turned around, and walked over to the window, where he looked down through the clearing fog onto Bryant Street. Returning to their front-to-front desks, he said, "Maybe we can get a rush on our copy of Stacy Holland's phone and computer drive."

"That would be nice. I was wondering when she was going to come up."

"She's up now."

"I see that."

Waverly cleared the corner of his partner's desk and lifted a haunch to sit on it. "Let's call them now. Put a rush on it."

"Better would be if we just showed up down in Forensics with Chang's thumb drive. If there's a name on both computers . . ."

Yamashiro was up and out of his chair. "I hear you. Let's blow this pop stand." He pulled out the thumb drive and started to come around the desk.

But Waverly stopped him. "You think we want to run this by Juhle first?"

"And say what? We fucked up the Jarvis thing? Let's let her walk? She couldn't have done it because this aconite guy did. It would be way better if we had another name to plug in."

"All right. Let's go find it."

"I'm with you."

34

Dismas Hardy never thought he would appreciate Phyllis the way he did today. After an all-nighter at home moving from family room couch to living room chair and back again, he had finally given up on sleep altogether, gone back up to his bedroom, and silently gotten dressed. He wrote Frannie a note saying that he loved her and made it down to the office at six thirty, leaving a message with Phyllis that he didn't want to be disturbed.

Not by anybody, not for any reason. Not until eleven thirty.

Since it sometimes seemed that her life's highest purpose was to deny people access to him, Hardy was certain that Phyllis had been waiting for just such a directive for the past decade or so, and nothing like it had ever been forthcoming until today. He'd probably made her week, if not month.

He didn't really remember taking off his

shoes, or loosening his tie, or hanging his suit coat on the back of his chair, or going over to the couch in his office and lying down on it. Nevertheless, when he opened his eyes, that's where and how he was. He checked his watch: eleven twenty-eight. Getting up, he crossed over to the sink at his wet bar and threw some water on his face, drying it with one of the dish towels. Tucking in his shirt, straightening his tie, he walked back over to his desk and sat down.

Let his shoulders settle.

His desktop, except for his in- and out-boxes and the three framed photographs of Frannie and the grown-up kids, was bare. He reached for Frannie's picture and pulled it a few inches toward him, then did the same with the others — first Vin at about twenty-three, in a tuxedo, clean-shaven and short-haired; then the Beck in a cap and gown on her graduation from law school. Both beaming, seemingly happy, well-adjusted.

The office phone with its direct line to Phyllis buzzed at his elbow. He checked his watch. It was eleven thirty exactly.

When he picked up the receiver, it took all of his willpower not to answer with his traditional and — to Phyllis, maddening — normal greeting of "Yo." Instead he said,

"Good morning, Phyllis. Thanks for the wake-up."

"You didn't say to wake you at eleven thirty," she said, "but I thought . . ."

"You did fine, Phyllis," he said. "Good job. Thank you again. Any calls?"

"Mr. Hunt and Lieutenant Glitsky."

"My wife?"

"No, sir. Were you expecting her?"

"Maybe a little later," he said. "Were the other calls urgent?"

"They didn't say."

"Well, then, let's go with 'No' on that one. How about that?"

"Yes, sir." A hesitation. "Can I ask? Is everything all right?"

"Fine. I just had a rough night of sleep at home, so I thought I'd come down here and try to catch up. Thanks for the gatekeeping. You're pretty good at gatekeeping. Has anybody ever told you that?"

"Mr. Freeman used to think so."

"And he was a wise man."

"Thank you, sir."

"You're welcome."

Hardy hung up, closed his eyes, let out a deep breath.

Quit?

The word that had pervaded his thoughts

and his psyche from the moment that Frannie had first mentioned it now came back to assault him with a vengeance.

He couldn't quit.

Not in the middle of a case, and a murder case at that. And especially not when he was more and more convinced of Abby's true, factual innocence. He also believed that the matching ballistics results on the bullets that had killed David Chang and Stacy Holland — even without an overt, demonstrable connection to the death of Grant Wagner — would be enough to provide reasonable doubt to almost any jury that he could imagine. But the connection between these elements was so tenuous that no judge would let it into Abby's trial.

He knew that he could make that not-quite-legalistic argument, and possibly make it more powerfully than any other lawyers of his acquaintance in the city. He couldn't palm Abby off on someone who wouldn't do the job he could do. Was this arrogance distilled down to pure hubris? Or was it simply an acknowledgment of the skilled lawyer he'd become after three decades in the trenches of San Francisco's superior court?

He knew the game; he knew the players, the rules, the strategies. He had no doubt that he was going to win on his no-bail motion next Monday and then he was going to win again at Abby's murder trial. He could not desert her — not ethically, not personally.

And yet . . .

Frannie was right. At Abby's arraignment, he'd made a "special" appearance. He wasn't legally bound to represent her, and he hadn't yet received one dime in payment. So, technically, there was no ethical issue. He was not Abby's attorney of record. He owed her nothing. He could even withdraw from the case without another word to Abby and turn her representation over to the court, to appoint a public defender or assign another private attorney to her as it saw fit. For that matter, he could help get her a referral to another high-caliber lawyer in whom Hardy had confidence and who might take the case for not much money as a favor to him.

How and when had he gotten up from his desk chair?

Now he was standing by his office window, his hands clasped behind his back, looking out over the busy downtown streets. The fog had nearly burned off up here on Sutter Street, although it was still hanging on in grainy wisps down by the Hall of Justice.

Were his children in danger?

Given his own history, how could he have never seriously considered that possibility? Wasn't the very first duty of a father to protect his children? Even after they were all grown up? Did they in fact need to be protected? Or was Frannie's panic an over-reaction to the situation they actually faced? And even if it was, how could he ignore her?

He didn't want to believe it, but she'd actually made it sound like she was talking about divorce if he couldn't bring himself to get out of the murder business.

And yet, every time he revisited the conversation, that's exactly what it sounded like.

You're not talking you and me . . . he'd said.

I love you. I will always love you, but this can't go on. I can't live like this any longer, she'd replied.

Reliving it now, the words had no trace of ambiguity. She was going to leave him if he persisted, if he couldn't abandon this case where Vincent was tangentially, but truly, in the mix.

While he was standing there, the goddamn telephone rang. After all, he hadn't told Phyllis to keep holding his calls, and now she was dutifully letting them ring through.

He strode to his desk and picked up. "Yo." Back to normal.

431

"Lieutenant Glitsky, sir."

"All right. Put him through."

"Diz, you got a couple of minutes? I think I might have come across something. Maybe nothing, but if it's anything, it's on your case."

"I thought you were so sure Abby's guilty."

"I still am," he said, "but that ballistics match has got me thinking about some other possibilities."

"Always a dangerous idea," Hardy said.

"Well, if you're interested, I'll be in my spacious cubicle."

Hardy caught a cab outside the front door of his office and was at Glitsky's space in the bowels of the Hall of Justice in under ten minutes.

"That was fast," Glitsky said, looking up as Hardy appeared in the opening that served as his doorway. "Did you come from your office?"

"Isn't that where you called me?"

"I thought so, but maybe Phyllis has some devious tracking device and called you while you were in court or something."

"Maybe, but probably not." He pulled the one extra chair around and straddled it backward. "In any event, I'm here. What do you got?"

"You remember yesterday we're having lunch at Lou's and your pal Wyatt Hunt brings up this new shooting victim who used to be the girlfriend of Grant Wagner in your Jarvis case?"

"Sure. Stacy Holland. What about her?"

"Well, it turns out there's a ballistics match. The same gun that did Holland killed David Chang."

"Yeah, I knew that."

"Well, thanks for sharing. I thought this was breaking news. That's why I called you."

"Well, not so much. But I still can't figure out what connection there is between Chang and Holland and maybe my case, the Wagner killing."

"And yet it's looking more and more like there has to be one."

"I think you can bet on it. So thanks for the ballistics information, and sorry I already knew about it. But I think we're good here, right?"

"Yeah, we are, but . . ." He hesitated.

"What?"

Glitsky took another second or two, collecting himself, obviously trying to figure something out. "Okay, so, backing up, I hear about the ballistics match and David Chang getting shot in the head in the Park district, and something started nagging at me all day yesterday. This reminds me of something, but I can't figure out what. Or why. And then this morning it comes to me. You remember the Engle case?"

Hardy squinted, recalling the name. "Vaguely, yeah. Here in town, right?"

"Right."

"It's coming back."

"It should. It was the murder of the year. It's also the last death penalty case tried in San Francisco. Right up until now. And I'm a little surprised it didn't come to me sooner. It was probably the nastiest case I've ever been involved in. I didn't think I'd ever forget it, even for a minute. In fact, it stuck with me so hard, I kept my own personal file on it."

Reaching over, pulling a file folder across his desk, Abe handed it to Hardy with a gesture that he should feel free to open it and take a look. Newspaper reports, police files, the whole sordid mess.

As Hardy turned the pages, Glitsky went on. "These two scumbags — Karen and Dan Engle — they killed their two-year-old daughter, Evelyn, for the insurance they'd bought on her. For a whopping half a mil. One shot in the body, one in the head. A baby, Diz. Even here in San Francisco, a jury found that sufficiently appalling to

434

justify a couple of executions."

"And they went through with them? The executions? I don't remember that."

"That's because they didn't happen. They both died in prison within the first year. Karen from pneumonia, and Dan hanged himself. It's in the folder there, if you've got the stomach to get to the end."

"I don't know if I do. Now hearing the story. How does any of this help me on Jarvis?"

"It doesn't. It was just an itch I couldn't scratch."

Hardy turned another page, randomly, in the folder, and suddenly froze. Looking down briefly, his lips twitched once, twice. Then, closing it, Hardy held up the folder. "Can I borrow this thing?"

"What for?"

"A little light reading."

Glitsky shook his head. "Sure. Not that it's going to do you any good."

Hardy hesitated, then opened his briefcase and dumped the folder there.

You never knew.

35

At two fifteen, Waverly and Yamashiro were at last in Devin Juhle's office, the door closed behind them. For the past couple of hours, the computer forensics people had been more than happy to work with the phone and computer records of both David Chang and Stacy Holland. Working backward and forward with names; phone numbers; usernames; emails; Facebook, Instagram, and Twitter accounts; and anything else they could think of, they had completely struck out. There was no indication that these two murder victims had ever met one another or even communicated in any way.

"That seems almost impossible," Juhle said upon absorbing the news. "What about those six degrees of separation we hear so much about?"

"Well," Waverly said, "apparently not this time. Besides, this was only two degrees."

"All right," Juhle said. "If that's the hand

we've got . . ."

Yamashiro and Waverly exchanged a glance that Juhle didn't miss.

"What?" he asked.

Again the two inspectors looked at each other. Then Yamashiro nodded and Waverly waded in. "You know how we have Stacy Holland with Wagner, and we also had her with Chang, since they both got shot by the same gun?"

"Right. Yeah. So?"

"So with nothing tying Chang to Wagner, we're stuck, right? So we thought we'd go down that road awhile, get a connection, see if we could find something on their computers, although now we know that's a dead end. We still had no way to get Chang back to Wagner."

"I'm hearing some past tense," Juhle said. "You're telling me you do have something?"

Yamashiro made a face. "We were hoping for a name before we brought it up with you."

"A name would be nice," Juhle said, "but at this point any lead is a good one."

"Well, this is real enough," Waverly said. He went on with the rundown of the morning's discovery: David Chang's friend and the aconite from his grandfather's shop.

When he'd heard it all, Juhle said, "So

your working theory is that Chang got himself killed because he knew that our guy had bought this aconite?"

Waverly nodded. "Right."

"What about Stacy Holland?"

"Still unknown," Waverly said. "But if our guy killed Chang to cover up evidence in the Wagner killing, maybe he killed Stacy Holland for the same reason. Maybe she knew or found out something that he didn't want her talking about."

"Maybe," Juhle agreed. "Good theory, in any event. Meanwhile, I need hardly remind you guys, we've got a suspect you arrested locked up across the way. We're going to need more than a theory before I'm comfortable going to the DA with a new story. And you two of all people ought to feel the same way until you've got this nailed down rock solid one way or the other. You hear me?"

After the inspectors had gone, Juhle sat in a brown study for several minutes, after which he got up and made sure that his door was locked, came back to his desk, sat down, and punched some numbers into his cell phone.

Wyatt Hunt picked up almost immediately. "Talk to me," he said.

438

"That connection we were waiting for to hook up David Chang with Grant Wagner? It just came through."

At his desk at Deloitte, Bill Kenney, way outside of the feedback loop as far as the police were concerned, finally in frustration placed a call to David's sister, Sara, who left out some of the salient, perhaps prurient details of her morning, but filled him in on the visit to her grandfather's shop with Inspector Waverly and the aconite that finally provided a connection — some possible context, at least — to something that might have played a role in his murder.

When he got finished with that first call, he wasted little time before punching up Vincent Hardy's number and passing along the information to him.

"Wait a minute," Vincent said. "You're saying, or Sara's saying, that the inspectors think this guy bought aconite and used it to poison Grant Wagner?"

"In a nutshell, yeah."

"Do you know about that case? The Wagner case?"

"Not really, no. Sara just now is the first I've ever heard of it."

"Well, it's my dad's case. They've charged Wagner's bookkeeper with killing him."

"But —"

"I know. This would take her out of the picture as a suspect pretty quick, wouldn't you think? This other guy."

"Unless they were in it together. The poisoning, I mean. He buys the aconite, she administers it."

"And then he lets her get arrested, looking at life without parole, and she doesn't give him up? I don't think so."

"You're probably right."

When Vincent got off the phone with Bill, he took a break from his office and walked down to the coffee shop on campus. Down here in Mountain View, the day was perfect: mid-seventies, cloudless sky. He got his latte, found a shady table, sat down, and opened his laptop.

Hardy and Hunt sat with their coffees at the enormous circular table in the firm's conference room, known as the Solarium. The walls were floor-to-ceiling glass windows and the dome of a roof soared eighteen feet up from the floor. Around the periphery, a plethora of potted plants proliferated: rubber trees, ficus, ferns, fiddleheads, three redwood trees.

Hunt, pumped up on the latest information he'd received from Juhle, was laying it all out. "In any event, this pretty well closes the circle on connecting all those dots: Wagner, Chang, and Holland. Even Juhle admits that we ought to be able to get this in front of Farrell and our client walks."

"I wouldn't count on that."

"Why not?"

Hardy, with a bit of asperity: "Because we don't have this mystery person who may or may not have bought some aconite and then used it to poison Grant Wagner."

"Sure we do. Chang's grandfather will swear to it."

"I'm sure he will. But that's not quite identifying him. Besides which, this can't possibly be the only guy Mr. Chang has sold aconite to. I mean, it's a staple on his shelves, right? He doesn't keep it there to sell some of it one time every six months. So, how do we know that this one guy bought it to go poison Grant?"

"Because he did. This ties it all up."

Hardy took a sip of coffee. "Don't get me wrong, Wyatt. I love this theory. It makes perfect sense. It hangs together. If this thing winds up going to trial, it's exactly the kind of explanation that will sing to a jury — provided, of course, that a jury gets to hear it. But unfortunately, for the moment, that's all it is: a theory. If I took it around to

Farrell now — especially after the big stink he made about the indictment with Abby — he'd laugh me out of the room. There's no proof for any of it."

"How about Stacy Holland? Tying her together with all of this."

"And how, again, does that work?"

"Even Juhle says she probably knew this guy — her eventual killer — and got in a casual conversation with him about how aconite can mimic a natural death. So when aconite gets back in the news, our killer is afraid that Stacy will remember that talk, and so he's got to get rid of her, too."

"How do we know that? How are we even sure that she knew aconite from aspirin?"

"Well, for starters, because she told me she did when I interviewed her."

Hardy's coffee cup stopped halfway to his mouth. "I don't think I knew that."

"I'm sorry. I should have mentioned it. But it had no relevance back then, except insofar as she was a suspect in Grant's murder. Until now, when suddenly again it does."

Hardy put his cup down and was drumming his fingers on the table.

Hunt pushed his chair back, lifted an ankle over its opposite knee. "Are you all right, Diz? Time was you would have

442

jumped all over this and been at Farrell's, jamming it down his throat."

"Time was, I probably would have. You're right."

"So?"

Hardy let the silence gather. Finally he sighed. "Frannie wants me to quit."

"Quit what?"

"This case, at least. Maybe the law entirely. She says she can't take it anymore." He paused. "She believes there's a multiple murderer running around out in the world: Grant Wagner's killer, Stacy's, and Chang's, too. And you know what? She's absolutely right. And since Vinnie was a friend of Chang's, she thinks my involvement in that case, tangential as it may be, puts him at risk, too."

"Well," Hunt admitted, "I can't say she's all wrong." He, too, had taken a bullet in a case several years before, and knew whereof he spoke. "So what are you going to do?"

Hardy sat back, twirled his coffee cup in its saucer. "I'm trying to do what's right, corny as that might sound. To Frannie, first, then to Abby, who I'm beginning to believe is completely innocent. But each one seems to cancel out the other. All in all, I think I'm going to have to drop the case. Given our new sets of facts, or the new theory, whatever you want to call it, I think she'll be all right. I'll get her set up with another lawyer, who'll probably be happy for the work."

"When are you going to do that?"

"Soon. Before next Monday and the bail hearing, anyway."

"So between now and then? Do you want me out, too? I mean, Devin's been calling me and keeping me in the loop on all of this. He thinks Abby's case has gone south just like we do, but he's got to cover his ass, since he's already got himself an indicted suspect."

"What's your question, Wyatt?"

"I guess it's are you really doing this?"

"I've been trying to avoid a decision on it all day. Now it's starting to look like I'm making one."

"All right. Let me know if and when you pull the trigger, though, would you?"

"I'll do that."

36

With the door closed and Phyllis at the reception desk undoubtedly standing guard outside, Hardy sat uneasily at his desk. He'd pulled the folder with all of its notes, records, transcripts, and reports on the Wagner murder out of his briefcase and placed it where he could have it there at arm's reach should the mood strike him. Then, while he was at it, he impulsively grabbed the folder Glitsky had given him that morning, held it for a moment, hefting its weight, then pushed it to the side of his desk.

He realized that if he was going to be done with this stuff, he had to start somewhere, and this twenty-two-year-old file really had nothing at all to do with Abby Jarvis, to whom he really needed to talk and inform of his decision.

But minutes went by and he just sat there, unable, as Hunt had characterized it, to pull the trigger.

Instead, his mind wandered, seemingly of its own volition.

Like a tongue returning again and again to a hole in a tooth, his brain would not shut down, flitting from topic to topic from the original autopsy conclusion, to Gloria Wagner's request that the medical examiner redo the blood scan, to those results and the aconite, to Abby's first interviews with Waverly and Yamashiro, to his bail motion, now half-written, perhaps never to be completed.

He had to quit.

He had to quit.

Pull the goddamn trigger already.

At the very least, he had to tell Frannie that it was done. He might not completely agree with her that to quit would be to save his family's life — her fear on that score struck him as a bit extreme. But clearly she had reached her own limit, and he felt he had no choice but to accept that if he wanted to save his marriage, he was going to have to live with that new reality.

But it felt deeply, unequivocally wrong.

He stood up, came around his desk, opened the panels in front of his dartboard, grabbed a set of his tungsten blue-flighted favorites, and began to throw.

Mindlessly.

Six rounds, nine rounds, fifteen.

Leaving three darts where he'd thrown them into the tiny wedge of "20," he stood eight feet back at his throw line, backed up a step or two, eased himself onto the corner of his desk. Reaching around behind him, he pulled the folder closer and opened it up again.

And suddenly it struck him.

He couldn't abandon Abby and, at the same time, Frannie needed him to quit that representation. The two paths were mutually exclusive.

Except . . .

The truth was right there in front of him and, with it established, Abby could walk free as early as tomorrow. With no need for his representation any longer.

Hardy had been thinking of it all in legal terms — the new evidence, the interconnections between the shooting victims and Grant Wagner — as eventual strategy for her trial, as a theory he could float to the court as a "third party culpability" defense, the one where "some other dude did it." The problem with that defense — and it was all but insurmountable — was that for any evidence related to another suspect to be admissible, it wasn't good enough to produce a motive, even a great motive. It wasn't even good enough to produce a motive and opportunity. No. The defense not only had to produce *a specific other person* who had motive and opportunity, but there must be direct or circumstantial evidence linking the third person to the actual perpetration of the crime.

Almost impossible.

But what if the theory Hunt had outlined for him was not a legal ruse that he could cynically play at trial but an actual blueprint of how these murders had come about? Hardy suddenly realized that this case — legalities aside and for all its apparent complexity — in many ways could not be more straightforward.

In reality, how many suspects could there be? Assuming that Abby had played no role in Grant's murder, and that neither had Stacy Holland, how many other people could have reasonably shown up without an appointment and been welcomed at Grant's home late in the evening? And once there, without arousing any suspicion, this person had mixed up and shared some herbal tea with him. It had to be a family member.

With Abby and Stacy out of the equation — and Gloria Wagner now as well, because there was no way that she called for a redo on her father's autopsy if she'd killed him

— well, then, this was getting to be a very finite universe indeed.

And it was about to get smaller.

Hardy picked up the Wagner folder and leafed through the early police reports from when Waverly and Yamashiro, before they'd settled on Hardy's client as the only possible suspect, had been doing their jobs as policemen and conducting elimination and alibi interviews with the rest of the G-Team — Gary, Grace, and Gene — all of whom stood to profit hugely from their father's death.

Hardy turned the pages:

Gary, the eldest sibling and heir apparent, had accompanied his wife, Eileen, and children to one of their school plays: *Our Town.* The play had ended at around ten o'clock. The family had driven home together and gone to bed. Corroborated by Eileen and all three kids.

Grace and her husband, James, had stayed at home helping their four children with homework. They ordered takeout pizza. Their oldest, Janey, kept the parents awake on her semester project — *The Great Santorini Caldera and the Demise of Minoan Culture* — until one a.m. Again, everyone alibied everyone else.

Gene had gone out with Teri and another

couple — Frank and Gina Seidl — to one of San Francisco's fine old French restaurants, La Folie. They were at the eight thirty seating and didn't leave the restaurant until eleven thirty, after which they went back to the Wagner home and the men drank a few single-malt Scotches — Laphroaig, Lagavulin, and Oban — and the women drank Chardonnay until one, at which time the Seidls took an Uber to their home and Gene and Teri staggered upstairs to sleep.

Which left Joseph "Joey" Engle. It was with some surprise that Hardy realized this was the first time he was aware of having come across that name, although he must have seen it on his first perusal of the discovery he'd received from the DA. Joey was apparently not a true sibling but was more or less considered such by the G-Team, although he played no role in the family business.

Since a couple of weeks had passed by the time Waverly and Yamashiro had questioned him about his whereabouts on the night of Grant's murder, Joey told the inspectors that he couldn't be too sure if he remembered any details too correctly or exactly: the days and weeks after his stepfather's death had been devastating, one day following the next in a kind of a fog. But, according to his calendar, he'd had a dinner business meeting at the Hotel Vitale with a venture capital guy named Art Howell (never followed up, since by this time the inspectors had settled on Abby as their suspect). After dinner, Joey had gone out to a SoMa dance club and bar named Gin Out. Home at two a.m., alone.

Perched on the corner of the desk, Hardy stared at the name.

Engle.

Joey Engle.

Almost gingerly, as though afraid of what he might *not* find, he retrieved Glitsky's folder from the corner of his desk. He didn't come across Joey Engle until the fourth article from the *San Francisco Chronicle*. But finally, sure enough, the name appeared in the file as a sidebar to what was now a steady drumbeat of articles about the parents who had killed their two-year-old baby for half a million dollars in insurance money.

The article didn't provide much in the way of hard information, instead concentrating on the mystery of why this ten-year-old boy had been spared when his sister had been so callously murdered; maybe, the article opined, it had been as simple as the fact that the baby had been colicky and difficult, and that had sealed her fate. In any event, her brother was currently in the care of his aunt, his father's sister, Ginger.

Closing up the file, Hardy booted up his computer and spent the next fifteen minutes doing some research on Joey and Ginger. She had married Grant Wagner shortly after her brother Dan had hung himself in prison, and the two of them had adopted Joey to somehow try to reclaim for him the semblance of a normal life with lots of brothers and sisters.

Now Joey was thirty-two, with a fairly large web presence, at least from Hardy's perspective, and was evidently promoting some kind of a gaming portal that he was calling Gamma. Apparently, about four months earlier, funding for Gamma's next phase had somehow been withdrawn — in any event, it had disappeared — although the Gamma web page tried to put a positive spin on it.

Hardy wasn't fooled. Joey needed money; he might even be desperate for it.

Getting out of Google, he stared at his screen saver, a slide show of Yosemite scenes in all lights and weathers. The top of his screen said it was four o'clock.

But so what? he was thinking. What did any of this mean? It wasn't as if anybody thought that ten-year-old Joey Engle had shot his baby sister twice the same way someone had later shot David Chang and Stacy Holland. (Although, still, Hardy wondered, what damage might that have done to a ten-year-old child? Might the awareness of his parents' effective but ill-fated MO have somehow imprinted itself on his unformed psyche?)

Again, like so much of this case, Hardy's now very strong suspicion about Joey as Grant's killer made no sense. There was no real connection between the twenty-two-year-old murder of Joey's sister and the Wagner case, and a connection was exactly what Hardy needed — some relationship between Joey and either one of the gunshot victims. Something that would at least provide enough probable cause to convince a judge to sign off on a search warrant for Joey's domicile.

His fingers went back to his keyboard.

There was Vinnie's email to him from last night, with its attachment, which Hardy opened. A couple of strokes got him to the "search" mode: all of David Chang's techie and gaming invitees for the past couple of years.

Hardy typed in "Engle" and pushed "enter."

The actual address was Jengle@gmail
.com.

Hardy sat back in his chair. "Son of a
bitch."

37

Frannie didn't share her enthusiasm for his progress. "This doesn't sound to me like you're dropping the case, Diz. It sounds like you're still working on it."

"No," he said, wondering if he was telling her even a decent portion of the whole truth. "I'm tying up some loose ends and then I'm going to be done. That's it."

"So you haven't told Abby you're getting out?"

"There's no need to. As soon as they get onto this guy Joey, they'll have to drop the charges against her, and she won't need any kind of a lawyer."

"And who, again, is going to 'get onto' him, as you put it?"

"Farrell, Devin Juhle, the homicide inspectors. Take your pick."

"These are the same homicide inspectors who arrested Abby? What is it exactly that's going to motivate them to undermine their original case?"

"Evidence," he said. "Real hard evidence carries a lot of weight, Fran."

"And what's all this evidence? David Chang once invited him to a party?"

"Yes." It seemed so obvious to him. How could she not see it? "That's all we needed," he went on. "Some connection between him and Chang, which, with any kind of reasonable magistrate over at the Hall, ought to get us a search warrant."

"Which will find what?"

"Best case, the gun. Then quite possibly gunshot residue on the clothes he wore, maybe even blood spatter . . ."

"Okay, maybe this and maybe that. But either way, his gun didn't kill Grant Wagner, did it? How do you know that whoever killed the gunshot victims also killed Mr. Wagner? Isn't that a pretty big jump?"

"Not once we get Chang's grandfather identifying Joey as the guy who bought the aconite."

"Nope. From what I'm hearing, Abby still needs a lawyer. And now — need I remind you? — you've gotten yourself into exactly what you said you wanted to avoid all along. An apparent killer who is not in custody."

"Not for long, I really don't think."

"You don't think? You know, I'm afraid

that's not too heartening, Diz. In fact, I'm thinking that this is a guy who could walk up to our front door anytime he wanted and open fire on whoever opened up, couldn't he?"

"That's not going to happen, Fran. How would he even —"

"Because he's going to figure out that you're the guy who's trying to put him in jail. That's how. Not the cops, not the DA. They've got their suspect, and as long as they're happy with her, they're not looking for him. But you are, because if Joey goes down for Grant Wagner, guess what? Your client gets off. You really don't see this? Do we have to go over this again and again? Why is this so hard for you to understand?"

He was back in Glitsky's cubicle, his eyes bleary, his tie loosened, his suit coat hanging over the back of his chair. "She didn't exactly tell me not to come home," he was saying, "but she made it clear it wouldn't be much of a warm welcome."

"After she leaves you, her next husband probably shouldn't be in law enforcement."

"Thanks. I'll tell her you said so."

"We deal with this every day, you know. We being police people. Dealing with actual threats to life and limb."

"I'm sure you do. But I'm not putting myself in that position."

Glitsky cocked his head to one side. "Hmm."

"I'm not," Hardy said. "I promise you that this guy Joey could be off the streets and in custody by tonight, at least on the Chang and Holland murders. This would have the desired effect of getting me out from under my client, which is what Frannie wants from me."

"And how again does that happen? Getting Joey off the streets."

Hardy ran down his search warrant scenario.

Glitsky listened with a polite show of interest; then, when Hardy finished, he said, "All good, to be sure, but I'm afraid I'm falling into Frannie's camp. Didn't you just tell me that when Hunt showed the elder Mr. Chang Joey's driver's license picture in a six-pack, he couldn't say for sure it was the same guy? So no one can say that Joey bought aconite from Chang's grandfather, and even with a rock-solid ID, which you don't have, there's no evidence on the table — none that I've seen — that he's killed anybody, much less Grant Wagner."

"Abe, I'm telling you he actually murdered all these people. It's a completely seamless narrative."

"I'm sure it is, and that's my favorite kind. But you've still got no evidence."

"Okay, but you and I know we don't need evidence to get a warrant. We need probable cause to go look for evidence. And Joey being on Chang's mailing list gets us over that hurdle."

"How does it do that?"

"It puts the aconite in Joey's hands. Which is what we need."

"No we don't, and even if we did, so what? Who's to say he didn't use it to make his own tea, which he has for breakfast every day? And don't keep saying 'we' and 'us.' I'm no part of this except as a sympathetic ear. And maybe even not so much of that."

"Come on. You can't tell me you still believe Abby was any part of this."

"I can't? I'm darn tempted, I'll tell you that."

"Then give me an alternative explanation of why Chang and Holland had to die. Answer: They had to die because they could tie Joey to the Wagner murder. There *is* no other answer."

"Well, except that there is, and we just don't know it yet."

"That's not it."

"No?"

"No. There's no sign that Chang and Holland had ever even met each other, Abe. I'm not the one stretching to find a reason here to put them together. This is the answer that makes the most sense."

"Diz." Glitsky ran a finger under one eye, then the other. "Enough already. We can go on all day with this stuff. The bottom line is that there's no evidence on Joey and darn little probable cause, either. You know this. And you know all these courtroom rules better than I do. It seems to me that the main thing is you don't want to drop your client."

"Not if I don't absolutely need to."

"Well, you might be getting close to that point."

"I know," Hardy said. "You don't need to remind me."

He stood in a corner of the lobby of the Hall of Justice, arms crossed over his chest as though he were waiting for someone. His face did not invite interruption. The usual riot was going on around him but, in its own way, all of the bedlam gave him cover.

He couldn't decide what he was going to do.

For most of the day now, since Frannie's ultimatum the night before, he'd been trying to talk himself into living with the idea of abandoning his client. He almost didn't care what the reason was, or — God help him — the consequences with his wife: the idea remained anathema to him. Okay, maybe if Abby's trial was truly a year away, and if he wasn't positive that she was innocent, he could justify stepping aside in favor of another defense lawyer for any number of plausible reasons.

But that was not his situation today.

He knew to a moral certainty that Joey Engle was a serial murderer. He would stake his life on it. And in fact, as the minutes ticked by, he found himself considering the possibility that it might come to that.

His client was utterly dependent upon him for her freedom. He'd been trying to work his way around it but kept coming back to what he felt in his heart and soul: that for him to stand by while she spent so much as an hour locked up in jail was a dereliction of his sacred duty, a denial of who he was as a man and a refutation of the job he'd sworn to do.

He had to take Joey down. Nothing else would both free his client and protect his family. And if there was some risk for him, then so be it. Risk came with the territory. He and Frannie could discuss his retirement later — and perhaps it was time to quit taking murder trials — but for today he was his client's only path to justice. To do less than try to obtain that for her was to abdicate the responsibility that fell to him and him alone.

He'd talk it all out with his wife when he was done. They'd make future changes, if any, in a different moral environment.

But for now he had no choice. He had to make something happen.

38

Hardy surprised Hunt. He had been ready to pull the trigger all right, but not on the plan to drop Abby as his client.

Now, in the pre-dusk at a few minutes before seven o'clock, Wyatt Hunt stood hidden in the recess of a doorway across the street from Joey Engle's condo. He thought he'd recognize his quarry anyway from the general description of hipster millennial poster boy, but just to be sure, at Hardy's suggestion Devin Juhle had printed out the ID picture from his California driver's license. Hunt had given it a good look and had no doubt when Joey appeared through the glass-fronted lobby.

Joey stood at the curb for a moment, looking back and forth, up and down the street, until what Hunt presumed to be his Uber ride arrived, stopped, and picked him up. Hunt gave them most of a minute to drive off before he sent a text to Hardy: On his way.

Putting up his cell phone, double-checking for the reassuring presence of his gun in the holster at his back, Hunt pulled his jacket snug around him. Crossing the street, he got to the street door, played with the lock for about ten seconds, then let himself in. The elevator opened at the push of the button and carried him up to the fourth floor as if he were spontaneously levitating, fast and silent.

The door to Joey's condo posed no more of a challenge than the one downstairs.

Hardy's plan contained quite a few moving parts, and at any time any one of them could fail and render the entire operation worthless. But Hunt wasn't worried about this. His task here at the condo was straightforward enough: find the gun.

Of course, it might no longer be there at all, but as irrefutable physical evidence tying Joey to both David Chang and Stacy Holland, it was in many ways the linchpin of the whole plan, and without it Hardy would have to rethink his strategy and put things off to another day, which he'd made abundantly clear he was not inclined to do.

Hardy acknowledged that after Joey had shot Stacy Holland on Sunday, he might very well have gotten rid of the gun. It would have been a reasonable and smart thing to do. On the other hand, he'd used it twice already and — who knew? — maybe he would have occasion to use it again. Hopefully he had no idea he was under suspicion and so there would have been no reason yet to dispose of it. There might have been no sense of urgency.

In all, Hardy thought it was worth a try.

Hunt wasn't going to toss the whole unit. In fact, his goal was to leave no trace that he'd been here. He'd start in the most obvious places and go from there. His first stop was the bedroom, where, somewhat to his surprise, the bed was neatly made. Hunt lifted the mattress but found no gun, then looked under and carefully replaced the two pillows. The dresser had seven drawers — three narrow ones at the top, then two rows of two.

Nothing.

Around the bed, on the bathroom side, Hunt very carefully pulled out the top drawer of the small bedside table and there, wrapped inside a green tartan scarf, was a semiautomatic Glock 40 handgun — a very common gun, but also a match for the caliber of the bullets that had killed Chang and Holland.

Nodding appreciatively, Hunt closed the drawer, stepping back to see if he'd left any record of his presence. Satisfied, he made his way back out through the living room, turning off the lights he'd turned on earlier.

A minute later he was back on the street. Taking out his phone, he texted Hardy again, the simple letter *X,* meaning he'd found a gun.

Hardy sat at one of the back corner tables of the Quiver Bar overlooking the bay from the Embarcadero. When he saw Joey come around the top of the stairs, he raised his hand, got a nod in return, and waited as the young man made his way around the center table and back to him.

"Mr. Hardy?"

"Guilty." Hardy managed to be raising his glass for a sip of his drink with his right hand and so avoided the moment when they would have normally shaken hands. Instead he said, "I'm having a club soda, but they've got pretty much anything you want in the way of liquid refreshment here."

The waitress miraculously appeared as soon as Joey got seated. He ordered a Bulleit Rye with two ice cubes, then gave her a tight smile and warned her that he'd count them: two and two only.

She left to go place the order and Joey came back to Hardy. "It shouldn't be that hard to remember and get right, wouldn't you think?" he asked. "You order two ice cubes and they either give it to you neat or on the rocks." He sighed. "Well, we'll see if she gets it. Meanwhile, how can I help you? Or Abby, since you said this was about her. Something about her bail."

"I'm writing a motion for a hearing next Monday so the judge will let her out on bail, which is unusual in a special-circumstances case. But before we go down that road, I wonder if you'd mind if I asked you about something else entirely?"

His brow furrowed slightly as if he did mind, but he recovered quickly. "Not at all. Shoot."

"I couldn't help but notice your last name and wonder if you were connected with the Engle case back in the nineties. I've been in law enforcement one way or another for most of my adult life, and that name's stuck in my consciousness, right up there with O.J. Simpson and Dan White." If Hardy's aim was to rattle Joey, and it was, he'd clearly succeeded. "So I run across somebody named Engle, it gets my attention."

"They were my parents," Joey said. "And it's not a topic I'm comfortable talking

467

about, if you don't mind, though I can tell you that I've thought of changing my name many times."

"To Wagner?"

"Among others."

"Maybe if your first name started with a 'G' . . ."

A bitter attempt at a smile. "I don't think that would have done it. But all of that has nothing to do with Abby."

"Not really. Well, except for the similar ways the victims were shot. One shot to the body, one to the head. That's the kind of detail that jumps out at me. It's kind of a too-much-information moment, where you wish you could somehow put the picture out of your mind. You know what I mean?"

"Actually, I'm not sure I understand what you're talking about," Joey said. "My step-father was poisoned, not shot."

Hardy, hand to his forehead, feigned forgetfulness. "That's right, of course. I was thinking about Stacy Holland and David Chang. You knew both of them, didn't you?"

Joey hesitated for a moment as the waitress returned with his drink, which he checked for number of ice cubes and, apparently satisfied, gave her a nod. "Thank you. It looks perfect," he said. Then after taking a good sip, came back to Hardy. "I'm sorry.

Where were we?"

"Stacy Holland and David Chang."

"Right. Right. What about them, again?"

"They were shot the same way as your baby sister," Hardy said. "That's really the only connection I can make with Stacy and David."

"I don't understand what you're getting at. None of that has anything to do with me."

"But you did know both Stacy and David, didn't you?"

"To talk to, to nod at. I can't say I was close to either of them. Maybe even less than that. And what do they have to do with Abby? Or Grant, for that matter?"

"From my point of view as her attorney, Stacy and David are important because they prove that Abby is innocent of killing Grant."

"How is that?"

"She couldn't have killed them because she was in jail. I don't know if this information has been released to the public yet, but Stacy and David were both killed by the same gun. Did you know that?"

"No."

"Well, it's true. And since they both had an independent connection to your step-father, the police now believe, and so do I, that all three murders are related."

"That seems a bit of a reach, if you ask me. How was this David Chang person connected to Grant again?"

"The same way that Stacy was. Through the aconite."

"Aconite was the poison?" Joey was still trying to brazen it out, although the stress was beginning to show.

"Stacy's the one who told Grant's killer all about it. How death from an aconite overdose looked like a heart attack."

"And David Chang?"

"David was with him when he actually bought the aconite."

"How do you know that?"

"The police have talked to David Chang's grandfather in Chinatown, that little place he lives in right above the store. He's the one who sold the stuff to Grant's killer and swears he'll be able to identify him as soon as they have a suspect. So meanwhile, before the police had put any of this together, Stacy and David both had to be silenced." Hardy spread his hands. "That's the connection among all of them. Which means my client is innocent and needs to be out of jail."

Joey leaned back in his chair, took another pull at his rye, placed it down in front of him. "If the cops think it's all one person," he said, "why don't they let her out now?"

"They're light on evidence for the shooter. They need something like the gun, or Grandfather Chang's ID of the guy who bought the aconite from him. Or both. That's why I asked you down here, Joey. I'm hoping you could give me some names of people connected to both David Chang and Grant. Then we can start showing photos to the grandfather. Once we get an ID, then the police can get search warrants and maybe find the gun, check our suspect's phone records to see if GPS puts him at Grant's the night of the killing. It's really important, Joey. Without that ID, we've got nothing and Abby's still looking at prison for a crime she didn't commit."

Joey asked, "Why would this person keep the gun if it's the only hard evidence tying him to the murders?"

"Because it's already worked twice, and it might be needed again. It wouldn't be smart to go out and buy a new one just now, while the investigation is still hot. The police might be checking gun sales or new registrations. Who knows? Better to lay low. Meanwhile," Hardy purposefully shifted the tone of his narrative, "you don't think you're a suspect, so nobody's connecting you with the gun, the murder weapon, anyway. It's a low-risk bet, and if everything works out and the investigation cools down and they never do find the shooter, two or three months from now you get rid of it down the nearest sewer or out in the bay. End of story."

Joey swirled his glass again and tipped his drink all the way up. "So," he said. "Abby. She told you there's some way I could help her, although I don't know why I'd be so inclined if she killed my stepfather."

"Because I just proved to you, or thought I did, that she didn't do it. The person who poisoned your stepfather is the same person who shot Stacy and David, and that couldn't have been Abby because she's been all that time in jail. You following me here?"

Joey nodded.

Joey didn't think he was a racist, but now he realized that he was in fact guilty of a kind of reverse prejudice whereby he believed that, just as he probably could not accurately differentiate between half a dozen elderly Chinese men, those same Chinese men would not be able to tell him apart from five other Caucasian men with roughly the same coloring and bone structure.

But what if he was wrong?

472

It was a stone he had left unturned and only now after his conversation with Abby's attorney was he beginning to appreciate the gravity of his error. Grandfather Chang, whose grandchild David he had killed, might in truth be deeply motivated and able to pick Joey out of a pool of even dozens of young white guys. Positively identify him.

When they'd been at the store on the day he bought the aconite, goofing around with David, checking out the herbs and teas and poisons — before Joey knew what he would be driven to do over the next few weeks — he'd been his charming, sarcastic self: cracking jokes, trying to earn the old man's approval or even affection, because you never knew for sure where and when you could run into a source of capital. In short, Joey was making himself visible, identifiable, possibly even unforgettable.

Even after a few weeks had gone by.

He knew from any number of television shows what was going to happen if that attorney, Hardy, passed along his suspicions of Joey to the police, which apparently he had not yet done. Nevertheless, Joey could count on them getting into their protocols before long. They would pull his California driver's license photograph from their database and put it in a "six-pack" of photos of young men who more or less matched his description, and then show that six-pack to Grandfather Chang. And even without the gun in play, that would be the beginning of the end.

He couldn't believe how Hardy had so precisely come to understand his reasoning for having to kill Stacy. Their talk about the mostly unknown drug called aconite had gone on for at least a half hour and he had no doubt that she had not forgotten about not only it but him by the time he came over to her place. To the extent that she'd almost not let him in at all when he'd shown up, but then of course her courteous nature and reasonability had kicked in and she'd opened her door to let him in and sealed her fate.

By the time he was back in his condo, Joey had made up his mind: he needed to act swiftly and decisively, the way he had with David and Stacy. And this time he would get rid of the gun immediately afterward. Hardy hadn't been lying when he said that there wasn't any other evidence incriminating Joey; the gun and the ID were the only way they were even hypothetically going to get him, and he could eliminate both of those possibilities that very night.

In his bedroom, he walked over to the

bedside table, opened the top drawer, and lifted the gun out of the shawl in which it was wrapped.

Luckily but understandably, Joey didn't take an Uber or a cab this time. Undoubtedly, Hunt thought, he would want no record of his whereabouts. There was also still enough light left that any driver would have no trouble identifying him. Finally, it was a small town, and walking from his condo to his presumed destination in Chinatown five or six blocks north would take no longer than ten minutes.

Even though every detail in Hardy's plan had thus far worked out — the trap appeared to have been set, and now all that remained was for it to be sprung — Hunt nevertheless had to tamp down the steady buzz of adrenaline that had accompanied Joey's return to his residence, the turning on and then off of the condo's lights, and finally Joey's exit at his building's front door, where he checked the street in both directions and then turned up toward Market.

Hunt's quarry had been wearing a sports coat when he'd returned from his meeting with Hardy, but now he wore a much heavier Warriors jacket, no doubt better to conceal the gun that Hunt presumed he'd picked up during his brief stop at his condo.

Falling in about a half block behind Joey, Hunt kept him in easy sight. A steady breeze off the bay chilled the evening, but thank God today the fog had decided to stay where it belonged, out over the ocean. Hands in his pockets, Joey walked at an even pace, not so fast as to call attention to himself. He gave no sign of awareness that he was being followed or that he was worried about it.

When Joey got stopped by the red light at Market Street, Hunt closed the gap between them to fifteen or twenty yards, then stopped to do a bit of faux window-shopping, tapping out a text on his phone: "Grant @ Market. 5 blks."

Hunt's stomach now roiled as they closed the gap between them and Grandfather Chang's shop. In spite of the chill, he felt a drop of sweat trickle down his back. It took all of Hunt's discipline not to reach behind himself and draw his weapon, just to have it in hand should things go wrong in the next few moments.

At the Chinatown Gate, Joey stopped again.

There was still a lot of ambient light, true sunset probably only fifteen minutes away.

Maybe he was going to wait until true dusk, when his getaway on foot had a much better chance of success. Maybe he was reconfiguring his entire strategy.

Blood pumping in his ears, Hunt stepped into the recessed doorway of the Triton Hotel and waited, watching. "Come on," he whispered. "Come on! Go!"

For the first time since he'd left his condo, Joey seemed to be taking in his surroundings, looking both directions on Bush, then up Grant, finally behind him, his gaze pausing at the glass window behind which Hunt stood in the hotel's entrance.

Finally, possibly realizing that lack of movement could be as conspicuous as its opposite, Joey squared his shoulders and started walking again.

Up Grant and into the heart of Chinatown.

Hunt exited the hotel and, held up by traffic coming up Bush, finally jaywalked through the light to a chorus of car horns. Coming around the gate, he scanned the street, now packed with pedestrians clogging the sidewalk in front of him.

He'd lost him!

"No, no, no."

Stepping down into the street and off the sidewalk where the strolling tourists weren't as thick as they were on either side, he picked up his pace, scanning first the right-hand sidewalk, then the left.

And now, suddenly, here Joey was again, not fifteen feet away, almost directly ahead of him, keeping pace with the glacially slow flow of the pedestrian traffic, hands still in his pockets, moving slowly but steadily. They would be getting to the alley at any second.

Hunt closed to within a couple of feet.

Joey's pace slowed and he paused, a full stop. He looked left at what appeared to be a narrow driveway between the buildings. One more second of hesitation. Hitching at his belt, he turned and headed down the alley.

Hunt kept walking straight ahead, nodding to Yamashiro, who returned the nod as he and his partner, waiting there for Hunt's arrival, stepped into the mouth of the alleyway and started down a few steps behind Joey Engle.

39

A little bit earlier, at around seven thirty on this Wednesday night, District Attorney Wes Farrell had taken his seat for a potentially romantic date with his wife, Sam, at one of their favorite restaurants, Prospect. They had just started splitting their gelato dessert when the cell phone in Wes's pocket went off and he made the mistake of looking at the face of it.

Dismas Hardy.

"I might have known," he said. "I love that guy, but sometimes I'm tempted to kill him. This would be one of those times."

"Just don't answer."

"I've got to."

"No you don't."

Without another word, he gave her a "What can you do?" look, touched the screen, and said, "Please tell me that you're not just calling to harass me."

"I'm not just calling to harass you," Hardy

dutifully replied. "Although the harassment thing might play a small role. What are you doing?"

"What am I doing? At dinnertime in the middle of the week? What did you think I'd be doing? For the record, I'm having dinner with my wife — or I was, anyway, until a minute ago."

"Say hi to your lovely bride for me."

"Maybe not now. She wouldn't take it the right way. What do you want, anyway, Diz?"

"Mostly world peace, but a close second is Abby Jarvis out of jail. Tonight."

"Are you shitting me? You call me up for that now?"

"I do."

"It can't wait for the bail hearing on Monday?"

"Not really, no. Justice delayed is justice denied and all that, as they say. They've just arrested Joey Engle —"

"Who did?"

"Juhle, Waverly, and Yamashiro. In the Chinese herb shop where he bought the aconite that he used to kill his stepfather, Grant Wagner."

"They already arrested him? Why were they even looking at him?"

"That's a long story that I'd be happy to share with you, but meanwhile my client is rotting away in jail and Joey Engle is down here in one of the interrogation rooms in Homicide even as we speak. Spilling his guts."

"I'm gathering you're there, too."

"Good call. But merely as an observer. Oh, and by the way and not so incidentally, Joey is also the killer of David Chang and Stacy Holland."

"Good for him. And who is Joey again?"

"Grant Wagner's stepson. He stood to make three or four million dollars on Grant's natural death by heart attack. And he almost did." After waiting through a short silence on the line, Hardy asked, "Wes? You there?"

"I'm here. What do you want me to do?"

"Best case, I'd like you to come down here and help get my client out of jail. I kind of made a solemn promise to my wife that I wouldn't come home until that happened and I was out from under this case. And I'd like to sleep in my own bed tonight if that's possible."

"That sounds like your problem, not mine."

Hardy dropped his semi-jocular tone. "Wes, you've got an innocent suspect in jail. I need hardly remind you that if something ugly happens to her in the slammer tonight

481

after we've had this little discussion, it's going to be your problem, not mine."

"Sometimes you are truly a son of a bitch, you know that?"

"I know. I'm working on correcting that. But in the meantime you really need to come down here pretty damn soon. Like now. And have somebody call the on-duty judge."

When Farrell showed up at the Hall at ten fifteen and it turned out that Hardy had not told him the truth, the whole truth, and nothing but the truth, the DA was fit to be tied. Now, in the wide-open homicide detail, he let a little of the reality he was facing seep into his consciousness before he exploded. "Let me get this straight. You pull me away from a long-awaited fancy dinner with my wife with this cock-and-bull story about the man who killed Grant Wagner, so I've got to get my sorry ass down here ASAP and let your client out of jail. When it turns out that your guy only confessed to killing David Chang — which, if you'll excuse me for saying so, has nothing to do with your goddamn client and is absolutely, positively not getting her out of jail tonight. Even assuming that what he told Yamashiro in the car is admissible, since I'm not completely sure what cause you had even to arrest this guy."

"With respect, sir," Devin Juhle said, "he didn't have a CCW permit and he was carrying a firearm concealed under his jacket. And he reached for it the minute he saw me and I identified myself. If I hadn't had my guys coming up behind me, I believe he would have shot me dead."

"Okay, so he's not a Boy Scout," Farrell said. "The gun's still registered to him, isn't it? And the point remains that Grant Wagner, if memory serves, was not a gunshot victim. Am I right? So may I ask what the fucking hell . . . ?"

Running out of steam, he turned to the room's other occupant, Abe Glitsky, whom Hardy had invited down at the last minute as a pocket ally.

Farrell spread his arms, pleading to Abe. "Am I right, here? Even if we eventually get a ballistics match with the two gunshot deaths, how is that match supposed to prove that your man in there" — Joey Engle was getting sweated by Eric Waverly behind closed doors in an interrogation room not sixty feet away — "had anything whatsoever to do with Grant Wagner's death by poison? Do you see that, Abe? And, if so, tell me what it is I'm missing."

"I admit it's not a perfect chain of evidence," Abe began, "but, on the other hand, can you think of another reason he shows up armed with a concealed weapon at this tiny shop on a side alley in Chinatown? Where, I might add, the owner could and in fact did identify him as the guy who'd come in with his own grandson David and bought a lethal amount of the same drug that killed Wagner? That, to me — and I'm on your side here, Wes — is pretty persuasive."

Hardy jumped in on the heels of Abe's response. "My client didn't kill him, Wes. Not even arguably anymore. The fact is that Joey ran down to Chang's shop as soon as he could get there after I made him see the danger to him that both Chang and his gun represented. I mean, he leaves me and without a minute of hesitation he's on his way and my guy follows him from his condo south of Market to Chang's in Chinatown. And now, all that leaves, as soon as we get the ballistics match on the gun . . ."

"*If* we —"

As if on cue, an exhausted Waverly came out of the interrogation room and walked across the expanse of the homicide detail. When he reached the little knot by his desk, he said, "He just gave it up. On tape. All three of the murders. That guy has got a serious screw loose. Completely emotion-less. Like it was all a video game. He's actu-ally kind of proud about how clever he is."

40

Even with Farrell himself leading the charge, it took the rest of the night to get Abby out of jail.

They still had the laundered clothes she'd been wearing when they'd arrested her, and she wore those as she stepped outside. Hardy put his suit coat around her against the chill as they walked to the parking lot. After her effusive thanks as things had played out at the jail, she'd first wanted to hear about everything Hardy had discovered about Joey and his arrest and de facto confession. When Hardy finished, they were virtually silent on the ride home.

At exactly five fifty-seven a.m. by his car clock, Hardy pulled up in front of Abby's duplex in the Marina District. Out on the sidewalk under the streetlight, a woman and a child stood in heavy coats, and before Hardy had even set the parking brake, Abby had thrown open her door and rushed out to hug her mother and daughter, whom Hardy had called earlier to alert them to Abby's imminent arrival.

They were all crying, holding each other in a huddle when Hardy got out of the car, walking around to close the passenger door. He then came back around and endured the hugs from Abby's mother and the awkward but sweet kisses from Veronica. At last, Abby gently extricated her daughter and stepped into Hardy's embrace.

"I don't know how you did this," she said, "and I don't know how to thank you."

Half teasing, he said, "Try not to get into any more trouble. Because I'm not taking any more murder cases. Other than that, seeing you out here with your family is thanks enough. Really."

"Oh." Abby's mother reached out and touched Hardy's arm, then her daughter's. "I just realized that in all the ruckus with our lives here, I've never even sent over the check to pay you. It's just inside on the hall table if you want to wait. Ten seconds."

"I wouldn't worry about it," Hardy said. "The first court appearance is on the house, and that's all we've had."

"No, really, Diz," Abby objected, "that doesn't seem —"

Hardy held up a hand. "Nonnegotiable,

I'm afraid. Except I could use my coat back." After Abby had taken it off and handed it back to him, he put it on and said, "There is one thing."

"What's that?" she asked.

"I expect the Christmas cards to keep coming."

"Deal."

He leaned in and gave her one last quick buss on the cheek. "You all take care of each other."

"We will," they chimed in unison.

"That's what I like to hear." Hardy stepped over to his car and opened the door. Sliding in, he started up the engine, lifted a hand good-bye at the newly reunited family, and pulled out into the street, on his way home at last.

In her bathrobe over her nightgown, Frannie opened the front door as Hardy trudged up the last step, hefting his heavy lawyer's briefcase, which, by the way it seemed to burden him, might as well have carried the weight of all the world. Stopping, he set it down on the porch and tried to give her a hopeful expression that wasn't altogether successful.

"Hey," he said.

"Hey."

"Sorry I'm so late. You didn't have to wait up."

"Yes I did. I am so sorry. I am such a bitch."

"You're not. Turns out, I think you were mostly right. The part about not taking on any more murder cases. You're right about the risk being too great. We don't need it. But I couldn't just abandon Abby, especially knowing she was innocent and that the system would likely eat her up, guilt or no guilt. She looked guilty enough, anyway. I couldn't let it happen. And on the other hand, I couldn't risk losing you."

"You weren't going to lose me. I just panicked."

"With some reason."

"No. Not reason enough to justify threatening us. That was so wrong."

"Well, we can fight about that later."

"I don't want to fight."

"Me neither."

She pointed to his briefcase. "Want to pick that thing up and come inside? It's a little cold standing here."

"It is, you're right." Reaching down, he picked it up and came into the hallway, then put it down.

Closing the door behind him, she asked,

"If I poured you a Scotch, would you drink it?"

"Normally I'd say it's too early, but I'm still on yesterday time. So thank you. I'll just sit here in my favorite chair a minute if you don't mind. I'm about done in."

"Sit," she said.

She was back in under two minutes.

He took the drink, thanking her, sipping as she set herself down on the couch. "So I take it you didn't quit, then," she said.

"Not exactly," he said. "Not in so many words, but maybe better." Hardy briefed her on the highlights, concluding with "In any event, Wes dropped the charges against her. And I just left her off at her home a half hour ago."

"Completely out of jail?"

"Out *is* completely out, Fran. There is no halfway."

"No. I know, but . . . Abby is just back in her life and you're no longer representing her?"

"Not even the brief appearance to have the charges formally dismissed. I'll send one of my associates. I'm stopping cold, as you suggest, before the job kills me, as it actually might if I keep at it. From now on, I hear 'murder case' and I run the other way."

Frannie broke a small smile. "Well, we'll see."

"We will see." Hardy tipped up his glass. "You wait."

41

Hardy did not wake up until three o'clock that afternoon. Frannie was off to her own job as a marriage and family counselor, and Hardy made his coffee in the kitchen, then fed the tropical fish, then finally took down his ancient black cast-iron pan and started cutting and assembling one of his famous omelettes. When he dumped his creation out onto his plate, the pan as it always did remained spotless — one swipe of a paper towel and it was ready to be used again.

When his cell phone rang, he was tempted to ignore it on general principles but then, seeing it was his son, he changed his mind.

"Yo, cowboy. What up?"

"I just heard from Bill Kenney, who read online this morning that they'd arrested a guy for the Dave Chang murder and also evidently a couple more murders, including his own stepdad. Which means they can let your client go, doesn't it?"

"Actually, that already happened last night. I dropped her off at her home around dawn. She didn't do it and Farrell finally saw the light and decided he needed to let her go."

"How'd Uncle Wes like that?"

"It wasn't his happiest moment, let's just say that. But in the end he did the right thing."

"So all these murders, they were all connected after all? As you always said?"

"They were."

"This bastard Joey, he just never should have used that aconite."

Hardy started to explain. "Well, he needed it to look like a heart attack so he'd get his insurance money and —" Stopping abruptly, Hardy said, "Bill Kenney's story had the connection to the aconite?"

"Not in so many words, but he and I had already put that together."

"Who put what together?"

"Me and Bill. That whole aconite thing, which is really why this Joey guy decided he had to kill David."

Hardy, trying to ignore the band of pressure that had suddenly appeared in his chest, asked, "And how did you do that exactly? Put that all together."

"Well, we got to talking about the source

of the aconite, and there really weren't that many options, so we went by Dave's grandfather's herb shop in —"

"In Chinatown. Yeah. I know it."

"Anyway, when I got back to the city yesterday, Bill and I hooked up after his work and went by there to check it out."

"To the shop?"

"Easy, Dad. It was cool."

Hardy, not thinking it was cool at all, said, "And when were you by there?"

"Sixish, six thirty. Somewhere in there. Anyway, it didn't take long to find out what we wanted, and we were out of there in twenty minutes. But if this hadn't all come down with them arresting Joey Engle last night, we figured we'd made the connection between David and your case, which could only help you. Right?"

"Right." Hardy let a small silence build.

"So?"

"So somewhere in the deep recesses of your mind, Vinnie, do you have any recollection of me mentioning rather strongly that you and your friends ought to keep away from anything to do with active murder cases?"

"Yeah, sure. But this wasn't like that. This was just following up on a couple of questions that seemed obvious enough to me and Bill. We couldn't believe that nobody was making any progress on who killed one of our friends. We were going to tell you whatever we found. And then it turns out we didn't need to anyway."

Yes, Hardy was thinking. But your couple of innocent questions brought you to the scene of Joey's arrest within, at the most, an hour of him showing up there armed and clearly ready to kill whoever he had to, to say nothing of the presence of three nervous and heavily armed homicide inspectors.

"We never got anywhere near to doing anything dangerous, Dad, if that's what you were worried about. We were just checking out some obvious stuff."

"Okay," Hardy said, "but sometimes . . ."

"Sometimes what?"

Sometimes your parents give you good advice and you'd be well advised to take it, he thought. Sometimes you're in danger and have no way of knowing about it. Sometimes really bad stuff happens with no warning to really good people. Sometimes simple curiosity really can kill the cat.

Hardy had these and a host of other answers ready to go.

Instead he bought himself a second or two by taking a sip of his coffee. "Sometimes nothing," he said. "Just me being old." He took a breath. "So what are the odds we're going to get some face time from you in the coming days?"

"Decent. Things are pretty chill down here lately. I'll let you know as soon as I do. How's that?"

"Fantastic," Hardy said, his enthusiasm in deep check. "Decent odds for a son sighting. Who could ask for anything more?"

The celebration of the successful conclusion of a case called for a better venue than Lou the Greek's, and now, at lunchtime on this Thursday, Hardy was sitting across from Glitsky in a booth at their favorite lunch spot, Sam's Grill. Stefano was their long-suffering waiter and he'd already delivered a Sapphire martini to Hardy and an iced tea to Abe. They were both waiting on their plates of sand dabs, considered by many — and certainly by them — to be the most flavorful flounder on the planet.

Hardy picked up his stemmed glass, enjoyed some gin, swallowed, and said, "There's one thing I just don't understand at all, though."

Glitsky nodded in understanding. "More than one, I'd bet."

Hardy ignored him. "Joey gets himself hung up in this classic copycat situation.

He's doing more or less exactly what his parents did twenty years ago."

"Twenty-two," Glitsky corrected him.

"Okay. Twenty-two. The fact remains."

"And what fact is that?"

Hardy's voice went up half an octave. "It didn't work, Abe. That fact remains. It didn't work for his parents and it didn't work for him. They killed for the insurance; he killed for the insurance. They got caught and never collected. Same thing with Joey. So why does this inspire their son, twenty-two years later, to try the same thing they so miserably failed at?"

"You're right," Glitsky said. "It doesn't make much sense."

"It's been gnawing at me."

Glitsky chewed some ice. "Maybe he wants to get caught at it and get punished. Maybe he's the only one left in his family and he suffers from survivor's guilt. Maybe he's a little lamb who's lost in the woods and he's looking for somebody to follow."

"Probably not that last one."

"No. Probably not. You want the honest truth? Probably we'll never know."

Hardy let out a sigh. "I hate that part."

Glitsky fixed him with a thousand-yard stare. "And who does not, my friend?" he said. "And who does not?"

ACKNOWLEDGMENTS

One of life's great joys is sitting down to write the acknowledgments portion of a book, not least because it probably means that the novel is done, but also because the process serves as a reminder of how many generous people contribute to the finished product, and what I owe to them.

For this book, I had an early vision that my plot would revolve around an exotic poison, so I called my good friend (and primary care physician) Dr. John Chuck at Kaiser Permanente in Davis, CA, and he put me in touch with Dr. Steven R. Offerman, an expert in poisons and toxicology. Steve and I spent a very productive and fun morning together, at the end of which I had a very good idea of the bones of my story.

This book also deals in some detail with quite a few financial concepts that were foreign to me until I got a good deal of clarification and insight from my brother

Mike, who just happens to be a CPA. I'm still not sure I "get" most of the jargon used herein, and any glaring mistakes are my own, but Mike gave me the confidence I needed to go ahead and make up the stuff I needed.

Similarly, when I started writing this book, I knew next to nothing about the culture of Silicon Valley, and particularly of Facebook, although you can reach me on my Facebook page, my website (www.johnlescroart.com), and several other sites (see following pages). Fortunately, my great friend, legal consultant, and *consigliere,* Alfred F. Giannini, Esq., has a fantastic daughter named Carolyn who works at Facebook and was kind enough to invite me to the campus and hang out with her and some of her colleagues there: Charlie Patterson, Seth Auser, Dan Yang, and (in New York, via video conference, which was way cool) Mikel Stevens. The whole field trip was an eye-opening and enjoyable experience that, I hope, contributed significantly to the verisimilitude of the finished book.

In the midst of my daily toil on this novel, one fine afternoon my computer crashed, threatening at least an entire day's work, if not my entire manuscript to date. In a panic, I called my son-in-law Josh Kastan and he called me back within minutes and walked me through a recovery ritual that worked! The finished book would not be the same without Josh's efforts on that day, and I cannot thank him enough for his calm confidence and extraordinary competence.

I am blessed to be a part of a wonderful community of writers in my hometown. Once in a while, we get goofy and challenge ourselves to insert little witticisms into our work. For you careful readers who noted the obscure reference in this book to a "turtle with a head cold," it comes courtesy of the Davis Roundtable. Check the books of Eileen Rendahl, Catriona McPherson, Spring Warren, and Kris Calvin for other appearances of this mysterious turtle.

I'd also like to acknowledge the incredible team of folks who work with me on a regular basis and help these books finally make it to publication:

Anita Boone, my assistant for over twenty years, is a marvel of organization and efficiency, to say nothing of tact, personality, and general good nature. She remains a joy to work with, and is a mind reader as well, which often proves critical.

Handling all of my social media, which in this world is such a large part of the publishing industry, is the talented and indefatigable Dr. Andy Jones. Aside from the website and Facebook listed above, he oversees my presence on Twitter (www.twitter.com/johnlescroart) and updates my blog. Also, on the hard print side, my two personal editors, Peggy Nauts and Doug Kelly, have given the final polish to many of my books, including this one, and I'm just so grateful to them for finding those last little glitches and dispatching them so completely.

My agent, Barney Karpfinger, remains the rock of my career. *Poison* is our twentieth book together, and he's been a fantastic friend and supporter every step of the way. I truly believe that my wonderful career would not have happened if not for Barney's unflagging efforts, energy, and enthusiasm.

Al Giannini (Carolyn's father, above) still fights the good fight with me on every book, and sometimes, it seems, every line of every book, keeping those pesky technical legalistic issues on the right side of reality. The reason that the legal and procedural stuff in these books reads like something that could actually happen is because of Al's expertise and experience in the real world of criminal justice. He's a true partner in these books, and I can't thank him enough for all of his effort and contributions.

Generous contributors to charitable organizations have purchased the right to name characters in this book. These people and their respective organizations are: Barbara Ohlendorf, Yolo Court Appointed Special Advocates (CASA); Bob Grassilli and Bill Kenney, Serra High School Fund A Dream; and Betty Lou Honaker, the Sacramento Library Foundation.

Penultimately, I must recognize and acknowledge the incredible enthusiasm and support of Atria Books and its terrific staff, from publisher Judith Curr to my editors Peter Borland and Daniella Wexler, and the amazing publicist David Brown. Working behind the scenes for the success of these books is the top-flight sales group of Janice Fryer, Wendy Sheanin, and Colin Shields. It is a pleasure and privilege to work with all of you. Thank you so much.

Finally, I love hearing from my readers. Please feel free to stop by any of the sites mentioned above and say hello — I really do answer my mail.

Thanks for buying my books!

ABOUT THE AUTHOR

John Lescroart is the author of more than twenty-seven novels, including the *New York Times* bestsellers *The Ophelia Cut, The Keeper, The Fall,* and *Fatal*. His books have sold more than ten million copies and have been translated into twenty-two languages. He lives in Northern California.